Knockout

"You were looking for my office."

She nodded. "Yes." It came out more breathless than she intended.

Something happened in his blue eyes. "Why?"

"I . . ." She trailed off, a half-dozen things she could not say on her lips. Serious things like *I believe members of the police are terrorizing the East End.* Extraordinarily unserious things like *I wanted to ogle your broad shoulders.*

Something dark and wicked flashed across his face. "Lady Imogen," he said softly at her ear, still not touching her. "What were you looking for?"

You. You you you.

Knowing she played with fire, she pressed her cheek to his, loving the feel of him, warm on her skin. "Your office."

A rough sound came from his chest and his fingers found her bent elbow, lingering there, on a place she'd never imagined had so many nerve endings. "Are you sure?"

"Yes," she said, not knowing what he meant. Not caring. Whatever it was, she was sure.

"Hmm," he rumbled, his free hand coming to her cheek, holding her steady as he pulled back, meeting her eyes, his fingers tracing the length of her arm to her wrist.

And then he was there, almost kissing her, torturing her with the promise of a caress . . . "And what were you going to do when you found me in my office?"

Kiss you.

No, wait. That wasn't right.

Was it?

By Sarah MacLean

Hell's Belles
BOMBSHELL
HEARTBREAKER
KNOCKOUT

The Bareknuckle Bastards
WICKED AND THE WALLFLOWER
BRAZEN AND THE BEAST
DARING AND THE DUKE

Scandal & Scoundrel
THE ROGUE NOT TAKEN
A SCOT IN THE DARK
THE DAY OF THE DUCHESS

The Rules of Scoundrels
A ROGUE BY ANY OTHER NAME
ONE GOOD EARL DESERVES A LOVER
NO GOOD DUKE GOES UNPUNISHED
NEVER JUDGE A LADY BY HER COVER

Love by Numbers
NINE RULES TO BREAK WHEN ROMANCING A RAKE
TEN WAYS TO BE ADORED WHEN LANDING A LORD
ELEVEN SCANDALS TO START TO WIN A DUKE'S HEART

THE SEASON
HOW THE DUKES STOLE CHRISTMAS

SARAH MacLEAN
KNOCK OUT

A HELL'S BELLES NOVEL

AVONBOOKS

An Imprint of HarperCollinsPublishers

KNOCKOUT. Copyright © 2023 by Sarah Trabucchi. All rights reserved. Printed in the United States of America. No part of this book may be used or reproduced in any manner whatsoever without written permission except in the case of brief quotations embodied in critical articles and reviews. For information, address HarperCollins Publishers, 195 Broadway, New York, NY 10007.

First Avon Books mass market printing: August 2023

Print Edition ISBN: 978-0-06-305679-4
Digital Edition ISBN: 978-0-06-305591-9

Cover design by Amy Halperin
Cover art by Alan Ayers
Cover images © vandervelden/iStock/Getty Images (chaise)

Avon, Avon & logo, and Avon Books & logo are registered trademarks of HarperCollins Publishers in the United States of America and other countries.

HarperCollins is a registered trademark of HarperCollins Publishers in the United States of America and other countries.

FIRST EDITION

23 24 25 26 27 BVGM 10 9 8 7 6 5 4 3 2 1

This one is for Jen.
Obviously.

KNOCK OUT

Chapter One

L ady Imogen Loveless enjoyed explosions.

To be clear, she was not a sadist. That an explosion might do bodily harm of some kind was not pleasing to her. No, if she was pressed, she would say that it was not exploded *things* that gave her joy, but rather *the means by which one* exploded things.

Imogen liked bright flashes of light and waves of heat and the particular smell and *the sound*—to the untrained ear a *boom* or a *crackle* or a *hiss* or a *whoosh*, but more often than not, some magical combination that made another word altogether. A *ratatoon*, a *frizzle*, a *tweel-pop*.

A body would be hard-pressed to find another in all of Britain who spent as much time thinking about the sounds of an explosion as Imogen did. (Her first word had been *Bang!*, though no one had been paying close enough attention to hear it.)

As she was a lady, however, and an aristocratic one at that, few paid attention to Imogen's peculiar fascination—nor any of the many other peculiar fascinations she'd accumulated over her twenty-four years of life. In truth, most people ignored the fascinations altogether when discussing the only sister of Earl Dorring, as *peculiar* was more than enough description to make a lady unappealing.

Not that Imogen thought *peculiar* much of an insult. She'd been labeled as such since birth, since her father brought her in pinafores to the Royal Society of Chemistry, where she'd wandered off, combined quicklime and water, and nearly burned the place down before the Earl was informed in no uncertain terms that children—especially young ladies—were not allowed inside the building.

Peculiar, they'd whispered as she toddled past, following her father into the street as he roundly praised her experimentation.

Odd girl.

Too clever by half.

If Dorring's not careful, she'll turn out worse *than too clever.*

She'll turn out to be too much.

And she had done just that. Lady Imogen Loveless was too much for society and too much for her brother, who became her guardian after her beloved father died when she was only sixteen, and *far* too much for any suitor who might have darkened the doorstep of her home in Mayfair—though none had as of that morning in January, one short month into her twenty-fourth year.

Which suited Imogen down to the ground, as she'd much rather be too much than the alternative. And if the wide world felt *too much* was not enough for their balls and dinners and teas and company, then Imogen was happy to be left to her workshop in the cellars of Dorring House with her tinctures and tonics, and to her friends, who understood just how entertaining and enterprising she could be with her tinctures and tonics.

No one ever discussed the sounds of explosions at tea.

So it was that on that January morning, just after dawn, the air brisk and cold with the night that had not yet burned away, Imogen was at the site of an explosion.

It was important to note that Imogen had nothing to do with the explosion in question. She did not know the sound it had made in the key moment—could only guess that it had been something of a *thunder*, considering that she was certain that the building had made a great noise when it collapsed to the ground.

There was no particular explosive smell—anything unique that might have lingered had been smothered by the acrid smoke of the fire the blasting oil had caused when it had been ignited, and the cloud of dust that had come from the building, now reduced to rubble.

Twelve hours earlier, the building had housed O'Dwyer and Leafe's, a seamstress shop tucked between a pub and a pie shop in Spitalfields, on a bustling little strip of East London that should not have thrived but for the popularity of this particular shop, and its skillful proprietresses, which attracted a constant stream of women. The loss of the establishment would be a loss to the businesses that had grown up around it. The building could not be salvaged; relocation was the only option.

A sad state of affairs, indeed, though not one that should rate the attention of anyone but those in the nearest vicinity.

It most certainly should not rate the attention of an aristocratic lady.

Even less the attention of four of them.

But this was not just *any* building, and these were not just *any* ladies.

And so, in the heavy grey of the London morning, made heavier by the threat of icy rain and the particular silence of a building that had been razed to the ground, Imogen and three others stood amidst piles of rubble in the now hollowed-out space, open to the street and sky, between The Hollow Drum and Mrs. Twizzleton's Savory Pie Shop.

The quartet was at once wildly out of place and entirely in control.

They were the Hell's Belles, whispered about in ball-rooms and barrooms throughout London—a team of women (Were there four? Forty? At times it seemed there were four *thousand*) who had made a name for themselves by bringing down the worst of the corrupt world when too often those in power refused to do the same.

Few knew the identity of even a single member of the gang, let alone the identities of the four who founded the crew—after all, when it came to women, people rarely paid attention. And the Hell's Belles, who'd been de-lighted to be christened as such by London's gossip rags (quoting unnamed sources at Scotland Yard), were very happy to take advantage of that lack of attention—and hide in plain sight.

If one were looking, one might find the foursome to-gether in Mayfair ballrooms and Kensington dining rooms and shops on Bond Street, where money and power and high fashion made for a certain kind of invisibility. They were just as commonplace in Covent Garden, where a good cloak and a better coachman could easily keep the identity of a woman hidden. But clad in brightly colored silks and satins and freshly pressed cloaks, mucking about in the grey morning soot of the East End?

That was a different thing altogether. Ladies did not go to the East End.

Then again, it was not every day a business bankrolled by a wealthy duchess—two wealthy duchesses—and the daughters of two equally wealthy earls was blown to bits.

And so . . . well. Needs must.

Needs, in this case, meant that Lady Imogen, lover of all things explosive—skilled explosive expert in her own right—was there to investigate. The smell. The sounds. The unique pattern of the blast.

She crouched in the rubble, considering the fierce fin-gers of black soot across what had once been the space behind the ribbon counter, which had been disintegrated beneath the strength of the blast.

Looking up, Imogen considered the partially collapsed brick wall behind her, where the mirror that had once separated the front of the shop from its rear rooms had been blown out and destroyed by the heat. Above, the wooden floors had been incinerated, leaving only the shell of the staircase between the ground floor shop and the sky—now visible through the disintegrated second and third floors.

She inhaled deeply, the air full of smoke and sulfur and cold rain. "They certainly got the job done, didn't they?"

The words hung in silence for a moment, before she turned to look at two women who watched her with vague censure.

She blinked. "What?"

"May I suggest you try sounding a touch less impressed about the destruction of an entire building?" the Duchess of Trevescan offered.

Imogen gave a little shrug. "Whoever did it knew precisely where to place the device—"

"And *when* to place it, as well." Sesily Calhoun stood in the now disappeared doorway, looking out at the street beyond, where a handful of early risers were already on their way to their day. "Late enough that anyone who saw anything—"

"—saw nothing." Adelaide Carrington, newly minted Duchess of Clayborn, appeared from the rear of the building. "The oldest rule of the South Bank. If you see something, say nothing." She brandished a stack of papers. "Found them. Lock box beneath the floor in the back room, just as Erin said."

"Excellent," Duchess said, unable to mask her relief as Adelaide joined her by the staircase. In the wrong hands, the documents—carefully preserved by Frances O'Dwyer and Erin Leafe and recovered by Adelaide— would destroy lives. "We don't need anyone to speak. Imogen will hear them anyway."

Sesily chuckled. "And the *News* will sing her praises."

It was not always praise, but no matter the newsprint—Respectable (The Hell's Belles), Salacious (Lady Vigilantes!), or Revolutionary (Defenders of the Common [Wo]Man)—the ink sold papers, thanks to an extensive following of people across Britain who enjoyed seeing truth finally shown to power. And a not insignificant following of those who held power . . . and had no interest in hearing truth.

It was the latter who set off bombs in places where women outside the seat of power congregated and shared ideas. Places like O'Dwyer and Leafe's.

There was no question that in the two years since the Belles had begun not only standing on behalf of those who were outside the power and privilege of Parliament—women, children, workers, poor—but also vanquishing those who wielded that power and privilege to punish, things had grown more incendiary.

A queen on the throne had inflamed the aristocracy; the idea that women might chip away at generations of power in other places, as well? Enough to turn that flame into something far more dangerous. Something explosive.

The result was more anger. An increase in rousing editorials about the weaker sex. More frequent cautionary tales about women gaining knowledge and strength, workers gaining rights, immigrants seeking equity, the poor demanding dignity, the dangers of sending children to school rather than work.

One queen, came the whispers, *and they all expect to be treated like royalty.*

And now, this. In three months, three explosions, at three such shops—each with a front and back room. A forward-facing business and a rear-facing one. One far more important than the other. And because of that, more dangerous.

A bakery in Bethnal Green that acted as a waypoint for women escaping men who wielded cruelty and power like weapons, a print shop in Whitechapel that made space for workers plotting for better treatment and wages, and now this, O'Dwyer and Leafe's seamstress shop, which hid one of London's secret women's health clinics.

All reduced to rubble in the hands of monsters with impressive science, rudimentary skill, and an absence of humanity.

"Watch those stairs," Imogen said without looking up from her inspection. "They're not sound."

Duchess snatched her hand back from the handrail that remained intact. "I hesitate to ask . . . but is any of it sound?"

Imogen did not reply, too focused on her inspection.

Adelaide adjusted her spectacles. "Imogen . . . is any of it sound?"

"Hmm?" Imogen looked up. "Oh, assuredly not." The three other women exchanged a look that was not uncommon when in proximity to their firebrand of a friend. "Sesily, would you bring me my bag, please?"

Sesily looked askance at the carpetbag Imogen had left at the once door to the space. "I'd prefer not to be flattened, honestly, Im."

"Don't worry about that." Imogen waved a hand toward the staircase. "You'll be fine if you avoid the stairs."

Duchess and Adelaide moved quickly to the opposite side of the shop as Sesily delivered the bag. Imogen opened the sack and rooted around within as Duchess looked to the street beyond, more awake than it had been thirty minutes earlier. "Quickly," she said softly. "The longer we linger, the more likely someone asks questions."

Extracting a small vial, Imogen collected a bit of soot from the blast, along with a shard of glass that she hoped held traces of the blasting oil that had been used. "Nearly there."

"It's not my father's work, is it?" Adelaide asked from her safe distance.

Imogen shook her head. "Your father's boys lack the finesse. No offense."

Adelaide laughed. "None taken. Finesse is not a quality that is required for running hired guns and heavy fists in Lambeth." That, and Alfie Trumbull, leader of The Bully Boys—the largest gang of criminals on the South Bank—had pledged to turn over a new leaf now that he had a duke for a son-in-law. It turned out that the hope of a grandson with a title made even the most hardened crime lord think about going straight. Or, whatever *straight* meant for crime lords.

"Who, then?" Adelaide continued, adjusting her spectacles.

"Someone competent . . ." Imogen said, using a boar-bristle brush to sweep away the dust, intensely focused, carefully searching. "But unimaginative. This is the same explosive device they used at the last one, and the one before that. Same blasting-powder. Same blast pattern."

"Unimaginative? Or unconcerned with being caught?" Duchess asked.

"Likely both," Imogen replied.

Sesily popped a lemon sweet into her mouth and wrapped her scarlet cloak tight around her. "Alright, so Imogen is close to the who . . . but *why*?"

"It's always the same. Those in power don't like it when the rest of us are beyond their control," Duchess said with distaste, toeing a pile of brick by her feet. "But the same villain? At three different places? With three different purposes?"

"I didn't say it was the same villain," Imogen said, standing up. "I said it was the same person who set the bomb."

"You mean a hired gun," Adelaide replied.

Duchess met her gaze. "You're going to have to see your father, Adelaide. If it's not The Bully Boys blowing up the place . . ."

Adelaide nodded. "Surely he'll have some idea of who *is* doing it. We need that name. And soon." She turned and looked to the street beyond, the sun up and the locals dressed and breakfasted . . . and coming to look.

Duchess indicated the papers in Adelaide's arms and tilted her chin in the direction of the waiting carriage. "You'd best get those inside, before someone notices we found something that did not burn."

The Duchess of Clayborn nodded and, slipping the hood of her cloak up over her flame red hair, made her way out to the street and into the carriage.

Sesily shivered. "Come on then, Imogen."

"These things take time!" Imogen said, not looking up from her work, moving quickly and carefully, knowing time was short. And then, "Aha! Got it!"

There. A bit of fabric. She lifted it from the dust carefully, extracting a second vial from her sack.

The other women straightened, Duchess taking a step forward, peering over Imogen's shoulder as she carefully packed away her treasure. "What makes that different than the yards of other fabrics charred to bits in this place?"

"Maybe nothing," Imogen said, placing the vials inside her carpetbag before extracting the small notebook and pencil she carried inside the ballooned sleeve of her bright blue coat. "But I've seen this particular fabric before. At the bakery. And the print shop. Where fabric doesn't come by the yard."

Opening the notebook, she ticked off several boxes: *tinder, fuse, soot.*

Sesily let out a little sound of admiration. "Well done, Im."

"Quite," Duchess said. "But as you have removed somewhat critical evidence from the scene of the crime, I think we'd best be on our way, and quickly. Scotland Yard will be round soon enough."

Imogen gave a little snort of derision. "When are they

able to make time for a seamstress shop in Spitalfields?"
She hefted her bag and made her way toward her friends,
already turning to join Adelaide in the carriage. "Not one
man in the Metropolitan Police wants this assignment."

"I'm afraid you are mistaken, my lady." The deep, rich
voice came from the rear of the building, behind them.
The trio stilled in the space between what had once been
indoors and what had always been outdoors. Adelaide's
face appeared in the window of the carriage, her eyes
wide, fixed on a spot behind them.

On a *man* behind them.

Something happened in Imogen's chest. A *thrum*. A
mark, unique and familiar, not unlike that of the explosion that had summoned them there.

That had summoned *him* there.

She turned, shoulder to shoulder with her friends,
and found his gaze, dark and exasperated beneath his
narrow-brimmed hat. As exasperated as the words he
grumbled. "Why are you here?"

Chapter Two

Detective Inspector Thomas Peck was having a bad day. It had begun at a quarter past five, decidedly the worst hour of the morning. Nothing good came of waking at a quarter past five. First, it was the coldest point of the night, too far from the fire in the hearth and not close enough to the sun breaking over the horizon. Second, it was early. Not so early that it seemed to be the dead of night, and not late enough to be considered a proper time for an early rise. It was early in the most irritating way, as if only the wide world could have held still another quarter of an hour, everything would have been perfectly in order.

The inspector, you see, thrived when things were in order.

The young constable from Scotland Yard's Detective Branch who had knocked on the door of Mrs. Edwards's rooming house in Holborn had been unable to wait, however, and so a quarter past five—that ungodly hour—it was. It was not the fresh-faced boy's fault, Thomas would acknowledge later, once he'd found strong coffee and brisk air. It was Thomas's. Because he'd been more than clear with the entirety of the Detective Branch; if there was an explosion anywhere in London, at any hour, on any day, he was to be summoned. Immediately.

But it did not mean he had to enjoy being roused before dawn.

Nor did it mean his landlady had to enjoy it. Indeed, Mrs. Edwards—who took great pains in berating the young constable loudly before shrieking *"Detective Inspector!"* up the central staircase of the rooming house—claimed not to enjoy it. Though she seemed to enjoy the shrieking well enough.

Never mind that. By twenty to six, Thomas was returned to his stern, perfect control: shaved, washed, dressed, and exiting the house, Mrs. Edwards at his back, shouting him out the door with her well-practiced sermon, *Why Decent Tenants Do Not Receive Callers Before Daybreak.*

It took a great deal more than a landlady's diatribe to deviate Thomas Peck from his course, however, and he closed the shining black door behind him, silencing the noise with a firm hand. He looked to the young constable. "Where to?"

Where to, was the East End, where a massive explosion had taken out a seamstress shop between a pie shop and a pub. Keenly aware of the police wagon in which he traveled, the Detective Inspector instructed the driver to drop him in the alley behind the building, so he could enter unseen.

The young constable did his best to hide his belief that the detective inspector was expecting more than was reasonable in Spitalfields—by all reports, the building had been razed in the dead of night; surely any culprit would be gone.

But Thomas Peck wasn't expecting a culprit. He was expecting something much worse.

Chaos. The kind that came in a pretty, plump, petite package, with bright eyes and glossy black curls. The kind that too often came with trouble. And mountains of paperwork.

And there she was, as expected. Lady Imogen Loveless, dressed in the bright blue of a summer sky (*had the woman ever worn a color that wasn't in the damn rainbow?*), holding the enormous carpetbag she was never without, between piles of rubble in an exploded building that was by no means stable, alongside two other ladies—the Duchess of Trevescan and Mrs. Sesily Calhoun—promising to make his bad day much worse, as she always did.

Thomas stopped them as they headed to their carriage, the newly married Duchess of Clayborn visible in the window of the conveyance. He would be lying if he were to say he did not enjoy the shock on the Duchess's face—and the way three sets of skirts swished around the ankles of the trio he'd frozen in their tracks.

Lady Imogen turned first. Of course.

She began in the same manner she always did, by offering him a bold, bright smile—one clearly intended to addle the mind of a lesser man. But Thomas Peck was not a lesser man, and he was immune to the woman's charms. At least, he was when he was prepared for them. "Why, Detective Inspector! What a surprise to find you here!"

"I wish I could say the same, Lady Imogen," he said, stopping next to a pile of fallen bricks that had once been a wall between the front and back rooms of the shop, resisting the urge to approach her. "But I have come to expect you wherever there is mayhem."

Her dark eyes went somehow brighter than they'd been, fairly twinkling. "What a lovely thing to say."

Her companions shared an amused look over her black curls.

"Careful," he said. "I'm not convinced you don't cause it."

She flashed him a smile that he might have thought was pretty if he weren't already braced for the full blast of it. "Careful yourself. I'm not convinced you don't come searching for it."

Mrs. Sesily Calhoun snickered at the retort, and Thomas scowled. He didn't come searching for it. He was an inspector of the Detective Branch of Scotland Yard. He had work to do and was too damn busy to follow this woman around, no matter how often they crossed paths. "I don't."

Lady Imogen shook her head, and Thomas had the distinct sense he was being patronized. "Of course, you don't."

"I come to places where *crimes* have been committed. Places where I am required to do my *job*."

"A job you do well," she said, her gaze sliding over him in a way that he should not have liked so much.

Hang on. Was she mocking him? He narrowed his gaze. "I do it *very* well, as a matter of fact."

That smile again, full of delight and secrets. "That's why I said it."

More snickers from the ladies who flanked her, and he'd had enough. "Ladies—why are you here?"

"Do we require a reason?"

"To be lingering in a hollowed-out building? Generally, yes."

"And what if my reason were simply that I enjoy explosions?"

"That's a ridiculous reason," he replied.

"Well. That's rather unkind. I *do* enjoy explosions."

"Enough to have caused this one?"

A pause, and she smiled again, admiration in her gaze—not that he was interested in the woman admiring him. Still, he did not dislike it when she said, "Oh, that was very well done."

His brows rose. "What was well done?"

"That quick response—an interrogation, wasn't it? So quick and casual that I might have answered it if I were a lesser woman. I imagine it works a great deal of the time."

It did, as a matter of fact. "And yet you didn't answer."

She grinned. "I did not."

He shouldn't like it, the way she sparred with him. The way everything went brighter with the battle of wits she offered. He shouldn't like the way her curls bounced about her face. He shouldn't notice how her cheeks flushed with her own pleasure.

And he most certainly should not wonder what other things made her cheeks flush with pleasure.

He cleared his throat and regained control of the conversation. "You are a woman with a confessed fondness for explosions, in the early morning hours in the rubble of a building that has been razed to the ground."

"Am I on your list of suspects, Detective Inspector?"

"No," he allowed. "But you cannot fault me for finding you suspect."

"Take heart, Tommy. Most of London finds me suspect."

He *absolutely* should not like it when she called him *Tommy*. He pressed his lips together, trying for his most intimidating look—one that regularly had hardened criminals rolling over. "This is the third exploded location at which I've found you in as many months."

The lady was unmoved. "And what a tale it will make for our future children."

It was only due to years of training that Thomas's face did not reveal his shock. He exhaled sharply and quelled the extraneous thoughts her teasing might have inspired in the mind of a lesser man. "Lady Imogen, I believe you know more than you are willing to share about this particular crime."

"It's plausible." Lady Imogen tilted her head in his direction. "Do you have a very serious plan for my interrogation?"

She was infuriating. So why was he considering all the ways he *might* interrogate her? Ways that began with tossing her over his shoulder and depositing her in the back of a dark carriage . . .

His thoughts were interrupted by a bark of feminine laughter as the Duchess of Trevescan moved to leave the building. "Truly the two of you make an excellent play. If your current careers go south, you could always take to the theater."

With the delighted pronouncement, she made for the street, Mrs. Calhoun at her heels.

Leaving Thomas alone with Lady Imogen.

He stepped closer to her, even though he shouldn't. "I could arrest you, you know."

"On what grounds?" she asked, matching his step with one of her own.

"Tampering with the site of a crime."

"Has there been a crime?" She took another step. Closer. Close enough for him to stare down at the top of her head, the roundness of her pink cheeks, the point of her pert chin, and beyond, to where the bodice of her bright blue dress peeked from beneath a matching cloak. A gleaming brooch made of black obsidian, set in a silver frame, was pinned to the velvet at her breast, soft and lush. As lush as she was.

He cleared his throat and dragged his eyes to hers, deep and brown. "I expect so."

She nodded, her curls bouncing to and fro. "As do I."

He tightened at the words, at the way she said them with such simple clarity, as though she was his equal. "And?"

"And . . ." She lingered on the word, and he hung on her hesitation, on the curve of her lips, the white edge of her teeth, the little hint of her pink tongue at the end of the word. "I have done nothing requiring a trip to Whitehall." A pause before she added, "Not *today*, at least."

Exasperation flared. "What do you know?"

"Nothing the police will help."

"You mean nothing that will help the police."

"Do I?" With a smile, she turned away, and for one mad moment, he reached for her, stopping himself as his fingers barely grazed the cerulean wool of her cloak. She was a *lady*. Sister to an earl. He couldn't touch her. What had he been thinking?

The woman should not be let out of the house, truly. She was chaos.

And *temptation*.

Not for him. He was perfectly in control. Perfectly able to resist her. He'd resisted worse.

Liar.

He snatched his hand back and found his voice, ignoring the feel of her name on his tongue. "Lady Imogen."

She did not reply, instead coming to a stop, her heavy winter skirts swirling around her ankles with the change in momentum. He stopped, too, his gaze tracking over her shoulder, past her curls, to the young white woman standing in Imogen's path, eyes wide in her pale face.

"Good morning!" Lady Imogen said happily, as though they were anywhere but here, in the shell of a burned-out building.

The young woman blinked, surprise and confusion and something heavier on her face—something made worse when she looked to Thomas. Instinctively, he took a step backward, giving her space. "Oh," she said softly, backing into the street, her gaze tracking over the building, the rubble, and finally the lady, out of place. "Oh," the young woman repeated, seeming to realize herself, and bobbed a quick curtsy.

"There's no need for that," Lady Imogen said, waving her up and tilting her head. "May I help you in some way?"

"I had an . . ." The woman—girl, really. She couldn't have been older than sixteen or seventeen—hesitated, looking to the building once more, eyes somehow going wider, like saucers, filling with palpable disappointment. ". . . appointment." She swallowed. Heavy. Desolate. "This morning. Wiv the seamstress. *This morning.*" The last came with panic.

Lady Imogen nodded. "I understand. As you can see, she is not here."

"Is she . . ." Another hesitation.

"Oh, she is quite well, don't you worry about that. Already setting up shop not far from here." Imogen set down her carpetbag and pushed her cloak aside to reach deep into the wide balloon of her coat sleeve, extracting a small book and a pencil.

Thomas wondered what else she might keep in that sleeve. He would not be surprised to discover a vial of poison or a sharp blade or a heavy candlestick ready for swinging within.

While he wondered, Imogen scribbled on a page of the book before ripping it out and passing it to the girl, who stared down at it for a moment before looking up once more, frustration keen in her eyes.

She couldn't read.

Of course, Thomas wasn't the only one to notice. Lady Imogen put a warm hand on the girl's arm and leaned in, whispering too softly for him to hear. Though he tried, dammit.

The girl's pale fingers—*no gloves*—grasped Imogen's—*also no gloves*—tightly. "Thank you, ma'am."

"Of course. The seamstress will have you sorted in no time. There's no need to worry."

The girl dropped a quick bob and spun away, hurrying back into the grey morning where the rain hovered on the brink of sleet.

"You know where Mrs. O'Dwyer and Mrs. Leafe are," Thomas said.

"Of course I do," Imogen replied, leaning down to collect her ever-present carpetbag. "You do not?"

He clenched his jaw.

"You know, Detective," she said happily, "you really shouldn't begin your day without breakfast. An empty stomach puts you on the back foot."

"I am in no way on my back foot, my lady."

A little smile appeared on her pretty pink lips. No. Not pretty. Not pink. Just lips. Ordinary lips. Not at all for noticing. "Forgive me. I would have thought you would have started with the location of Mrs. O'Dwyer and Leafe."

He scowled. She wasn't wrong, but he'd be damned if he admitted it. "Where are they?"

"That would take the fun out of it, don't you think?" And then, the absolute madwoman headed for her carriage, no doubt thinking she'd won the battle.

He turned away, determined to restore quiet reason to the morning, looking immediately to a clear spot amid the rubble, a spray of dark soot marking the location where the blast originated. And circling the perimeter? A set of fresh, small footprints.

His gaze traced the area, registered a disturbance in the blast pattern—new marks in the dust.

He turned as the carriage door opened from within, welcoming Lady Imogen to safety, her black ringlets bobbing, her lovely bottom swaying as she reached to pass her bag up into the carriage.

Not that the loveliness of her bottom had anything to do with him stopping her. "Lady Imogen," he called out.

She turned back.

"Your bag."

She tilted her head. "My bag?"

"I don't suppose you'll show me what's inside?" He would have wagered a year's salary that she had found something useful in the rubble, and it was now tucked inside that enormous carpetbag she went nowhere without.

Since he'd met her fourteen months earlier (he wasn't counting—precision was his job), Lady Imogen Loveless had produced any number of remarkable things from that bag. Explosives. Weapons. And a series of files that had helped Thomas put the newly formed Detective Branch of Scotland Yard on the map. Information on an earl who'd killed his wives. More on one who'd kidnapped children to let them die in his workhouses. Files thick as Thomas's thumb, each one stamped with an indigo bell and filled with enough evidence to send both of the men away for a lifetime.

What is in there today, Imogen?

And more importantly, why wasn't she willing to share it?

She looked down at the bag in her hand, as though she'd just discovered that it was there. When she returned her gaze to him, there was a playful twinkle in her eye. "Really, Mr. Peck. You ought to know better than to ask a lady about the contents of her reticule."

He slid a look at the bag—capacious and nothing close to a reticule—and replied dryly, "An odd thing to call a reticule—a bit more inside than a handkerchief and an extra hairpin, I'm guessing."

"I carry it with me on outings, and it is full of items that are of a personal nature," she said. "If that is not a reticule, I don't know what to call it."

"Well, I don't think you'd be out of line calling it luggage, considering," he said.

"Nevertheless," she retorted, "a lady never tells."

She turned and passed the bag up through the open door, following it into the dark interior of the carriage.

He watched, but not because of her lovely bottom. Instead, he watched to ensure that she left. Her presence was a continuous distraction. He had work to do, and he knew where to find her.

Mayfair. Where ladies lived. With aristocrats and money. Ladies who had no place in the East End.

Though turning away required more effort than he would ever admit, Thomas did just that, returning to the wreckage of the building to investigate the source of the blast—which had already been investigated by Imogen Loveless, who kept more secrets than a criminal mastermind.

Walking the perimeter of the formerly front room of O'Dwyer and Leafe's Dressmakers shop, he moved toward the staircase—all that remained of the building itself—looking for any evidence left by the architect of the blast. His discerning gaze tracked the floor, searching for clues that might be revealed among the ash and soot and rubble.

More footprints. Heeled boots. Blue, no doubt. Like her dress. Ladies like Imogen Loveless wore shoes that matched their dresses, because they were not beholden to practicalities. They could swan about in bright colors and never worry about soot on their hems or dirt on their heels, as they had all the money and access and privilege they required to buy new skirts or boots or carpetbags or whatever else they required whenever they required it.

Ladies like Imogen Loveless could turn up in Spitalfields to play at investigating an explosion on a whim, because they had no reason to ever be here for legitimate work. Or life.

"Spoiled," he grumbled, deliberately sidestepping the footprints in the dirt, as though in doing so, he might sidestep the woman herself.

A creak sounded above, and Thomas looked up, icy rain coming down through the charred rafters above. He narrowed his gaze and considered the missing upper levels. Somewhere, surely, there was something that had survived the explosion. Some clue to what had happened here—so similar to what had happened to two other buildings in the past three months.

He moved closer to the staircase, wondering how sturdy it might be—

"No! Don't!"

He turned at the shout—too loud to have come from

a lady and yet . . . Lady Imogen was there, leaping from the carriage into the street below, without waiting for the coachman to deliver a step. Into the mud. Not caring that she was ruining her skirts. Proving his point.

Except she didn't seem to be uncaring in that moment. There was something in her eyes—something like . . . concern? He shifted his movement, reversing his course, heading toward her.

Another creak sounded from above, this one louder—more like a rumble.

"Imogen!" The Duchess of Trevescan was leaping down from the carriage, reaching for her friend. "Wait!"

Another rumble. Louder. Closer. He looked up at the stairs.

"Tommy! Don't get too close to the—"

Christ, they were coming down.

And Imogen Loveless was running toward him.

He moved without thinking, heading directly for her, lifting her clear off her feet, barely registering her little "Eep!" as he made for the street, where her trio of friends stood shoulder to shoulder, eyes wide, as the staircase collapsed with a thunder, sending up a cloud of soot and ash behind them.

He turned once he was outside the footprint of the building, looking back at the place where, not ten seconds earlier, he'd been standing. Where she'd been heading. The stairs had collapsed into a heap of wood and brick—enough to have killed a man. And a woman. An emotion he did not care for flared and he looked to the lady in his arms, unable to stop himself from asking, loud and irritated, "Do you see now? That you have no place inside exploded buildings? That you might be hurt?"

Imogen's eyes were wide, and for a heartbeat, he saw something there. Something like fear. And he loathed it—the way it muted her.

Her fire returned, hotter than before. "I wouldn't have been in there if you had taken more care!"

He barely contained a roar of frustration. He should put her down. Put her down and leave her there, on the street in Spitalfields. The madwoman.

And he would. In just a moment.

Just as soon as he was certain she was out of trouble.

"Oh, my," Sesily Calhoun interjected from afar. "Would you look at the muscles on him?"

"I wonder if I could convince Henry to grow a beard again?" the Duchess of Clayborn said. "It is so exciting when they let you shave them off."

Thomas looked to the women watching them. "Aren't you married, ladies?"

"Ah, but not dead," Mrs. Calhoun replied as the Duchess of Clayborn nodded happily. "We're simply admiring the fine way you saved our friend."

Their friend, still in his arms, the soft, lush weight of her a perfect reminder that she was safe. That they were alive. That his heart thrummed in his chest.

"Not that I needed saving," Imogen said softly. "Or, rather, not that I *would* have needed saving if you hadn't ventured so close to the stairs."

He could not stop the growl that came from deep in his chest at the words.

Her brows rose. "Of course, since you *did* get so close to the stairs, and I *did* come back inside, thank goodness you were there to save me, Tommy."

He ignored the way the diminutive—one only his mother and sister used—sounded in her soft, aristocratic voice, and corrected her. "Detective Inspector."

Christ, she was so soft, and she smelled so sweet, like tarts in a shop window, like pears and cream. And as he held her and told himself to *set her down, dammit*, the feel and scent of her took control of the situation. Making it impossible to do anything but feel her. Smell her. Look at

her—all pink cheeks and dark, sparkling eyes and a smile
he should not commit to memory.

When she put a hand to his chest, he couldn't help his
flinch. For a single, wild moment, Thomas Peck was out
of control. And he did not like it.

"That's a lovely sound," she said. "A *harumble*." She
was talking about him. About the sound he'd made.

He put her down. Immediately.

Chapter Three

That evening, just before dinner was served, Imogen received a missive from her brother. That she lived in the same house as her brother—the sixth Earl Dorring—and had done since their father was the fifth Earl Dorring, was no matter. In the eight years since their father died and her brother had assumed the title, Charles Edward Loveless had done all he could to avoid having to interact with his younger sister.

Nine years older in body and what Imogen calculated as approximately ninety years older in soul, when their father died, Charles had left the care and feeding of his younger sister to well-paid governesses, cooks, and housekeepers—a battalion of servants who were more than happy to leave Imogen to her own devices in the upper levels of the east wing of Dorring House and in the depths of the stone cellars beneath the house.

Periodically, it occurred to Imogen that her brother simply might not know where to find her—but whether or not Charles was able to find the east wing or the cellars, he hadn't attempted it before, so it was no surprise that he did not begin doing so that evening.

Instead, he sent a note.

Sister, it read. *Come and see me.*

"Charming," Imogen said under her breath at the summons, which signified two things: first, something serious was afoot, as her brother never initiated their interactions; and second, he was in residence for dinner, a rare occasion, as Dorring had little interest in dining with his sister and often took the meal unsentimentally at his club or with his mistress.

It should be said that Imogen was perfectly happy with such an arrangement, as she'd much prefer eating whatever was warm and delicious in the kitchens than sit in the cold dining room at opposite ends of the enormous gleaming table there, doing her best to pretend her relationship with her brother was anything other than nonexistent.

That, and when Charles was in residence for dinner, they *always* had lamb.

She made a face and pushed the heavy protective spectacles she wore to her forehead, sliding back from her workbench in the Dorring House cellars. She looked to the footman who'd delivered the note. "Please tell my brother I'll be happy to join him just as soon as I am finished here. I am in the middle of something, as you can see."

Geoffrey, the red-cheeked young footman in question, who could not seem to look away from the bubbling pot on the makeshift stove nearby, spoke in the direction of the fire, worry clear in his voice. "Yes, I see that, my lady, but the earl, he was quite insistent . . ."

Imogen sighed. "I see. It is urgent."

"Yes, ma'am."

Fetching a rag, Imogen lifted the pot from the fire and set it on a large, flat stone in the corner of the cavernous space. Wiping her hands on her apron, she waved in the direction of the stairs. "By all means, then. Let's hear what the earl has to say."

The footman did not reply, except to cast a skeptical eye in the direction of the pot, still steaming. He swallowed, his large Adam's apple bobbing in his long, thin throat. "Is it . . ."

"Perfectly safe." Imogen smiled. "I've only ever accidentally exploded it once."

"What is it?" he asked, relief palpable.

"Nothing to worry about. Just a bit of light gunpowder."

His eyes went wide. "My lady—"

She waved away his concern. "No need to worry, Geoffrey. It's not nearly as dangerous as the ordinary stuff. This is more for exploding small things. Locks and safes and whatnot."

He did not look convinced.

She smiled. "Perhaps let's keep it a secret between us, though, hmm? Shall we find my brother?"

After a heartbeat of consideration, the young man seemed to decide that keeping the earl waiting was a more serious infraction than allowing the earl's sister to explode the house, and so Imogen followed the footman up the stairs and down the long hallway to her brother's study, a place she rarely visited.

The footman opened the door to the imposing room appointed with high ceilings, dark wood, and the rich smell of leather and tobacco—a room that had been inhabited by generations of earls prior to the one who currently claimed it—and announced, "Lady Imogen, my lord."

Imogen rolled her eyes and stepped past the young man. "Thank you, Geoffrey. Though my brother and I do not often cross paths, I feel confident he will recognize me."

"Ma'am." Geoffrey offered a tiny, perfect bow and left. At a clip.

Imogen couldn't blame him. She rather wished she could do the same.

Seated at the great Dorring desk—carved from the hull of a sunken Spanish galleon that some distant Dorring had attacked on the high seas—her brother did not look up from the letter he was reading. "Sit."

Imogen did not sit. She waited, taking in her brother's pristine aristocratic perfection.

If a traveler from the past somehow turned up and said, "Do please point me in the direction of a modern gentleman," all of London would lead them directly to Dorring House. Charles was thirty-three, tall and slim with hair the color of a sandy beach and eyes the color of the sea belonging to that sandy beach. He had a long straight nose that would send portrait painters running for a brush, and in her lifetime, Imogen had never seen him with even a thread out of place.

As for Imogen, she was eight inches shorter, and a fair bit rounder, with unruly dark curls and deeply ordinary brown eyes and a face that, should it send painters running for their brushes, would serve as an excellent template for a perfect circle.

All this, even before they opened their mouths, and Charles revealed himself to be deeply proper and miles-deeply boring. Imogen, though she was many things, was neither of those.

That they were siblings was a testament to the Lord's sense of humor.

She grew tired of waiting. "Do you ever wrinkle?"

Silence. Unsurprising, really. Charles did not make unexpected noise. There was nothing even near explosive about him.

"Have you ever stained a sleeve with ink?"

He turned his letter over and continued to read, as though she was not speaking.

Imogen tossed herself into one of the chairs facing his desk. "How often do you require a haircut?"

Charles sighed and raised a hand, indicating she should wait.

"You summoned me, Charles. If you are otherwise oc-cupied I can return to—"

He lowered the letter to the desk and looked up. "You were— Good God, what are you wearing?"

She looked down. "An apron."

"For heaven's sake, why?"

"For the same reason most people wear aprons, I imagine—protection."

"Most people wear cloth aprons to protect their clothing from being stained with soup. You are wearing a *leather* apron."

"Am I to praise you for your powers of perception?"

He set both hands to his desk. "Why are you wearing a leather apron?"

"To protect myself from soup?"

He did not rise. "Imogen."

"Charles."

They stared each other down for a long moment, as he seemed to weigh the length of the conversation if he pressed her on her attire against the length of it if he simply got to the point . . . and chose the shorter course of action. "Alright."

"Are you staying for dinner?"

"I had planned on it."

"Lamb."

"I expect so." He lifted his letter. "If I may?"

She sighed. "Go on."

"You were seen."

"I am seen in a great many places, Charles. Where?"

He looked down at the paper. "Spitalfields." He shuddered. "What a ghastly name for a place."

Imogen froze. She'd been seen at O'Dwyer and Leafe's. Honestly, it should not have come as a surprise. A building had been exploded in the night—people were bound to take notice of it in the morning. But she had not been simply seen—she had been identified. And more than that, *named*. Which meant . . . a number of things. Including the possibility that someone who did not belong in Spitalfields had been there with them that morning.

"Who told you that?"

"As your response confirms it, I see no reason why it matters."

It mattered quite a bit, in fact.

Had it been Tommy?

It wasn't an impossibility. He might be an absolute bear of a man with dark hair and blue eyes and an ability to verbally spar *and* carry her all over Christendom, but all those excellent characteristics did not change the fact that he was exactly the kind of man who would decide to follow some sort of idiotic code after saving her from a falling building, and hie off to tell her brother to put her under lock and key.

"And when was I allegedly in Spitalfields?"

Charles looked her straight in the eye. "This morning."

She tilted her head. "It's not ringing a bell."

Charles pinched the bridge of his nose. "Imogen, this conversation is beneath us both." If there was one thing Charles disliked, it was nonsense. "You were seen in Spitalfields at the"—he read from the paper—"former site of O'Dwyer and Leafe's Dressmakers."

She sighed. "Fine. I was there."

"Why?"

"I was having a dress made. Obviously."

"Difficult to do when the building had been exploded, I imagine." They stared at each other in silence until finally, he stood. "Right. I blame myself, really."

"For the explosion? You really ought not to say that aloud if you expect to get away with it, Charles."

"Especially considering the friendship you appear to have struck up with some *Peeler.*" The last came with dripping disdain.

Well. With an attitude like that, Imogen highly doubted Tommy Peck had told her brother anything about the morning. Which was heartening. Somewhat. At least in the sense that she could return to thinking about Tommy's legs and his eyes and the way he carried her to and fro.

She wondered if he was the strongest man she'd ever known.

He certainly was the handsomest.

Ugh. She shouldn't be thinking about how handsome he was. Or strong. Or the color of his eyes. "He's a detective inspector at Scotland Yard," she corrected her brother and reminded herself. "We are *not* friends."

"No, I don't suppose you are," Charles replied. "Considering you're practically feral."

It took a great deal to insult Imogen, but even she had her limits. "I beg your pardon?"

"As I said, I blame myself, as I understand this is one of any number of places considered inappropriate for ladies at which you've been seen recently."

"For example?"

"One would think I should not have to enumerate them beyond a demolished building, but I shall. I have heard news of you at a ladies' gaming hell in Covent Garden—"

Seventy-Two Shelton Street was much more scandalous than a gaming hell, but she wasn't about to correct him. "Alongside half of Mayfair."

He ignored her. "I'm told you were seen swanning about in Lambeth—"

"At the Duke and Duchess of Clayborn's *wedding*," she interjected.

"I'm to believe the duke and duchess were married in *Lambeth*?"

They had been. Well. Close enough. "Yes."

Her brother waved away the discussion. "Alright. As I understand it, you've been carousing in a ladies' only tavern somewhere on the South Bank."

It was in Covent Garden, but she wasn't about to tell him that either. As it was, he knew far too much about her whereabouts. "It's ladies only, Charles. How much trouble do you think I can get into there?"

"Frankly, there's a difference between ladies and *Ladies*, sister, and I think it's time you start behaving like the correct one."

She wondered how he'd respond if she chloroformed him.

"Father let you roam about and hired you science teachers and God knows what else instead of governesses and . . . dance instructors and whatever else proper young ladies require."

"Whomever," she said.

"What?"

"Not whatever. Whomever," she repeated. "*Dance instructors and whomever else proper ladies require* are people, you know." In his shocked silence at having his grammar corrected, she added, "And I know how to dance."

"Do you?"

"Yes. I took lessons for many years."

"Not do you know how, Imogen. I know you learned. I paid the bills. *Do you dance?*"

"I—" She didn't. "Well, not for lack of knowing, is my point."

"Because you were too busy with your damn laboratory. Mrs. Madewell informed me not three hours ago that she believes you're keeping gunpowder in the cellars."

"I am not!" She was *making* the gunpowder in the cellars. She knew better than to *keep* it there. It was good to know the housekeeper was a spy for her brother, however.

"Of course you're not," he said.

"I'm not?"

He was already moving forward. "But you are far too wild for your own good."

She supposed *wild* was better than *feral*. "I'm perfectly happy, Charles."

"No, you are not."

"I'm not?"

"No. You are four and twenty, and it is well past time to shorten the lead I've allowed you since our father died."

Feral, wild, and now leashed. "That's the third time you've referred to me as though I am an animal of some sort, Charles. I'm beginning to take offense."

"You've soot on your face, and your hair . . ." He trailed off and slid his gaze up to her hair, where her curls were no doubt doing what her curls did. Which he would not understand, as he had perfectly straight hair. She wondered if he even combed it. Perhaps it just fell into place at all times for fear of being criticized.

She narrowed her gaze on him. "If you're quite through, brother."

"I'm not, as a matter of fact. I've made a decision."

"About what?"

"You require a husband."

"A *what*?"

"A man. To take you in hand."

She couldn't help it. She laughed. "Charles. I do *not* require a husband."

"Yes. You do. It's time you were married, Imogen."

"I've been out for six years!" She shook her head. "I'm not . . . marketable." She'd worked quite hard to not be marketable. She was rather proud of it, if she was honest.

"While I don't disagree, I assure you, it has nothing to do with you having been out for six years."

She scowled at him. "And here I was, thinking that a time traveler would think you a gentleman."

"Tomorrow—" He stopped, her words sinking in. "What?"

"Don't worry, I no longer think it."

He shook his head. "Fine. Tomorrow, we make up for lost time."

"What are you going to do, hire me a governess?"

"Not a governess, no," he said calmly, taking his seat once more and extracting a collection of letters from the desk drawer. "But a chaperone would not be out of line."

"A chaperone!" Imogen shot from her chair. This was madness. "I am twenty-four!"

"I'm also restricting access to your private cellar."

"Why?"

"Because husbands do not want odd wives."

"There's nothing odd about being interested in—" She cut herself off, and he waited for her to finish.

When she didn't, he tilted his head toward her as if to say, *You see?*

Chloroform—a brief knockout—was too good for him. Something worse. Something that sent him to the chamber pot for a few days, perhaps. She took a deep breath and did her best to make him see reason. "Charles. I've no need for marriage. I have a home. I have money."

"On the contrary, sister. *I* have a home. I *give you* money."

Her eyes went wide. He couldn't possibly mean— "Are you threatening to cut me off? Because I took a drive to Spitalfields?"

"Not at all. I fully intend to provide you with a large dowry. Enormous enough to get even you married. Quickly." He brandished the stack of envelopes, setting them to the desk one after another. "A chaperone. A dance instructor. A lady's maid—"

"I have a lady's maid."

"Not one with a skill for hair and maquillage, clearly." No, Hillary had a skill for listening when other servants gossiped, which was far more valuable, if you asked Imogen.

Charles was still stacking envelopes on his pile. "A

dressmaker—one whose shop is *not* exploded, last I checked . . ."

Imogen wasn't listening any longer. She was exiting the room. Already making plans.

Her brother couldn't marry her off if he couldn't find her.

Chapter Four

Three mornings later, Thomas Peck's day was boding extremely well. He had slept deeply, uninterrupted by either late night or early morning summonses from Scotland Yard, and woken to a bright January morning, blue skied and unseasonably warm. He'd fetched water, had a quick soak and a quicker shave, and dressed in a navy coat and trousers, his world in perfect order. Precisely as he liked it.

Yes, all was right with the world. No explosions, which meant no lushly curved ladies smelling of pears and cream in their wreckage, which meant no disorder. Everything as it should be, he thought, stroking one hand over his freshly oiled beard as he pulled his hat and greatcoat from the peg just inside the door and left his rooms, making his way downstairs. *An auspicious beginning.*

At which point, everything went sideways.

First, his landlady bid him good morning. Authentically— without any hint of her usual surly censure, and without even a whiff of the long list of grievances she kept so close at hand relating to his tenancy, and that of everyone else in the rooming house.

Instead, she'd offered him breakfast. And not day-old toast and the end of the marmalade, neither. No, Mrs. Edwards had cooked. Eggs. Bacon *and* blood pudding. Bread that was, if his nose was not deceiving him, freshly baked. With butter.

She'd set a salt cellar next to his plate.

A plate that was, when he touched it, *warm*.

It was the warm plate that summoned the whisper of cold dread, which became even more icy when Mrs. Edwards did not return to the kitchens, muttering about how the terrible tenant in room three (a German barber who seemed a perfectly decent fellow) had woken her in the dead of night when he'd come in from *Lord knew where*.

No, instead, the very tall, very slim, very taciturn white woman had lingered. And Thomas Peck, known for being one of the most skilled detectives in the Metropolitan Police Force—so skilled he had been made detective inspector in its newly formed Detective Branch two years earlier—had no choice but to notice . . . Oh no. Was the woman *blushing*?

The freshly baked bread scent went acrid.

Mrs. Edwards's brows rose, expectantly, and Thomas had the unsettling sense that he was in a play, the lines to which he had never learned. "Erm," he said, clearing his throat. "Thank you?"

His landlady smiled a wide, brilliant smile—one he'd never seen before. One that made her seem younger, more handsome, and . . . Was it possible she seemed *friendly*? "Oh, Inspector Peck, it was my absolute pleasure," she gushed, and he froze, recognizing the tone in her voice.

Something had happened.

Before he could decide how to respond, she continued. "I confess, I had no idea I had such a *hero* in the house."

Thomas frowned. *What on earth?*

"I am afraid I do not—"

"Carrying a lady from a collapsing building! To think!"

The memory of Imogen Loveless—*Lady* Imogen Loveless, he reminded himself—in his arms three mornings earlier, dark eyes on his, dust in her silky curls, came unbidden. There'd been a witness.

Of course there had been. There was nothing involving that woman that *wouldn't* summon attention. She was pure chaos. His frown turned to a scowl. "How did you—"

"The *News* even has a sketch!"

"A *what*?"

"Shall I fetch it? So you can see?"

Dear God, no. Peck stood, eager to leave this conversation. This room.

Before he could say no to his landlady, whom he found he liked far better when she was consumed with grouchiness, she was off, into the kitchens. Excellent. A perfect opening for escape. Before she returned with the sketch.

Peck left the breakfast room at a clip—he'd never again be tricked by warm food—barreling past the barber from room three, who tipped his hat with a "Good day, Detective Inspector! Off to keep us all safe, I see!"

Little did the man know that in that moment, Thomas Peck was thinking only of escape.

Dammit.

There had been a witness to the collapse . . . to his carrying Imogen—*Lady* Imogen, he corrected himself once more—from O'Dwyer and Leafe's . . . and they'd gone to the *News.*

Who? It could have been anyone.

And, more importantly, *why?* These days, did there need to be a reason?

But, perhaps even more importantly, *was there any earthly way he could avoid anyone who had seen it?*

That, at least, had an answer: *Absolutely not.*

But he was one of Scotland Yard's best regarded men, the head of the Detective Branch, in line for a promotion to superintendent of his own police division, and big as a house. So at least he could bank on some segment of his colleagues being terrified enough to keep their mouths shut.

Head down, he headed to work, slightly surprised when the two sergeants at the front desk of Whitehall— the building that housed the headquarters of the Metropolitan Police—ignored him altogether, deep in discussion about something else. As he climbed the steps to the row of glass-paned offices that housed Whitehall's senior inspectors, no one seemed to notice his arrival. And by the time he'd made it to the end of the wood-paneled corridor—to his own office in the rear corner of the building, where the Detective Branch was situated, it appeared possible that no one in all of Scotland Yard had seen the *News*.

Or perhaps Mrs. Edwards had been mistaken. Doubtful, that.

"Ah. You're here."

Peck paused in unlocking the door to his office, looking over his shoulder to find John Phillips, a senior Whitehall inspector, coming round the corner, thick file in hand. A tall, dark-skinned Black man with a wardrobe full of perfectly tailored suits, Phillips had been at Scotland Yard a mere two weeks fewer than Thomas had, having joined the Metropolitan Police eleven years earlier after a stint in Her Majesty's Navy. For his part, Thomas had joined the police fresh-faced and green, nearly as green as the force itself—only three months after Parliament had voted for a new, publicly funded police unit to replace the private Bow Street Runners, which had grown rampant with corruption.

Phillips and Thomas had become fast friends, when they'd discovered their mutual love of boxing and ale. After that, they'd chased each other up the rungs of Whitehall, honing each other's powers of deduction as they unofficially competed for the most cases solved in a given month—a tradition that only ended when Peck was assigned a post as an inaugural detective inspector of Scotland Yard, two years earlier. Phillips could have easily joined the Detective Branch, but instead elected to continue his rise through the rungs of the formal Metropolitan Police, overseeing the uniformed members of the Whitehall precinct—five dozen sergeants and constables. While their work now differed, the men remained colleagues and friends.

"I am here," Thomas replied, entering his office and shucking his coat and hat. "And I've work to do."

"No doubt," Phillips said, following him into the room and dropping into a chair as Thomas rounded the desk. "Your explosions won't solve themselves, will they?"

"They will not, in fact." Thomas lifted a stack of files from the desk—seven explosions. Four on one day late last October, no witnesses. No deaths. Just clean explosions taking out some of the cruelest workhouses in the city, on the same morning Imogen Loveless delivered him a file thick as his thumb, indicting their owner in more than one murder.

And now, three more. Different from the October bombings because of their cruelty—November's killed eight at a bakery in Bethnal Green. December's razed a print shop in Whitechapel, sending two to their death and another dozen to surgeons across the East End. And now, the most recent, a seamstress in Spitalfields—in the middle of the night, thankfully, luckily, when the building was empty.

No witnesses. Explosions just as tidy, with little, if any, evidence pointing to a culprit. And just as connected to Lady Imogen—but in a different way. Thomas couldn't prove it, but he was fairly certain she had orchestrated the first round of bombings, ensuring no victims but the wealthy, powerful, titled monster who owned the workhouses. But the recent ones . . . it was almost as though she knew more than he did.

A vision flashed. Lady Imogen in his arms as he stood outside the building, smiling up at him as though everything had gone just as she'd intended. Lush curves, bright laugh, and somehow, always at the center of the chaos.

He'd be fascinated by her if she wasn't so infuriating.

Eager to think of anything but Imogen Loveless, he looked to his friend. "Do you not have an office of your own?"

Phillips ignored the dry question. "Adams is asking for you."

Superintendent Wallace Adams oversaw the Detective Branch along with the rest of the Whitehall police division, but rarely came to this corner of the building, allowing Peck nearly complete control over the Detective Branch, a decision that could not be faulted for Thomas's legendary unflappable nature and keen investigative skill. Adams had been Thomas's superior officer for years before the branch had been formed, and he was happy to turn up to praise the team for a crime well solved, or to deliver a few claps on the back, but he rarely, if ever, summoned his detective inspector.

"What's he want?" Thomas asked.

"Dunno," Phillips said. "Maybe it has something to do with your newfound celebrity?"

Peck froze at the words, full of dry humor, his gaze immediately meeting his friend's. "Dammit."

Phillips grinned. "A proper hero if I do say so myself."

Thomas cursed under his breath. "I don't understand how anyone knew I was there. I was alone."

"Alone, with the lady."

Alone with the lady.

Thomas did not reply, and Phillips filled the silence. "From what I read, she was lucky you were there. She ought to send you a thank-you note."

"No, thank you," Thomas said, making a show of

sorting through the files on his desk. "Knowing her, it would arrive delivered by a wild bear, and explode upon reading."

Phillips's black brows rose in amusement. "Really? Sounds like a worthy adventure."

At first glance, she didn't seem like mayhem. She seemed pretty as a damn picture, with her enormous brown eyes and her full pink lips and her rosy cheeks, all set in a perfect round face atop a lush body that made a man wonder before he remembered she was a lady and ladies weren't for wondering.

And just then—just when he was telling himself not to wonder—that was when she'd knock him over the head with her chaos.

She wielded distraction like a weapon.

In that moment, Thomas would have done anything to distract from the conversation and, more specifically, from the woman herself. He looked down at his desk, hoping for a robbery, perhaps. Some light counterfeiting. He'd settle for a missing hound.

What he got was far worse.

He went hot with . . . something. It wasn't embarrassment. Thomas Peck did not get embarrassed. But truly, he'd take an exploding missive over this. Because there, in all its glory, was the morning's *News*, a front-page headline reading:

SPITALFIELDS GETS A PEEK OF PECK!
*London's Favorite Detective Proves
Fascinatingly Fearless in Building Collapse!*

And as if that weren't atrocious enough, beneath it was a caricature that made Thomas seriously consider going door to door throughout the city to collect every damn issue of the rag, stopping only when they were all deposited into the Thames.

Set against a sketch of the hollowed-out carcass of

the building that had once housed O'Dwyer and Leafe's Dressmakers, an illustrated Peck stepped from the rubble into the street, looking like a giant, with broad shoulders and long legs. In his arms, a woman, plump and dark-haired, her legs kicked up in the air, skirts scandalously askew.

Imogen Loveless. Though, thankfully, she remained unidentified. If she'd been named . . . Well. While he didn't care for the way she turned up constantly in the midst of his working day, he didn't wish her ruined. Indeed, he wished she'd go back to the world into which she'd been born. Where she belonged.

Where he decidedly did *not* belong.

They'd gotten it wrong, of course. Oh, they had the curls right—a riotous cloud—and the lush drape of her in his arms. He could still feel the warm weight of her, soft and curving, even though he absolutely should not remember any of that. But she was unconscious in the picture, dark eyes and full pink lips closed instead of as they'd been—open, with a delighted gleam in one, and a cacophony of chatter in the other.

In one corner of the frame, a gaggle of women of all ages and ilk—old and young, bejeweled and in rags, one holding a squalling infant, another with a basket of posies—stood wide-eyed and sighing, hearts floating up from their clump.

"Fucking hell," he said quietly. He'd never live it down.

"Really, Tom," Phillips said, and Thomas did not have to look to know his friend was smiling a wide and irritating grin. "You'd think you'd embrace such meteoric fame."

"Fame is for artists and dandies," Thomas said. "I've actual work to do. As do you, for that matter."

Phillips—one of the hardest working men at Whitehall—did not rise to the bait, instead ignoring it altogether. "One question," he began, and Thomas clenched the paper in one hand. "Could you explain the physics of your clothing coming off your body as the building came down around you?"

Thomas's gaze returned to the giant in the caricature— no doubt supposed to be him—half naked, his shirt and coat shredded to bits as he stormed from the building.

Phillips tilted his head and considered the cartoon as well. "Or perhaps we are to think it was the lady who could not stop herself from . . . before the rafters came down around you . . ."

"Bugger off."

His friend grinned. "Nah. I think I'll stay." He whistled long and low. "But I shan't stop thinking about whether or not the lady in question had such a nice ankle."

Nicer. "And how do you think your wife would respond to that?"

"I hope by showing me how well her own ankles compare. But your lady would be hard-pressed to match my Susie." No man in the wide world loved a woman like John Phillips loved his wife. It was enough to give anyone in the vicinity a toothache.

"She's not my lady," Thomas grumbled. He simply happened to have the ill fortune to run into Lady Imogen with alarming frequency.

"Of course not. You're simply an everyday hero, rescuing a damsel in distress."

Thomas scoffed. "There was nothing distressed about that particular damsel."

"Rescuing hapless women, then."

The scoff became a little huff of laughter. "If she heard you call her hapless, I'm not sure she wouldn't challenge you to a duel."

"Pistols or swords?"

"Blasting powder, more likely."

"Really." The word was drawn out, as though Phillips were considering his options.

Thomas didn't like that. And he liked the fact that he

didn't like that even less. Clearing his throat, he stood up from the desk. "You know, I think I'd prefer a conversation with Adams over this one, after all."

Philips waved a hand in the direction of the superintendent's offices. "Go on then." He leaned forward and snatched the paper off the desk. "I'll be here. Reading."

"Again, you've an office of your own."

"Yours has better light." Phillips brandished the paper. "And better material."

Thomas rolled his eyes and left the office, in search of more important business, his long strides claiming ground as he pushed thoughts of newspapers and aristocratic women and one lushly beautiful one in particular out of the way. He was a serious man with a serious job and a serious future. And he did not have time for whatever one madcap hour with Lady Imogen Loveless threatened to bring into his life.

Certainly not here, at his place of business.

Satisfied with the resolution, Peck made for the long corridor that led to the rear corner of Whitehall, where the superintendent's office overlooked the mews behind the building.

And that's when she appeared.

For a moment, he thought he'd imagined her. After all, there was no reason for Lady Imogen to be inside Scotland Yard at all, let alone down a long, dark passage full of storage closets and unused interrogation rooms.

But there she was, exiting the uniform room, as though everything were perfectly normal.

As though Thomas himself had summoned her.

And perhaps he had.

She was wearing green this time, a bright, happy emerald with luxurious skirts and the wide ballooned sleeves and her ever-present obsidian brooch. The dress was so bold that it seemed impossible that she was

skulking about down the dark corridor. Surely someone attempting to stay out of sight would have chosen a
less . . . flamboyant color.

"What in hell?" he said, immediately changing course
and heading for her.

And damned if the woman didn't flash him her bold-
est, brightest smile and say, "Hello, Detective Inspector! What brings you here?"

Chapter Five

She hadn't been expecting to see him, but she'd be lying if she said she wasn't *hoping* to see him, and Imogen tried very hard not to lie to herself.

The truth, as anyone with a reasonable amount of sense would agree, was that she rather *liked* seeing the detective inspector. Big and broad and rough-hewn, with a blue gaze stern enough to inspire the kind of thoughts that had landed many women into serious trouble over the years.

Lustful thoughts.

Enjoying a glimpse of the detective inspector was like witnessing an explosion, all color and sound. There was no denying the breathless excitement that came as he bore down on her in a darkened corridor of Scotland Yard as she slipped out of the uniform room, where she'd been snipping small pieces of coats and trousers to inspect in her makeshift lab at Trevescan House (as the one in her own house was off limits since she'd left home). Excitement that had her pressing her back to the doorjamb and watching him come for her, wondering what he might do when he reached her.

The fact that he was more likely to arrest her than anything else was irrelevant.

Pasting a bright smile on her face, she greeted him. "Hello, Detective Inspector! What brings you here?"

"Don't *hello* me, you madwoman," Tommy said,

sounding simultaneously fierce and exasperated, his long gait making up so much ground that it was impossible to run . . . even if there was an escape. *Even if she wishes to escape.*

"That's not a very nice thing to call me," Imogen said. "Or anyone else, for that matter."

"What in hell are you doing here?"

"Scotland Yard is a public building," she said, brazening it through. "I am allowed inside."

"Inside, yes. Inside the uniform room, no."

She made a show of turning to look at the room through which she'd just finished rifling. "Oh, is this where you keep uniforms? I didn't realize."

"The door is open, Lady Imogen."

She should not enjoy exasperating him, but there was little she enjoyed more. "Is it? Oh, so it is. Well. You can see how I might have been confused."

His brows furrowed. "Why are you here?"

"I am looking for you," she replied, the lie coming more naturally than expected. Perhaps because it was not such a lie.

When she and Duchess had decided that the best course of action to prove Imogen's hunch that the navy wool used as tinder at each of the explosions was, in fact, the same weave as the wool specially designed for uniforms at Scotland Yard, Duchess had offered to send someone else to collect samples from Whitehall. Instead, Imogen had volunteered for the task, telling herself it was because she needed something to do now that she was no longer living at Dorring House.

That a trip to Whitehall would allow her to wander past Tommy's windowed office once or twice was simply an added feature. She didn't intend to bother him, only to confirm whether the bulk of his arms when he was holding her in Spitalfields was as she remembered. Maybe to confirm the line of his beard, the color of dark mahogany. Just to check on the firm set of his jaw. The serious weight of his scowl.

For science.

And here he was, assisting her research as he glowered down at her, looming nearly a foot above her, brow furrowed, jaw tight, lips in a straight line. "You were looking for me."

She nodded. "Yes." It came out slightly more breathless than she intended.

Something happened in his blue eyes, their black centers going wide. "Why?"

"I . . ." She trailed off, a half-dozen things she could not say on her lips. Serious things like *I believe members of the police are terrorizing the East End* and *I am here doing some light uniform vandalism.* Extraordinarily unserious things like *I wanted to ogle your broad shoulders.*

Tongue-tied—irritating man; Imogen Loveless did not get *tongue-tied*—she settled on, "I cannot remember."

His brows rose. "Just as you did not remember that you were inside the uniform room?"

She nodded once. "Precisely."

One side of his mouth kicked up—a movement so quick that she would not have noticed it if she was not paying very close attention. But she was paying attention, and the expression set off something in her chest. Something like a *thrumboom.* He stepped closer, and she caught her breath, craning to look up at him as he neared, as he crowded her back through the open door, into the dimly lit space behind—barely a room. "Do you remember now?"

Remember what?

Honestly, Imogen. Focus. She made a show of looking around the tightly packed shelves, carefully avoiding the pile of trousers from which she'd snipped a strip of fabric. "I must have taken a wrong turn."

"Mmm," he said, continuing to stalk her back, the sound a low rumble. "A wrong turn down a dark hallway as far as one can get from the entrance to the building."

Her bottom bumped against a shelf at the back of the small room. She looked up, his face in shadows and somehow, impossibly, his eyes on her. How was he *so* handsome? She cast about for something to say. What would a woman of the world say in this scenario?

The answer came immediately.

"Maybe not such a wrong turn after all."

Oh, my.

Something dark flashed across his face. Dark and wicked. And he was so close. She lifted a hand, setting it to his chest, warm and firm, where his heart beat in a strong, even rhythm. *Bumpbump. Bumpbump.*

"Lady Imogen," he said softly at her ear, still not touching her, every inch of him statue still. "What were you looking for?"

You. You you you.

Knowing she played with fire, she pressed her cheek to his, loving the feel of his smooth beard on her skin, and sighed. "Your office."

A rough sound came from his chest and he did touch her, finally, his fingers coming to her bent elbow, lingering there, on a place she'd never imagined had so many nerve endings. "Are you sure?"

"Yes," she said, not knowing what he meant. Not caring. Whatever it was, she was sure.

"Hmm," he rumbled, his free hand coming to the other side of her face, holding her steady as he pulled away, meeting her eyes, his fingers following the length of her arm to her wrist, against his chest.

And then he was there, a hairsbreadth from her mouth. Almost kissing her, torturing her with the promise of a caress . . . "And what were you going to do when you found me in my office?"

Kiss you.

No, wait. That wasn't right. But now, that was all she could think of. She wanted to kiss him. She wanted him to kiss her. And she didn't care for a moment that they were in the uniform room at Scotland Yard. All she cared was that he was there, and he smelled like leather and amber, and he radiated heat like the sun, and her heart was banging about in her chest, and his fingers were stroking over her wrist in little circles that were going to make her mad if he didn't . . .

"Tommy," she whispered, unable to hold it in.

"My lady," he said, the words so close she could almost feel them on her lips.

And then he was gone. Stepping away from her, leaving her feeling off balance as he brandished a small pair of gold embroidery scissors and strip of navy wool in his hand.

"Hang on—" Her eyes went wide. The piece of uniform fabric, snipped from a pair of trousers, had been safely tucked away in the balloon of her sleeve. "That's mine!"

He tilted his head. "Is it?"

"You thief!"

"Would we say *I* am the thief?"

Her gaze narrowed on him and she reached out to snatch the scissors from his hand. "We would absolutely say you're a scoundrel." She shoved them back into her sleeve.

"Be careful," he said instantly. "You'll hurt yourself."

"Oh, now I am to believe you are concerned about me?"

"Someone ought to be," he retorted. "At any rate, I was simply doing my job; stopping a crime in progress."

She lifted her chin and gave him her coolest look. "The only crime committed here was the crime of my thinking you were worthy of my attentions." Something flashed across his face—too fast for her to identify it, though she hoped it was regret. "To think . . . I nearly let you kiss me."

"I had no intention of kissing you," he said.

The words stung, harsher than she'd ever admit. The whole situation had unsettled her, and she didn't care for it. "Stand aside."

"What were you planning to do with this?" He inspected the fabric.

She did not answer him, instead pushing past.

He grabbed her arm. "Imogen—"

They both froze at the familiarity—her name without her title, combined with his touch. Ignoring the sizzle that threatened, Imogen raised her eyes to his and let her aristocratic upbringing fly. "I beg your pardon, Detective Inspector. Remove your hand."

He did, as though he'd been burned.

Triumph warred with regret. Won. Imogen stepped into the hallway, moving at a clip away from him. Toward the exit. Would he follow? Would he make a meal of what he'd found? Would he insist on searching her person for more? He'd find it. In her pockets, in her other sleeve. She wasn't a fool. When taking samples, she took as many as she reasonably could. He'd found only one, but it was enough to make things difficult.

He caught up with her where the dark hallway met with the bright main thoroughfare of Whitehall. "My lady, you owe me answers."

"I owe you nothing of the sort," she said.

"I could arrest you," he replied.

She stilled. The absolute gall of the man. He'd addled her brain and nearly kissed her in a dark room, then manhandled her forearm and stolen her loot, and he thought *she* was the villain? She turned to meet his gaze. "On what grounds? Tailoring trousers without a permit?"

He scowled down at her. "Attempted theft."

"It's better than attempted kissing."

"I didn't attempt to kiss you," he said, as though that were a perfectly reasonable and not at all hurtful thing to say.

As though it didn't ring with the truth about her. That she was not for kissing. It was not a surprise; Imogen had been in proximity to plenty of men in the six years since her brother had insisted she come out, and she knew she was more than most people were able to accept— even people who were not looking to kiss her. But there had been a tiny part of her that thought perhaps Tommy Peck was different. He was strong and noble and larger than life, and if anyone was able to handle Imogen's *too much*, it would be Tommy, for whom nothing seemed impossible.

But in that moment, holding the fabric he'd thieved from her under the guise of seduction, it became clear that even Thomas Peck had his limits. And Imogen was one of them.

The realization hurt, making her angrier than she expected. "You know, I actually considered having lustful thoughts about you earlier."

He looked as though she'd delivered him a strong facer. *"What?"*

"Peck! Come on, then—we haven't got all day!"

The blessed interruption came from behind Tommy's massive shoulders—too broad for Imogen to see, even as he stiffened and turned toward the speaker, all detective inspector once more.

"I'll be right in."

She took the opportunity of an audience to step out from behind him, surprising the stern-faced white man who stood at a distance, his eyes immediately going wide at Imogen's appearance.

"Oh!" he said.

She waved. "Don't mind me! I am just leaving. I was simply here to—"

The older man interrupted her with a knowing chortle, as though she'd told a joke that only he had understood. "I can imagine."

What did *that* mean?

No matter. She dipped a little curtsy and made for the stairs leading to the exit. She should have known better than to think any trip to Scotland Yard would be easy.

"This isn't over," Tommy whispered as she passed, but he let her go.

"Oh, I think you'll find it absolutely is," she replied.

She did not turn back to see if he watched her leave. It did not matter if he did.

Imogen did not care in the slightest.

Chapter Six

Thomas told himself he was watching her leave to make sure she didn't cause more trouble, as it was a miracle the woman had survived this long with the way she simply marched through the world doing whatever she wished.

Like flirt with him. Like touch him. Like go soft and sweet and tempting in his arms.

No.

Like whatever she'd been doing in the uniform room.

Attempted kissing.

He hated the memory of her face after he'd denied attempting to kiss her. Hated that, for a heartbeat, she'd seemed hurt by his denial. By his lie. Because he absolutely was intending to kiss her before he found scissors in her sleeve.

If he hadn't been so intent on kissing her, he would have been more focused on what the hell she was doing skulking about in Scotland Yard, shredding clothing and whatever else she might have been up to. She was into something. Possibly in over her head with something.

Why didn't she tell him what she knew?

Had he not proven that he was a decent man, willing to take on villains of all ilk? Had he not leapt into the fray in the past, when she and the ladies with whom she spread mayhem came up against a villain?

What was she up to?

And whatever it was, *why in hell didn't she ask him for help?*

The question screamed through him as he watched her leave, resisting the urge to marvel at the sway of her hips beneath that bright green frock, the color of summer grass. Absolutely not hoping that she'd turn back to look at him and give him one more glimpse of her fire—all dark eyes and flushed cheeks.

He had no interest in that. At all.

When the last bit of that bold color disappeared around the corner where the building's central staircase led to the exit, Thomas looked down at the strip of navy wool he'd found inside her sleeve. What did she want with this? He carefully folded the fabric into a small square and tucked it into his palm along with the memory of her soft skin, promising himself he'd go after her that afternoon. He was through letting the lady spread her chaos about the City. These were actual crimes, dammit. And he wasn't going to stop until she told him everything she knew.

Decision made, he followed Adams into the superintendent's office—and a meeting already in progress.

"Ah. *Finally.* Peck," Adams said, waving Thomas in and indicating the other man in the room. "You know Commissioner Battersea, of course."

Whatever this meeting was, it was not good.

"Yes, sir." Thomas nodded in the direction of the commissioner of police, an older, ruddy-cheeked, craggy-faced white man who rarely turned up outside of honor marches or events requiring newspaper reporters. Battersea waved a dismissive hand in his direction, as if to stay any unnecessary chatter—which suited Peck just fine.

The commissioner motioned Peck into a nearby chair. "Have a seat."

After his run-in with Imogen, he was fairly vibrating with pent-up frustration and something altogether too close to desire to be appropriate for the halls of Whitehall and a meeting with the commissioner of police. He did his best to restore the cool exterior he donned whenever dealing with higher-ups at Scotland Yard. "I'll stand, thank you."

It was not a question, and the commissioner immediately looked to Adams. "You weren't wrong about this one."

Adams turned a proud gaze on Thomas. "I told you."

Thomas wished the two of them would get to the point.

"Fair enough. We've a situation." Battersea leaned forward in his chair. "Late last night, I received a visit from the home secretary." Thomas did not reply—years of training had taught him that silence was power—but the home secretary never came down from his place in the House of Lords to fiddle with Scotland Yard, despite having the authority to do just that. Whatever the *situation*, it was not a minor one.

"The home secretary, it seems," Battersea continued, "received a visit of his own yesterday, from Earl Dorring."

Dorring. Recognition slammed through Thomas, though he did his best to hide it. Imogen Loveless's brother. His heart began to pound. It couldn't possibly be a coincidence. The commissioner was here because of what had happened three days earlier. Likely to do the man's bidding and string Thomas up for the caricature in the paper that morning. Or worse. To get him sacked.

"At any rate, the earl has a sister. Isobel or some such."

Imogen. He bit his tongue.

He'd nearly ravished her in the uniform room, not ten minutes earlier.

Battersea waved a dismissive hand, unaware of Thomas's riot of thoughts. "No matter, Adams has a file."

"A file?" he asked, surprised. His attention flickered to Adams. "Has she committed a crime?"

Besides defacing uniforms?

"She's missing," Battersea replied.

A beat. "Who's missing?"

"The girl," Battersea said, as though it was all perfectly clear. "The sister."

"The earl's sister," Thomas clarified, disliking the words on his tongue. Disliking the reason he was required to speak them.

"Isobel," Battersea clarified.

Imogen. Thomas tamped down any evidence of his confusion related to the conversation, which was beginning to feel more farce than anything else. How on earth had Imogen Loveless, who had been standing in Scotland Yard minutes ago, somehow convinced the home secretary, the commissioner of police, and the superintendent of Whitehall that she was missing?

And more importantly . . . why was Thomas involved?

Battersea sighed and turned to the superintendent. "I thought you said this was your best man?"

Adams sputtered and said, "One of the finest detectives Scotland Yard has seen, sir."

"Well, he's rather slow on the uptake." The commissioner met Peck's gaze. "Perhaps you're exhausted from all the attention you received from the papers today."

Though the snide comment ignited a flame of anger, Thomas stayed quiet, knowing it best to keep any relationship to Imogen Loveless under wraps.

The commissioner tamped out his cigar, obviously nearing the end of his patience with the discussion. "Point is, the earl wants the girl found, which is where we come in."

He had found her, Thomas wanted to say. She hadn't been even close to lost mere minutes earlier. Indeed, she'd been in Scotland Yard. In his grasp.

Literally.

"Does Dorring have reason to believe she is in danger?"

"That depends on one's definition of danger," Commissioner Battersea said.

"I assumed we all had the same definition," Thomas said, clenching his teeth, some of his anger slipping through his tight control as he stared down the commissioner and added in an unyielding tone, "Is the lady in danger?"

The air in the room altered subtly, going taut and heavy long enough to make Battersea blanch around the eyes, before Thomas reined himself in.

Control. It was the key to everything, in Thomas's experience. He would not allow himself to lose it again, no matter the provocation.

No matter the brief, petty satisfaction of seeing his so-called superior's pupils widen in instinctual fear—before his bushy white brows lowered and his cheeks stained an even darker red.

Sensing the tension, Adams rushed to clarify. "There is concern the lady's reputation might be sullied if she is allowed to . . . cavort about."

Considering all the places the lady frequented on a normal Thursday evening, Thomas thought that waylaying her cavorting was an impossibility. Nevertheless, his brow furrowed and he said, "And so, they came to Scotland Yard to protect . . ."

"Her virtue, my boy," the commissioner blustered in a clear attempt to reclaim his own power before turning back to Adams. "Truly maybe you were wrong about this one."

Thomas, for his part, had trouble hearing anything after *protecting her virtue*. His fists clenched. Surely this was some kind of wild jest delivered by the universe, considering he'd been in a dark room alone with Imogen Loveless minutes earlier, and neither of them was thinking about her virtue.

He met Battersea's gaze impassively as the commissioner puffed himself up importantly. "I'll make it plain for you, Peck. The Met is planning to assign a superintendent to the Detective Branch. Your name is at the top of the list, thanks to Adams, who swears you've a brain in your head and a fair bit of honor in the rest of you."

Thomas lifted his chin, the pride and satisfaction that burst through him making a small thing of allowing Battersea to feel he'd regained the upper hand. A promotion to superintendent of the Detective Branch would allow Thomas to implement a dozen new ideas—to think about crime in new ways, and not just in the places Whitehall prioritized. "Thank you, sir."

"Don't thank me yet," Battersea sniffed. "Superintendents must be approved by the home secretary."

Everything clicked into place. He looked to Adams, who gave him a knowing smile—his mentor's pride clear as day.

"No one will deny you're regularly making Whitehall look heroic," Battersea was saying in a grudging tone. "Though we could do with more solving crime and less carting ladies about in the *News,* if you ask me."

Thomas resisted the urge to tell Battersea to shut his damn mouth—instead reminding himself that he could suffer the commissioner's bluster if it meant the promotion and control over the Detective Branch. A far more important endgame than putting the man in his place.

The man, who was still talking. "That . . . and I'm not sure the House of Lords is wild about your heroism— what with the fact that you've made something of a habit of sending aristocrats to prison."

"Only the aristocrats who make a habit of committing crimes," Peck pointed out, avoiding the way the conversation continued to weave around Lady Imogen and her crew of chaos, who'd delivered him the evidence to send an earl and a marquess to Newgate in the last year.

"Point is, if you're going to become a superintendent," Battersea intoned, coming to his feet, "it's time you learn that aristocrats get what they want, my boy. And as the lady is causing her brother some worry, and her brother and the home secretary play carom together, her disappearance is now *Whitehall's* worry. And seeing as you're tempted by the idea of a promotion?" Battersea prompted.

"Yes, sir." More than tempted. Thomas had been aiming for this from the moment he'd begun working for the police eleven years earlier. A promotion would give him the funds and the freedom to secure his family's status—to do what his father had been unable to do all those years ago, and set a new course.

"Well, then . . . it seems the girl is *your* worry, Inspector."

Imogen. Not missing, whom he'd been planning to chase down as soon as possible anyway. Get the information she had relating to his investigation and secure a promotion in the balance? There was no way to lose. Thomas focused on the press of the fabric he'd found in her sleeve, warm in his palm. "Yes, sir."

Battersea clapped him on the shoulder. "Good man."

Thomas stared down at the older man's hand, where it lay pale and heavy. He did not move, except to return his gaze to the commissioner, full of disdain and steel.

The commissioner removed his hand like it burned, and made a meal of exiting the room, leaving Thomas waiting, standing rod straight, until the door closed behind the man. He rounded on Adams, who was already heading to the table in the corner to pour himself his first drink of the day.

Adams shook his head as he poured. "You'd better find the gel, Tom. Don't give that man any reason to make good on the way he feels about you."

"I was perfectly respectful," Thomas protested.

"You were fucking terrifying. You always are," Adams said. "Drink?"

Thomas shook his head. "She won't be difficult to find."

"You seem sure of yourself." Adams turned an amused look on him. "Is she one of your acolytes? A lady with a penchant for a Peek of Peck?"

Peck grimaced at the question—a reminder of both the fact that Adams did not know anything about his prior interactions with Lady Imogen, and the fact that Thomas's embarrassing celebrity was becoming unavoidable. "She isn't. But finding people is my job."

Adams made an affirming sound. "And how's that bit of the job going? I understand you're paying rather close attention to the explosions in the East End."

"Three in as many months," Thomas said. "Someone ought to be paying attention."

"Probably some landlord looking for a way to build something new and raise rents," Adams said. His gaze sharpened. "Do you have reason to believe they are connected?"

Imogen has been at all three. Ordinarily, he would tell Adams just that—Adams was the man who had taught Thomas that coincidences were rarely coincidental. The Hell's Belles turning up at sites of three explosions that already felt connected was enough to prove that there was something amiss.

But there was a reason Imogen hadn't revealed her findings to him.

In the past, the lady had helped take down two separate aristocrats terrorizing their families, employees, and more. Perhaps she was into something now. Perhaps she was deeper than she was willing to admit.

Perhaps she was in danger.

Whatever it was, she hadn't confided in Thomas. And so, for the first time in his long career, he found himself withholding information from Adams. "I think they're connected, but I cannot prove it."

"No evidence?" Adams said. "That's a surprise."

"I'm closer every day," Thomas replied.

"Well, don't let it consume you. There are plenty of crimes west of the Garden that need solving." Thomas didn't care for the implication that the East End was less worthy of Scotland Yard's investigation than the west of London, but he didn't reply. Not even when Adams added, "And *that's* how a man gets a promotion—not the other." A pause. "Now for the interesting bit—who was your visitor?" Adams tilted his head toward the door. "The girl who came to see you?"

Thomas's fist tightened at his side, the only indication of the discomfort that flooded him at Adams's mention of Lady Imogen. "No one."

Adams cut him a disbelieving look. "Was she? Funny that. I couldn't help but notice the likeness to the illustration in the *News*. The curves and the curls . . ."

"She's no one," Thomas said, more firmly than he intended, not liking that Adams noticed anything about Imogen. Especially not the curves. Or the curls.

Imogen Loveless was a lady from Mayfair, and she wasn't for noticing by men who came from the gutter.

A pause, and Adams lifted a file from his desk. "Fair enough. You worry about finding this girl then. The earl's sister."

"I'm already making plans." He had been since he'd seen the edge of her dress disappear down the corridor. Even without the assignment, he would have sought her out. To uncover her purpose. To divine her games and how Scotland Yard played into them.

"Take heart. Finding one girl can't be more difficult than robbers and murderers," Adams allowed.

Adams didn't know that Imogen Loveless was just as dangerous as robbers and murderers when she wanted to be. Thomas had no doubt she kept myriad weapons in her carpetbag full of mayhem.

Adams extended the file to Thomas, who stared at it for a long while, a single name taunting him from the corner closest to him: *Loveless, Lady Imogen*.

"This is it, Tom," Adams said. "Think of how proud your da would be."

The words tightened Thomas's chest, welcome and bittersweet. David Peck and Wallace Adams had come up alongside each other on the streets of the East End, picking and scraping to make ends meet. When Adams had become a Bow Street Runner and then joined the police, Thomas's father had been a street sweeper, working all hours of the day and taking extra work wherever he could to care for his wife and three children.

From the moment Thomas had been old enough to hear it, David Peck had made sure his son knew that every sweep of his broom was to ensure a better life for his children. Thomas would learn to read. He'd get a good job—one that paid well for food and heat and a wife and children. And he'd live better than his parents.

Longer, too, it turned out. David had died when Thomas was nineteen, leaving his best friend, Wallace Adams, who promised to care for the wife and children he left.

Adams had done just that, becoming a new kind of father—bringing Thomas into Scotland Yard, making sure Rose met and married a decent man, and paving the way for Stanley to become a vicar. Without their father, they might not have learned to work and love, but without Adams, they wouldn't have survived.

"He would have been so proud, Tom," Adams said.

Thomas nodded. His father. Who'd done all he could to lift his children out of the gutter. Whom Thomas tried to make proud every day. And it wasn't just David Peck's memory Thomas made proud with the promise of a promotion. It was Adams, too, his mentor and friend.

"You make it sound like a hero's quest," Thomas replied, taking Lady Imogen's file.

Adams gave a little chuckle. "When it comes to the aristocracy, hero's quests come in various shapes."

He opened the file to read. A thin dossier. A few aristocratic acquaintances, a handful of sweets shops and haberdasheries that she frequented, the name and age of the lady's maid. None of the important bits. No reference to files inked with blue bells, to a carpetbag full of explosives, to vigilante justice.

Either Dorring didn't know much about his sister or he didn't care much about her. If he did, he'd have already found the lady—whom Thomas expected to find before sunup—along with all she knew about the explosions in the East End.

He looked to his superior. "And when I find her?"

"Deliver the chit home and collect your accolades from the toffs. And your promotion from Battersea." Adams paused, and for a moment, let their personal history into the room. "You're the best detective in the Yard, Tom, and you're this close to getting what we've always wanted for you. What we've always known was for you."

Thomas did not misunderstand that *we*—Adams, yes. But his family, too. And most of all, his father, no longer here to see it.

"All you have to do is bring the girl to heel. How difficult can it be?"

Peck nearly laughed at the words—the easy suggestion that Imogen was meek and biddable. That he might turn up wherever she'd decided to hide and she'd follow him directly home. Wallace Adams did not know that Lady Imogen Loveless was not the kind of woman who was easily brought to heel. Indeed, she was the kind of woman who might bite if she was given the chance.

He'd be doing the rest of Scotland Yard a favor taking this project. If it went to someone else, someone who was not familiar with the lady's particular brand of chaos . . . Well, if she did bite, Thomas would be prepared.

He might just like it.

He tried to tell himself the thought was unwelcome. Tried to push it away. But the idea of Imogen Loveless coming for him with her smart mouth . . . Well, it made a man wonder about that mouth . . . what it would feel like. What it would taste like. What it would take to stop it . . . and turn all her clever little retorts into pretty little sighs.

It made a man wonder how Imogen sounded when she sighed.

Lady Imogen. She was not for wondering.

She was for finding. Quickly. And without spectacle.

For purely occupational reasons.

Chapter Seven

"To freedom!" Imogen announced happily that evening, lifting a pint of ale with gusto and toasting her friends.

"To freedom!" The women around her—Sesily, Adelaide, and Duchess—matched the toast . . . and Imogen's excitement.

In the three days since she'd left her brother's home, Imogen had made herself comfortable in her friend's enormous and mostly empty town house on South Audley Street. Duchess had suggested that Imogen select one of the dozen guest rooms in the house for herself, as well as providing her free rein of the cellars for a new laboratory should she desire. Which of course she did.

Truly, there were benefits to being dear friends with someone rich, powerful, beautiful, and married to a long absent husband who paid his wife's bills and never came to town.

That night, the quartet of women, along with Sesily and Adelaide's husbands, were ensconced around the large table in the rear corner of the large central room of The Place, a tavern for women and others for whom the rest of the world could be a danger, tucked away in Covent Garden—difficult to find if one wasn't searching for it in the tangled web of streets between Bedford Street and St. Martin's Lane.

Over the years, The Place had become *their* place—a

safe haven from the wide world where they could meet beyond the censorious gaze of society . . . without worry of discovery or disdain. They'd begun meeting there several years earlier, when Duchess had gathered them together for a common purpose—to help those whom society ignored, or worse, injured.

It had begun simply—helping women who came to them with a wish to change their fate. Wives looking to escape abusive husbands. Daughters and sisters seeking a way out from cruel fathers and brothers looking to trade them for power and money. Women looking to marry as they wished, to stand up to their employers, to escape their lot, to live their lives on their own terms.

Women from all walks. The daughter of a duke who'd found herself with child. The wife of a butcher who was a violent drunk. A shopgirl who'd witnessed a crime and needed protection. A rich merchant's daughter looking to escape a loveless aristocratic marriage.

But soon, word was out. And their work became more complicated. Assisting a brothel full of girls out from under the thumb of their vicious employer. Rescuing children from workhouses. Providing safe havens for powerless workers. Sending aristocrats to prison for embezzling funds from orphanages. Sending others to prison for murder. Sending still more to . . . well, to other places entirely. In only a handful of years, the Hell's Belles had become legendary.

They did their best to help as many who needed them as could find them . . . and they did it more often than not from the corner table at The Place, where people went not to be seen, but to live. There, those who were rarely welcomed in the rest of London could drink and dance and laugh and be welcomed freely, and no one cared that Sesily Calhoun had once been Mayfair's brightest scandal, or that Adelaide was daughter to one of London's greatest crime lords, or that Duchess spent her absent husband's money like it was water. Nor did they care that Imogen was odd . . . or in hiding from her brother.

In short, The Place was perfect.

And it was one of Imogen's favorite spots in all the world.

She set her glass down on the scarred table with a *thunk* and pronounced, "I refuse to be governed! Can you imagine! He actually thought he could marry me off to some . . ."

"Toff!" Sesily helped.

Imogen pointed at her friend. "Yes!"

"Good for you!" Adelaide said.

"I beg your pardon!" The Duke of Clayborn feigned offense. "*You* married a toff!"

"Yes, my love, but there is hope of your reformation," his wife retorted. Everyone laughed and she leaned into his kiss—a public display of affection that would have shocked the House of Lords down to their well-heeled shoes.

"How long do you intend to keep your location from your brother?" Sesily asked.

"My *brother*," Imogen spat, "has absolutely no reason to care about my whereabouts as long as I remain undetected."

Adelaide adjusted her spectacles and said, dryly, "Well, considering how meek and biddable you are . . . that should not be difficult."

Everyone laughed, and Imogen tossed her friend a look. "Well. Let's say I shall do what I can to steer clear of him," she said before looking at Duchess. "If Duchess does not mind a tenant . . . at least until I find my own footing."

Brows raised around the table. "Find your own footing—" Sesily said, disbelief in her voice.

"Imogen—" Adelaide began.

They both stopped, and Duchess finished their thoughts. "I think this *is* finding your own footing, my friend. Leaving your brother's house. Deciding to captain your own fate."

"Oh," Imogen said, feeling rather emotional in the wake of her friends' responses. "That's a terribly nice thing to say."

"Speaking of your footing," Adelaide began. "How was your trip to Scotland Yard this morning?"

Unsettling.

"Productive," she said, meeting the eyes of the women around the table. "No one stopped me on my way to the uniform room—and I was able to take four samples of fabric that I believe match the same stuff that has been used as a fuse in two of the three explosions. Between that and the common blast patterns and the type of blasting oil, I no longer have any doubts—Bethnal Green, Whitechapel, and Spitalfields were set by the same people."

"Truly, Lady Imogen," the Duke of Clayborn said, "your understanding of explosives would be terrifying if I were not on your side."

She flashed him a bright smile. "And who said I was on your side, toff?"

Everyone around the table laughed, and Imogen finished articulating her plan. "I'm going to take them to O'Dwyer and Leafe's, and see if someone there can match the weave of the fabric. I've a dozen tests to run, but I'd wager the contents of my carpetbag that we're dealing with skill, means, access, and information."

"If you're right, that sounds like power, and a lot of it," the Duke of Clayborn interjected, looking to his wife. "I assume you've spoken to your father?"

Adelaide nodded, eyes wide behind her spectacles. "As suspected, it's not his crew."

"Who then?" Clayborn asked.

The women around the table shared a look, and the

duke sat back. "Ah. As usual, the Hell's Belles are one step ahead."

Caleb Calhoun, Sesily's husband, tipped his ale in salute and said in his dry, American accent, "You get used to it, Duke." He looked to the table. "Who?"

"We don't know," Imogen said. "Not with certainty."

"But Imogen has a hunch," Adelaide said.

"I have a hunch." She looked at Duchess. "But none of the evidence I have is proof. Not yet. And even if it were, we don't have the important bit."

Sesily chimed in. "We don't know who's paying them."

Someone was absolutely paying them. There was no coincidence involved in three businesses hiding secret, revolutionary activities going up in flames. And even if Scotland Yard was doing the exploding, it was at the behest of others. Far more powerful others.

"That's where I come in," Duchess said, extracting a piece of paper from her pocket and setting it on the table. Everyone leaned in to read the three names on the paper. A marquess and two earls.

Clayborn shook his head. "Three of the most powerful men in Lords." He looked up at Duchess. "Can you prove it?"

She shook her head. "Not yet."

"If it's true," Imogen said, looking at her friend, "it's more dangerous than anything we've done before."

Duchess nodded. "And we can't use your man."

Her man.

Tommy.

Duchess's meaning was not lost. As helpful as he'd been in the past—arresting a handful of aristocrats after the Belles had provided him with unimpeachable proof of their crimes—Tommy Peck was first and foremost a detective inspector at Scotland Yard. And as such, he could not be trusted to help should they produce proof of corruption at Whitehall.

Which made Imogen's already inconvenient fascination with him all the more bothersome.

"So if we cannot go to Scotland Yard . . ." Adelaide began.

". . . then we shall have no choice but to go higher," Duchess replied. "But we'll need as much proof as we can find."

"We need to get into their houses," Sesily said simply, as though it were a perfectly normal course of action. "If they're making payments to Scotland Yard . . . there will be proof. Who can get us invitations to dinner?" Her husband groaned beside her, and she patted his leg. "Don't worry, Caleb darling. You won't have to dine with aristocrats."

"No one is dining with aristocrats in January," Duchess said. "Parliament isn't back in session until March. No Parliament, no season. No season, no balls, no dinners, no teas, none of it."

"We can't wait until March," Adelaide said. "These places—the people who use them—who *need* them—they are in danger *tonight*. Right now."

Duchess nodded. "But not even I can manufacture a social season."

"You can't," Imogen said, staring down at the list of names—names she knew from six years in society, and twenty-four as Charles Loveless, Earl Dorring's sister. "But my brother can."

Everyone looked at her, a collection of confusion and curiosity on their faces. She looked to Duchess and set her finger on the first name. "Unmarried." The second. "Youngest son, unmarried." The third. "Brother, unmarried."

She pointed to herself. "Are we not lucky that my brother has an unmarried sister and is willing to call in virtually every chit he has to cure her of the affliction? And quickly?"

Understanding dawned around the table. "Imogen

Loveless," Sesily said. "Are you suggesting that you fabricate a search for a groom?"

She looked to Sesily. "I'm certainly not suggesting I search for a groom in earnest. But I can tolerate a few balls if it means we can get to the bottom of whatever is happening in the East End."

"And so?" Duchess asked.

Imogen met her friend's expectant gaze. "And so . . . I think you should throw me a ball."

"Wonderful," Duchess said, as though she'd lived her whole life dreaming of just that. "Let's get you married, Imogen Loveless."

"Or at least let's get the unmarried men of London panting after you," Sesily retorted. "That's the fun part!"

"Hang on," Adelaide interjected. "What of captaining your own fate? What of charting a new course?"

The course could wait. Imogen looked to Duchess. "May I come and stay again, Your Grace? At a later date? When I've fully aggravated my brother into never wanting to eat lamb at the same table again?"

"Whenever you like, for as long as you like. You know that," Duchess said, all certainty. "In the meantime, I believe you continue to require a place for your experiments? You are welcome to explode my cellars all you like, whenever you like."

Imogen grinned. "Your husband might feel differently."

"What my husband does not know, he cannot protest. What was it you said?" Duchess lifted her glass, fizzing with champagne. "To freedom!"

"To freedom!" the others cheered, turning heads nearby as Duchess downed her drink.

"As though it isn't loud enough in here!" Maggie O'Tiernen arrived, a twinkle in her dark eyes as she settled a hand on Caleb's shoulder and leaned in to top up Duchess's champagne.

A Black woman who'd left Ireland for London the moment she was able, Maggie had arrived with the clothes on her back to build a new life, where she could live freely as a woman, embodying her true self. Knowing what the world could do to those who wished to live authentically, she'd built a safe haven here, on the edges of Covent Garden. The rules were simple: If you were looking for a place to live out loud, and you could find it, The Place would have you, however you came, whomever you loved.

"Alright, ladies?" Maggie asked, before turning to Clayborn and Caleb where they sat, looking bemused. "Lads?"

The duke and Mr. Calhoun were the rare exception to the rule that The Place was largely for women, but Caleb Calhoun had won Maggie's heart when he'd taken down a handful of thugs who'd tried to burn it to the ground fourteen months earlier, and the duke and Adelaide paid handsome rent to keep the apartments abovestairs where she once lived, so Maggie looked the other way as long as they stayed quiet and didn't upset the customers.

Imogen was also fairly certain Maggie had required the two men to take a blood vow that they'd enter the fray if anyone ever threatened The Place while they were there . . . so that helped as well. Though, truthfully, no blood vow was necessary, as there was no doubt that both men would happily put themselves in front of a bullet to keep their wives safe.

It was very sweet, really.

Sweet enough to make a woman wonder what it might be to have a man worried about her safety. Not that Imogen needed it. And definitely not that she ever dwelled on it. Late at night. When the world was quiet and thoughts were loud.

As she attempted to recall the exact feeling of being carried out of a building as it collapsed around her, cradled close to a broad, warm chest.

"Alright, Maggie." Duchess's response rose from the back corner of the table, where she was tucked into enough darkness that it would be difficult to identify her. "Packed to the gills tonight, I see."

"Aye. Have been every night for the last two weeks. Had to ask The Bastards to loan me three of their bruisers—they're on every door." The Bareknuckle Bastards ran Covent Garden—protecting its people and keeping out anyone who wished them ill . . . all while running contraband beneath the eyes of the aristocracy and doing their best to fleece the worst of it. If Maggie's security had come courtesy of them, it was the best there was.

Which was why Duchess asked, "Is there a worry?" It wouldn't be the first time Maggie had required security—The Place had been knocked over several times since it had opened. Imogen thought of the explosion of O'Dwyer and Leafe's. Men in power did not care for places beyond their control.

There was always a worry.

"Nothing specific," Maggie agreed, sounding less than pleased. "The city appears to have discovered that the ale here at The Place is better than the ale anywhere else in town."

"Mithra must be thrilled," Duchess offered.

"So thrilled, she's increasing her prices," Maggie said, looking over her shoulder at the Punjabi brew-mistress holding court at the bar, and shouted the next. "As though we haven't been carrying her swill from the start!"

Mithra turned with a bright smile and shouted, "Don't seem like swill now, does it, Mags?"

"You'll have to make The Place members-only if this goes on, Maggie," Caleb said.

"You'd best hope not, Calhoun," the tavern mistress retorted. "I'm not sure you'll make the list."

"Ah, but my wife will," he said. "And then you'll have no choice but to have me."

"You're lucky to have married so high above your station," Maggie replied, already returning to the bar.

"I am, indeed," Calhoun said, now looking directly at Sesily. Imogen ignored the little twinge of envy that came with the portrait the two of them made.

"Before the two of you decide to rush home to bed," Adelaide said dryly, "I've something I'd like to discuss." Everyone turned attention to her as she held her newspaper up like a trophy. "Have we all seen today's *News*?" Before anyone could answer, she set the paper on the table and pointed one long, slim finger at the illustration there. "It seems our friend is famous."

Confused, Imogen leaned in along with everyone else, tilting her head to make sense of the drawing. The enormous man. The woman in his arms. Their clothing's mutual state of disarray. And the building behind, reduced to rubble. *Was that—*

Her face was instantly hot. "Oh . . ."

"Oh, my!" Sesily turned the paper on the table to get a better look. She burst out laughing and repeated, "Oh, my!"

"Really, Sesily," Duchess admonished, snatching the paper from its place, looking down at it for a long moment before saying, "This clearly isn't you, Imogen. The woman the detective inspector is carrying from the building is unconscious."

"Someone was unconscious?" Caleb looked to his wife. "Sesily—"

She waved a hand. "No one was unconscious, Caleb. That's the point."

"But someone did carry Imogen from the building?" the Duke of Clayborn prompted.

"Detective Inspector Peck," Adelaide said. "But it wasn't really a carry. More of a . . ." She paused, considering. ". . . running lift. He had no choice really."

"Oh?" asked the duke. "And why not?"

"Well, it was falling down."

"The building." This from Calhoun.

"Yes," Sesily said.

"Fucking hell, Sesily—"

"Dammit, Adelaide—" The curses came in unison.

"It wasn't me in the building!" Sesily.

"I was in the carriage! It was Imogen!" Adelaide.

The two men turned on her, looking simultaneously concerned and outraged. "Fucking hell, Imogen!"

"Dammit, Imogen!"

Imogen looked to her friends. "Traitors!"

Sesily and Adelaide had the grace to look chagrined.

Imogen extended her hands to the two men who, very sweetly, had claimed her as one of their own after marrying into the crew. "For what it's worth, you two . . . this is why we don't tell you everything."

"What in hell—" Caleb.

"I would like to bring this conversation back to what is important," Duchess interjected, summoning everyone's attention to where she was holding the paper in their direction. "Leaving aside the fact that Imogen is unconscious here—an absolute insult, if you ask me—"

"Thank you," Imogen replied. She'd been perfectly conscious. Indeed, if it hadn't been for her, it was the inspector who would have been knocked out by the falling staircase.

"You're welcome," Duchess said, a twinkle in her blue eyes. "I will say this: I am quite impressed with how well they portrayed the detective inspector's muscles."

A chorus of feminine laughter was met with masculine groans, and Imogen wondered if she would be missed if she crawled beneath the table.

She covered her face. "Do you think he's seen it?"

If he'd seen it, what did he think?

Did he remember the feel of her in his arms as well as she remembered the feel of his arms around her?

No doubt he was not remembering anything of the sort. Instead, he was likely imagining how much easier his life might be without Imogen skulking about in burned out buildings and Scotland Yard uniform rooms. He was probably furious about the caricature and, by extension, with *her*.

She really couldn't blame him.

Though, she didn't want him furious with her.

She wanted him, full stop.

Of course, she would never admit it. Never in a million years would she tell anyone—not even her friends—how, late at night, when she lay awake in her bed, thinking about all that might be and all that she might have, she sometimes allowed herself to imagine the very ridiculous and absolutely impossible possibility that she might, one day, have Detective Inspector Thomas Peck.

Thighs and all.

"Maybe the sketch isn't the worst thing to have happened," Duchess said.

"It isn't?" Imogen looked up.

"Maybe . . . if we are correct about the explosions . . . about who is setting them . . ."

Detective Inspector, Scotland Yard.

Adelaide understood at the same time. "Enemies closer."

The words ran through Imogen, a little blast. A tiny *whooom*.

Tommy Peck . . . close. Tommy Peck, in the dark, his beard against her cheek, his broad chest warm at her hand, his voice low and dark at her ear. Coming for her. *Claiming her.*

Kissing her.

"Imogen?" She looked up to find Duchess's icy blue gaze on hers.

"Yes?"

"You said no one stopped you on the way into Scotland Yard."

Imogen held back her wince. "Yes."

"How did things go on the way out?"

She cleared her throat. *She'd been too much.*
I didn't attempt to kiss you.

She'd been so sure he was going to kiss her. It was all so embarrassing.

Sesily leaned forward. "*Lady Imogen!* What are you hiding from us?"

Imogen shook her head, her heart beating a *tapatap* in her chest. "Nothing happened."

It was the truth. And also a lie.

Adelaide's brows rose. "In my experience that is precisely the kind of thing people say when something absolutely happened, Imogen."

"Nothing happened," she said again, trying to make it sound as insistent as possible. "It's just that I . . . ran into . . . Tommy."

The ladies around the table shared knowing looks.

"You needn't look so amused," Imogen grumbled.

"Where did you run into *Tommy*?" Duchess asked.

"In the uniform room." She paused. "It was dark. We were alone."

"That sounds like the kind of place where something absolutely happened," Sesily said.

"Nothing happened!" Imogen said for the third time. "He discovered one of the strips of fabric in my sleeve."

"In your sleeve," Duchess said. "How did he find it?"

"He tricked me."

"How?" Adelaide said.

"The way men trick women, I imagine," Imogen said, frustrated. "He leaned in and he was warm and big and broad and he smelled like sunshine and darkness altogether, and his beard was against my cheek, and the next thing I knew, he'd stolen my sewing scissors and a strip of the fabric I'd cut from a pair of trousers."

There was a beat of silence as the words landed around the table, and Imogen decided that if she was in for a penny, she might as well be in for a pound. And then she said, "But he didn't kiss me, the wretched man. In fact, he told me he had no intention of even attempting to kiss me."

"Awful," Adelaide replied.

"Monstrous," Sesily agreed.

Their husbands shared a look of confusion. Caleb started. "Wait. He was to kiss her?"

"He made a tacit promise to," Sesily said. "With the warmth and the delicious smells."

"And the beard," Adelaide said. "Once it touches you, there must be kissing. It's a rule."

"Perhaps he was attempting to remain a gentleman," Clayborn offered.

The women around the table scoffed, and Sesily said, "Awful."

Imogen had never felt more vindicated. "Thank you."

"And what happened?" Adelaide said.

"I left," she said.

"And he didn't follow you?" Sesily asked, all affront. "No!"

"Monstrous," Sesily announced dramatically.

"Thank you," Imogen said, immensely grateful for good friends.

"As much as all this is fascinating," Duchess interjected, "may I point out, Imogen, that Thomas Peck is a high-ranking member of the Detective Branch at Scotland Yard and, as I understand it, the only viable name on a list of potential superintendents for that branch?"

Imogen's gaze flew to Duchess's. "Really?"

Duchess tilted her head, blond hair gleaming in the candlelight. "Really. If I had to wager, he's looking for a way to secure that promotion."

Imogen did not misunderstand. If the Belles were right—*and they were right, she knew it*—and the police were being paid by members of the House of Lords to lay waste to places in the East End that kept women and others who fought for power safe . . . every policeman in London was suspect.

Including Tommy Peck—especially him, if he was looking to a promotion.

No matter how noble he seemed.

Imogen's gaze dropped to the sketch again. They really had drawn him beautifully—his sleek beard and his dark hair and his muscular arms . . . He'd been wearing an overcoat, but she could distinctly remember how easily he'd held her—and she was not exactly light as a feather. His arms were likely just as they were in the sketch. Bulging muscles the size of small linden trees.

She wouldn't dwell on his thighs—despite the way they tempted her, even in an illustrated format.

"In that case," Sesily said with a laugh, "I cannot imagine serious Mr. Peck enjoyed this illustration even half as much as we did."

He must have loathed it.

Imogen met Duchess's glacially blue gaze as she said, soft warning—soft *understanding*—in her tone, "Once a Peeler, always a Peeler, Imogen."

She nodded. The police couldn't be trusted. "I know."

And besides, it didn't matter. He hadn't even kissed her.

"Imogen." Maggie returned, a welcome interruption, blessedly plonking an ale in front of her. "Warm in here, don't you think?"

Everyone around the table stiffened at the words. It was January in London, and the table where they sat was up against an outside wall. While it wasn't cold, it also wasn't warm. And even if it had been warm . . . Maggie wasn't talking about the weather.

Caleb and Clayborn were out of their chairs, a wall of shoulders flanking Maggie, considering the room beyond.

"I shall never grow tired of that response," Maggie said with a wink at Duchess. "Stand down, lads. My bruisers have someone outside; they say he's been asking for Lady Imogen." She met Imogen's gaze. "There's a back door."

Charles had found her. And to add insult to injury . . .
he'd found her *here*. In this place she loved. Disappointment flared. "Maggie—don't let him in. His censure will
turn the whole place cold. I'll meet him outside."

"Oh, I'm not letting him in," Maggie replied. "His
kind ain't welcome here and he knows that. All they do
is cause trouble."

His kind? Charles was subtle. He had never caused
trouble in his life. Suspicion threaded through Imogen.
Suspicion, and something like excitement. "Who is it?"

"Well, he's wearing more clothes." Maggie tipped a
chin in the direction of the paper on the table. "But I
know that Peeler when I see 'im."

Chapter Eight

Peck stood on the far side of Bedford Court, back against the brick front facade of the building that overlooked The Place, and waited for Lady Imogen to exit the tavern. She couldn't stay inside forever.

He rubbed his hands together and bounced twice on the balls of his feet. It was past ten and growing bitterly cold, but The Place was bustling. Every time the door to the tavern opened, music and raucous laughter poured into the street along with groups of happy women and a handful of others Miss O'Tiernen had deemed worthy of entrance.

More worthy than he was, clearly. Since the Detective Branch had been formed, he'd had several occasions to turn up at the tavern deep in the winding streets of Covent Garden, but he'd rarely been allowed inside, and even less often been given a welcome of any warmth.

The last time he was in Maggie O'Tiernen's pub, he'd been trying to get information on a street gang that, by all accounts, had tossed it over several times. Miss O'Tiernen had poured him a pint, patted him on his head, and sent him on his way as though he were an errant child.

But another thing had happened on that evening, fourteen months earlier, before Miss O'Tiernen had declined his offer of help.

He'd met Lady Imogen.

He could still remember it, the way she'd appeared in front of him, her round face tilted up to his from where she stood, five feet if she was an inch. Standing a foot taller than her, he shouldn't have even noticed her.

Except she was not a woman who went unnoticed; she was a woman who was impossible to miss.

Plump, pixie-sized, and pure pandemonium, she'd sized him up immediately and placed a wager on him to win in a bout . . . one she was attempting to arrange. And if he was honest, in that moment, he'd almost been willing to fight . . . just to prove to her that absolutely, he would win.

Luckily, sanity had reigned that evening, and he'd escaped whatever sway she'd had over him. The same would happen tonight, he vowed.

If she'd come out.

Perhaps he had miscalculated the situation—he could have skulked about in the darkness, entered through the rear entrance. But two things had kept him from that. First, he didn't like the idea of breaching the perimeter of The Place without permission. He appreciated the value of security for those inside—a value that could not be overstated considering how frequently the tavern was threatened by outsiders who resented its unconventional power.

Second, he didn't want to have to find her, or collect her. He didn't want to play at being her keeper. The lady was clever and bright, and when he interacted with her, he wanted her to trust him. Yes, he wanted her to share what she knew about the explosions in the East End . . . but he also wanted her to meet him on equal footing.

When they played, he did not imagine them cat and mouse, but cat and cat, and he never wanted her to doubt it.

So he'd asked the bruiser at the door to tell her he was there.

The downside? He had to wait in the damn cold.

And then the door opened and the enormous man guarding it stepped aside, and she appeared, and he wasn't cold anymore.

Thomas stilled, surprised for a moment by the strange calm he felt when she appeared. She wasn't wearing the green from earlier in the day any longer. She was now in a bright ruby red dress and a black overcoat the color of the night sky and the obsidian brooch she always wore at the line of her dress. There were no colors in which she was not beautiful, and his calm slid into deep satisfaction . . . the kind that came with looking at a beautiful painting, or a perfect flower, or a sunset.

Whatever her idiot brother had told the home secretary—whatever he believed—Imogen wasn't missing. She was barely even hiding. If one paid even a modicum of attention to her, they'd have known exactly where she would be.

Peck was not interested in analyzing how much attention he paid to the lady. That way lay danger.

Instead, he relaxed against the wall, motionless. He did not signal to her or call out, instead using the moment to take her in when she paused beneath a lantern that marked the unassuming door to The Place. The small fixture cast a barely-there circle of glowing candlelight on the street below—just enough for him to drink her in.

The golden light that gleamed on her glossy curls did nothing to hide her red cheeks—a product of the warmth inside the pub. Perhaps she'd been dancing within. Or maybe just laughing and drinking and enjoying a respite from the rigid world into which she'd been born. God knew Peck was exhausted every time he had to stand on ceremony with aristocrats; who could blame the woman for relishing a day or two of freedom?

She pulled her coat tighter around her—was that a shiver?—and looked down the street, where it curved back around to Bedfordbury. Looking for him? A trio of giggling women tumbled out of a hack just at the bend and Imogen smiled in their direction, stepping out of their path, into the street. Heading straight for him.

She'd known where he was from the start. "Really, Detective Inspector. If you wish to see me, you are welcome to call at normal hours."

"The question is not *when* to call, my lady," he said, coming off the wall and standing straight, feeling as though he was to submit for inspection. "But *where*." He paused. "Unless you plan to toss over Scotland Yard again on an upcoming morning?"

Her brown eyes lit with delight, as though they played her favorite game. "All you have to do is ask."

She stopped, close enough to touch if he reached for her. Not that he had any intention of reaching for her. She was not for touching.

This morning had been a special case. He'd been working. She'd been suspicious.

"Why were you in the uniform room?"

Her pretty lips curved in a tiny, secret smile, like she had a hundred secrets that she'd share if only he said the right words. "I told you, it was a wrong turn."

"I don't believe you."

Her dark eyes twinkled. "I have ideas for a new uniform design."

He scowled.

"I think you'll like how it fits in the thighs."

He should have kissed her that morning. It would have been a mistake, but he would not have regretted it. Not like he regretted how the morning had gone.

Because now he had to face the truth. That women like Lady Imogen Loveless, no matter the way they took hold of the world and flouted convention, were not for men like Thomas Peck, born in the streets of Shoreditch, without money or title or power to recommend them.

"Your brother is looking for you."

If he weren't watching her so intently, he would have missed the little flutter of her lashes as the words landed.

"So you have uncovered my hiding place."

"Does it count as a hiding place if it is simply *your place*?"

"Don't sell yourself short, Detective Inspector," she said, lifting her pert little chin—turning her round face into a heart. "Perhaps I'm excellent at hiding, and you're just a very good detective?"

"I am an exceedingly good detective," he agreed. "But you are in no way hiding." He indicated The Place. "Half of London is in that room, my lady. You think they have not seen you?"

"Certainly, but none of them are looking the way you do."

The air shifted between them, the silence and darkness growing heavier in their wake. He knew what she meant, of course. Knew she referenced his detective skills. And still, it felt as though she was saying something else entirely. Something that he could never acknowledge was true.

Thank God, the chatterbox continued. "*Why* are you, anyway?" she asked.

"Why am I . . . what?"

"Looking? For me?" She paused. "Is it about the *News*?"

He didn't like the way her tone softened with the question, as though this woman who was always so certain of her next move suddenly did not know what to do. The damn gossip rags. No wonder she'd gone into hiding. Christ. "No," he said quickly. "Hang the *News*."

"If it's any consolation," she offered, "Duchess thinks it's a very flattering likeness."

"I prefer you conscious," he said without thinking, immediately regretting it when her brows shot up.

"Do you?"

He scowled and ignored the question. "They made me the size of a small house."

"But in a good way."

"I shall take your word for it, my lady." A pause, and then, "Did you report the incident to the *News*?"

The horror in her voice was answer enough. "Absolutely not!"

"I am here because your brother has reported you missing."

"And is it possible for me to report him cabbage-headed?"

He couldn't help his own huff of laughter. "I'm not sure I could arrest him for it."

"A pity," she said. "No chance of a slow ship to New Zealand?"

"Not for earls who have committed the crime of looking for their sisters, no."

"Ah, but he is not looking for me," she said. "He asked *you* to look for me."

He looked down at the top of her head. At her sooty black lashes on her round, rosy cheeks. "Not me. He asked the home secretary, who asked the commissioner of police, who asked me."

"An impressive chain of command, and all to find me? Who is in no way hiding?"

"You are one of the easier missing persons I have been assigned to find, I'll be honest, considering I saw you not ten minutes before I was asked to seek you out."

He'd seen her. And he'd touched her. And he'd breathed her in. And he'd seriously considered kissing her before somehow, impossibly, finding his nobility.

Like an imbecile.

"Next time I shall endeavor to make it more difficult for you," she quipped, and her smile returned—the one he liked. She patted his chest. "I will admit, Inspector, exciting as this has been, as you can see, I am not missing."

He really ought to let her go. "Your brother says otherwise."

"My brother will think otherwise when I am in my bed tomorrow morning."

An image of Imogen Loveless in bed flashed, her dark

curls against white linen, her pretty, soft curves like pure temptation against the counterpane. One soft, lush arm beckoning to him.

Thomas swallowed, pushing the image away. "You are going home?"

"Indeed," she said.

"Why?"

"As it turns out," she said, pulling her black coat tight around her and ducking into the collar to avoid the wind, "I am to be married."

"To whom?" The question came quicker and harsher than he'd intended. He hadn't intended to ask it at all.

"Someone my brother no doubt believes is perfectly suited for me. I expect someone titled, or wealthy, or with some kind of family estate that makes people desperate for a country house party."

"I'm not sure your brother knows anything about what will suit you."

Her eyes went wide with surprise. "And you do?"

"I don't think it's a country house party, that's for certain."

She grinned. "Don't be so sure. You'd be surprised by how many murders happen in the country."

"I assure you, I would not be surprised by that at all. But your delight at the statistics is not a small amount concerning."

"If there were a murder at my country house party, Detective Inspector, would it be alright if I summoned you to investigate?"

She could summon him wherever she liked, he feared. He ignored the question. "If you intended to go home and let your brother matchmake you . . . why did you leave home to begin with?"

"I am ungovernable."

"Would you believe I've noticed that?"

She smiled. "If you must know . . . we were having lamb."

"An excellent reason to leave home."

"Lamb means that my brother is home for dinner. And when my brother is home for dinner, he tends to be . . . aggressively dictatorial." She paused. "As though I am an errant child who needs a firm hand."

Thomas wasn't so certain she did not need a firm hand, but he knew better than to say so.

"Usually it's something silly." She waved a hand. "Admonishing me not to explode the library, or not to take the carriage to the South Bank after dark. Not to wager on bareknuckle fights in Covent Garden."

"Mmm. Callous overreaching."

"Precisely. I usually smile and agree and force down a bit of mint jelly"—she made a face—"and then we both go about our business. But this time someone told him about the explosion in Spitalfields. *Before* the illustration." Thomas did not imagine that an earl would care for his sister being found at the scene of the crime. "And that was, as he put it, *the last straw*. And he threatened me."

The cold night immediately felt warmer. Hot, even. "Threatened you how?"

Imogen's gaze turned curious. "You are turning red."

"Threatened you how?" he repeated.

"Marriage." She paused. "Honestly, it would not have surprised me if he sent you not to find me, but to *affiance* me."

He laughed. The very idea of an earl thinking Thomas Peck worthy of his only sister—of *Lady Imogen Loveless*—was unimaginable.

"You needn't find it so amusing," she grumbled, and for a hot, wild moment, he misunderstood. Imagining for a remarkable heartbeat that she thought him a fine man. One worthy of marrying so far above himself it was absolutely impossible to fathom.

"Anyway," she said, a touch too loudly, "a bit of time away and my head is clear. I've had a change of heart."

He had never heard such a terrible lie. "Have you?"

"Indeed," she said. "I'm headed home this very night and cannot wait to meet a battalion of suitors. You shall no doubt be unable to miss the crush of them when you drive past the house. I hope the place can sustain the weight of the hothouse flowers."

He couldn't help his amused look. "Though I sincerely doubt you feel that way, my lady, you must return home. There are actual crimes being committed in London. And I would like to go back to solving them."

He didn't like the look she gave him, as though she had very clear opinions about those crimes, and his role in solving them. "What happens when I go home?"

"I imagine your brother will buy you a new frock and send you to a ball or two."

"No," she said, suspicion in her round face. "I mean, what happens to you? A new carriage? Larger rooms at Whitehall? Do they name a horse after you at the Palace?"

"A man can dream," he retorted, not liking the way the questions suggested he had an ulterior motive for finding her. He was a detective with an assignment. This was his job.

"Rooms outside of Holborn?"

"How do you know where I live?"

She tilted her head, her brown eyes large and lovely on his. Not that he cared about how her eyes looked. "I think you'll find I know a great deal about you, Detective Inspector."

"Because of your chaos ladies, no doubt."

"I don't know what you're referring to."

He raised a brow.

She grinned. "Though I daresay they would enjoy the name."

The woman was impossible.

"You should ask for something very valuable," she said. "My brother is terrified of scandal and drinks with the home secretary, and if you've been assigned to keep

our family name out of the muck, that should be worth
at least a *promotion*."

A pause. A telling one. How did she know that? "You
do know a great deal about me, it turns out."

"To what?"

"Head of the Detective Branch."

"Impressive." It did not sound as though she meant
it. It sounded as though she was disappointed in him.
"Strange, is it not, that Scotland Yard does not offer you
a promotion for solving serious crimes in places that
need it, but finding one peculiar, madcap, errant aristocratic lady from Mayfair buys you an entire division of
the Yard."

He hated how the words made him feel, as though he'd
done something wrong. As though he hadn't spent his entire adult life on a straight, narrow path in the hope that
he might be able to lift himself and his family from their
station. Trying to earn the opportunity he'd been given.
To convince everyone around him that he deserved it. "I
have done far more than find a girl from Mayfair."

"No doubt." She nodded. "But they only care about the
bits in Mayfair, don't they?"

He could change that. A promotion meant the ear to
the commissioner of police. It meant he could prioritize
the injustices of the East End . . . injustices he knew firsthand. Of course, he didn't tell her that. Instead, he said,
"Not all of us are born with the world at our feet, able to
play at justice when we don't have a tea party to attend."

Her brows rose at that. "Do I look like the kind of
woman who attends tea parties?"

No. She didn't.

"And in your experience, Detective Inspector, have I
ever treated justice as though it were a game?"

He set his jaw. Why did this woman set him off so well?

"I do not begrudge you your promotion. I am simply
saying that if I am the means to such an end, I deserve
something as well."

He didn't like the direction of the discussion. "Is it a return journey to your brother's house?"

She smiled one of those overwhelming smiles and stepped closer. The wind whipped up the street, sending her curls into chaos. "No. I've plenty of friends inside who can do that."

Thomas Peck had been a detective long enough to know that this woman was up to something. And that his evening was about to go very, very sideways. And still, he asked, "What then?"

She shook her head. "I would like the kiss you did not attempt this morning."

Chapter Nine

In all the years that Imogen had loved explosions, she'd never quite felt a thrill like this—like coming toe to toe with unflappable, immovable, perfectly controlled Thomas Peck and daring him to kiss her.

Enemies close, she told herself. Wasn't that what they'd decided inside?

Oh, the request was wild and reckless—her brother would lock her in a tower if he knew she'd made it—but if Imogen was to return to Mayfair and have to attend *balls*, she could at least have this, could she not?

She practically deserved it.

What if this was it, after all? Her only chance to kiss this man she'd watched for more than a year, unable to keep herself from cataloguing all his delicious qualities. She knew ladies weren't supposed to notice them . . . the broad shoulders, the thick thighs, the sleek beard, the eyes that flashed like he knew every mad thought in her head before she thought it. Like he knew she was thinking of kissing him at that precise moment.

At many moments, if she was honest.

Though, he couldn't be too surprised by that. She imagined most people who found themselves in Thomas Peck's company imagined kissing him. He was tall and strong and stern and clever, and he smelled like leather and amber and the sun. Imagining kissing him was simply the product of good sense.

Yes, Imogen had given some thought (a great deal of thought) to kissing Thomas Peck in the past. But until that night, she'd never considered actually *asking* the man to kiss her. That way, Imogen knew, lay madness.

After all, Imogen was not the kind of woman men simply hauled off and kissed. She was too peculiar and too perplexing, and altogether too much for most men. For most *people*, if she was honest. Oh, she had the Belles, who welcomed her particular brand of chaos, but it did not escape her that when their husbands looked at her, it was with the curious fondness one might offer an overexuberant Labrador retriever.

Thomas Peck had never once looked at her with even curious fondness. Instead, he looked at her with stern resolve. With steady calm. And, in the thick of it, with unflagging irritation.

Except for now. Now, as her request hung between them in the cold air, and her heart was pounding, the sound like blasting powder in her ears, the poor man looked as though she'd slapped him directly across the face.

Which wasn't the most flattering response, if Imogen was being honest.

"Are you . . . drunk?" A response that could only be described as *unflattering*.

Yes. The escape whispered through her. *Yes, I am drunk. Why else would I ask you to please kiss me?* And somehow, despite knowing she should say yes, she told the truth. "Not at all." And somehow, despite knowing she should stop talking, she added, "I am perfectly capable of handling my liquor."

His brow furrowed as he watched her. "You must be drunk," he said, his jaw setting in a firm line. "It's the only reason why you would have made that request, in a pub in Covent Garden."

"Technically I'm outside a pub in Covent Garden."

"That's even worse," he said. "It's the middle of the

night. Tell me, are you attracted to danger? Or is it simply a lack of sense?"

"I'm perfectly sensible."

He gave a little humorless laugh. "In the last fourteen months—"

"Has it been fourteen months?" she asked. It had been, but she didn't think he would have *also* been counting them.

He didn't reply. "I have found you in the midst of a turf war between two of the most powerful gangs in London, inside this very building as it was raided by thugs, inside a hollowed-out shell of an alleged seamstress's shop—"

"Not alleged," she pointed out.

"Absolutely alleged," he said, "as I don't believe that was *all* it was for one moment," he retorted before continuing, "as the building fell down around us—"

"I haven't properly thanked you for that—"

"I don't require thanks," he said. "I require you telling me what you know, so that I can prevent it from happening again."

She wasn't going to do that. She couldn't be certain he was for trusting. So Imogen stayed quiet.

He understood. "But I know better than to expect you'll do that, so tonight, I'll settle for not worrying that you're going to turn up and explode Scotland Yard!"

"Point of order," she said. "You cannot prove I did that the first time."

She had done it the first time, in fact, but Scotland Yard deserved exploding, if you asked her. Not that she was about to tell him that. She was supposed to be keeping enemies close, after all.

He looked to the sky and cursed, dark and soft. Irritated? Exasperated?

"If you don't wish to kiss me, that's fine," she said. "I only thought it might be diverting."

When he returned his gaze to hers, it was full of something else entirely. "Diverting."

Even Imogen knew she could not say *life-altering*. "Yes."

Something rumbled in his throat, and even in the shadows, she could see the color washing over his cheeks. "*Lady* Imogen."

"You needn't emphasize it," she grumbled. "I don't need a reminder that I'm a lady."

"I didn't emphasize it to remind you that you're a lady."

She looked away, down the street.

He went on. "Nor did I emphasize it to embarrass you."

"Why, then?" She looked to him, her gaze finding his for a heartbeat before his slid away, over her shoulder, to the door to The Place.

"I did it to remind *me* that you're a lady."

Her mouth dropped open on a little "Oh." The full meaning of the words became clear. Meaning, if she wasn't a lady . . . *what then?* In her lifetime, she'd never been more curious. She repeated herself. "Oh."

"Dammit," he grumbled. "Go back inside."

She had no intention of going back inside. Instead, she stepped toward him, filled with courage. "I thought you wanted to take me home. To my brother."

"I think you should find someone else to do it."

Fascinating. She took another step toward him. Close enough to touch him, now. Close enough to feel his warmth. "But what of your assignment?"

"My assignment was to find you. You have been found."

"Seems a bit like a half-measure if you ask me." She looked up at him, her breath quickening at the way he stared down at her, his jaw steeled. His brow set. Stern. "What of your promotion?"

He shook his head. Once. "I'll get it another way."

And in that breathless moment, Imogen was over-whelmed with something she'd never felt before. *Certainty.* This man *wanted* to kiss her. And for someone who had reached the age of twenty-four without ever having been so certain of such a thing . . . it was . . . explosive.

"Do you hear that?" she asked.

He shook his head, and she watched the knot in his throat move as he swallowed.

"It's a *frizzle*." She stepped closer.

A low sound from deep in his chest.

How exciting.

She put her hand on the place where the sound had come from. "But that . . . that was a *rumble*." It turned into a low hum.

"Tommy?" she asked quietly, the word so soft that the wind would have stolen it if they weren't so close.

"Mmm." She wasn't sure the noise was meant as encouragement, but she took it as such. After all, she might never feel like this ever again. What if this was an irreproducible phenomenon? A chemical equation that only worked with these particular variables?

Imogen plus Tommy plus moonlight equaled . . .

How else was she to prove her hypothesis? She'd never ask him again. She took a little breath and said, "Would you kiss me, please?"

His eyes were closed before the words were even out, and for a heartbeat, Imogen thought she had miscalculated.

But then he cursed. Low, dark, and absolutely wicked. And as the word hovered between them, one strong arm snaked around her waist, pulling her tight to him, and his other hand clasped her face, his thumb pressing beneath her jaw, tilting her face up, and his eyes opened, and he was staring into her, and suddenly, Imogen didn't feel at all sure. Or at all safe. She felt very much unsure, and very much in danger . . . but in the most thrilling way possible . . .

She sighed as his lips touched hers, and he pulled away, just enough to speak. "Christ," he whispered. "Don't make noise."

Confusion flared. "Why?"

"Because it's bad enough you feel the way you do . . ." he said, as if it were an explanation.

Which it absolutely wasn't. "How do I feel?"

He didn't answer. Instead, he kissed her, and Imogen forgot the question because she was too wrapped up in how *he* felt—one hand at his broad chest and the other to his soft beard, holding his face as he held hers. She let her thumb slide over his cheek as she pushed herself up onto her toes, and it was his turn to make noise, another of those delightful rumbles, punctuated by his pulling her tight to him and deepening the kiss.

The January wind whipped around them, lifting the edge of her coat, and somehow, Imogen felt nothing but his heat. He was big and warm, and the lips she'd imagined so many times were impossibly careful with her, sending pleasure pooling deep within. Imogen had spent years with Sesily, and Adelaide was recently married, and she'd had reason to see dozens of lovers in embrace, which is why she'd always imagined kissing a pleasant way to pass the time . . . but as Tommy's hand went wide on her back, pulling her impossibly closer, and his tongue stroked across her bottom lip, as though asking for entrance . . .

Boom.

She gave it without hesitation, reveling in the way he claimed her, stroking deep, scattering her thoughts. Her heart was pounding in her chest, and the rest of her was in chaos, consumed by this man, who she'd imagined kissed very well but was perhaps . . .

Was it possible he was the greatest kisser to ever live?

She couldn't stop the laugh that came at the thought, another exclamation of delight that distracted him—dammit. He lifted his head, his breaths matching hers with their weight. "You laugh a great deal at odd times."

She shook her head and smiled. "I am enjoying myself. What else would you have me do?"

He watched her for a long moment and then said darkly, "I can think of a few other things I would have you do."

Oh, that sounded *delicious*. Before she could ask him to elaborate, a cacophonous noise came from behind her. Someone had opened the door to The Place.

"Eep!" She let out a little squeak as he lifted her nearly off her feet and turned her, placing himself between her and anyone who might be leaving the pub. Not that Imogen could imagine anyone having any interest in what they were doing. "What on—"

"Hey! Peck!" Caleb Calhoun shouted from across the street, his broad American accent impossible to miss.

Tommy rumbled again, making sure she was properly out of view before turning to look over his shoulder. "Get gone, Calhoun." Imogen shivered at the power in the command.

"When I tell you there's nothing I'd like to do more . . ." Caleb trailed off, stepping into the street anyway.

Imogen made to step out from her spot and speak to him, but Tommy held her firm. "Let me—" she began.

"No," he said softly, looking down at her. His face was shadowed, and she shivered at the conviction in the word. "He doesn't get to see this."

Of course Tommy wanted to hide what they'd been doing. He'd only kissed her because they had a deal. To send her home to her brother and clear her name from his list of assignments. Witnesses would complicate things, and the last thing Detective Inspector Peck needed was more gossip in the *News*—especially relating to kissing unmarried ladies.

Imogen reveled in the privacy for a different reason. With no one to witness it, this wild moment was theirs alone. To be kept between them, safe, for as long as they could remember it. And Imogen would remember it forever, she had no doubt. Long after Tommy had forgotten she'd ever existed.

Once she'd gone back to being too much for the rest of the world—this kiss would be enough.

Still, Caleb Calhoun was married to Sesily Talbot, and if Imogen knew one thing, she knew that if her friend had sent him to find her, Caleb was not going to be deterred—even if he very much wanted to be. Sure enough, the American stopped several feet from them and said, "Alright, Imogen?"

Tommy released her, taking his heat with him when he turned to face the other man. "That's *Lady Imogen*, to you."

Calhoun's brows rose. "Is it, now?" He stepped to the left and peeked around Tommy's broad shoulders. "Ah. There you are."

She blushed.

"Do you need assistance, *my lady*?"

She shook her head. "No, thank you, Mr. Calhoun. I'm quite well."

Calhoun nodded and took a step back, a broad grin on his handsome face. "I shall head back inside, then, shall I?" He paused, then said to Tommy, "And we'll call that my debt repaid?"

Tommy's shoulders shook with a quick laugh. "It will take more than a few moments' privacy to repay your debt, American."

"You'd best name it soon, Peck. I don't like owing a Peeler."

"Why, are you afraid I'll come for your wife's crimes?"

Imogen stiffened. It was the wrong thing to say. Caleb's good-natured grin disappeared, replaced with cold threat. "Come for my wife, and I'll destroy you."

"Keep her out of trouble, and I won't have to."

A pause, and then Caleb's grin returned. "You'd be lucky to have me come for you, Peck. I can promise that the more likely alternative would be far less welcome and far more entertaining."

"And what's that?"

"Imogen will come for you. And she'll knock you out." Caleb tipped his head to the side and winked at her. "Alright, *Lady* Imogen?"

She couldn't help her little smile. "Alright, Mr. Calhoun."

"Don't be long," he said in a mock whisper. "Next time, it will be one of the women coming to check on you." He turned his back on them, sauntered back across the street, and disappeared inside The Place.

Silence fell as the door closed behind him, and Imogen wondered whether she could convince Tommy to return to their prior activities before he stepped away and looked back at her. "You should go with him."

Apparently not.

She'd received her kiss, and now Thomas Peck was back to being detective inspector of Scotland Yard. Man of serious business.

Which meant Imogen was to pretend that everything that had just transpired was in the past. Doing her very best to seem like the kind of woman who regularly kissed handsome men and lived a perfectly normal life afterward, she said, "Of course."

He gave a little grunt in reply, and moved away, returning to his place at the wall, putting several feet of distance between them.

"Mr. Peck?" He did not reply, so she added quickly, "You needn't worry that I'll renege."

"Renege?"

Had he forgotten the kiss so quickly? The offer she made? "On our deal. I'll return to my brother. Tonight."

He was quiet for a long moment, before he said, "Yes. Our deal." Reaching up and pulling his collar up to cover his neck, he added, "You should get inside, my lady. It's cold."

It was cold. Colder than it had been when she'd exited The Place a quarter of an hour earlier. Colder, now that she knew how warm it was in his arms. Imogen catalogued him in the chill, in the shadows of the lantern light, knowing, instinctively, that this was likely the last time she would be alone with Detective Inspector Thomas Peck, who did not take risks with his future or his reputation, and who resented being made to do a lesser man's work.

It was ridiculous how handsome he was. His beard should have made him seem rough and unpleasant, but instead did the opposite, its sharp edges proving his skill with a blade and his care for his person. She knew how soft it was. How well oiled. Knew, too, the feel of it on her skin, sleek where his voice had been rough.

That she'd never feel it again made her almost regret the first time.

Almost.

He lifted his chin. "I won't leave until I've seen you inside."

Of course he wouldn't. She nodded. "Good night, Mr. Peck."

"Good night, my lady."

Turning away, she made her way to the door, suddenly eager to get inside and find her friends, who would distract her with laughter and stories and plans for tomorrow and the next day and the day after that. She, too, had work too important to risk.

She'd nearly reached the door when the bell rang from high above, loud and urgent, and Imogen stilled, looking to the rooftop. The signal had come from one of their lookouts—close enough that whoever it was could clearly see that she was with Tommy. Everyone in the Belles' operation knew Thomas Peck was a Peeler. Not to be trusted.

Another reason not to go around kissing the man, but that was a thought for another time.

Imogen turned back as the sound of thundering hooves and clattering wheels came from around the bend in the street. She looked toward the noise, knowing even before she understood that the carriage tearing toward her that it was coming too fast. There was no way the driver would stop the unmatched pair before it reached her.

Everything happened at once.

More bells. Loud and chaotic.

"Imogen!" A shout from a distance.

Was Tommy out of the path of the carriage?

The clatter of wheels, the harsh crack of a whip.

And then an immense force, knocking her back, off her feet, turning her in the air.

A thundering crash. Bright light. Loud noise.

And then absolute silence . . . broken by a deafening cheer.

Imogen opened her eyes. She was on the floor inside The Place, atop Tommy, who was atop the door he'd ripped from the hinges as he'd pushed her from the path of the runaway carriage, being sure to put himself between her and the worst of the fall.

He'd rescued her.

Again.

Only this time, London wouldn't need the *News* to report it.

Chapter Ten

W hen this works, I expect a commendation from the queen," Imogen said, tucking herself behind a potted fern and surveying the crush in the Trevescan ballroom. "You do know how to put on a show, Duchess."

The Duchess of Trevescan turned a bright, practiced smile on the room. "You are not wrong. Have you been enjoying yourself?"

Adelaide arrived, pressing a cup of ratafia into Imogen's hand. "Drink."

"Well, as you know, balls are my very favorite thing in the world," Imogen replied dryly before doing as she was told.

"Not everything can end in an explosion, Imogen."

She slid a look at Duchess. "Is that a challenge?"

"My husband would notice if we took down the place, Imogen, so let's keep our focus on the actual goals, shall we?"

The trio stood shoulder to shoulder, assessing the crowd in the ballroom, all bright colors and delighted chatter and swaying bodies. At the far end, a group of men stood deep in conversation. "Interesting that they are all together, no?" Imogen said.

A marquess and two earls, all summoned to this particular ballroom under the guise of the very best of aristocratic celebrations—a ball in which one powerful man finds another to take his sister to wife.

"Like follows like," Duchess said darkly. "I saw you dancing with Oakham."

The marquess. Unmarried, and for good reason, if the Belles had properly done their job. He owned a string of shirtwaist factories in Whitechapel that mistreated their workers beyond imagining. If the Belles were correct, it was his money that had taken out Mrs. Mayhew's print shop, where workers had been secretly organizing to protest his cruelty—he'd caught wind of the meetings and made sure they could not inspire others. No one ruled with an iron fist like an aristocrat looking to keep the status quo . . . status quo.

"He didn't say a word." Imogen shuddered. "I assume he was deigning to dance with me because he could not say no to Charles."

"As long as Oakham's here, Sesily and Caleb are at his home," Duchess said. "Don't forget that."

It was the only reason Imogen was willing to suffer the man and his ilk. "If you ask me," she said, "it is much less complicated to knock him out, tie him up, and see him oublietted."

"Yes," Duchess replied matter-of-factly, "but think of how digging such a deep hole would ruin our frocks."

"Speaking of frocks," Adelaide said. "You shan't avoid attention looking the way you do, Imogen. That color is beautiful on you."

Imogen looked down at the mandarin Dupioni silk, trimmed in gold thread. It was the first of an extensive order her brother had placed with Madame Hebert, Mayfair's most coveted dressmaker, the very moment that Imogen had arrived home and told him she had rethought the situation and decided, indeed, marriage was a worthy goal.

Charles, in a fit of senseless joy, had immediately summoned the dressmaker, irrationally certain that a collection of silks and satins and cottons and wools would convince some fool to marry her.

The finest dress had arrived that morning and there was no denying Imogen was wild for the brilliant color—a mix of oranges and reds and yellows that she'd immediately loved . . . irritating, honestly, considering she did not want to have to wear that dress to this evening's event. She wanted to wear it to The Place, and laugh and jest and dance the night away with people who accepted her for her peculiarities.

She wanted to know what Tommy would think of it.

She imagined his stern gaze moving over her, taking in the slide of the silk, the ruching of the bodice, her ever-present obsidian brooch. He wouldn't say anything about the dress, but he would notice it. Because he noticed everything.

And maybe he'd kiss her again.

Not that she should be thinking of that now, when she had other, far more important things to be thinking about. But she was not dead, was she?

If she were dead, she would not have spent the last hour in the arms of a half-dozen unmarried aristocrats, cataloguing all the ways they were not like Tommy Peck. Not as tall as him, nor as broad.

Not as delightfully bearded.

Not as taciturn. Not as stern.

Not as deserving of this particular frock, in which she looked quite excellent indeed.

But six years ago she'd agreed to work with the Duchess of Trevescan and help vanquish bad and powerful men, so . . . here they were, looking out on a field of suitors comprising the best and worst of society.

"Imagine thinking you'd marry any of them," Adelaide said, pushing her spectacles higher on her long, straight nose. "The very idea you wouldn't blow a hole in the side of the house if you were forced to reside with one of them!" She rolled her eyes. "How did it go with the others?"

Imogen understood immediately. The final two suitors

Duchess had made certain would be in attendance. Imogen's gaze fell to the bright golden hair of the youngest son of the Earl of Leaving. "Considering his father, Lord Waite seemed remarkably decent."

Clever and intelligent. Not remotely swayed by her knowledge of chemical reactions. Really a perfectly nice man. The kind of man any other woman with Imogen's eligibility would have moved directly to the top of her list, if they didn't know the truth—that the man's father hadn't blinked when he'd hired muscle to kill eight women attempting to leave his employ at brothels in Seven Dials—another message delivered, clean and terrifying.

"And the other," Imogen began, referring to the younger brother of Earl Haverford, who was so cruel that his wife did all she could to keep clear of him, and end his line. "He was . . . fine? Appears to have the mental capacity of a brighter than average toad, but showed no signs of his brother's sadism being hereditary."

"Well. I suppose that's something," Duchess said, looking to a gleaming clock in the distance. "Now we simply wait until I'm able to see them out of my home."

Imogen looked to her friend. "Honestly, I'm shocked that my brother agreed to allow you to host, Duchess." She smiled at the idea of Charles having to interact with Duchess for any reason. "You're far too . . ." She trailed off.

Adelaide offered, "Clever?"

"I was going to say powerful."

"Let's settle on *fun*," Duchess said.

The Duchess of Trevescan had been blessed with money, beauty, and a husband who never showed his face in London, which made her gatherings scandalous and her invitations coveted by the brightest stars of the *ton*.

What those bright stars did not know, however, was

that the balls the Duchess held for the aristocracy were nothing compared to the ones she held for those who worked for the aristocracy—monthly festivities devoted to the staff who saw and heard everything.

Those maids—the ones who attended the ball held at Trevescan House on the last Tuesday of every month— were the most important part of the Hell's Belles network, and Duchess, Sesily, Adelaide, and Imogen knew it. Without them, there would be no ball this evening—no hint of which of the men in the aristocracy were behind the crimes across the East End.

Imogen laughed. "God knows my brother does not know what to do when faced with *fun.*" A thread of sadness whispered through her at the thought, as she cast a gaze across the ballroom once more, finding him at the other end, alone and unyielding. His stern blue gaze met hers; the message was more than clear. *You should be dancing.* "This night is *endless.*"

"Maybe Adelaide and Clayborn could cause a scene," Duchess said, waylaying a footman with a plate of tartlets, selecting one with a little asparagus tip at the center. "Clayborn gives an impassioned speech, Adelaide finds an East India investor and gives him a swift kick."

"I wouldn't mind that plan," Adelaide said, depositing a glass of champagne on a nearby table.

"Perhaps I could chloroform myself," Imogen offered. "You could pretend I was dead."

Duchess pretended to consider the idea. "It wouldn't be the first dead body we had to deal with."

"I wouldn't even be dead." Imogen waved a hand dismissively. "Fifteen minutes, and everything would be back to normal."

"Just enough time to get you into a carriage," Adelaide laughed. "You'd be halfway to Bath before anyone realized you'd gone missing."

"We would need a strong gentleman to carry you out

of here, though," Adelaide interjected. "Unfortunate that the detective inspector isn't in attendance."

"Mmm," Duchess agreed. "I'd like to watch him crash through one of these doors, a trail of timber and glass in his wake."

Imogen's cheeks blazed at the none too subtle reference to the other night at The Place. The memory of soaring through the air and landing against his firm, muscular body a week earlier was not one that Imogen would soon forget. Nor, apparently, would the rest of the Belles. "Must we rehash it? Again?"

"I intend to rehash it until the end of time," Adelaide replied. "All that concern for your person. All that risking his life to protect you."

"Top notch," Duchess agreed.

He had been concerned. *Are you hurt?* he'd repeated again and again as he'd run his hands over her arms, down her back, along her legs. All beneath the shocked gaze of those inside The Place.

He'd been concerned until he'd realized she was fine. And then he couldn't have escaped her more quickly.

"Considering the way he resisted remaining in my company for even a moment longer than Duchess insisted . . . just long enough to see me home to Dorring House," Imogen said, "I don't think he was interested in anything but seeing me returned to my brother, in one piece. I was an assignment. Passed down from the home secretary to one very unlucky Detective Inspector Thomas Peck."

"Considering all the places his hands were when you *crashed through a door*, I don't think anyone would use the term *unlucky* to describe that man," Adelaide said dryly.

"A pity he's Scotland Yard," Duchess said. "I don't like that at all, considering."

"He does the right thing with Imogen's dossiers, though, so that's something," Adelaide replied, referencing the files the Belles had compiled on particularly criminal peers recently. Peck had been more than happy to arrest aristocrats and see them to justice. "Makes one wonder if he'd do the right thing with other things belonging to Imogen."

Cheeks flaming, Imogen cast a look at Duchess. "Please make it stop."

"You must admit it's been an exciting week." Duchess laughed.

"Could we perhaps discuss the bits that did not leave Thomas Peck so eager to get away from me?"

The duo shared a look but gave her what she wished. Duchess began, "Would you prefer to discuss O'Dwyer and Leafe's?"

"Mithra's given them a place until they can set up a new shop," Adelaide said, keeping her head down as she led them along the edge of the ballroom to a quieter corner where they would see anyone approaching. "They're already seeing clients."

"And how long before they're discovered and Mithra's is in danger?" Imogen asked, looking to Duchess.

"Mithra's doubled the security she usually has, and she's got half the brewmasters in London after her already."

"Ah, so it's to be two birds with one stone," Imogen muttered in frustration.

"This is how it is, Imogen," Duchess snapped. "They come for us. We move. And we do our best until they find us again. And we're close. Tonight, after Sesily and Calhoun are through, we'll be even closer."

Imogen nodded, swallowing her frustration. "Every day."

While she did not yet know *who* had set the bombs, she knew the hallmarks of the explosions were the same. The spray of the blast. The tinder. The strips of fabric used to soak the blasting oil and ensure the fire would catch, the oil would explode, and the whole building would come down, along with anyone inside.

But she could not identify the culprits. Even though

she was virtually certain that whoever it was had been trained by Scotland Yard . . . or was Scotland Yard. So certain that she would marry the first man her brother introduced to her if she was wrong.

No proof was no proof, however. O'Dwyer and Leafe's had the fabrics she'd taken from the Scotland Yard uniforms and the ones she'd taken from the sites of the explosions.

"I don't have it yet."

"You will," Duchess said with certainty. "In this, there is no one cleverer than you. And when you sort it out, we shall have all the proof we need."

"And if I'm right?"

"You're right," Adelaide said. "Think of how your brother commandeered your detective inspector to find you at The Place. Parliament thinks of Whitehall as their personal footmen."

A memory flashed, the look on Tommy's face when she'd guessed why he was there, searching for her. He hadn't simply been irritated that she'd guessed her brother had commandeered him, as Adelaide called it. He'd been ashamed of it. As though he hadn't had a choice in the matter. And then she'd made him another deal. Stolen another piece of the honor that oozed from him even as she'd bartered for that kiss that she had no business taking.

Without thinking, she raised her hand to her lips, as though she could will the caress returned. The softness of his beard. The warmth of his lips. The crisp taste of him. The clean scent of him.

"Imogen?"

At Adelaide's prompt, Imogen dropped her hand as though she'd been burned. "Hmm?"

"What are you thinking about?"

"More like *who* is she thinking about," Adelaide teased.

"I am not above chloroforming you two," Imogen replied.

"You would never." Adelaide again. "We are far too diverting."

They were, but she wasn't about to admit it.

"Oh, dear," Adelaide said, looking into the crowded ballroom.

Imogen followed her gaze to find her brother bearing down on them, irritation clear on Charles's face. He clearly did not appreciate seeing her tucked into a dark corner. She looked to her friends. "Help!"

Duchess leapt into action. "Let's take a quick turn and see if we can lose him in the crush."

They ducked behind a row of potted ferns just long enough for Charles to lose sight of them, and popped back out in the middle of a cluster of young women. "Good evening, ladies," Duchess said, sounding positively regal. "It appears Lady Imogen has misplaced her dance card, so we're off to fetch a new one. Do tell her brother as much should you see him."

The group of young women agreed instantly, their willingness growing exponentially when Duchess lowered her voice to a whisper and said, "As I understand it from an *excellent source*"—she tilted her head toward Imogen—"Dorring has decided to make the long trip to the altar this year. You'd best be certain to save a dance for him. Young, handsome, titled, and *wealthy*."

She paused and looked to Imogen, who immediately nodded and chimed in, "If only he weren't my brother!"

They pushed through the tittering crowd, Imogen smothering a laugh as Duchess grinned and said, "That should buy you a bit more time to choose your next partner."

"You decide." She didn't care for balls or whether she was the belle of them, but she had a bit of self-respect. Before Duchess could reply, Imogen added, "Someone who has a brain in his head, though."

Duchess looked down at her, a single blond lock falling

over her brow as she smirked. "These are aristocratic men, Imogen. You might wish to lower your expectations."

Imogen groaned. "You're certain faking my own death is not an option?"

Her friend's blue eyes went wide. "Do you have the means to chloroform yourself?"

"In fact I do not. Charles made me leave my bag in the carriage. Something about *not appearing odd*," she replied. "But I have faith that you *do* have a way to render me unconscious?"

"Of course I do," Duchess replied, looking out across the room again—tall enough to see more than Imogen could in what had become a crush. "But I've no intention of doing it. *Interesting*."

Imogen looked up at that, Duchess had seen enough of Mayfair over the years that she did not often find things *interesting*. Her friend's attention was locked on something across the room. "What?"

Duchess met her eyes. "I think you should choose."

Imogen blinked. "Choose what?"

"Not what. *Whom*." Duchess smiled. "Think on it, my friend. Anyone in London—who do you choose?"

She pushed the answer away.

Duchess seized it, nonetheless. "Do you have someone in mind?"

"No." The answer came quickly. As quickly as the image had come to Imogen's mind.

"No?" Duchess replied, sounding completely disbelieving.

"No one. Of course not. Who would I have in mind?" Knowing she sounded completely nonsensical, she bit her tongue. "Certainly no one here."

Duchess looked down at her as they were jostled by a group of older women pushing them back, making more room on the dance floor. "But someone somewhere else?"

No one.

No one here, no one anywhere else. Certainly not anyone with broad shoulders to crash through doors and arms strong enough to carry her out of buildings and thighs that were . . . in a word . . . *impressive*. She cleared her throat. "No."

"Interesting," Duchess said, looking past her. Toward the entrance to the room. "I only ask because there is a new arrival who seems . . . promising."

Before Duchess finished her sentence, Imogen noticed a change in the women gathered around her at the edge of the ballroom. They were no longer simply watching the dance. They were . . . tittering.

"Where did he come from?" someone whispered behind her.

Something tumbled in Imogen's stomach. She looked to Duchess, whose blue eyes were twinkling with an expression Imogen recognized as *scheming*.

"Duchess . . ."

Blond brows rose in pure innocence. "Yes?"

"Who is it?"

"Have a look for yourself." Duchess leaned in. "Imogen Loveless, you are the bravest woman I know. It's perfectly safe. Really. It's not as though anything is going to explode."

She did as she was told, feeling not at all brave. And when she turned, it was to see that the dance floor had cleared enough for her to get a good look at the entry to the ballroom, where just inside the door, Detective Inspector Thomas Peck stood, all in black, looking like a man who had spent his life in Mayfair ballrooms.

Duchess was wrong. It was not safe. Imogen sucked in a breath, and though it was completely impossible, it seemed as though he heard it, his gaze crashing into hers from across the damn room.

What was he doing here? Looking like he belonged here?

No. Not like he belonged here. He didn't look anything

like any of the simpering aristocrats scattered about the room. He looked like the antithesis of them. He looked like a man with purpose.

What purpose? Was it her?

It couldn't be her.

He set off another explosion in her chest. *Tweel-pew.*

And then Duchess was in her ear.

"I take it back. Perhaps things will explode, after all."

Chapter Eleven

Tommy Peck entered the Trevescan ballroom feeling a dozen kinds of fool, like a small boy trying on his father's too-large coat and too-large boots, clomping around the house in delight. But there was no delight that night.

The clothes and shoes he wore fit him perfectly, though they were no less a costume. If anything, they were more of one—one with a heavier weight. Not to be stripped off and left in a pile beneath the kitchen table, forgotten until the next morning, when Father was late for work, but instead to be worn like they meant something. Like they were truth.

There was nothing about that evening that felt like truth.

He almost hadn't come. He didn't belong anywhere near the place and its people. But he'd had no choice. He'd come because of her. Everything Tommy had done in the last week had been because of her, if he was honest—from the moment he'd carried Imogen out of O'Dwyer and Leafe's on that rainy morning.

He'd told himself it was because she clearly knew more about his investigation than she was willing to share. Confirmed it when he'd found her at Scotland Yard. But then, the carriage had nearly taken her out outside The Place and his desire to interrogate her had become something else. A desire to keep her safe.

That night, Tommy had gone home and attempted sleep until he'd had no choice but to hire a hack and head to Dorring House, where he'd kept watch all night, awake in the cold after taking a beating thanks to The Place's well-reinforced door, until Imogen had exited the next morning, clean and coiffed, looking no worse for wear.

And still, Tommy had been certain something wasn't right.

In his more than a decade with the Metropolitan Police, Tommy had been near death on more than one occasion, and this feeling . . . it was not the same. He saw the event again and again, over and over. Imogen, frozen in the lantern light, looking to the bend in the road. The thunder of the horses. The clatter of the wheels.

All night long, a single thought, repeating over and over: *She was in danger.*

By sunup, he'd convinced himself that what he was about to do was good sense. Yes, she was in danger—he was sure of it—but she had also collected evidence relating to the crimes in East London that he needed to access.

What better way than to offer his services to her brother? The earl wanted his sister married? Wanted her protected? Who better to do so than the Scotland Yardsman who'd found her the night before—there was no need for her brother to know that she hadn't really been missing.

So, when she'd disappeared into the carriage that had taken her to the dressmaker or the haberdasher or the library or wherever beautiful young women went on Tuesday mornings, Tommy had stepped out of Berkeley Square and asked for an audience with Earl Dorring.

As he'd waited in the marble entryway, he'd catalogued the space—an enormous chandelier hanging from the ceiling of the first floor, which was accessed by a massive staircase. The walls teeming with portraits, ancestors of not only the humans in the house, but it seemed the horses and hounds as well. He did his best not to linger on the hallways above, knowing he would not find a sliver of jewel-toned skirts or a hint of black curl.

Which was fine, as he had not been there to see her. He had been there to see her brother. To offer his services.

Off hours.

Just until the lady was married, he'd agreed with Earl Dorring. Just to make sure she was safely traveling from one place in Mayfair to another. To keep her out of harm's way. To keep her reputation as pristine as that house in Mayfair.

To keep her safe.

It had all seemed simple enough until that evening, when he'd dressed in trousers and shirts and waistcoats softer and better fitting than anything he'd had before— thanks to the earl, who insisted he dress for the occasions at which Imogen would require guard.

Tommy had ignored the roiling in his gut as he'd shaved and oiled his beard and brushed his teeth and descended from his room to the wide-eyed astonishment of Mrs. Edwards.

And now, Tommy Peck, a boy from the streets of Shoreditch, entered the home of the Duke and Duchess of Trevescan through the main foyer and up the grand central staircase to the ballroom within. Allowed in alongside money and title and power, because he had put on the costume.

He stepped into the ballroom, the air thick with the perfume and heat of those assembled—all of whom seemed to sense that he'd entered, as though they could smell the lack of title and money and power on him— and steeled himself for what was to come.

Looking out over the ballroom, Tommy leaned on his instincts as a detective, tracking the space. Cataloguing its size and scope. The exits, one doorway at one far corner, leading to a dimly lit corridor. Another hidden

in the wall paneling on the opposite side. The windows
along one wall, black with the night beyond and reflect-
ing the hundreds of candles within that dripped wax on
those assembled below.

He wondered how they cleaned their clothes—neither
silk nor satin nor dark wool made for easy washing after
wax had cooled in the threads. The thought had barely
formed before he realized his folly. No one in that room
worried or thought about washing their clothes. That
was the purview of servants. And even then, only if these
people had interest in wearing the same clothes twice.

His gaze fell to the crowd below, with their impeccable clothes and impeccable hair and their collective
unwavering gaze, focused directly on him as if to say,
Imposter. Intruder.

As though he didn't know it already—that he didn't
belong here, with these people.

And then he saw her.

Her frock was the color of a summer sunset over
the London rooftops, not orange, not red, not gold, but
somehow all three, and somehow in constant flux, setting the sky aflame, just as she set the room aflame, making it impossible for him to notice anything else. Not the
women around her, not those who tittered near him, not
the liveried footman who took his invitation and passed
it to another, who announced him, as though he were a
valued guest and not a servant, just like them.

"Mr. Thomas Peck."

His name clanged through the room, loud and
discordant—when was the last time the place had heard
the name of a resident of Holborn?—followed by absolute silence.

Collective shock.

Across the room, Imogen's enormous brown eyes
remained on his. Her cheeks flushed almost instantly,
sending a thrum of awareness through him. *He'd done
that.* He'd put the wash on her cheeks, and as he watched,

the flush traced down her neck, over her shoulders, and to the pretty, smooth expanse of her chest, disappearing beneath the line of that gown . . . the one he feared he would think of whenever he saw a sunset, for the rest of his days.

The rest of the room was cold, but Imogen Loveless was fire.

For one wild moment, Tommy wondered how it might be if, instead of being there to watch over her, he was there to be with her. He didn't have time to linger on the thought—which was likely for the best—as Imogen was already turning away from him, pushing through the crowd. Disappearing.

With that, Tommy no longer felt out of place. He knew his purpose. He was there to watch over Imogen Loveless, and if she was running, he was there to chase.

What he did not expect, however, was half of London stopping him from getting to her.

It began easily enough, with the Earl of Dorring meeting his eyes from across the room and offering a quick nod—Tommy had no qualms about avoiding conversation with the man—but within seconds, someone else called out to him, stopping him in his tracks.

He couldn't very well ignore Commissioner Battersea.

"Sir," he said, accepting the firm handshake that drew him closer to the group of men assembled.

"Can't slip past me, my boy." The man laughed heartily despite not having made a jest. "Come, come. Everyone wants to meet you—the brightest star in the Yard."

Tommy gritted his teeth and shoved the promotion to the forefront of his thoughts as Battersea made introductions. The trio of white men with the commissioner—a marquess, and two earls—were known throughout London as powerful, vocal members of the House of Lords. They were trotted out every time a reform bill was even whispered about in the news—workers' rights, women's rights, immigrants' rights, compulsory education—to shout down the truth and drum up anger from any who would listen.

Tommy had been at more than one gathering-turned-riot incited by the trio. Seeing the commissioner with them did little to change Tommy's view—entitled toffs.

"I confess—it's not every day we see a Scotland Yardsman in a Mayfair ballroom!" Lord Oakham said.

After a round of *harhar*ing, Earl Leaving added, "Indeed! A bit like inviting a horse to dinner!" He clapped a hand on Tommy's shoulder, and it took all Tommy had not to smack the touch away. "A jest, Peck! A jest! You're the cleverest horse in the field!"

"Clever enough that he must be back to the race, gents," Battersea interjected. "As I understand it, Mr. Peck is on the job." He leaned in. "Dorring's sister needs minding until she finds a man to do the work for free." He lifted a chin toward Tommy. "Peck has offered his skills for the task."

"Good man," Leaving said. "Odd thing, the Loveless girl."

"*Loveless* is right—can't imagine anyone wishing themselves saddled to her," Oakham agreed. "Bad enough I was required to heave her about the ballroom tonight."

Tommy's jaw clenched; any one of these men would be lucky to have Imogen Loveless. But they wouldn't, because Tommy had no doubt that the woman wouldn't give them a second look. There was no way Lady Imogen was marrying anyone even in the same universe as these men.

He'd stop the fucking wedding himself, and take immense pleasure in ending the goddamn groom.

"You ought to take care," he said, drawing the sharp attention of the quartet with the quiet threat he could not keep from his tone. "It is my job to keep the lady safe, and that includes silencing those who disrespect her."

Collectively, the men blanched, trading nervous looks as they attempted to assess whether Tommy was serious.

"Watch your tone, Peck," Battersea blustered, having no choice but to attempt to control Tommy and prove his worth to the assembled lords. "You'd do well to remember this isn't your place."

"I assure you, sir," Tommy replied, his words like steel. "I could not possibly forget that."

Battersea narrowed his gaze as Lord Haverford jumped in. "Nonsense, Battersea. He's just doing his job. Not that he needs to play the watchdog with us." He waved a limp hand at the room beyond. "We're all of us throwing hats in the ring. Proximity to Dorring's name and fortune is worth . . . making an effort . . . for the girl."

A false chuckle from Oakham. "Certainly. All we are saying is that she'll need a firm hand from a husband."

"Spare the rod, spoil the wife, isn't that how it goes, Haverford?" Leaving said, the implication in them turning Tommy's stomach.

The group laughed again—fucking ghouls—and Tommy imagined what it would be like to take a rod to the lot of them. His hand clenched at his side. He wouldn't need a rod. His fists would do just fine.

A growl sounded low in Tommy's throat as he considered the full repercussions of putting a fist into the man's face, turning the Trevescan ball into a brawl, and ruining his career.

Battersea must have heard it, for the nervous look he cast in Tommy's direction. "Alright, Peck. You are released. Be sure to give the ladies the full show—we need them telling their husbands to vote for additional Home Office funding, eh?"

Oakham chortled and reached for Tommy's shoulder, missing it when Tommy sidestepped the touch. "Well, not *the full show*. Though Lord knows you'll be asked for it. Do try to keep yourself in check, Peck. These *ladies* . . . they're not for you."

Was his career worth not delivering these men a

well-deserved facer? Everything in him told him to do it and hang the consequences. And then he saw it, a flash of fiery orange silk at the far end of the room.

Imogen.

If he started a brawl, he wouldn't get to her.

If he started a brawl, he would no longer have a reason to get to her.

Except he did have a reason. He could see the carriage bearing down on her. The building coming down around her. These men, insulting her.

If he started a brawl, he wouldn't be able to protect her.

But he deserved a damn medal for not starting one.

Without farewell, he left them, vowing to open investigations into all three of them. What was it Imogen had asked for the other night? A slow boat to New Zealand? Tommy could not think of three more deserving passengers.

Where was she?

"Detective Inspector, what a lovely surprise."

Fucking hell. A man couldn't get three feet in this damn room.

Gritting his teeth, he turned to discover the Duchess of Trevescan, tall and blond and lithe—dressed in an ice blue gossamer gown that only made her seem more of a queen than she did on a working day. He dipped his head. "Your Grace."

"If we weren't in this particular ballroom at this particular ball, I would tell you that considering all the ways we've met before now, you really needn't stand on ceremony. Alas—"

"While I'm wearing such a complicated cravat, I expect I have no choice but to stand on ceremony, ma'am."

She grinned. "It's very well tied. Well enough that someone might come looking to steal your valet."

He didn't have a valet. He had Phillips—who was a clotheshorse and had delighted in teaching him to tie this particular knot, which he was sure would delight the

Duchess—a renowned detective inspector with a penchant for bespoke waistcoats. "Thank you."

"Since we are here playing our roles," she said quietly, "I confess I am surprised you are dressed for an evening of play, when you are surely here for work."

He coughed a little laugh, then immediately qualified, "Forgive me, but I can see no scenario in which tonight's festivities might be considered *play*."

She smiled. "Mr. Peck, I think you'll find that most things are play when Imogen is involved."

He met the woman's knowing blue gaze. "I know better than to think you'd tell me where she is."

"I'm sure I couldn't say."

Of course not. He exhaled harshly, biting his tongue before he said something inappropriate.

"But the last I saw her," the Duchess added, tipping her head in the direction of the doorway nearby, leading to a dim corridor behind, clearly not meant for guests, "she was on the hunt for some air." Before he could leave she added, "Mr. Peck?"

He met her gaze, no longer light and curious, but instead hard like steel. "Know that Imogen is not to be trifled with. Where her brother falls short, I assure you her friends . . . do not."

A vision flashed, the duchesses and Sesily Calhoun, clad in silks and satins in the rubble in the East End. At The Place. Shoulder to shoulder.

"Make no mistake," the duchess added. "Where others might be impressed by your position—I am far more interested in the man you are outside of the uniform." She let her gaze linger on the men he'd left only moments earlier. "I noticed your self-control with that odious collective."

Tommy didn't need to look. The hot fury that came in the wake of her words was enough. "I did not wish to ruin your party."

She nodded. "While I can assure you I would not

have thought it ruined in the slightest, I appreciate your aplomb." She leaned in. "Though I would have happily lent you a weapon."

"I assure you, I would have done the job without it."

Her brows rose. "I can see why Imogen thinks you're a decent man."

The words warmed him in a way he did not expect. "And you?"

The woman's gaze narrowed thoughtfully. "I reserve judgement." But she nodded in the direction of the corridor again, which was something.

Tommy did not need further instruction. He nodded once and faded into the crowd and, when he had a chance, slipped away, down the winding hallway, undetected. He followed the winding corridor around a corner, trying all the doors along the way. He silently discovered a card game in progress and the stairs leading to the kitchens before another corner revealed what he was looking for—an unlocked door, a dark room, and Imogen.

Chapter Twelve

Ignoring the triumph that coursed through him as he found her in the darkness, on the far side of the room—a library—looking out the window, he closed the door behind him, taking care to make enough sound that she would hear. He didn't want to scare her.

Did she scare? She was a woman who faced down the worst of men without help or hesitation, much to his own frustration, so Tommy highly doubted he would scare her.

Still, she turned at the sound, the darkness of the room hiding her face. A beat of silence, fairly crackling with anticipation. And then, "You found me."

Of course he'd found her. He was beginning to think it was all fated—following her, finding her.

Christ. It wasn't fair that she looked the way she did. Like a treat in a shop. Sweet and lush and more tempting than was sensible. The dress that made her look like a sunset in the light was a different thing altogether in the dark. With the moonlight streaming through the window, it was the color of summer peaches—the kind that sent rivers of juice down one's chin.

Tommy's mouth watered.

"As I've said before, my lady, you are very bad at hiding."

He imagined her lips curving in the darkness with the memory of their conversation the other night, and resented the shadows for keeping him from seeing it. "As *I* have said before, Mr. Peck, I am not trying very hard."

He turned to lock the door—he wasn't a fool, and he knew that if they were found alone in the dark, it would destroy them both—before approaching her slowly, knowing he shouldn't and, as usual, not being able to resist her temptation. "If not hiding, then what?"

She lifted her chin, and admiration burst in his chest. Whatever she was about to say would be all truth. Pure Imogen. "Perhaps I was waiting for you to find me."

Something burst in his chest. Dangerous, like her explosions.

"Why are you here?" she asked.

"I was looking for you."

She shook her head. "No. Why are you here, at Trevescan House? Dressed like . . ."

He held his breath as her gaze tracked over him in the dim light, realizing that while he'd hated donning this costume earlier, now . . . he wanted her approval.

". . . like a rake about to lure a lady into the gardens."

A delicious vision appeared. Imogen in the gardens, looking like the sun, him on his knees, worshipping her.

They shouldn't be there. Together. Alone.

He shook his head to clear it, even as he went hard as stone. He cleared his throat at the discomfort and cast about for something to say to bring the conversation away from darkness and the things husbands and wives did within it. "Should you not be . . . dancing?"

She looked to him. "Are you offering to take me for a spin?"

His brow furrowed. "No."

"Do you dance, Detective Inspector?"

"Not here," he said.

"You ought to learn," she said. "What with how you look . . . ladies will want to dance with you."

He didn't care what ladies wanted to do. He wanted to know what *a lady* wanted to do. "I know how to dance."

Her brows rose. "Did they teach you that at Whitehall?"

"No," he said. "My mother taught me."

On Sunday afternoons around the scarred oak table in the main room of their flat in Shoreditch. A vestige of his mother's former life, before she'd been swept away from her home in Marylebone by David Peck, a street sweep who'd promised her the wide world.

And delivered none of it.

Not that Esme Peck had ever seemed to mind as she'd sent Tommy and his sister, Rose, around and around the table, clapping her hands in time to an imaginary orchestra. His parents had made music all on their own.

But his father had never been able to make good on his promises, and when he died, Esme had been left with far less than she'd been born with.

He cleared his throat, willing the thoughts away even as he welcomed the lesson in them. This place—it was not for him.

This lady—he could never give her the life she deserved.

Imogen was studying him. "That's an unexpected education for a policeman."

"Considering how you spend your time outside of Mayfair, my lady," he replied, "I would think you are expert in uncommon education."

Her brows rose at the question—no doubt she'd heard the edge in it . . . the one he hadn't meant to be there. "What education should I have received?"

"Training in all the typical useless nonsense."

Her eyes were lit with fire now, as though she'd never been so entertained. "Define *useless nonsense*."

She was baiting him and he took it. "Embroidery, dancing, menu planning . . . French. *Dancing*."

She made a face. "Menu planning. Awful. We only ever have lamb when my brother dines at home."

"You don't enjoy lamb?" Why did he ask that? He didn't care how she felt about lamb.

"I enjoy lamb even less than I enjoy dancing if I'm being honest."

He blinked. "And French?"

She shook her head. "I did not take to it."

"What did you take to?"

"Chemistry."

He couldn't help his surprised laugh—or the pleasure that came with the way her gaze brightened, as though she liked making him laugh. He liked it, too. Even though he shouldn't.

"And a bit of Old Norse."

His brows rose. "I'm sure that comes in quite handy."

"Less handy than chemistry, equally as handy as menu planning," she said.

He shook his head, unable to stop himself from saying, "You are like no woman I have ever known."

She grinned, pride in her bright eyes. "So I have been told."

His chest was tight with the look of her. With the way she did not hide her curiosity, but instead took pride in it. "When I was a little girl, my father used to boast to his friends about me. Rubbish at embroidery, excelled at equations. No grace whatsoever on the dance floor, but more than able to handle combustible liquids. Unable to wrap my head around menu planning, but an excellent addition to a discussion of animal husbandry. Could converse with a Viking, but not with the French ambassador." She paused for a long moment and then quipped, "And would you believe not a single visit to Reykjavik?"

They laughed together, softly, the sound curling around them like a promise. And then, like a fool, Tommy said, "I would have been proud of you, too."

"Thank you." She dropped a tiny bob of a curtsy, her black ringlets bouncing as her smile turned bittersweet.

"But when he died . . ." She shook her head. "Well. Suffice to say, Charles did not find me so worthy of discussion."

Her brother was an idiot.

She took a deep breath and let it out. "My friends, luckily, have found me quite useful." She tilted her head in his direction. "And I know my way around an explosion."

"A fact I fully intend to discuss with you."

She nodded. "I am not a fool, Detective Inspector."

His brows shot together. "What does that mean?"

"Only that I assumed you were here for business, rather than pleasure."

In that moment, Tommy decided that women like Imogen Loveless should not say the word *pleasure*. It was distracting and dangerous. And it filled a man's thoughts with visions that were absolutely unbusinesslike.

He let out a breath that might have been a laugh if he weren't suddenly consumed with the need to tell her the truth. "Lady Imogen, I am here because your brother invited me."

"Ah." Something unpleasant coursed through him at the little response, as though he'd said something wrong, even though it was the truth. Even though it was not a secret. Before he could speak, however, Imogen added dryly, "My brother certainly has a way with the home secretary." She stood straight, her little sigh like gunshot in the quiet room. "And so? You are to play companion until, what . . . I choose a husband?"

"That is what we discussed."

"So you are to be my keeper. My brother is afraid of the rest of the world discovering what I do with my time, if not hours of embroidery and dancing lessons. And you are to ensure I do not leave the limits of Mayfair."

He nodded. "Yes."

She shook her head. "Really, Detective Inspector.

I would have thought you'd have no patience for this whatsoever. Playing nursemaid to me, as though I am an errant child."

"You have been nearly killed twice in the last ten days, my lady, so—"

"Don't call me that," she said. "Not if you're to be my governor."

"Stop," he said, disliking the words. He should leave this room. Wait outside for her. If they were caught, Dorring would call them both on the carpet. Hell, if they were caught, they'd both be ruined. Frustration flared and he thrust a hand through his hair. "He didn't come to me, Imogen. I went to him."

She sucked in a breath at the words. At her name, which felt forbidden on his lips without her title preceding it. "Why?"

Because you aren't safe. "Because I want you to tell me what you know about the explosions in the East End."

Understanding dawned. "So you convinced my brother I required a keeper."

"Not a keeper. A guard." In the darkness, the word took on new meaning—not an assignment. Not business. Something else. Something more powerful.

As though he were her protector. And hadn't he been? Hadn't he taken an arrow for her as he'd carried her from a collapsing building? Hadn't he raised his broadsword as he'd saved her from the carriage careening down Bedford Court?

Hadn't he donned chainmail for her that very evening, and headed into battle in Mayfair?

"Is there reason to believe I need one? Besides my brother's bid to keep me from besmirching his own reputation?"

"Considering the trouble you and your friends discover regularly, and the fact that you've put at least two aristocrats in Newgate, a guard is not the worst of ideas."

"I haven't needed one yet."

"You need one all the damn time!" he said sharply. "If I hadn't been in Spitalfields . . . in Covent Garden . . ."

"If you hadn't been in those places, *I* wouldn't have been in danger, Detective Inspector." The woman was enraging. But before he could say so, she added, "And I am to be grateful for you offering to play shadow to me until I am packed off to the country to be a wife to someone who neither loves nor understands me?" She gave a little laugh. "No, thank you."

It hadn't occurred to him what would happen when she found a husband, but he didn't like the idea of Imogen Loveless—who'd once marched into the jail at Scotland Yard and blown open one of its cells—whiling away her days in the country.

Though she wouldn't be forgotten.

That, he was sure of.

She shook her head. "I'm very sorry, Detective Inspector, but you have hitched your wagon to the wrong horse. I've no intention of being *kept* or *guarded* or *nursemaided* or whatever it is you're intending."

In his silence, Imogen nodded and crossed toward the door, the only sound in the room the silk slide of her skirts. He moved to let her pass, telling himself it was for the best. The sooner they were out of this room, the sooner he could return to the comfort of his job.

Except he couldn't stop himself from speaking to her retreating back. "You've no intention of marrying, either. So why are we here, Lady Imogen?"

She stopped, lifting her gaze to his. "I don't know what you mean."

He approached her, slowly. Certainly. "Your brother may be easily fooled, my lady, but I am not. You've no intention of marrying anyone in that ballroom. What are you up to?"

She worried her lip, watching him. Considering her reply. Choosing her words. He waited, ready to unravel whatever lie she was about to tell.

Except, as usual, Imogen Loveless was not predictable. One of her lovely round shoulders lifted and fell in a little shrug. "Perhaps I am proving to my brother that I am not the marrying kind."

It was nonsense, of course. "And when half the eligible men in Mayfair ask for your hand?"

She laughed. "For all the time you spend in Mayfair, you don't spend much time in ballrooms, Mr. Peck. And it shows."

"What does that mean?"

"I am too much for marriage. Were you not listening when I told you about the Old Norse?"

The words filled Tommy with indignation and no small amount of anger. The idea that someone might find her to be too much—when he could not find a way to look away from her—it was infuriating.

Bollocks.

Before he could find a less foulmouthed response, she lifted her attention to his chest. "I blame my ancestors."

"Your ancestors?"

She nodded. "Imogen Loveless. It's in the name, after all. My destiny."

"Bollocks." Turned out, he couldn't keep it in. "You're perfectly loveable."

Her gaze flew to his at the words, and he drank in the look of her, eyes wide, mouth parted on a surprised little gasp, her shocked expression there and gone in an instant, replaced with a secret little smile. "That's kind of you."

Tommy had never in his life felt less kind.

They stood in silence for a long moment, and then she took a step toward him, closing the distance between them. He caught his breath, knowing he should back away. Knowing he should end this—whatever it was about to be. Knowing that if they were caught . . . everything would go sideways.

Except she spoke, the words barely a sound, "I disappeared from the ball." He could not move. "And I wanted you to come looking." He shouldn't be so close to her. Shouldn't be able to feel her heat. To scent her perfume, lush and mouthwatering. "But I should have hidden from you."

"Why?" He shouldn't ask.

"You scare me." He stiffened, but before he could pull away, to put space between them, she lifted her hand and brushed her fingertips along his cheek. "Wait. Not like that. Let me . . ."

"Explain." The word came harsher than he intended. A demand rather than a request, and he forced his hands into tight fists at his sides. He shouldn't touch her. That wasn't the job. The job was to protect her.

It didn't feel like a job.

"I—" she started, then stopped, collecting her thoughts. Her lips pursed into the prettiest little bow he'd ever seen. He bit the inside of his cheek. Christ. The woman had just admitted he scared her, and no wonder; he was imagining all the ways he wanted to devour her. "I am used to chaos."

He offered a crooked smile at the words. "I expect you are."

She shook her head. "You don't understand. I am used to being the *source* of chaos. But you . . ." It killed him to wait in that pause that seemed to stretch on forever. "You make me feel . . . like the chaos is outside of me. Like I can't control it."

The pleasure that came at the confession was acute. "You make me feel that way all the time," he said, unable to stop himself from reaching for her. "Out of control."

"I don't like it."

"You shall get used to it."

Her brown eyes found his in the darkness. "Does it go away?"

"No," he said.

"I'm sorry."

He didn't tell her the truth. That if she was like him, she would start to hunger for it.

She tilted her head, as though she was thinking of a solution. Of a cure. "Perhaps if . . ."

His brows rose. "If?"

"If there were some way to embrace it."

"Embrace it?" She couldn't possibly mean what he thought she meant.

She nodded and stepped closer, looking down at his hands, his fists clenched tightly even though she was close enough to touch. *Because* she was close enough to touch. He could lift one hand and stroke his fingers up her arm. Over the soft skin of her cheek. Into her curls. Tilt her face up to his. Claim those pretty red lips again. Revisit the taste of her, fresh and sweet.

He *could*, but he *wouldn't*.

This was his job. He was to guard her. To keep her from danger.

But in that moment, somehow, he had become the biggest danger to her.

Her head was bowed now, staring down at the floor. No. Not at the floor. At his hand. She reached for it, her fingers stroking over his fist, tracing the ridges of his knuckles. How was it possible that her touch felt like that? Like fire, rushing through him.

Like mayhem.

He released a shaking breath and she looked up at him, realization in her dark eyes, rimmed with sooty lashes. "You feel it, too. The *ratatatat*."

Yes. *Yes.*

But he wouldn't admit it.

"Perhaps," she started again, "if we just . . . let it take us . . . for a moment . . . once more . . ."

A terrible idea.

"Maybe it will calm it." Her fingers were sliding up his arm now—scattering his thoughts with her soft touch, so soft he had no doubt he could resist her. She a foot shorter than he. He'd proven he could lift her. He should do that. Immediately. Lift her up and set her aside and leave this room.

"Calm it," he repeated, instead.

"The chaos," she whispered.

He wasn't sure he'd ever be calm again. "Once more," he said. Surprising himself. He hadn't meant to say that.

He hadn't meant to return her touch. Hadn't meant to stroke over the lush curve of her waist. Didn't mean to pull her closer. To slide his other hand up to the soft skin of her jaw, to tilt her toward him.

"Just once," she said. "And maybe then . . . it will feel . . ."

"Better." It wasn't a terrible idea; it was a brilliant one.

"Right." She nodded, coming up on her toes, meeting him as he leaned down.

"Just one kiss," he said. "And then—"

She closed the distance between them, and he forgot the plan.

Chapter Thirteen

It should be said that Imogen was generally quite brilliant.

She was extremely good at maths, a scientific genius to rival any man at the Royal Society of Chemistry, and in the past two years, she'd discovered three separate chemical reactions that proved extremely useful when it came to catching criminals, distracting peers, and rendering unconscious men who . . . well . . . deserved it.

So it was not without thought that she proposed that Thomas Peck kiss her again. The way he made her feel was so uncommon—so out of the realm of her prior life experience—that she really did hypothesize that kissing him might calm the wild beating of her heart and return everything to normal.

The moment his lips found hers, however, his arms coming around her waist and pulling her tight to him, it was clear that Imogen did not need to complete the experiment to prove that her hypothesis had not only been incorrect, it had been nonsensical.

But she was going to complete the experiment anyway. Obviously.

For science.

Because the kiss might not have calmed the chaos inside her . . . but it was the closest thing she had ever felt to an explosion.

A wild *ka-boom* of an explosion.

And as a woman who enjoyed explosions, she was keen for more.

She ran her hands up around his shoulders and tilted her head, opening to him with a little sigh of pleasure, delighting in the way he received her, sliding his tongue over her bottom lip with a sinful lick and dipping inside, bringing flame with him.

Imogen sucked in a breath at the touch, stilling for a moment, unable to move or think or respond because *it was happening*. He was kissing her again. Not outside of The Place after she offered him a trade. But because he felt it, too—this wild pull.

And that knowledge, along with the feel of him, warm and strong and for this mad moment *hers* . . . was enough to set her aflame.

She met the kiss, and they burned together, sliding, stroking, clinging, their breath coming hard and fast and his hands moving, slow and deliberate, a smooth promise of pleasure down her spine, over the lush curves of her hips and around to her bottom, pulling her tightly to him, lifting her into his kiss, making her forget everything but this man, this kiss, this moment.

No, there was nothing calming about Thomas Peck's kiss.

It was the opposite of calming.

It was . . . *exciting*.

So exciting that she couldn't keep the discovery to herself.

She pulled away with a quick "Oh," her fingertips running through the soft pelt of his beard.

He stroked one thumb over her cheek and caught her eyes. "Oh?"

"It's just—I was wrong."

He stiffened and made to pull back, to put distance between them.

"Oh, no. I don't mean . . . Don't do that," she insisted.

He stopped and let out a quick exhale. "I think I ought to."

She clutched his arms to stay his movement, and couldn't ignore the steel of his muscles beneath his beautifully tailored coat. "Oh," she said again, unable to keep the approval from the word.

A low sound rumbled in his chest. Something suspiciously like pleasure. Her gaze flickered to his, and he said, low and rich, "What were you wrong about, Imogen?"

She blinked. "I thought the kiss would solve everything."

He cursed, soft and wicked in the dark. "It didn't. It was a mistake."

No. It wasn't. That much, she knew. "It should have," she insisted. "It's a matter of science. Of exposure."

One dark brow rose and he cut her an amused look. "Exposure."

"Precisely. In the same way one exposes a child to a disease. To get it done with."

"Lady Imogen," he said, the words slow and easy. "Am I a disease in this scenario?"

"You don't have to be," she said. "I am happy to be the disease."

"You are not a disease," he replied, the words clipped, as though she'd offended him.

She smiled at that. "That's a lovely thing to say."

"I should not be here with you."

"My brother hired you as my guard," she said. "Where else would you be?"

"I remain a man. An unmarried man outside of your world. If we were discovered—"

She would be ruined. Without doubt. "Sesily would be thrilled," she muttered.

"What?"

Imogen lifted her chin, dismissing the question. "Mr. Peck, are you my guard? Or not?"

His hands—still holding her tight to him, as though he could not find the willpower to release her—flexed at her round bottom. "I am."

"And you have reason to believe it is necessary?"

He closed his eyes at the question. "I do," he said softly, more to himself than to her. "Though I am not sure *you* aren't the danger."

Feeling wicked, she pressed back into his grip, reveling in the way his eyes opened and his fingers tightened, sending a thrum of pleasure through her. "I like to think of myself less as a danger and more as an *adventure*."

He huffed out a laugh. "You are that."

"And if you are to be my guard on this adventure," she said quietly, "perhaps the solution to this particular problem is a longer exposure." The words fell between them, and she knew they were a risk, but she added, "An *investigation*, of sorts."

"Ah," he said, lifting one hand to stroke over her cheek, back and forth in a slow, maddening slide. Imogen held her breath, waiting for his answer. And then he dipped down and pressed a hot, openmouthed kiss to her jaw, just beneath her ear, where he whispered, "We have established that I am very good at investigating . . ."

"Tommy," she whispered, wanting more. Wanting him.

He stilled at the sound of his name, and then, with another low growl—frustration? desire?—he lifted her off her feet, into his arms. Imogen couldn't remember ever having been carried about in her entire life, and this man had done it three times in a little over a week. She shouldn't have liked it. She should have resisted it—she was perfectly capable of moving herself from place to place. She did not require some brute from Scotland Yard to carry her about.

But every time he did, she couldn't help but marvel at his enormous muscles—she was not small, after all—and the way he seemed to have absolutely no trouble at all with lifting her, carrying her, touching her . . .

She loved it.

Tommy set her on a nearby table, where she knocked into a heavy brass lamp.

She gasped and turned, but before she could reach to catch the heavy fixture, Tommy was there, his reflexes instantaneous, grabbing it from midair with one large hand before it hit the ground and the glass shade smashed.

In one smooth movement, he returned the lamp to the table and set his hand to the side of her face, pressing his thumb beneath her chin, and tipping her face up to his.

She couldn't help her breathless."That was impressive."

"Mmm." He dipped his head and stole another kiss, acknowledging the compliment before he whispered at her lips, "I like impressing you."

"I am impressed," she said softly. "By so much of it."

He pulled back, barely. Just enough that she could look into his eyes. "For example?"

She gave him a little smile. "Are you searching for compliments, Mr. Peck?"

He didn't hesitate, his blue eyes going deep and liquid. "Yes."

She lifted a hand and stroked one finger down his nose. "This bump."

"Bar fight."

"Did you win?"

His shoulders straightened, chest broadening at the question, as though he were a champion presented to his queen. *Her guard.* "Yes."

She nodded. "It suits you."

"Winning?"

A little smile. "That, too."

He matched her smile. *That suits you, too.* But she didn't say it. Instead, she let her fingers trail down to his beard, smoothly oiled, loving the sound that rumbled in his throat. "You like that."

He pressed against her hand, urging her on. "Mmm."

"It makes you look"—he took hold of her hand and pressed a kiss to the center of her palm, stealing her breath as she finished—"wild."

Another rumble in his chest and he leaned down to coast his lips along the soft skin of her neck, the barely-there kiss punctuated by the stroke of his beard and the slow slide of his tongue tasting the pulse that hammered there. Without thinking, she lifted her chin, giving him permission to continue, and added, "It makes me *feel* wild."

"Shall I tell you what makes *me* feel wild, my lady?" The words were low and lazy, as though they were not at a Mayfair ball at which she would be missed. As though he had a lifetime to be distracted by her shoulder, to trace the curve of it to the edge of her dress.

She wanted to tell him not to call her that. Not to put the distance of her title between them. But she liked it too much, the claiming in it, the idea that she was his. That it was his choice. "Please," she said, the word barely there as his fingers returned to the edge of her gown, tucking inside, setting her on fire.

"Here?"

She nodded, looking down at the place where he tugged at the rough silk, at the gold thread. "Wait—" She reached for the brooch she always wore—obsidian set in silver. Removed it, slid it into her pocket. And when that was done, she whispered, "Yes."

The fabric stretched as he followed her silent instructions, hooking his finger and tugging it lower. "*You* make me feel wild," he said, and she could hear the surprise in his voice. "You upend all my good sense. I'm to question you. I'm to watch you. I'm to keep you at a distance."

She tugged on his hair until he looked up at her. "Why?"

"You've been tampering with my crime scenes." Another tug, and the fabric scraped across her nipple, baring it to the cool room and his hot gaze. He stared down at her, and she recognized the emotions on his usually well-guarded face.

Recklessness. Chaos. Desire.

"You've been tampering with my bodice."

He shook his head. "I can't help myself."

She nodded. "You know what they say . . . best to keep enemies close."

Tommy didn't reply, and for a moment, she wondered if there was something wrong. She had never done anything quite like this . . . never revealed herself to another, let alone a person who made her feel the way he did. But she'd heard plenty about the act—difficult not to with Sesily and Adelaide nearby—and as far as she knew, men did not . . . stay still for it.

Was it . . . was she . . . acceptable?

The thought crashed through her and she released him instantly, moving to cover herself.

"No," he said, the movement unlocking him. He caught her hand in one of his, strong and warm and unyielding. "Let me look."

Her cheeks went red with embarrassment. "Is it . . ." She paused. Rethought. "Am I . . ." *Oh, no,* she couldn't ask that. She took a deep breath. "Are you . . . satisfied?"

He looked up at that, meeting her gaze. "Am I *satisfied*?" He gave a little laugh. Barely there, but recognizable as a laugh nonetheless, and Imogen wondered if it was possible to perish from embarrassment. "No, my lady. I am not satisfied."

Perishing from embarrassment would not be the worst outcome, she decided. At least she would not remember that reply when she was dead. "Oh."

"Imogen," he said softly. When she did not meet his eyes, he said, "Look at me."

The demand was raw enough to tempt her, and when she did, it was to find him stern and serious. "I am not satisfied by looking, because looking isn't enough. I want . . ." He looked down at her breasts, bare and aching for him, and stroked one hand over his mouth, like he was starving. "Christ, I want to touch you more than I want my next breath." His eyes found her, light with desire. "May I touch you, my lady?"

That honorific again. Asking permission. Setting her on fire. "Yes," she replied. "Please." She bit her lip, unable to ask for what she wanted.

She didn't have to. Because he knew. He wanted it, too. And when he gave it to her, his tongue painting over the straining tip of her breast like a promise, it was *glorious*. She gasped, sliding her fingers into his hair, finding purchase as he bent her back over one arm and turned his attention to her other breast, taking the peak into his mouth and—*Oh!*—sucking in lush, lovely pulls, again and again, sending pleasure pooling deep within her, making her ache for more.

"That is . . ." His gaze found hers at the words, but he did not stop, instead licking over her with the broad flat of his tongue, daring her to finish. She did. ". . . *wicked*."

He smiled at the assessment. "Not wicked so much as an adventure, no?"

She couldn't help the little laugh as he notched her legs wide beneath her skirts and pressed closer, worshipping her. He scraped his teeth across one nipple, soothing it immediately with tongue and lips, and her fingers clenched, holding him tight to her as she begged, "*More*."

He didn't hesitate, his hands stroking down her legs as he lifted his head to claim her mouth in a wild kiss—one she matched until his fingers found her ankle beneath her skirts and she gasped at the sizzle the touch sent through her.

His lips slid across her cheek to her ear, where he repeated on a low whisper, "May I touch you, my lady?"

She wanted to scream her approval, but settled on a quick, harsh "Yes, please."

"Mmm," he rumbled, his tongue tracing the curve of her ear. "These stockings are so smooth," he marveled, stroking up her leg, palming the curve of her calf as his teeth worried her ear. "And here." He played at the back of her knee, and she laughed. "Ticklish?"

She lifted her chin to give him more access—aching for more of his touch, his kiss, whatever he would give her. "I didn't know until now. No one has ever . . ."

Breath punched out of him. "No one has ever touched you here," he finished for her, the words dark and full of something like pride. "No one but me."

She turned her head to meet his gaze. "You like that."

"I shouldn't," he said. "I have no right to." And still, he pushed her thighs wider, pressed closer, let his fingers travel higher.

"But you like it, nonetheless."

"I do," he said harshly. "It makes me want to lay claim to you."

"You already have," she said. "You do every time you call me *my lady*."

He stilled at the words, turning his face to the ceiling and closing his eyes. "*Fuck*," he whispered. "Imogen . . . don't say that. This . . . it's one time. After this . . . we must . . ."

"One time. For exposure." She reached down and pressed her hand to his, where it lay just above her knee. "But I am glad it is you, Tommy. Touching me. First."

He stole her lips for another deep, wild kiss, exploring higher, until—

He stopped, breaking the kiss. "Imogen?"

She grinned, knowing what he'd found. "Tommy?"

"Is this a blade?" His fingers stroked over the leather strap at her thigh.

"It is."

His brow furrowed. "Why?"

Her fingers tangled in his hair. "One never knows when one might meet a nefarious character in the darkness."

His touch traced the holster on her thigh. And then a gruff, "You don't need a blade."

"I don't?"

"Not tonight."

She shivered at the words, punctuated by the stroke of his beard at her neck, and then replied, breathless, "Experience tells me it's much better to have a weapon and not need it than it is to need one and not have it."

A beat. And then, "This is your weapon of choice?"

"No, but they tend to frown upon explosives at balls."

"Mmm," he said. "Unfortunate."

His hand was still on her blade, unmoving. "Isn't it? But if I have to carry a blade, that one is quite special." His nearness turned the words to breath more than sound. "It was made for me by a lady bladesmith in Scotland."

"I am unsurprised you have a lady bladesmith."

"I have a lady most things," she replied. "You should try it."

"Mmm. I confess, there is a lady I am tempted by right now." The words sizzled through her. "But you misunderstand," he added. "When I say you don't need a weapon tonight, it's because I am your weapon, now. You have me."

Her eyes flew open and she pulled back to meet his, intensely blue. "My guard?"

"Your blade."

She shouldn't have liked it, but it sounded so . . . *romantic.* As though he were a Scottish warrior and they were in the wilds of the North Country and he was

about to wrap them both in his plaid for the night—
putting his back to the cold with the single purpose of
protecting her.

His lady.

Her man. Not for long, of course. She was not being
coy when she said marriage was not for her. That she
was too wild for marriage. But tonight, in that moment,
in that place, he was hers. And so she did what any self-
respecting woman would do—she reached down and
grasped his hand, guiding it off the hilt of her blade,
higher, along the curve of her thigh, to the tops of her
stockings. Where she stopped, because he'd reached
skin, and she'd never felt anything like it.

They both groaned, and he added a second hand to the
first, toying with the ribbons. "Tell me . . . are these tied
with pretty bows the color of fire?"

It was difficult to find her voice. "Yes."

"May I see them?" A pause, and then, "My lady?"

She trembled at the question, but caught her skirts in
her hands, lifting them up, over her thighs, revealing
herself. He watched, his body tense, jaw set like steel
as he stroked over the wide satin ribbons. "I wondered
how soft it would be," he said, more to himself than to
her. "Your skin. And now I have my answer. Too soft
for hands like mine."

She instantly shook her head. "No." His rough fingertips were strong and work-hewn and perfect, stroking along the edge of her stockings, tracing her inner
thighs.

He cursed again. "So soft. How are you softer than
silk?" He traced further over her skin, and her thighs
opened wider, giving him access to the place where an
ache had begun that she did not recognize but absolutely
understood.

Tommy also understood, his blue eyes capturing hers
in the darkness as he followed her silent instruction.

"Here," he said, the word a marvel. "I wondered about this."

He was so close—a fraction of an inch from where she wanted him. "What else did you wonder?"

"It would take a lifetime to catalogue all the ways I have wondered about you, Imogen Loveless," he said. "I have wondered about the color of your skin and the shape of your body and the feel of you against me . . ."

She should have been embarrassed by the whimper that came at the words, but she couldn't find room for embarrassment for all the desire that coursed through her. "Tommy—" she said, urging him on.

"I wondered how soft your skin would be. And now, I wonder . . . how soft will you be . . ." He trailed off, his words hot at her ear as he moved in exquisite torture to—

She gasped and he growled, low and dark and full of arrogant pride, like he'd known what he would find and was more than pleased to be proven right. "And now I don't have to wonder," he whispered, holding her gaze. "Here . . ." His fingers stroked over the seam of her and she couldn't keep her eyes open. "Impossibly soft, aren't you? And so wet."

His words threatened to undo her even as he gave her the kiss she was aching for, a long, lush claiming that captured the cry of pleasure she couldn't keep in when he parted her folds and delved inside, painting over her again and again until he found the place she strained for him and circled once, twice, pausing only when she rocked her hips into his hand, urging him closer. He broke the kiss, lingering on her full lower lip with a little suck before he said, "There?"

Imogen sucked in a breath. "Yes."

Another circle, devastatingly slow. "Like this?"

The breath punched out of her, ragged and fierce. "Oh, dear God."

"He's not here, love," he whispered like sin. "It's just me." Her hand scrambled down his arm to his wrist, clutching it tightly. "Go on, then," he urged. "Show me."

Her fingers tightened on him and she rocked her hips against him, searching for his touch, wanting him to resume it. "Please, *Tommy*." He gave her what she wanted—what she could not find the words to ask for, the slow, unyielding circles that tracked the movement of her hips. Over and over in a rhythm that she couldn't have imagined for herself—like in all the time he'd wondered about her, he'd somehow divined the exact way she liked to be touched.

He knew it in detail when, if she'd been asked an hour earlier, she would have said, simply, *By him.*

Soon, her thoughts were scrambled, nothing but the pure pleasure he wrought as he teased and tempted and played without purchase.

The muscles of her thighs tensed as she held him in the exact place she wanted him, and he widened his stance, holding her open. "No," he said. "I want to watch it hit you."

It was coming—roaring toward her as she held him tight to her and said, "Don't stop."

"I wouldn't dare," he said, low and dark, the words barely more than a growl. "It's yours, love. Claim it. Use me."

And she was using him, rocking against him, along his strong, knowing fingers, as his thumb continued in perfect rhythm. "That's it." He caught her jaw in his hand, tipped her up to him. "Look at me. I want to see you—"

"I'm—" She gasped, and he caught her scream as she pressed her mouth to his, going wild against his hand and his lips, needing him to guard her—to guide her—through her pleasure as she came hard and fast against him, rocking against his touch as he drank down her cries.

As she returned to herself, he held her, pressing soft kisses along her jaw to her ear, where he praised her for what she'd done, calling her a half-dozen things that no one had ever called her. Magnificent. Beautiful.

"*Like fire*," he spoke at her ear, moving just slightly, just enough to send a shock of pleasure through her before he lifted his hand and, looking directly at her, sucked his fingers into his mouth.

It was wicked and sinful and made her want to do it all over again. Her eyes went wide and he grinned. "Like fire, and like honey."

She couldn't stop herself—she reached for him, pulling him down for another kiss, knowing even as she did that it was a very bad idea. That she was supposed to walk away from him now—that they were to go back to their lives, having achieved a level of exposure that afforded them some immunity.

Except she was not immune to him.

She feared she was the opposite.

But she kissed him rather than think about it, and he seemed perfectly satisfied with the plan, tipping her back, licking into her mouth, stroking down over her chest to toy with her breast, which sent a fresh jolt of excitement through Imogen, making it her turn to wonder . . . if perhaps they could continue their investigation. Immediately.

Before she could suggest it, however, he lifted his head. "Do you hear . . ." She opened her eyes and met his gaze, feeling unmoored. He cursed, soft and wicked. "Christ, Imogen. You are so *pretty*."

It was not a word that was ever used to describe her, and so she couldn't help the way she dipped her head, looking away from his attention.

And then she heard it, too.

A bell. In the hallway beyond.

She froze for a moment, at once knowing what it was, and wishing it to be anything else. Anywhere else.

Not now. Not while she was here in Tommy Peck's arms, and he was telling her she was pretty.

The bell sounded again, and it was her turn to curse.

"What—"

She released him and pushed him away, and he went, the gorgeous man, watching as she lowered her skirts and hopped down from the table, and made for the door.

Imogen threw the lock and opened it a crack, peering out to discover Adelaide in the hallway beyond. "Oh!" Adelaide said. "Good. You're still here."

"Where else would I be?" Imogen asked, pulling the door tighter around her as Adelaide craned to see inside the room.

Her friend cast an amused look at her. "You realize you are quite short, Im . . . and that man is very tall. And directly behind you."

Imogen turned. "One moment, if you will, Detective Inspector."

He stepped back and spread his hands wide, and she stepped into the hallway, closing the door behind her.

Adelaide's brows were halfway to her hair. "When we have more time, I shall want every detail."

"I don't know what you're talking about," Imogen said, nodding at the bell in her friend's hand. "What is it?"

Her expression grew serious. "No time. Duchess has the carriage waiting."

Imogen looked over her shoulder, toward the closed door.

"Your body man won't like it," Adelaide said softly.

"No, he won't," Imogen agreed, already moving down the hallway. "But there's no reason to make it easy for him."

A wide grin broke across her friend's face. "It's to be a hunt, then?"

Imogen's heart was pounding at the idea that he might follow her. She shouldn't like him chasing her. She should want him to leave her alone. And still, she couldn't stop her reply. "I prefer to think of it as an *adventure*."

Chapter Fourteen

Tommy was furious.

He'd realized his mistake less than a minute after she'd left him alone in the library, and he'd headed immediately for the door, fairly ripping it from its hinges to reveal the empty hallway beyond. He'd gone for the ballroom first, full of the misguided hope that he was wrong, and that he'd find Imogen starry-eyed, in the arms of some toff with dreams of squiring her straight out of Trevescan House and directly to the nearest altar.

God knew that scenario would make everything easier.

Even if it made Tommy want to put a fist into something.

She wasn't in the ballroom. A quick glance around the crowded space revealed that she was not alone in her disappearance. The Duke and Duchess of Clayborn were gone as well. Tommy had no doubt they were all together, and that they were headed toward trouble.

Like followed like, did it not?

Goddammit, she was headed into trouble without him, and he had to navigate a roomful of aristocrats to find her.

Fucking hell.

Through his frustration, Tommy saw a flash of silver blue at the far end of the room, near the hidden door he'd catalogued earlier in the evening. He knew that color—had noticed it on the Duchess of Trevescan not an hour earlier, before everything had changed. Before he'd manhandled Imogen Loveless in the darkness, in absolute defiance of his responsibility toward her safety and his investigation.

Responsibilities he continued to fail now that she was out of his sight.

He was already headed for the door, ignoring a half-dozen calls for his attention, eyes trained on the place the Duchess had disappeared. The woman couldn't leave her own ball in full swing, could she?

Apparently she could. By the time he'd made his way down the dark servants' stairs to the rear door leading to the Trevescan House mews, he was moving at a clip, having gained enough ground to catch a glimpse of the ice blue hem of the Duchess's gown as she disappeared into her carriage.

Her *unmarked* carriage.

Tommy cursed in the darkness and ran for the street, flagging down a hack and shocking the driver when he climbed up on the box to offer the man half his monthly rent to relinquish the reins.

"'S madness," the older white man said before passing him the leather straps and blowing into his hands, chapped red and raw with the cold. "But I'll take your money."

The Duchess's carriage turned out of the Trevescan mews and Tommy followed at a distance, growing more and more enraged as they traveled farther and farther from the lights of Mayfair.

"If we get robbed," the driver said as they crossed through Seven Dials, "I'll be chargin' more."

Where were they headed?

Thirty minutes later, Duchess's carriage turned into the Docklands and Tommy swore and stopped. This was no place for a lady. Even less of a place for three of them—a husband with them or not.

Imogen didn't have a husband.

She didn't have Tommy, either.

He tossed the reins to the driver and leapt down from the hack. He'd be quicker and undetected on foot. "Thank you."

The driver didn't say anything as Tommy counted out the coin he'd promised. Only once the money had exchanged hands did the older man tip his chin toward the river and say, "In there . . . friend or foe?"

Tommy looked over his shoulder at the looming dark warehouses of the Docklands. "A bit of both, I expect."

"You know what you're in for?"

Tommy told the truth. "I expect it's trouble."

The driver looked down the dark alley toward the water. "Worth it?"

A vision of Imogen came, unbidden, head back, dark curls gleaming, eyes half closed as she took her pleasure. Perfection. He pushed it aside and it was replaced with another. The carriage bearing down on her outside The Place, along with the fear that had consumed him at the possibility that he might not reach her.

"Yes."

The old man nodded sagely. "Must be a fair bit of money . . . or a fair bit of woman."

Tommy didn't respond, already moving toward the labyrinthine streets of the Docklands, telling himself that hack drivers knew next to nothing about the world.

Tucking himself into the shadows of the warehouses along the river, he listened for carriage wheels—and heard something else entirely. Shouting.

He followed the sound—the noise becoming louder and more cacophonous as he drew closer, a handful of bellows melding into a symphony of sound. The Docklands were a maze of dark, narrow alleys and cobblestone streets that bounced against the looming warehouses, making direction impossible to discern.

It took Tommy several moments to find the path—feeling his way toward the noise in the pitch black—

finally arriving at a wide street connecting the docks and the high land of Whitechapel. And there, with a straight shot to the river, he found what he was looking for . . . though he felt no triumph in the discovery.

Something was on fire.

The river gleamed with the reflection of the flames on the slick surface of high tide, and a dozen men rushed back and forth, their faces gilded in the light. At the end of the street, Tommy stopped to take stock of the damage, flames licking out of a high window on the upper floors of a riverfront warehouse.

Where was she?

At a distance, the Duchess of Trevescan—now out of her carriage—was deep in conversation with Sesily and Caleb Calhoun—who hadn't been at her ball—and a young Black woman who wore a heavy leather satchel at one hip. As he watched, the woman extracted a thick stack of papers from her bag and passed them to Calhoun.

Tommy's gaze narrowed. What were they? He should stop them. They might contain valuable information related to whatever had happened. But he didn't. Calhoun was already headed in the opposite direction at a clip—Sesily at his side—and Tommy made a decision he knew he would not regret.

He went looking for Imogen.

Frustration and something close to panic in his throat, he scanned the assembled crowd—difficult, as everyone appeared to be in motion. A few dozen men were rushing to and from the river, enormous buckets in hand. To one side, several others wheeled a cart full of heavy casks away from the building, following the direction of a dark-haired, brown-skinned woman Tommy did not recognize.

All around him, dockworkers were arriving in groups, each one heading for a small group in front of the building. There, the Duke and Duchess of Clayborn stood with Saviour and Henrietta Whittington. Above the line, the couple were owners and operators of Sedley-Whittington, one of the largest shipping companies in Britain, with stake in more than half of the river berths. Below the line, Whittington was known as Beast, one third of The Bareknuckle Bastards, the most successful smuggling operation England had ever seen. Not that anyone could prove it.

Point was, nothing happened in the Docklands without the couple knowing. Apparently, that included fire.

Tommy headed for the quartet, vaguely thinking that it wasn't every day dukes and known smugglers spent time together, though considering the Duchess of Clayborn's father was widely believed to be the head of The Bully Boys, the biggest gang of thugs on the South Bank, maybe it wasn't so impossible a friendship.

He didn't care much about it then, however.

He wanted to know where Imogen was. Immediately.

"Detective Inspector!" He gritted his teeth at the bright words from the Duchess of Clayborn, who was the first in the group to notice him. She broke away from the others and approached him. "What brings you here?"

"I did not have a chance to thank my hostess for this evening's ball," he said dryly, summoning a little laugh from the lady as he looked past her to survey the crowd for Imogen. "That, and it looks like you may want Scotland Yard here soon enough."

From a distance, Saviour Whittington let out a humorless snort. "Oh, yes, Scotland Yard is always a welcome presence in the East End."

Tommy turned a stern gaze on the other man. "Do you have a reason for wishing me gone, Beast?"

The other man rocked back on his heels and said, "Besides the fact that every time Peelers turn up here, something goes sideways? Hear me, Peck—if any one of our men are harmed tonight, I'm coming for you personally."

"I didn't set the fire," Tommy replied.

"Clearly not," Beast said, rocking back on his heels. "Too busy playin' at being a toff tonight, it seems."

Tommy looked down at his clothes—made for dukes and not Docklands—and felt his face heat.

Mrs. Whittington took pity on him. "We haven't time for the two of you to spar, boys. We've a blaze to prevent." She looked to Tommy. "We can use your help, Inspector."

His and that of every other able-bodied person in the Docklands. Fire in London was the hand of God, superseding every other concern, no matter how dire. If it was not caught at the start, it would consume every building and body it could—and no one would be able to stop it.

He looked to Beast. In this, at least, there was no line between them. "Set up a line from the river," he said, shucking the coat that cost more than his entire wardrobe, tossing it aside as he moved to help. "We'll need more men."

"Oy!" Beast shouted to a boy running past. "Take the boys and get the bells ringin' on all these ships. We're going to need as many hands as possible to keep the whole thing from burnin'. And send word to my brothers. All free hands are needed here. Now."

The boy was already running, and the rest were spurred into action, knowing time was running out, and if they did not get the fire in check soon, the whole of the Docklands was threatened. At the entrance to the building, the woman he did not recognize waved off the men who'd been ferrying casks, driving them in the direction of the line of dockworkers forming to pass water from the river—thankfully at high tide—to stop the fire.

The Duke and Duchess of Clayborn were headed in that direction as though they'd done this exact thing a dozen times before. Tommy knew the job. He joined them.

Adelaide threw him a look as he stepped into line next to her, taking a bucket of water and passing it to her. She took it, immediately passing it to her husband. "It isn't every day you find a Peeler down here," she offered. "Imogen is going to enjoy finding you on this particular line, Mr. Peck."

Tommy took an empty bucket from her and sent it toward the river. "Where is she?"

She looked over her shoulder in the direction of the warehouse, squinting against the flames. "Not far. She went looking for . . ." She trailed off and looked back at him. "She'll return presently."

"Where?" The question wasn't soft. But neither was his temper at that moment. Every inch of him wanted to find her first, and join the line second, but he knew that the fire was the first and most important task.

Water sloshed over his hand, ice-cold from the river. Adelaide took the bucket and waved away the question. "It's not important."

"I think I'd just as well be the judge of that."

Apparently his tone revealed how he did not care for the Duchess's response, as Clayborn leaned around Adelaide's figure to level Tommy with a glare. "Careful, Peck."

Lord save him from love-struck men. Tommy took a deep breath, doing his best to swallow his frustration, not entirely believing that if the Duke of Clayborn decided to come for him, the entirety of the Docklands wouldn't happily see Tommy into the river. He looked to the warehouse, where a dozen men were now carrying water inside. "What's inside?"

"The entire stock of Mithra Singh's new brewery."

Ale. He looked to the woman at the entrance to the building. "Miss Singh, I imagine?"

"The finest brewmistress in London," Clayborn said.

"Brewmaster, too," his wife pointed out as she passed another empty bucket down the line.

Clayborn nodded and clarified. "Better than *anyone* making ale today."

Men who'd made a fortune brewing and selling ale wouldn't like a woman claiming that crown. "Rivals?" Tommy asked.

Neither responded.

"What else is inside? Besides the beer?"

More silence.

Goddammit, if these women would stop keeping secrets from him, he could help them. Did they not see it? Several buckets passed in silence before Tommy caught Adelaide's eyes. "The fire isn't an accident."

When she did not reply, her husband spoke. "Do you think they'd be here if it was?"

Them. The women the papers called the Hell's Belles. Tommy snapped his attention to the duke. "And you allow them to come?"

Clayborn offered a humorless laugh. "*Allow* them? You think for one moment these women *ask permission* for what they do?" He shook his head and looked down at his wife. "All I can do is be grateful *she* allows *me* to fight by her side."

It was madness. If he'd known where Imogen was headed earlier in the evening, he would have tied her up with the ribbons of her own stockings to keep her safe.

Where was she?

The Duke and Duchess of Clayborn were now making eyes at each other, but Tommy couldn't keep in his retort, quick and angry. "And so, what? She says she wants to walk into fire and you simply—"

"Oy!" The shout came from above, in the direction of the building, and Tommy recognized it instantly.

Except, of course, he couldn't have.

Because it wasn't possible that he was hearing correctly.

"How is it looking from out there?"

It wasn't possible. There was no goddamn way that

Imogen Loveless was *inside* a burning building, calling down to the street below, as though she were casually hailing a hack.

"What in hell?" The Duke of Clayborn's words rang around them.

For her part, the Duchess of Clayborn turned calmly and looked up into the dark space that marked the second floor of the building, where Imogen's face peered out like a little moon in a sky about to turn into an inferno, and said, "From out here it still seems like it's confined to the upper floors, but it's more important how it looks from in there, Imogen!"

"Right as rain! No fire at all where I am. I just require a bit longer!" Imogen said. "I've nearly sorted it!" Her gaze fell on him and her eyes lit up, as though they were meeting on a stroll through Hyde Park. "Tommy! I didn't expect you to arrive so quickly!"

Tommy couldn't find the words to reply. He wasn't sure he'd be able to find words ever again.

Adelaide slid a nervous look at him. "Do be quick about it, Imogen; the detective inspector is . . . growling."

"Sometimes he does that," Imogen said. "Usually when he is irritated with me."

"I think he might be irritated then, Im."

Irritated was not even in the same universe as how Tommy was feeling. Tommy was feeling unhinged.

"I'm perfectly safe, Tommy!" Imogen said happily, as though two floors above her the whole building weren't threatening to cave in. "No need to worry!"

He didn't look at her. He couldn't look at her.

Instead, he turned on Clayborn. *"You let her walk into fire."*

"I didn't know." Clayborn's eyes went wide, and he immediately pushed his wife behind him, keeping her from whatever Tommy had become. "Fucking hell—*I didn't know.* Dammit, Adelaide!" he tossed over his shoulder. "What is Imogen doing *inside*? The whole place could—"

Adelaide didn't let him finish, her voice clear and crisp and certain. Like she'd seen Imogen do this kind of thing a hundred times before. "She insisted. She didn't want another building to—"

Tommy went cold when she caught herself from finishing the sentence.

"Another building to *what*, Adelaide?" her husband roared, passing water with more vigor.

Tommy finished for her. "To explode."

Adelaide looked to him. "Exactly. She went in to—"

Tommy didn't hear the rest. He was too busy running for the building.

Chapter Fifteen

He found her on the first floor, crouched by an enormous wooden silo, in a pool of lantern light, in a room that smelled like wheat. She was holding a jar of beige powder and leaning over the damn bag she carried everywhere.

Tommy pulled up straight just inside the entrance to the room, sucking in a deep breath—what felt like the first one he'd taken since he'd opened the door to the Trevescan library and discovered she'd given him the slip.

He rubbed one hand across his chest as he exhaled—trying to ease the tightness there, even as he knew it would not dissipate. At least, not until this woman was out of his life and had taken her chaos with her.

Christ.

"I've changed my mind; I am going to make it my life's purpose to get you married."

She did not look up from her task as she lowered the jar into the bag, slowly. Instead, she said, "While I am sympathetic to your deep-rooted sense of responsibility, Tommy, and more than impressed with your commitment to your promise to my brother, I would appreciate it if you did not distract me."

His brow furrowed and he took a step closer. "What is that?"

"Mercury fulminate."

He stilled. Tommy had been investigating the explosions throughout London long enough to know that mercury fulminate had been used in the other two in the East End. He also knew that, in the wrong hands, it could cause the whole place to go, and them with it. *Her* with it. "Dammit, Imogen—leave it. I'll handle getting it out of here."

"No need. It's perfectly safe when handled properly."

"And is carting it around in a carpetbag proper handling?"

"Not for most people, no. But I am not most people." Was she *smiling*? He couldn't see it in the dim light, but he could swear he heard it. She finished seating the jar within the bag and returned to the silo, ignoring the bag and him, as though this were all completely normal.

"You do realize that I've just discovered you inside a burning building with an explosive."

She stood and wiped her hands on her skirts. "And do you have reason to believe I have taken enough leave of my senses to be inside this burning building, with an explosive, by design?"

He didn't. Despite the proximity this woman seemed to have to murder and mayhem, Tommy had never believed she was responsible for it. Not even at the beginning, when he hadn't understood her. What he understood was that he wanted her out of this place.

He wanted her *safe*. And not only because it was his job.

Not that he was willing to admit it to her. "I have reason to believe you've taken leave of your senses in any number of ways," he said.

"It is remarkable how everyone thinks *I* am the mad one," Imogen grumbled.

Before he could ask her to explain, there was a rumble outside the room, where a half-dozen men climbed the stairs, buckets in hand, to fight the fire.

"They'll need salt and alum to keep the fire from spreading while they fight it," she said, all casual, as she snatched up the lantern and crouched low to look under the silo.

Tommy did not move. "They know."

"I assume Beast and Hattie have it under control." She paused, reaching a hand into the darkness, and Tommy held his breath. "They've handled fire here before."

He didn't want to talk about what the Sedley-Whittingtons had handled before. Not when this woman was destroying him, pulling words from him like "When I get you out of here, I'm going to turn you over my knee."

"I'm nearly done," she replied, the words entirely lacking in concern.

"Nearly done—" His indignation strangled the words in his throat. "Imogen, the whole place is aflame."

"Not the *whole* place," she said calmly into the darkness under the silo as she reached beneath it, feeling about for something. Hopefully not something flammable. "And when I am through it will remain largely un-aflame."

"Imogen. Look at me."

He wanted to see her eyes. Wanted to know she was as unconcerned as she sounded.

"I cannot, I'm afraid," she said, pressing her cheek to the floor.

"Why not?"

"Because, you are a distraction, Tommy Peck," she said. "And I would like very much for my friend to have as much of her brewery as possible in the morning."

Satisfied, she came to her knees and pressed her hands to her thighs, one hand clenched in a fist. She took a deep breath. "I would like to have as much of the *Docklands* as possible in the morning," she said, to herself more than to him.

And then, before he could reply, she said softly, with a voice that threatened to crack, "I would like very much for them to *lose* tonight."

He recognized the frustration in the words. The quiet, barely-there admission that she was tired. But more than that, he recognized the meaning in them. Imogen knew who was behind the explosions. He was sure of it.

"Who? Who are they?" He took a step toward her, wanting to help her up. Wanting to get her out. Wanting her to see that they were on the same side. "Tell me—"

"No," she said firmly, holding up a hand, and did not look in his direction. "Don't move. If you knock the bag—"

He stilled at the words, wanting to take her by the shoulders and shake her and carry her out of this building and off the docks and out of fucking *Britain* until he was sure she was safe.

But he did as she asked, and did not move.

Instead, he watched her, silent sentry, ready to carry her from yet another building if it was required. She stood and moved to the bag, fussing within before snapping it closed.

Tommy held his breath when she lifted it, even as she moved toward him with smooth purpose, as though she were carrying a basket of baked goods for a church tea and not a bag full of explosives.

She lifted the lantern when she drew close, and he fought the urge to rub at the tightness in his chest once more as she smiled, bright and beautiful and unconcerned.

With a little head tilt, she inspected him. He knew what she found—the opposite of her own demeanor. Frozen in place, fists clenched, every muscle in his body strung tight like a bow. Ready to fight any villain if it meant keeping her safe.

His jaw ached with tension.

"You are angry with me."

He shook his head. "Angry does not begin to describe how I feel about you right now."

Something softened in her gaze and it made him come even further unstitched. "You were concerned."

"Am. Am concerned. Present tense," he said, the words tight in his throat.

"Don't worry," she said. "I shan't tell my brother I gave you the slip."

He released a harsh breath. "You think I care about what your fucking brother thinks right now?"

Her brows rose at his foul language. "Do you not?"

His throat worked, and her gaze flickered to it. He hated what she saw there. How it revealed more than he would ever admit. "I want you out of this building. Now."

She waved the lantern in the direction of the door. "I am not the one blocking the exit, Detective Inspector."

The words were punctuated with a creak from above—a sound Tommy did not like, all things considered.

He stepped aside to let her pass. "Down, Imogen."

"And here I was thinking the street was up," she quipped.

Swallowing his irritated growl, Tommy followed close behind her as she descended the narrow staircase, keeping his gaze on the carpetbag that was the most serious threat to her person.

At the base of the stairs, ten yards from the entrance to the warehouse, with a straight shot to the outside, Tommy could see Mithra Singh standing, wringing her hands. Inside, the great, cavernous warehouse was circled with stairs, circling up to the top of the building, allowing for access to the windows and a wide open view to the roof, but Tommy didn't look to where the fire brigade was doing their best to keep the flames at bay—all he could look at was Imogen, curls bouncing, hips swaying and carrying that infernal bag containing a deadly explosive device, as though everything were perfectly normal.

If he hadn't been so focused on the damn bag, he might have looked up. Might have heard the massive crack a heartbeat earlier.

By the time he heard it, she'd slowed, turning her face up to the ceiling and the chorus of warnings shouted from above. He didn't follow her gaze, not even when she turned wide eyes on him in what seemed like impossibly slow motion.

Instead, he ran for her, snatching the bag from her hands and pushing her toward the door with the singular goal of keeping her safe. Miss Singh came forward to catch Imogen as she stumbled over the threshold, even as Tommy dropped the bag and kicked it away, just in time, as a too-large hunk of wood came down on top of him, the jagged edge of it scraping over his arm, leaving a wicked sting in its wake as it sent him to his knees.

Imogen, the madwoman, was coming back for him. "Tommy! Are you—"

And then he was mad, too. He pointed to the docks beyond and shouted, "Get the hell out!"

She blinked at the words, at the wild shout of them. And then she squared her shoulders, lifted her chin, and said, "Not without you, you lummox."

In all his years brawling his way through East London, followed by nine as a Scotland Yardsman and two more as a detective inspector—no one had ever called Tommy Peck a lummox. He didn't care for it. "What did you say?"

He struggled to his feet, as she came to help him. "I'll be happy to repeat it once we get outside and you are safe."

"You don't keep me safe, Imogen Loveless. I keep *you* safe."

"Oh, right. In this play, you act the part of my nurse-maid. I forgot."

This damn woman. Did she not know how she'd incited him in the last three hours? Did she not understand that such things had repercussions?

She bloody well would. He would tell her. In great detail. But first, he snatched her bag from where he'd kicked it and pulled her from the building at a clip, passing her friends and his foes, ignoring them as they called out, finally stopping where their lights faded and the shadows began.

Only then, when they were as far from mayhem as possible, did he risk looking at her. And that was when he realized his mistake. As long as he was near Imogen, mayhem was not far.

And in moments like this, he would not be able to resist it.

He set the bag on the ground and pulled her far from it, a flood of emotions coursing through him—fear and fury and frustration and relief, acute and intense.

And *need*.

It was the need he could not deny.

He pulled her to him, not caring that half the Docklands could see them, not caring that any number of people who could orchestrate the end of his career were in shouting distance.

All he cared about was having his hands on her.

She came without hesitation, her own hands sliding to find purchase on his shoulders, fingers threading through his hair as she released a little sigh and turned up to his kiss.

He searched her face, running his thumb over her rosy cheek, marveling at the softness of the curls that clung to his hand. "I should take you home."

"Do you want to take me home?"

He didn't. For one, wild moment, it occurred to him that he didn't want to take her anywhere . . . because here, in this place, surrounded by her friends, no one was interested in separating them.

But he *should*.

"I should bring you home and tuck you into bed," he said to himself more than to her. "I should see you safe and asleep."

And damned if this magnificent woman didn't flash him the sweetest smile and say, "Whose home?"

The question thrummed through him—no longer in a bed with fluffy pillows and pristine bedclothes fit for a princess born into her world, but now in his bed in Holborn—big enough for a man of his size, but without the frills and frippery suited to a woman like Imogen.

Still, they'd make do.

He closed his eyes against the image, which was a mistake, because the action only clarified it. And when he opened them again, she was looking up at him with those enormous brown eyes rimmed with those impossibly long lashes, and he had no choice but to kiss her.

Before he could lean down and claim her mouth, however, she stopped a hairsbreadth away from him and whispered, "Thank you."

He was too full of her to understand. "For what?"

She smiled, and he imagined he could taste it, slow and sinful and sweet. "For coming to rescue me."

He claimed her mouth, needing the feel of her, the scent of her, the taste of her, the softness of her lips, the sweet way they opened to let him in as though he belonged there, inside her.

Pleasure thrummed through him, pooling hot and deep, and he was instantly hard with the wildness of the evening—the memory of her coming around his fingers crashing into the knowledge that she'd been inside a burning building and could have been hurt. Desire was a wild riot inside him . . . a need to claim her. To mark her safe. To mark her his.

Madness.

He'd never felt this way. Never wanted anything the way he wanted this woman in this moment. It was unsettling and infuriating and terrifying.

And irresistible.

And he didn't care. God knew he should. God knew he was on the cusp of ruining this glorious woman—of making it impossible for her to live the life for which she was born.

But she'd been in danger, and he'd been out of control, and now he had his hands on her, and, *Christ*, he could feel how much she liked it in the way her hands trembled at his skin as they slid over his shoulders, and her tongue slid over his, and he wondered if he'd ever be able to stop.

She gripped his arm, using his strength to press herself closer. To kiss him properly, and he reveled in it—in being strength for her use.

Until pain lanced down his arm, a lick of fire that had him ending the kiss on a gasp. Her eyes went wide and she released him, turning her palm up, revealing fingers dark with blood. His blood.

"Dammit, Tommy!"

He shook his head and tried to pull away. "It's nothing."

"It's absolutely not nothing," she said, taking his hand in a firm grip and tugging him toward the light once more. "Frances! Help!"

The woman who'd been in conversation with the Duchess of Trevescan turned at the urgent cry, already moving toward them.

"Imogen, it's fine." He'd had worse. Like having to let her go.

Ignoring him, she said, "He's been hurt."

Embarrassment coursed through Tommy. "I'm *fine*."

"Where?" the woman named Frances asked Imogen.

"His arm." Imogen held out her hand. "He's bleeding."

"Best get him out of that shirt," Frances said.

"I'm perfectly able to hear you both," he cut in.

Frances looked to him. "Excellent. Then please remove your shirt, Mr. Peck."

He absolutely wasn't doing that. "I don't think—"

Before he could finish refusing politely, a tear sounded in the darkness, and he stared down at Imogen, the wicked blade he'd found beneath her skirts earlier in the evening now in her hand . . . and the sleeve of his shirt now hanging in pieces at the shoulder.

"Something fell on him," Imogen said to the other woman, who was already turning him to inspect his arm in the light from a nearby lantern.

"Mmm," Frances said thoughtfully. "You'll need stitching, I'm afraid."

"I can do it myself," he said. It wasn't the first time he did such a thing, nor would it be the last.

"And no doubt that would be pretty indeed," she replied, already reaching into the heavy black satchel that hung across her body.

Tommy had the clear sense that he was not being given a choice as she extracted a brown glass bottle and a handkerchief. Uncorking the bottle, she announced, "Water," and then poured a liberal amount of the liquid on his arm and the handkerchief, soaking it through. "Let's get a good look at this wound." He hissed as she poked and prodded at him.

"Really, Tommy," Imogen said, sounding altogether too happy. "You are making a meal of it."

"All men make a meal of it," Frances replied. "Why do you think I choose to work with women?"

"I think most women would dislike someone rooting around in their wounds," he said through gritted teeth. "Ow!" he said as she squeezed the edges together.

"Well!" The Duchess of Trevescan clapped her hands as she approached, something close to joy in her voice.

"The fire is contained, and though it will take a bit of time, Mithra won't lose everything."

Imogen let out a sound that was close to delight, and he couldn't help but look to her, and revel in the relieved, bright eyes she turned on her friend. "We win," she said.

I would like very much for them to lose tonight.

Imogen's words from earlier.

"Tonight," the Duchess said, the words rich and warm and triumphant in her Mayfair accent. "What's happening here? Are you hurt, Detective Inspector?"

"Yes," Imogen said, as he replied, "No."

Duchess looked to Frances. "There appears to be some confusion."

"No confusion. He's a nasty slice on his arm."

Duchess looked to him. "That's what you get when you take off your expensive coat, Mr. Peck."

Tommy gritted his teeth as Imogen laughed. "Don't needle him, Duchess. I hear he was hauling water."

"He was indeed. It was difficult to miss," Duchess said, looking at him. "Making Scotland Yard look like a worthy endeavor tonight."

He didn't care what Scotland Yard seemed like that night, if he were honest, but he did not reply.

"You shall have to tell me all about it in great detail," Imogen quipped, and Tommy thanked his Maker for the beard that hid the heat that spread across his cheeks at the words. "Just as soon as Frances sews him up."

As if on cue, Frances reached into her bag for a second bottle and looked to him. "You're not going to like this bit."

"Because men make a meal of things?"

"No, because it's going to hurt." Frances looked to Imogen. "Perhaps you ought to distract him."

Imogen nodded and stood directly in front of him, setting one warm hand to his cheek, tipping his face up to look at her, her black curls blowing wild around her face, cheeks red with the cold wind coming off the river.

Christ, she was pretty.

He resisted the urge to put his hand over hers on his cheek.

"You did very well on the water line, Tommy," she said softly.

Why did that make him want to preen?

He didn't have time to think through the answer, because Frances took that moment to pour the liquid over his wound. He cursed, low and foul, and said, "What is that?"

"Gin," she said with a shrug. "There is a growing belief that alcohol on a wound aids healing."

"I would have preferred to drink it," he grumbled, rolling his shoulder in an attempt to shake off the pain.

"I feel the same, truly," Frances said. "But my partner is legions smarter than me, and I do what she says. Now, let's get you stitched."

"I'm afraid you won't be stitching Mr. Peck, Frances," Duchess said. "We've a few men with burns from the fire who need tending, and they take precedence over the Inspector."

Imogen patted Tommy's cheek. "Duchess doesn't mean to insult, Tommy."

"Of course not," Duchess agreed. "I'm leaving you in more than capable hands, Mr. Peck."

She meant Imogen's hands. Hands that Tommy knew were more than capable. Hands he'd experienced earlier that evening. Hands to which he would happily turn himself over if given another opportunity.

Except the opportunity that presented itself didn't seem pleasurable.

Indeed, as he looked at the women, considering him with a collection of suspicious smiles, he realized the opportunity that presented itself involved Imogen taking a needle to him.

He shook his head. *"No."*

Frances was already turning away—heading to patients in more serious circumstances. But he heard her as she tossed over her shoulder, "I wouldn't fret. Imogen is excellent with a needle."

Chapter Sixteen

"Was that O'Dwyer or Leafe?"

Imogen did not flinch at the question, and he saw the surprise that came on the heels of it. She hadn't expected him to so easily sort through the identity of the doctor.

Without answering, she adjusted his arm on the table between them, inside the captain's cabin of one of the Sedley-Whittington ships docked for the night. Even as Beast had blustered and balked at the idea of a Peeler inside one of his boats, his wife had recognized Imogen's predicament—Tommy needed stitching, and driving anywhere to do it was out of the question.

And so, here they were, in one of the lushest cabins he'd ever seen, adorned with silks and fabrics and leather and mahogany and a table full of maps that rivaled Magellan's.

She continued threading the needle Frances had given her, grateful for the excuse not to meet his eyes. "O'Dwyer."

"Frances O'Dwyer, seamstress, hmm?"

Imogen met his eyes then, lifting the needle in her hand. "Does she not do a fair amount of stitching?"

He eyed the gleaming silver weapon and said, "I could do with some of that gin she wasted before you start."

Imogen stood and crossed the room to the captain's

decanter filled with amber liquid, and he couldn't resist watching her hips, swaying beneath her skirts. She poured it into a glass and walked it back to him. "Will whisky do?"

He knocked it back and coughed, screwing up his face. "Not whisky. Rum."

"The risk one takes when one drinks stolen spirits," she replied with a laugh.

He nodded to his arm. "Go on then."

She adjusted the light and leaned over his arm, her deep focus making it easy to watch her. He wondered at her stillness—this woman who knew the ins and outs of explosives and raucous taverns and who carried a blade at her thigh and a bag full of danger at her side and who turned up wherever chaos threatened and who was always *moving*.

But now . . . as she investigated the slice on his arm, a little furrow at her brow where a curtain of perfect curls fell, tempting him with the idea of pushing them aside and letting them twine around his fingers, she was still, and he drank her in.

Sensing his attention, she met his gaze. "This won't be pleasant."

"Have you done it before?"

"Many times."

Somehow, he simultaneously hated the answer and loved it. Hated that she'd *many times* been in proximity to the kind of danger that required a skill for stitching a wound. Loved that she was able to do the stitching—that for this moment, she would turn her skills to him. That they were somehow, for a heartbeat, partners.

Partners who held a single breath in anticipation of the first stitch.

"I'm sorry," she whispered, the words barely there as she began her work, and the softness of them, the truth in them, made him ache.

"Go on," he urged her, and she followed the instruction, placing the first stitch with a smooth, clean motion that proved her earlier claim. She'd done it before. "Who else have you stitched, Imogen Loveless?"

"Enough that I know the score," she said, looking up through her curls. "Do you want names?"

Yes. He wanted names. He wanted to know whose skin she'd touched. Who she'd studied without shirts, or trousers. Or more.

"Would it help to know that your arm is one of the more impressive ones I've stitched?"

Yes. Yes, that helped very much. *Though it shouldn't.*

"We shouldn't be here," he said, willing them both to hear the words. "Your brother will come looking for you."

She shook her head. "He never comes home after events in society. He goes to his club, or to his mistress, to wash off the scent of matchmaking mamas." A pause and then, "Ironic, that, isn't it? That he is more than willing to play the part of matchmaking mama for me, and refuses to offer himself up to them."

A pause, silence heavy in the room. And then Tommy asked, "Why don't you wish to marry?"

She placed another stitch before she spoke to her work. "In my experience, husbands come in two flavors. The first is the kind my brother seeks for me. Full of bluster and power, lord of the manor, with a desire for a wife as a broodmare and a hostess and, at best, a pile of money."

Tommy did not reply, even as the idea of Imogen in such a marriage—set high upon a shelf and brought out only when she was required—unsettled him, and he could not deny the instant relief that coursed through him when she wrinkled her nose and said, "The roasted lamb of men."

He rumbled his amusement, urging her on.

"The second flavor," she said, "I did not believe existed outside of storybooks."

"Until your friends," he replied, understanding instantly. "Lady Sesily. Miss Frampton."

"Mrs. Calhoun. The Duchess of Clayborn." She smiled. "They neither of them intended marriage, and then . . ." She paused and collected her thoughts before finishing, the words incredulous. "And then they met husbands who wished to stand by their side. Partners. Who believed in them. Who wanted them to . . ."

He waited what seemed like an eternity as she sought the word. When she found it, her eyes lit with satisfaction, gleaming deep and brown in the lantern light. ". . . to *thrive*."

He couldn't help repeating her. "To thrive."

She nodded. "It is beautiful."

More beautiful than he'd ever admit. "You mean husbands who love them."

Another slow, methodical stitch. "A rare quality for husbands, these days."

"It shouldn't be."

Her brows shot up.

Why had he said that?

Why was he suddenly imagining how it would be to stand by a woman the way the Duke of Clayborn had done on the water line earlier in the evening? How it would be to pull a woman he loved close and press a kiss to her temple, the way he'd seen Caleb Calhoun do a dozen times inside his Covent Garden tavern?

She looked to him. "You sound as though you've seen husbands like that, as well."

"I've a counterpart at Scotland Yard. Loves his wife to distraction. Can't go a day without singing Susie's praises."

"Lucky Susie."

"And my father," he said, immediately stopping. He didn't know why he'd said it. He shouldn't have. There was no reason for it.

Imogen peeked up at him, then returned to her work. Quiet.

A trick he'd used a hundred times in his work. A thousand. And still, he filled the silence. "He loved my mother wildly—convinced her to run away from the life into which she'd been born. Promised to carry her dreams with him."

She smiled. "And then you came along."

"And my sister and brother." He watched the top of her head, curls gleaming in the candlelight. "He worked every day, until he died. To give us the life he wanted for us."

And he never got there.

Tommy left the last unsaid, instead settling on, "So. Husbands who love their wives should not be rare. They should be everywhere."

"There, at least, you are right," she said, thoughtful. Still. "There is great joy in seeing my friends loved."

"They love you, as well," he said, remembering the Duke of Clayborn's anger when he'd realized Imogen was inside the warehouse. The way Calhoun came into the street outside The Place to check on her.

Something threaded through him at the memory. Something that, if he inspected it too carefully, would be close to envy.

"I am lucky that loving my friends meant loving me." She gave a little shrug. "But they do not understand me. I . . . baffle them. They think me curious and entertaining. Perhaps diverting. But madcap. Chaos."

He didn't like the way she said *chaos*. Didn't like the resignation in it. The way it sounded, suddenly, like the word was a mantle she'd been given, not chosen.

How many times had he thought of her as such? Chaos? Mayhem? Havoc?

And yet, now, as they sat in a captain's cabin on a ship docked in a berth on the Thames, as the world turned in the city beyond and she performed her calm, measured task, Tommy realized that it was the first time he'd ever seen her this way, still and calm and focused. And it felt as though she was revealing a piece of herself—one she'd hidden from him before now.

How many more of those pieces were there?

And how could he discover them all?

"So that is the flavor you prefer?" He shouldn't have asked. None of this conversation was for him.

Except, she placed another stitch, clean and careful, and said simply, "It is not for me."

He blinked. "Love?"

She met his eyes. "You are surprised."

"In my experience, women want love."

Instead of answering, she leaned back and considered her handiwork. "Not bad."

He'd pushed her too far.

Resisting the urge to curse in the darkness, Tommy followed her gaze. "I thought you said you were rubbish at embroidery."

The clouds in her eyes were replaced with a grateful gleam, and she clung to the change of topic. "As long as you do not expect an iris, or a chrysanthemum, or an inspirational quote, we should be fine."

"What kind of inspirational quotes are you offering?"

"How about *Beware falling rafters*?"

He nodded, sagely. "A cautionary tale."

"In ancient Greece, the oracles inked their prophecies on fabrics. I could make you my canvas."

A vision flashed, unbidden, her fingers painting over his skin, her whispers at his ear. Desire thrummed through him. "And so you would paint me with your truth?"

Her thumb stroked along his arm, turning him carefully toward the light. "You would not like my truth."

The words sizzled through him, a teasing glimpse of something more than what the rest of the world saw of Imogen Loveless. "Tell me."

"I am not the kind of woman men love."

Tommy sucked in a breath at the unexpected confession. "What does that mean?"

She sat back. "I think you are done."

He set his free hand on hers, holding her firmly until

she looked into his eyes. "What does that mean? That you are not the kind of woman men love?"

It was rubbish.

Something flashed across her face. Disappointment. She sighed and shook his hand off, reaching for a pair of scissors. "You are through, Mr. Peck. Do try not to get hit with falling rafters in the future."

He sighed and released her. She was not going to answer. Another layer of Imogen Loveless that was not for him. And not for now. Hiding his frustration, he replied, "I make no promises."

She tucked the scissors into her bag, followed them with the spool of thread and the needle before turning back to him. "What of you?"

"What of me?"

"What flavor of wife do you have a taste for? The one who marries for prestige? Or the one who marries for love?"

"There isn't much prestige to be had with me, I'm afraid."

"Nonsense," she said. "The hero of Scotland Yard—you must have dozens of women chasing after you in a constant state of excitement."

He raised a brow. "It might surprise you, my lady, that I am not interested in women suffering from excitement at a mere glimpse of me."

"Ah. Then love it is."

"Love would . . ." He paused. ". . . be nice."

It wasn't an appropriate conversation. Not when he should be asking her about the bomb she'd found in the warehouse. In the fire that the docks had narrowly escaped. His investigation and all the ways she turned up a part of it.

Not when he should be apologizing for taking advantage of her mere hours ago, his mouth on her skin as she came apart on his fingers.

She looked away, and he would have given a year's salary to know what she was thinking.

"So there it is," he said softly. "My truth for yours. Tell me the rest."

"There is not much to tell," she said. "It is not complicated or secret. I am, simply, a bit more than anyone bargains for."

It wasn't true. "How so?"

She wrinkled her nose, and he could tell he'd unwittingly disappointed her as she sat back, that hand sliding across the scarred table. "Really, Inspector, you embarrass us both."

He reached for her, his hand landing on hers, keeping her still. Her gaze flew to his, surprise flashing in them in the strange, swinging light of the cabin. "I swear that is not my desire."

She looked to their hands and he tightened his grip, resisting the urge to lace his fingers through hers. To kiss her again, as he had at the ball. To pull her into his lap and touch her. To play with her.

"The wide world thinks me chaos," she said, searching for the words to explain. "But it is not chaos when it is simply . . . the way one is. I am . . . too much for most people."

She was nothing close to too much.

Before he could say so, she held up a hand, a knowing gleam in her eyes. "When I say I am too much, people wish to comfort me . . . *no no, Imogen, you're not too much!* But I am. I am big and bold, my laugh is loud and my hair is wild, and I am peculiar. I've a penchant for chemistry, and an instinct for danger, and if there is an adventure in the wind . . . I *want* it. All that, and my passion for explosives . . . which you have witnessed firsthand."

He watched her with fascination, his brow furrowed, trying to understand. Trying to make sense of this wonderful woman. She smiled, a tiny, wistful expression, and reached for him, stroking her thumb over the furrow in his brow. "You're trying to understand me." She laughed. "Don't. No one ever has. Not my family, not society, not even my friends—though they come closest, and love me in spite of my . . . peculiarities."

"I want to," he said. And it was the truth.

She nodded. "I know. But I wish you wouldn't. It makes me wonder what it would be like if someone did." She looked down at their hands.

The way those words tempted him . . . when he knew they should not. When he knew there was no way he could give her the life she deserved.

"Tonight, Imogen . . . I—I took advantage of you."

Her eyes went wide. "You did?"

"Yes," he admitted. He should have been stronger. Should have been able to resist her. But even now, with her pretty gaze on his and her soft fingers stroking over his arm, he couldn't quite find the disappointment he should feel. "My job—I was to keep you safe."

"I didn't ask—"

He didn't let her finish. "I was to keep you from harm, protect you. And instead, I practically ruined you in a Mayfair library and then failed to notice you were headed into a burning building."

She met his eyes as she stroked his arm a second time. "Of my own doing."

"It remains my fault."

Another stroke, her fingers like fire. "Forgive me, Tommy, but you are—quite dim when you wish to be."

He blinked. "I beg your pardon?"

"If you think for one moment that you could have kept me from here tonight . . . you really have not been paying attention. You needn't carry the weight of the world. You could not stop us tonight."

"You knew. You knew before anyone told the police. That the building was aflame. You knew there was an explosive inside."

She nodded. "I did."

"They came to tell you at the ball."

"Yes."

"And it wasn't an accident." He knew all this. He wasn't a fool.

"Of course it wasn't an accident," she said. "We wouldn't be here if it were an accident."

"What in hell are you up to?" he asked, softly. "Tell me. Let me help you. Tell me why you are here. How you knew to come here. How you knew what was inside." He paused. "Tell me how you've always known where to be. Where I *should* be. Tell me how you are always there first."

"Because I receive the information before you do," she said.

"How?" he asked, frustrated. "It isn't your job to find the culprits. To keep them from doing it again."

She shook her head. "It is not. And yet it falls to me, because there are too few others who care about the East End. Who can be trusted here."

"*I* care, dammit. *I* can be trusted."

"Perhaps," she said. "You, Tommy Peck, detective inspector and hero of Scotland Yard, beloved of the *News* and half of the population of London for your strong arms and enormous thighs and your penchant for carrying women away from danger—"

"Woman," he said.

"What?"

"Not women. I've only ever been seen carrying one woman from danger. If you're going to mock me, I'd appreciate you getting your facts straight."

"Fine," she said, and he could see her cheeks darkening with a blush even in the dim light. "Carrying *me* from danger. Perhaps you could be trusted. But how are we to know when you work for them?"

"For whom?"

She gave a little, humorless laugh. "For power. For the police. For Parliament. For the legions of men—and their countless wives—who would rather see the East End destroyed than help lift it up."

"That's not what I want. I want the East End safe. But to keep it so, someone must let me in."

Her brows rose. "And you wish for me to make the introduction?"

"They trust you. And the women you run with."

"The women I run with." Her lips twisted in amusement. "Did you not name us?"

"I didn't," he said with a scowl. "The papers named you. It's a ridiculous name."

"I rather like it," she said. "Hell's Belles—it makes us sound like we've teeth."

He couldn't stop a bark of laughter. "No one who's spent any time with you would think you don't have teeth, Imogen."

Her eyes went wide. "You really must stop saying such nice things to me."

"So they trust you. The people here. They trust you with the news of explosions in seamstress's. In print shops. At bakeries . . . but shall I tell you what I think?"

She looked up at him, the focus in her big brown eyes threatening to distract him. What would it be like to have that focus—that unabashed interest—on him at other times? When he wasn't discussing explosions. When he was simply . . . with her?

He pushed the thought aside. "I think that they were not a print shop, a seamstress, and a bakery."

"Of course they were," she said without hesitation. "I have seen the press, the fabric, and the milled flour myself."

"I am not a fool, Imogen," he said. "I know things, as well. And while I don't know what was going on inside Mithra Singh's brewery, I know that Frances O'Dwyer was not summoned to treat a man suffering from burns because she was a seamstress. I know women seek doctors like her when they have no other choice."

"You're wrong," she said, standing once more, her stillness gone. "Women seek doctors like O'Dwyer and Leafe when they have made their choice, and they want someone to believe them."

He nodded, grateful for the reply. Feeling like she was bringing him closer. He pressed on. "I know Mrs. Linden housed girls on the run in the back of her bakery—girls desperate for a better life. I know that's where they received money and clothes and food, and papers to start a new life. And I know Mrs. Mayhew used her print shop to organize groups of workers in the factories across the city."

Imogen stiffened and he knew he was right. "Who else knows?"

"No one," he said softly. "Because I also know to keep my mouth shut until I have all the information. But more importantly, because I know *you* have that information. I think you know the whos and the whys and the hows. And I wish you would trust me enough to let me in."

She remained silent, but her gaze did not waver.

In the two years he'd known Imogen Loveless and her gang of women, they'd been instrumental in bringing down some of the most powerful men in Britain, each one with a collection of evidence that Tommy himself could not have amassed.

Their access to the West End and their welcome in the East End gave them a particular skill for collecting information. They did not always come to him. But when they did, it was with irrefutable evidence.

Evidence he had no doubt they had been collecting. Evidence he had no doubt *Imogen* was collecting. Evidence he could use, dammit, to stop these crimes. "You cannot always do it on your own, Imogen. Surely you understand that. At some point, the four of you will find yourselves too close to danger."

"We've done just fine in proximity to danger so far."

He shook his head. "You think you will remain unnoticed? Unnamed? Your brother can see you are up to something. How long before he tells his friend the home secretary? How long before someone notices what I already have? That you four turn up like bad pennies?"

"I beg your pardon. There's nothing bad about us. If anything, Detective Inspector, when I turn up, you make arrests. Your star rises," she pointed out, fire in the words and in her eyes. "Indeed, when you are named superintendent of whatever nonsense division of Scotland Yard they intend to give you, it shan't be because you found me in plain sight. It shall be because you've sent multiple aristocrats to prison on the backs of *our* work. And if we don't think you are ready to know everything . . . perhaps you are not ready to know everything."

"You aren't wrong," he said. "But what has changed? You brought me in before—why not now?" His fist clenched on the table and he resisted the pain that shot over his newly stitched wound. "Dammit, Imogen, what happens when you run out of luck? Whoever they are— these are not good men. These are men with destruction in mind. What happens when they decide to make you their next target?"

She was quiet.

"You will need me, then. To keep you safe."

"And if you cannot keep me safe?"

The certainty in the words infuriated him. "I am extremely good at my job."

"And I am extremely good at mine."

Frustration consumed him, roaring in his ears like one of her explosions. "Imogen. Do you know who it is? Who threatens you? Who threatens these places?"

She didn't reply.

Goddammit.

"Imogen." Her name came on a whisper. "Whatever this is . . . I can help."

She shook her head. "*Can* and *will* are not the same."

Frustration rumbled through him. Caught in his throat. In his chest. "I *will*. I will help."

"How?" She reached the end of her fuse. "You come back tomorrow? Pick through the ash and round up the witnesses for questioning. Frances O'Dwyer? Erin Leafe? Mithra Singh? You question my friends—a collection of aristocrats and criminals, businessmen and sailors? The half-dozen women who work the docks when the ships are in port? You trust that someone knows something about how warehouses burn. About how explosives threaten."

"I don't have to do any of that," he said. "I only have to question you. You know everything they know, don't you? You were here before me. You are always here before me. I can help you. I can keep these places—these people—safe. It is my *job*."

A beat. And then she burst out laughing. "You expect these people to believe Scotland Yard will help? These people in this place where Peelers rarely show their faces except to round them up and carry them off to Newgate for crimes ranging from being poor to being desperate? You think one evening on the water line, preventing a warehouse from burning, will uncouple them from their safest adage?"

"Which adage?"

"The one that tells them not to trust the police."

He stilled. He knew that the new police force and the residents of the East End were often at odds. But still—the idea that they thought they could not trust him? That *she* could not trust him? "I've no intention of taking anyone to Newgate tonight."

"And how are we to know that, Detective Inspector?"

He hated the way she lingered on his title with disdain

here, in the East End of London, where he had been born. Where he'd brawled as a child and again as a young man. Where his father had been born before him. Where his father had died.

This place Tommy had once vowed to protect.

She continued, standing and smoothing her skirts, straight and regal. "Does your truncheon strike a different kind of blow? Does your whistle sing a different note?" Something shifted in the air between them. Something angry. Something important. "Are we to believe you are good because you tell us so?"

Yes.

The word stuck in his throat.

He'd worked for the police for eleven years, and he was not a fool. He had been pulled from the streets of the East End, only months after the Metropolitan Police were formed in response to the Bow Street Runners growing more and more corrupt and less and less in service to justice.

Adams had hired Tommy with the promise that this was a job that would allow him to build something. To be something. To change something.

So, *yes.* They could trust him. She could trust him.

But he knew better than most that he could vow it a dozen times in a dozen ways, that he could beg her to believe it, and the vowing, the begging, the willing it to be true would change nothing.

If he wanted Imogen Loveless to trust him—to believe that he was a decent man with a just goal—telling her she could would never be enough.

Tommy would have to show her.

Chapter Seventeen

"You told him *what*?" Adelaide squawked the question the next afternoon from her place on a small settee in the back room of Madame Hebert's shop on Bond Street.

"I told him the truth," Imogen said, doing her best not to squirm as the modiste let out a seam on one of the many frocks Charles had ordered in his eternal quest to tempt Imogen into marriage. While the quest was going poorly, Imogen would not complain of its spoils. "That he could interrogate the entire East End until he saw himself into the grave, but that he'd gain no new information from any of them."

"Well then," Sesily said dryly, picking another chocolate out of the box on her lap. "I would wager Inspector Peck didn't take *that* lightly at all."

"He didn't," Imogen said as the modiste waved her assistant over with a box of thread. Madame Hebert peered in and selected a perfect match for the silk Imogen wore, and returned to work. "He was quite angry, I expect, though I did not linger."

"The way Imogen came stalking off that boat," Adelaide confirmed, "looking like a queen. The poor man didn't have a chance. He likely felt clubbed directly over the head."

"I do love it when they're left flummoxed by our brilliance," Sesily said.

"Poor Mr. Peck," Duchess interjected from her place

on a stool at the far end of the modiste's shop, where she inspected the line of her stunning black silk in the looking glass. "He's been flummoxed by Imogen's brilliance since the beginning."

"And yesterday he was flummoxed by something else of Imogen's entirely," Sesily said dryly.

"Sesily!" Imogen protested, her cheeks going red as she looked to the seamstress.

"Oh, please," Sesily retorted. "It's just us. And Madame Hebert would never repeat it."

"Repeat what?" the modiste said with a wink before she indicated that Imogen should turn around. "I think that, in light of any flummoxing that may or may not have occurred, yesterday or in months prior, or I daresay in the weeks to come, I would like to take a second look at your undergarments."

Adelaide and Sesily exchanged delighted looks and the modiste wandered off to fetch ribbon or whalebone or whatever it was dressmakers went looking for while their customers collected themselves.

"No one is going to see my undergarments," Imogen protested.

"Certainly not with that attitude," Sesily said, getting up from the settee and passing Adelaide the box of chocolates. "That color is gorgeous on you, Im. Wear that out, and you'll gather a collection of admirers. Peck will have to fight them off if he wants to keep you."

Imogen considered her reflection. The peacock blue was flattering, and while Madame Hebert had not hesitated to lower and broaden the neckline of the garment, she had made sure to include a long sleeve that ballooned to a fitted wrist—a perfect spot for a hidden item. The bodice was gathered and ruched, well complemented by the undergarments Madame Hebert was planning to reconsider, accentuating every one of Imogen's curves— curves she knew were entirely out of step with the current fashion, yet had always pleased her.

The frock highlighted her softness and the way it layered over her strength, allowing her to take up more space in a world that was constantly telling her to take up less. To be less.

Imagine what Tommy would do if he saw her now.

Would his eyes go dark like they had yesterday? Would he run his hand over his mouth the way he had in the ship's cabin last night, like she was a meal to be devoured?

She cleared her throat.

"Even if you are right, and this dress summons interest, Tommy Peck has no interest in fighting them off," she said, forcing any hint of disappointment from her tone. "He wants me married as much as my brother does, so he can pack me off to the country and pack himself back to his desk at Whitehall."

"Tommy Peck wouldn't even have a desk at Whitehall if not for you bringing him two of his most lauded arrests of the past year," Adelaide scoffed. "He ought to get on his knees and worship your brilliance, Imogen."

"Agreed," Sesily said around another chocolate. "And while he's down there—"

"Sesily!" Duchess admonished with a laugh.

"I'm simply pointing out that Tommy Peck owes her for making him seem far cleverer than he is."

"He is clever, though," Imogen replied, searching for anything to stop her cheeks from blazing.

"Not cleverer than you," Sesily argued. "They're none of them cleverer than you."

"He's sorted out that the businesses that are being attacked have something in common—that they're where women find safety."

"And has he sorted out who might want those places destroyed?"

"Have we?" Imogen said, meeting Duchess's eyes in the looking glass.

Duchess looked to Adelaide. "We think so."

Adelaide nodded. "And you, Im? Are we close to knowing who's setting the fires? Did you get the rest last night?"

Imogen nodded. "I've got the mercury fulminate, which was used in all the other bombings. I've the fabric fuse . . . doused in blasting oil. Frances is looking at it now to see if it's a match."

Sesily let out a low whistle. "So we're close."

Imogen nodded. "And there's something else; when Mithra startled our man, he dropped something."

"Too much to hope it was a calling card, I suppose," Sesily said.

"Sadly, no." Imogen waved a hand at her carpetbag, at Adelaide's feet. "Inside pocket."

Adelaide fished out a gold disk, no larger than a ha'penny, and embossed with a haloed man, robed and holding a sword and shield. At the bottom of the oval, hammered Latin. *Quis ut Deus.*

"A saint," Imogen said. "But which one?"

She looked from one friend to the next. Sesily laughed. "You cannot imagine *I* ever paid attention on Sunday mornings."

"My experiences in church inevitably ended with someone getting stabbed," Adelaide said.

Duchess considered the medallion for a long moment. "We require a man of the cloth, it seems." She winked. "Never a dull moment for the Belles is it?"

Madame Hebert returned to consider the back fastenings of Imogen's gown as she replied, "And so? When we have all the proof? What then?"

Duchess met her gaze, all serious. "If it's Parliament and the Yard together? There's only one option."

"We take it to the people," Imogen said, watching as Adelaide returned the medallion to her bag.

"I don't think Imogen's detective will be thrilled with that." Sesily shot from her seat, circling the fitting room, fiddling with bits of ribbon and lace, before peering through the curtain that separated the room from the shop itself.

"He's not my detective," Imogen said instantly.

"Mmm." Sesily humored her for a moment before turning back with a look of absolute delight on her face. "Tell me, do you think that we have developed special powers of some kind?"

"Why, is it a vicar?" Duchess said, fiddling with a bow at the base of her spine. "Do we think this is too much?"

"It's 1840. Nothing is too much. Why are you even wearing black, Duchess?" Adelaide said. "Are you planning to be widowed?"

"One must always be prepared."

"Everyone, do listen to me," Sesily said, her attention on the front room of the shop. "I've made a discovery."

"What kind of discovery?" Adelaide asked, eating another chocolate from Sesily's box. "*Is* it a vicar?"

"It is not a vicar," Sesily said. "And don't eat all those chocolates. He's here."

"Who's here?" Imogen said, turning her back to Madame Hebert, who was now considering the inside placket of the dress.

"Your detective."

The modiste took that moment to yank on the ties of her stays, and Imogen let out a little squeak of surprise, summoning the attention of everyone in the room.

"Interesting," Duchess said.

"What do you mean he's *here*?"

"Interesting that she didn't deny that he's her detective that time," Adelaide said.

"Yes, I noticed that, too," Sesily replied, turning back to the front room.

"He's not my detective."

"Too late." Sesily opened the curtain a touch more, and the modiste indicated that Imogen should move to a more private space. "Good Lord, look at the size of the man. Do you think he believes he's unassuming?"

"He absolutely does not believe he's unassuming," Imogen grumbled, stepping out of the gown to allow the modiste to work on her stays. "Where is he?"

"Across the street, leaning against the milliner's and glowering."

Imogen knew that particular glower well. "I expect people are doing their best to avoid him. Do you think he is waiting for me?"

Silence fell and she turned to face her friends, who were staring at her in disbelief. Duchess began. "Imogen. The man practically took you on the docks as the whole placed burned last night."

She blushed. "He did not."

Adelaide's brows went up in a silent question.

"He didn't!" Imogen protested. "It was a kiss! That was all!"

"Have you forgotten that I'm the one who found you in the library at the Trevescan ball?"

Imogen opened her mouth to argue, and then closed it.

"Well, I for one am not thrilled with Scotland Yard following us all over London," Duchess interrupted, making her way to stand next to Sesily. "It will only summon more attention. Do you think he will leave?"

"I don't, as a matter of fact," Sesily said, watching him through the window. "Do you think we ought to invite him in?"

Imogen's brows shot up. "In here?"

"It is where we are," Sesily pointed out. "He could wait in the front room. Perfectly aboveboard."

"Absolutely not," Imogen said.

"Hmm," Duchess said, not sounding at all convinced.

"What's that supposed to mean?"

"Only that I'm not sure you have a choice in the matter."

The bell rang at the front of the shop and Imogen's chest tightened immediately. "Is that—" She came to stand next to Sesily, holding her dress to her body, her back bare to the fitting room.

He was *inside*.

Her brow furrowed. "No! Absolutely not!" She made to approach him, but Hebert was there now, working on the buttons, unbothered, as though policemen big as trees frequented her shop every other day.

"Good afternoon, Lady Imogen," he said, the words deep and rich. "Duchesses. Mrs. Calhoun."

"Do come in," Adelaide said, sounding thoroughly delighted by the way the afternoon was shaping up.

"No. Do not come in," Imogen said. "You cannot simply wander into a dressmaker's shop on Bond Street, Tommy. This is not done."

Everyone looked to her.

"It's not!"

"Well, no," Sesily said. "But since when have you worried about such things?"

Never. But she was considering starting now, even as Sesily turned to Tommy. "Are you looking for Imogen?"

"In fact, I am. As you know, I have been asked to look after Lady Imogen's safety for the time being."

"Hired, no?" Duchess corrected, the cool disdain in her voice marking her rich and fearless even before she added, "Parliament loves to put Scotland Yard on a lead, do they not?"

He had the grace to look slightly uncomfortable. "I wouldn't describe it that way."

"But what's important is that you tracked her here," Sesily said, raising her voice so Imogen would clearly hear. "How very *clever* of you."

"Oh for heaven's sake," Imogen muttered, wishing she were wearing literally anything but the half-open dress Madame Hebert had left her in. "Is it your belief that I might find trouble here, Mr. Peck? Shopping for ribbons and silks?"

"I would never presume to think you couldn't find trouble wherever you wished it, Lady Imogen," he said, and everyone tittered.

Everyone but Imogen, who wished she was closer to her carpetbag.

"I do like him," Sesily interjected. Of course Sesily liked him. Sesily liked anyone with a quick tongue. And if they were beautiful, all the better.

"Mmm. Too bad he's a Peeler." Duchess, on the other hand, was a woman of sense.

"Well, you've sorted it," Imogen said, meeting him dead in the eye, and trying very hard not to be embarrassed by her state of half dress. Or, rather, full dress but half fastening. "There is no trouble and we're not in hiding. We're on Bond Street."

She watched him for a long moment, disliking the way he dwarfed the large room with his broad shoulders and his thighs, which were . . . not insignificant. And his *hands*. In Imogen's experience, men never knew what to do with their hands in situations such as this. They were always holding gloves or hats or walking sticks. But not Tommy Peck. He simply . . . stood there. Like he was perfectly comfortable waiting for her and would do so, forever.

Which was odd, if one really thought about it, considering he was standing in a room with four women he knew to be, at best, mayhem, and at worst, vigilantes.

Narrowing her gaze on him, Imogen said, "Last I checked, you had more than one unsolved crime to sort out. Hard to believe you've chosen nursemaiding a spinster happily on the shelf over actually . . . inspecting."

His brow furrowed. *Good.*

And then he said, "I don't think it's difficult to believe at all, actually. You see, Lady Imogen, if I had any faith that you could keep yourself out of trouble, perhaps I would have left you alone. But I don't have faith in that, even a little. And so, here we are."

They stared each other down for a long moment before she repeated him. "Here we are."

With that, she turned, revealing her still scandalously

open back to him, returning to the little platform where she'd been standing. At which point, she realized he had followed her into the room. Clutching the bodice of the dress to her, she said, "I am not finished, Tommy. You may wait in the front room."

"If it's all the same, I'd rather not, considering how quickly you are able to give me the slip—particularly when you're in the company of this lot."

"I beg your pardon, this *lot*?" No one spoke with such accusation as Duchess.

"Do you deny your keen ability to disappear from beneath the noses of most people, Your Grace?"

A pause. "I do not, as a matter of fact, Detective Inspector. And the only reason you will survive referring to us as *this lot* is because you spoke of that ability with deference."

"I would never dream of anything less." He sat, folding his enormous frame into the spindly little jewel-toned chaise in the corner. "It's only because of my admiration for your quick reflexes that I am choosing, as a serious man with a serious job, to sit in a fitting room and wait for Lady Imogen."

"Well, Lady Imogen has had quite enough," Imogen said. "You cannot stay here. It is not *appropriate*."

Sesily snorted at the word.

"You've three married women and a modiste playing chaperone. What could possibly happen that is inappropriate?" Tommy asked.

"You'd be surprised," Sesily said slyly.

"Sesily!" Adelaide protested. "You'll embarrass the poor man."

"Oh, please. Look at him! This is not a man who is surprised by where people . . . get mussed." Sesily looked to Tommy. "Are you, Mr. Peck?"

He wasn't looking at her. He was looking directly at Imogen, one dark brow raised in a perfect dark slash. "I am not."

Imogen's cheeks were instantly aflame and she was suddenly very aware that the dress she wore was unfastened to the waist and she had nothing into which to change, and not ten feet away was Thomas Peck, who, not twenty-four hours earlier, had his hands in her skirts.

In other things, too.

And suddenly, it was not only her cheeks flaming, it was the rest of her, too, as though the temperature in the whole place had gone up.

"What are you here for, then, Tommy? It cannot be to protect my reputation."

A beat, and then he said, "I'm very glad you asked, my lady. You see, I am here for your bag."

Silence fell in the room.

She looked toward him instantly.

This infernal man.

She'd been wrong before. He wasn't simply sitting on a ludicrously small chaise in the corner, looking tall and strong and handsome and . . . stupidly perfect.

He was sitting next to her carpetbag.

And then, as they all watched, he reached down and lifted it without hesitation, as though it weighed nothing.

"And I thought you might like to take a drive."

Chapter Eighteen

She thought she couldn't find trouble on Bond Street? In the past two weeks, he'd met Imogen Loveless in the shell of a building that had been exploded, in a burning warehouse, and outside one of the most raucous pubs in Covent Garden—where a carriage had nearly run her down—and somehow, the most trouble she'd been in was in the back room of a Mayfair dressmaker's.

Because if there was one thing that was trouble, it was Imogen Loveless, smart-mouthed, fresh-faced, and half-dressed.

Just asking to be *mussed*.

In all his thirty years, Tommy had faced any number of temptations. In his youth, he'd been offered easy paths to money—fixing fights, running contraband, stealing. As he'd aged, there'd been others: women, cards, food, drink. But every single temptation he'd faced paled in comparison to the temptation of Imogen standing before him in a stunning silk in a color so decadent he knew, instinctively, that he couldn't name it. A stunning silk that was obviously held up by nothing more than the woman's soft hands and softer breasts.

And then, as if that weren't enough—as if he didn't deserve a damn sainthood for not looking, for not *touching*—she'd turned around. And the back . . .

He swallowed, mouth dry.

It had been open.

And he'd *looked away*.

Aristocrats called themselves noble? There was nothing nobler than looking away from the beautiful skin of Imogen Loveless's back, smooth and silky and lush enough to make a man wonder what his fingers would look like pressed against it.

Tommy deserved a goddamn title.

He'd waited in the front room of the modiste's shop while she dressed, holding her carpetbag, telling himself he was not straining to listen to her soft instructions as she ordered the dress she'd barely been wearing. Holding back his suggestion that she order eight to twelve additional versions of it, and hang the back fastening.

Telling himself that he was simply waiting for her to finish and join him. Making sure she didn't sneak out a rear exit and go on the run with the help of her gang.

Telling himself it was all in service to his job, even when she pushed through the curtain and into the front room smelling like pears and sunshine. She was wearing a bright yellow day dress and matching coat the color of the summer sun.

"You did not have to come inside," she said to him, as she headed for the door, eyeing the carpetbag in his hand.

"Considering the fact that every place you go is more than it seems and, too often, the location of something nefarious," he said, coming off the wall and pretending not to be called to her like a dog on a lead, "I think I did need to come inside."

"The most nefarious thing that happens at Hebert's is an unwieldy amount of aristocratic gossip."

"Who danced with whom at the Trevescan ball?"

"Come now, Mr. Peck," Sesily said from behind him. "We all know that's not the best gossip to come from the Trevescan ball."

He looked to Sesily, unable to keep his surprise at bay.

She grinned. "I'm still here."

"Is there a name for a group of you? Like a murder of crows?"

"A murder would be delightful, come to think of it," Imogen said, turning back to him. "I assume you've a carriage somewhere?"

"We'll have to make do with a hack." He pointed down Bond, to Bruton Street. "You're too brightly colored for murder."

Her lips curved in a knowing smile. "You underestimate the value of distraction."

He wanted to kiss her again. Surely his memory from the night before was incorrect. Surely her lips weren't so soft. The taste of her wasn't so sweet. The feel of her against him wasn't so good.

What had she said?

"Distraction," she repeated. "A Distraction of Belles." Sesily laughed delightedly. "Perfect."

It was perfect. There had never been a collective noun better suited to these women. To this woman. Imogen, ever the distraction.

He looked to the brightly colored carpetbag in his hand, willing himself to focus on what was inside. On the information she had that would help his investigation. That would bring the culprits to justice. That would cement the reputation of the Detective Branch, and of Tommy himself, in the minds of the Home Office.

He hailed a hack and reached up to open the door.

Keeping the lady safe, getting her to share the information she had. That was the job. Not falling for . . . whatever this was.

Imogen held firm on the street.

"Inside, if you please," he said.

"Are you mad? It's broad daylight," she argued. "Half of London is watching. I can't go anywhere without a chaperone."

Sesily snorted. "Since when are you worried about chaperones?"

"Since right now," she said, scowling at Tommy. "Since Scotland Yard has taken an interest in my personal effects."

"For what it's worth, I think Mr. Peck has been interested in your personal effects for quite a while, Imogen." Sesily pressed a kiss to her friend's cheek and whispered, "Have fun."

Once inside, the carriage clattering away from Mayfair, Imogen looked to Tommy. "Where are we going?"

"I thought you might enjoy a drive."

"With a policeman looking to rifle through my personal effects?"

He leaned down and moved her carpetbag from his feet to hers. "There," he said. "An olive branch."

She narrowed her gaze on him and moved to prop her feet on the bag. "An olive branch that already belonged to me."

"That dress you were wearing," he said. "In the shop."

Her eyes flew to his.

"You look beautiful in that color."

Her cheeks went pink and he felt like a goddamn prince. "Thank you."

He resisted the urge to say more. He shouldn't be talking about that dress. He shouldn't even be thinking about that dress, which likely cost more than a month of his pay. That was the point of this drive, was it not? To prove that their lives were so different, they might as well be from different continents?

Imogen was titled and beautiful, born into a future filled with dresses that cost more than a month of his salary and balls in Mayfair filled with people he'd never do anything but work for. And he was Tommy Peck, who'd come up on the streets of the East End and hadn't even seen Hyde Park until he was seventeen.

Looking out the window, Imogen noticed that they were on a straight shot east. "Am I being kidnapped?"

"I know better than to think that you would be a well-behaved captive."

She tossed him a smile. "Oh, Tommy, you know better than to think that I would be a captive at all."

He looked to the bag at her feet. "With whatever you keep in that bag, I would believe it."

"You'll never know," she said. "Where are we going?"

"Nowhere. We're just taking a drive."

She looked out the window. "To Holborn?"

"Shoreditch."

Her brows rose, but she did not speak, and he found himself marveling once again at the way this woman who so often brought chaos around him could simply . . . be. Like calm in a storm. When she asked, simply, "Why?" it was with that same calm, like the sea on a cloudless day.

There were a dozen reasons, he knew—and most of them impossible to confess. Impossible to consider. So he settled on the one that felt the safest. "You don't like the police."

She cut him a dry look. "You've noticed."

"And yet, you've provided me with plenty of evidence relating to criminals you wished brought to justice." A half-dozen blue files, the outside of which were inked with an indigo bell, filled with evidence that would send some of the most powerful men in Britain to prison.

She tilted her head as if to acknowledge the strange balance of truth. "There are times when the punishment must come from within."

"Aristocrats."

"A man murders his wife. Another murders his peers. One steals from an orphanage. Still another stands by while workers die in his factory." She paused. "Heinous crimes at which the aristocracy can turn up their noses—at least in public. Whatever punishment your arrest and their subsequent trial metes out . . . it is acceptable to the House of Lords."

"Then why not let me play a part in this one?"

After a pause, she said, "Because this one is more complicated. When we pull on this thread, it may well summon us to a place you do not wish to go."

"I will find my way there, eventually," he said. "It is my job."

A little smile. "And therein lies the rub."

His brow furrowed. "You think my loyalties lie elsewhere from justice?"

She watched him for a long moment, the only sound the clattering of carriage wheels on the rough streets of the East End. Crafting her reply carefully, she said, "You are *exactly* what I think of you, Tommy Peck. Noble and good, and with a sense of justice that I have seen in too few people, and only a handful of men."

He shouldn't care that she thought it. Praise should not feel different when it came from her. It shouldn't make him flushed. Shouldn't make him want to ask her for more of it. But somehow, inexplicably, it did.

Somehow, inexplicably, Imogen Loveless's approval had become more meaningful than all the rest.

"Then let me in. Tell me what you know. Let me work with you."

She chewed the side of her full bottom lip for a moment, and he was transfixed by the movement—wanting simultaneously to watch her do it forever and also pull her to him and take over the task.

When she stopped, she said, "Punishment from within. You understand what I mean."

"Men of power, brought before their peers. Punished by them."

"And what if the punishment cannot come from within? What if it must come from . . . without?"

He shook his head. "You're talking about vigilante justice."

"Another good option," she said. "A Vigilante of Belles."

Anger flared. "No. Dammit."

"Why not?"

"Because I am here. Because I can be—"

"The long arm of justice? Is that what they call it?" She looked out the window at the buildings flying by— the driver was moving at a clip, eager to drop them at their destination and get back to safer parts of the city. "And what does that look like in Spitalfields? What does it look like on the docks? Or here? The arm of justice seems only long enough to reach the borders of Covent Garden. It does not extend so far when those who require it live too far south or east."

"Justice looks the same everywhere," he replied, hot with frustration.

She tilted her head and leveled him with a look. "It is blind, they say."

"Yes," he agreed.

A ghost of a smile flashed across her lips. "It rarely sees the East End, at least." He didn't misunderstand, but before he could reply—before he could find an argument against the point she was making so clearly, she said, "It's alright, Tommy. We can do it without you."

Goddammit, he hated that.

Hated that it hadn't even occurred to her to turn to him for help. To bring him into whatever information she had. Whatever plan they'd concocted. Hated that she put herself at risk when he was here, and he could help keep her safe.

He could keep her safe.

"Imogen—" he began, but she stopped him from saying whatever it was he was going to say.

Which he would never be able to recall, because he was so flummoxed by her asking, "May I ask a question about intercourse?"

If the woman had set off a bomb in the carriage, she could not have shocked him more.

He coughed. "What?"

"That is the word used in polite society, is it not?"

"I don't believe any word is used in polite society."

"Hmm." She considered the words. "Probably not, but in truth, we're above polite society, wouldn't you say?"

He honestly did not know what he would or would not say.

Imogen did not have the same problem. "I assume you have performed the act at one point or another."

"Lady Imogen."

"Yes, well, that is the problem with polite society. We too often prize what we mustn't say over that which we absolutely must. No matter. There's no need to be polite here."

On the contrary, Peck could think of nothing needed more in this situation than politeness, as if he allowed himself to go down an impolite path with this woman, he might never wish to return.

He cleared his throat and stayed quiet.

"And so?" she asked. "Have you had intercourse?"

A peculiar sound was strangled from his throat. "Yes."

"Yes, of course you have. You seem very skilled at all the bits leading up to it."

The woman hadn't witnessed his skill at even half of the bits leading up to it. Not that he was going to say that.

"Is it as delightful as it seems?"

Victoria herself ought to turn up at Whitehall complete with crown and scepter and knight him. Directly into the Order of the Magnificently Restrained.

"My lady." He forced the words from his throat.

She looked out the window and said wistfully, "Back to polite society I see."

When he did not reply, she said, "It's just that I've never had it, and after last night . . . and some of this afternoon . . . I find myself . . . curious."

It was possible the woman was trying to kill him. This

was it. She had a plan to vanquish Scotland Yard by seeing those who worked for it directly to their demise. Starting with him.

He cast about for literally any reasonable explanation for her change of topic. And then, with a bolt of realization, said, "Hang on. Are you attempting to dissuade me from discussion about whatever you and your *distraction* of ladies are up to?"

She was silent for a moment, watching him carefully, and he would have done anything to know what she was thinking. And then she said with a big, bright smile, "Clever man."

Except as he watched that smile that did not quite reach her eyes, he didn't think he was very clever. "Imogen—"

She waved that small hand once more, as though she could brush it all away. "You needn't worry about me, Tommy."

"I *needn't worry* about you?" Frustration turned to indignation and then anger in his chest. "You've nearly been killed three times in the last two weeks, Imogen. You put yourself in danger every day you don't let me help you."

"And you worry my brother won't pay your fee?"

The question sent a sizzle of defiance through him— an urge to protest every thought she seemed to have about him—and he shot forward in his seat, coming closer to her than he intended. "Don't. Don't do that. I didn't go to your brother for a fee, or because of his relationship with the home secretary, or because I had a yearning to dress myself like an idiot and march into Mayfair."

She licked her lips, and it was like a blow to the gut. He looked. He couldn't not look. They were pink and plump and wet, and *Christ* he wanted them. "Why did you go to him?"

It took a moment for the question to unscramble his

thoughts, thoughts he would blame for why he answered truthfully. "Because I want you safe."

He could have stopped at *I want you*.

She smiled, slow and sinful, as though she understood. "You don't look like an idiot when you're dressed for Mayfair."

She'd taken notice of him the night before. She'd catalogued the trousers and waistcoat and cravat he'd worn . . . and liked them.

He shouldn't care that she liked them. It didn't matter. Tommy Peck wasn't made for Mayfair, and Imogen Loveless wasn't made for Shoreditch, and neither of them should be in this carriage, and they shouldn't be this close, and he definitely shouldn't be thinking about hauling her into his lap and kissing her until they could no longer see straight.

"Why are we here, Tommy?" she said quietly, her gaze flickering to his lips. "Headed to Shoreditch as the sun sets?"

"I was born there," he confessed, the words heavy in the quiet carriage, weighed down by her surprise. "You think I don't know what it's like. To be outside the view of those in power. And I was born there, to a street sweep and his wife, who took in washing to make ends meet. So when you say I cannot be expected to stand on the side of those who have no access to title or privilege . . ." He looked out the window, the late afternoon light setting the buildings aflame with the promise of sunset. It would come early and cold tonight. "When you say I cannot be trusted . . ."

She nodded. "It doesn't sit right."

"No."

"I did not know. Your file—" She stopped herself from finishing the sentence.

"My *file*?"

She waved a hand in the air. "You're a detective in-

spector at Scotland Yard, Tommy. In all the time the
Hell's Belles have delivered evidence to help you bring
a man to justice, it never occurred to you that we might
have done a bit of inspecting *you*?"

"What *is* in my file?"

She smiled and teased. "It will take more than an
outing to Shoreditch for me to reveal that, Mr. Peck."

God, that smile. It wrecked him every damn time.
"Name your price."

Her lids lowered, those sooty black lashes hiding
everything as she looked to his lips, as her own lips
parted on a little breath that he couldn't hear but knew
was perfect. "I don't know if you'd pay it," she whispered.

He would pay it. He would pauper himself to pay it.

"Tommy," she whispered, and the tiny, desperate
plea in the word made him instantly, impossibly hard.
He shouldn't respond to it. He'd just collected her from
Mayfair's most popular dressmaker, surrounded by her
titled friends in her gilded world. Any way he touched
her would be less than what she deserved. He couldn't
give her what she deserved.

But then her hand was on his beard, soft and sweet and
pulling him across the barely-there distance between
them. And she was whispering his name again, and
opening to him, and meeting his kiss with her own.

And he might not be able to give her what she deserved.

But he was willing to do anything to give her what she
wanted.

He growled into her mouth and she sighed into his,
and he was stroking deep, and reaching to pull her to
him, atop him, thinking of nothing but pulling her dress
down . . . or up . . . or both . . . and giving them both what
they wanted. Again and again.

The carriage began to slow, ready to make its turn
and bring them back to Mayfair. Away from this place
that he'd wanted to show her, and he knew he should
be grateful for it. Instead, he pulled away from her and

swore, thick and harsh in the dim light. And Imogen—
perfect, wonderful Imogen laughed low and smoky, like
sex, and said, "I could not agree more."

He could make love to her right there. He could spread
her across the seat and go to his knees and bring her
pleasure with fingers and tongue, and leave her feeling
soft and lush and loved.

But not here. Not in this place that should remind him
every moment why Imogen Loveless was not for him.

He knocked on the roof, indicating that the driver
should stop.

Imogen sat forward, confused. "We're stopping?"

"I'm going to ride up top," he mumbled. "We can't—"

"Tommy, we can—"

He was out of the carriage before it was even stopped,
leaping down into the street, already calling up to the
driver. "I'm joining you. Back to Mayfair."

He snapped the door shut, closing Imogen in.

Steeping himself in this place that had raised him.
That still housed his family. Steeping himself in the
reminder he should not have needed.

And then, as though he'd summoned it, he heard
the little, excited cry. "Uncle Tommy! Gran! It's Uncle
Tommy!"

And there, not ten yards away, were his niece and his
mother, the latter calling out, "Tommy!"

He stopped, one foot on the block, and the driver
looked down at him. "Oy! I ain't lingerin'. If you're doin'
callin' hours, the gel's got to get out."

"I won't be a moment," Tommy said. He was here for
a heartbeat. Just long enough to—

"Tommy!" his mother called again.

The door to the carriage opened, and he turned back to
tell Imogen to stay inside—the last thing he needed was
her asking questions—but before he could save himself
from the mess that was about to get made, his mother
took charge. "Thomas David Peck, did you think you

could bring a woman to Shoreditch and not introduce her to your family?"

Tommy froze, a mask of horror falling over his face.

It was a terrible miscalculation.

One made worse when he caught a glimpse of Imogen's broad, bright smile, impossibly visible in the fast-fading light. And then she spoke and he was doomed.

"Hello! You must be Tommy's mother."

Chapter Nineteen

In all the time Imogen had imagined Tommy Peck outside of Scotland Yard—and Lord knew that was a great deal of time—it had never occurred to her that he might have a family.

She'd imagined him at a pub in Marylebone after work with the men from Whitehall, drinking a pint and mulling his next case. She'd imagined him at home, in the small apartments she knew he let in Holborn, reading by candlelight, a whisky at his elbow.

Once, while on a walk in Hyde Park, she'd imagined him swimming alone in the Serpentine lake, his broad body cutting through the water, rivulets of water sluicing over his muscles.

Imogen liked that one very much.

From time to time she'd imagined him with a woman. Nameless and faceless, but tall and graceful and stunning—with endlessly long locks that defied gravity and a level of sophisticated understanding of the mechanics of intercourse that made her all any man desired.

Imogen didn't like that one at all.

But she'd never imagined that there might be a flat in Shoreditch where his mother lived, a beautiful white woman—tall and lithe and lovely, who looked impossibly young, as though there was simply no way she had a son Tommy's age—who greeted them with a warm hello and an even warmer smile, then opened the door to their flat and welcomed her son in from the cold, along with the total stranger with whom he'd arrived.

Perhaps it was the bizarre, unexpected discovery that made Imogen so happy to accept his mother's invitation inside. Curiosity was a quality Imogen was rarely able to control.

He stepped to the side to let her enter before him, the little girl—his niece, Annabelle, who proudly announced she was seven—in his arms. As she passed, he said quietly, "We're not staying."

Imogen nodded, ignoring the disappointment that came at his words, and his clear discomfort with her being there. Whatever coincidence had brought her here, following his mother up the stairs to the small flat, her gaze focused on the striped broadcloth of her workaday skirts, he didn't want Imogen there. But she couldn't stop herself from stealing this glimpse of him—a glimpse she'd never get again.

At the top of the stairs, a door stood ajar, and Mrs. Peck pushed through. Imogen hesitated on the threshold, suddenly nervous. She paused and looked back over her shoulder, to where Tommy stood two steps below her, Annabelle in arms, his eyes level with hers.

One of his dark brows rose in a silent question. This whole thing was unsettling and unexpected—the last thing he'd done was kiss her senseless and then leave her alone in a carriage to ride up with the driver. And now she was standing in his mother's flat. But she couldn't find the words to say all that, so instead she settled for "Is it alright?"

Hesitation flashed across his face, and she held her breath. If he told her no, she would leave. The whole world might think Imogen Loveless lacking in grace or tact or an ability to understand her place, but she did not want him to think those things. She did not want him to think of her as chaos or mayhem or anything embarrassing at all right now.

Right now, for some reason she would consider later, it was important that he chose for her to be there. That he be just a touch impressed with her. Just as he would be for that nameless, faceless, graceful, sophisticated woman with whom Imogen sometimes imagined he kept company.

He nodded. Tiny. Barely there. And paired it with a low, rumbling "Go on."

Imogen stepped over the threshold.

The flat was as warm and welcoming as Tommy's mother had been outside, a glowing fire in the hearth, several heavy pots arranged within, three chairs placed around the fire, each covered with a brightly colored knitted blanket. Next to the chair closest to the fire was a basket full of a smoky grey yarn, a project in progress. Small carpets overlapped all throughout the space, keeping the floor warm; the multicolored patchwork headed away from the room, down a small hallway to another room, where, through the open door, Imogen could see an iron bed, carefully made and adorned with another homemade blanket.

Tommy set Annabelle down, and she went racing down the hallway, shouting their arrival. Imogen couldn't help but laugh. "It's rare I get such an excited introduction."

Mrs. Peck shook her head with a laugh. "Please, come in! Coats, Tommy!"

Imogen passed her coat to be hung on a peg by the door.

The centerpiece of the front room was a wooden table large enough to dwarf the space, scraped and scarred and stained from what looked like years of use, set carefully with four places.

The sun was setting and tomorrow Shoreditch would have to work, so it was nearly time for dinner, which explained the delicious smell. Heavenly. Like bread and ale and a mix of delicious things bubbling away in pots on the stove, where Tommy's mother paused to stir whatever was in the largest before covering it once more, and turning to level her son with a curious look. "What a treat, Tommy. It's not every day you bring a guest to supper—"

"We're not staying for supper."

His mother continued as though he had not spoken. "Are you going to introduce us?"

There was a horrifying beat in the wake of the question—one Imogen immediately understood. Tommy did not wish to introduce her—for no doubt a dozen reasons. But the truth was, there was no easy way for him to explain her presence there. A lady he was to be watching because the home secretary played cards with her brother, who wished her to stay out of trouble long enough to be married off, but also a lady who happened to have taken evidence from the scene of a rather serious crime . . . and worse, an aristocrat! Imogen was not ordinary dinner guest material.

But she was in his mother's house, so he cleared his throat and said, "This is L—"

"Loveless!" Imogen interrupted, dropping into a small curtsy. Knowing what would happen if he said *lady*. Not wanting this woman, in her perfect, wonderful, immaculate home, to have to feel she was required to stand on any ceremony whatsoever. "Imogen Loveless," she added, realizing that a given name was important in moments such as this. "Please. Call me Imogen. I'm so very pleased to meet you, Mrs. Peck."

There was a beat as the older woman took her in—women weren't supposed to interrupt men in the East End, either, Imogen imagined—and then her beautiful face broke into a smile. "Well. If I'm to call you Imogen, you must call me Esme."

"Oh, no," Imogen said, turning a wide-eyed look on Tommy. "I couldn't."

"Then Miss Loveless it is," Esme said, turning away

and waving a hand at the table. "Tommy, we'll need the bench from the other room if you are staying for supper."

"We're not staying for supper!"

"Why did you come here at suppertime then?" His mother tossed him a look that even Imogen, who did not remember her mother, knew was best described as maternal certainty.

"We didn't—" He bit back the retort, seeming to know, with the keen instincts of a child, when a battle with a mother was simply unwinnable.

They were staying for supper, apparently, which suited Imogen quite well.

Any further argument from Tommy was interrupted by a loud scream of "Uncle Tommy!" Annabelle was back, propelling herself down the hallway and directly into Tommy's outstretched arms.

Imogen watched, eyes wide, as Tommy Peck, pride of Scotland Yard, feigned weakness and cried out an exaggerated, "*Aarghhh-oof!*" before lifting a little girl into his arms once more, making a meal of it.

The girl patted Tommy's beard and laughed with unrestrained glee. "Higher!"

He laughed and did as he was told, lifting her again in his strong arms, his eyes crinkling at the corners in a way that made Imogen wish she could draw closer and get a better look.

"Annabelle!" A dark-haired white woman was coming down the hallway now. "Stop yelling in Uncle Tommy's ear. So sorry," she added, brushing at her skirts. "We were attempting to get the cat out from under the bed."

Annabelle yelled directly into Tommy's ear. "Did you bring me something?"

"Let's see," Tommy said, reaching into his pocket and extracting a small round tin.

"Peppermints!" the little girl shouted, snatching them

from her uncle's hand, squirming to get down, and thundering past her mother.

"Don't spoil your supper!" the woman called after her. "It's hard to believe that the cat doesn't wish to come out from under the bed, with all this quiet calm, isn't it?" She reached out to shake Imogen's hand as she tipped her head in Tommy's direction. "Rose Lowry."

"My sister," Tommy added, seeming to understand that introductions remained in order.

"Pleased to meet you, Mrs. Lowry," Imogen said. "Imogen Loveless."

"That's a beautiful color." Rose's gaze tracked over Imogen's yellow dress, lingering on the brooch pinned to the neck. "And that brooch is gorgeous."

Imogen lifted a hand and brushed her fingers over the obsidian design, but before she could thank her, Rose pressed a kiss to Tommy's cheek. "Alright, brother mine? I saw the *News* made you famous!" She looked to Imogen with a mischievous gleam in her eye. "Dark curls are en vogue I see."

It was decided. Imogen liked this woman.

"Don't you have other things to do than read the *News*?" Tommy grumbled.

"Difficult to do those other things when every lady I know is finding time to bring baskets of teacakes over in the hopes that she might get a Peek of Peck!"

Imogen couldn't hold in her laughter, and Rose tossed her a grin. "I see you know of the game."

"Not only do I know it," Imogen said, "I very much enjoy teasing your brother about it."

"Excellent!" Rose laughed. "Now. How did you and Tommy meet, Miss Loveless?"

Imogen looked to Tommy, wondering what to say. She couldn't tell his family the truth—that they'd met any number of times in the course of his investigations into crimes across London. And she couldn't tell them the rest of it, either . . . that the moment they'd met, it had been Imogen who wanted a Peek of Peck. That she'd wanted a Peek of Peck for fourteen months. And the affliction was growing worse. Not better.

Luckily, Tommy answered for her. "We are work colleagues."

Imogen barely held back her grimace. *Work colleagues?*

Rose's eyes went wide. "They've women working at Scotland Yard now?"

"No," Tommy said.

Everyone waited for him to continue. When he didn't, Rose looked to Imogen. "Do you have brothers, Imogen?"

"One," she said.

"And is he as insufferable as mine?"

Imogen had been in this room with Rose and Tommy for less than ten minutes, and she knew that there was nothing remotely similar in their circumstances when it came to their siblings. Even if it didn't seem like they properly adored each other, in his lifetime, Tommy would never dream of marrying Rose to the highest bidder.

Nevertheless, Imogen played along with a grin, ignoring the way her throat tightened at the thought. "Oh, absolutely."

Rose laughed and Imogen was consumed with eagerness—a desire to stay in this warm room full of food and family and charm, so different than the home that awaited her when Tommy brought her back to Mayfair.

"Go into the bedroom and get the bench by the window, Tommy. And Rose, set two more places."

He moved instantly, but not to do his mother's bidding. Instead, he came for Imogen, bearing down on her with a look that was part concern and part desperation. He placed a hand at her elbow and pulled her aside.

"We do not have to stay," he said quietly, bending close to her ear. "You are not obligated to be here."

The words were soft—more breath than sound—and

they sent a shiver through her as she looked past his
shoulder to the other women in the room, who were doing
their very best to pretend they were not noticing how close
Tommy and Imogen stood to each other.

And it occurred to her that in all her years in the house
in Mayfair, occupied by generations of Earls of Dorring,
Imogen had never experienced this kind of kinship. And
she couldn't help a heartbeat of nearly unbearable envy.

She looked up at him, meeting his beautiful blue eyes—
eyes she now knew he shared with his sister and mother—
and realized that she wanted, for just a moment, to pretend
that she was welcome here. That he wanted her here. That
she might belong here.

"I want to stay," she said softly. "Very much."

With a wary look—did he think she was going to
steal the silverware?—he nodded once and turned away,
heading to do his mother's bidding.

The moment he left the room, Esme pounced. "So
Imogen, how long have you and Tommy been . . ."

"Mother!" Rose said with an apologetic laugh as
she fetched two additional bowls from a high shelf.
"Leave it!"

"Och, leave it." Esme waved a hand in the air. "The
boy has never brought a woman into this house before.
A mother's allowed to be curious!"

Imogen couldn't help the little hum of pleasure that
came at the revelation that, whomever Tommy Peck spent
his nights with, there was no one particular. At least, no
one he brought to family dinner. *He didn't bring you either.* She cleared her throat. "Oh, I am not a woman."

Rose and Esme turned curious eyes on her, and Imogen
wrinkled her nose in frustration. "I mean, I am a woman.
Of course. But I am not . . . Tommy's . . . Mr. Peck's . . .
woman. That is—he is not—I do not—" She let out a
little sigh and brushed a curl from her forehead. "You
understand."

"Understand what?" Tommy asked as he reentered,

carrying a long wooden bench to the end of the table, where Rose had set the bowls.

"That we are not—" She waved a hand between them. "You know."

He looked up from where he was straightening the bench but did not speak.

"Lovers," she said pointedly, before clapping her hand over her mouth as though she might belatedly keep the word in. "I didn't mean that, either! I meant . . . you know . . . lovers in the poetical sense. The point is—"

"You are not a woman, you and Tommy are not lovers—in any sense—and there is no reason for our mother to make meaning of you joining us for a perfectly normal Thursday night dinner," Rose said.

Imogen nodded, feeling very relieved. "Yes. Precisely."

Tommy's lips twitched in amusement. "I missed quite a bit in the forty-five seconds I was away."

"Life moves quickly," Imogen said, flustered and frustrated. Because it was a lie, was it not? They were, in fact, if not lovers, then *something*, weren't they? They'd been kissing in the hack not thirty minutes earlier. They'd only stopped kissing because he'd stopped the damn carriage. Nobly, she supposed, even if she'd been disappointed.

Not that she was disappointed any longer.

Well. Maybe a *little* disappointed.

"As I said"—Tommy cut his mother a pointed look—"we are . . . friendly . . . through work."

Rose scoffed. *"Work."*

"Not work?" Imogen asked.

"Not work," Rose said. "Tommy hates bringing work home. You wouldn't be here if it was work."

Tommy nodded. "Sometimes, a particular case requires a more personal touch." He met Imogen's eyes. "This investigation happens to cover the East End, and we were nearby."

They'd been in Mayfair. But she understood what he

was reminding her. She was there for work. She was there because he was attempting to show her that he did care for more than money and power and privilege and Parliament. That he had come from here. Wasn't that what he'd said in the hack?

But he'd intended a drive, and now it was dinner.

And his lovely family.

And it was delicious.

"Well, if you're in the East End at dusk, it's a good thing you've Tommy with you. The boy knows every nook and cranny out here, and will keep you out of trouble."

Imogen looked to him, perfectly straight, perfectly groomed, perfectly serious. Perfect. "I imagine he was the kind of child who was always out of trouble."

"I imagine you were the opposite."

She grinned. "I remain the opposite."

He gave a tiny exhale of laughter, as though he couldn't help but like her reply. But like *her.* "Oh, I know."

Rose and Esme shared a look before Esme said, "In fact, Tommy *wasn't* always out of trouble."

It was as though Imogen had won a prize. "He *wasn't?*"

"Mother." The word was a gruff warning.

It did not work on Esme, whose blue eyes gleamed. "No. Indeed, I recall one particular knock at the door one afternoon when he was about fourteen . . ."

"Mother . . ." Now it was a growl.

Imogen thought she might perish of curiosity. "Who was it?"

Tommy's ears were turning red. "It's not important. Where's Annabelle?"

Rose was already snickering. "You want Annabelle to hear this story?"

He bit back a curse and turned away, the red now coloring his cheeks.

"At the time, the house had a laundry line that was

shared between our place and the facing building at the rear," Esme said, delighting in the story. "A building that housed . . . a number of ladies."

A bawdy house.

It was decided. This was the best dinner party she'd ever attended. No one ever talked about bawdy houses at dinners in Mayfair. "Go on . . ."

"This is not appropriate."

"It most certainly was *not* appropriate, Thomas Peck," his mother retorted. "I opened the door, and the lady of the house was standing there, primped and painted. And very concerned because several pieces of the girls' laundry had gone missing from the line over the past few weeks. A stocking. A petticoat. That morning, one of the girls had seen a corset go in through our window."

Imogen turned wide eyes on Tommy, who looked as though he might throw himself into the fire. "Oh," she said, feeling for the young boy, tempted by all those underthings on the line. And now, for the man, horrified by the story of his childhood antics.

"My boy, a thief!" Esme said. "And not just a thief—an unmentionables thief!"

"Funny how you are able to mention it now," he said dryly, heading for a bottle on a nearby shelf.

"The important thing is, for all the stealing he'd done, when the poor thing took one look at Mrs. Farrell, he confessed immediately. The missing clothing was returned the moment the interrogation began." Esme reached for him and patted his cheek, red above the smooth line of his beard. "And thus ended his misguided life of crime."

Rose laughed. "Wasn't his punishment having to sweep the front and rear of that particular building for the better part of a year? Not the worst punishment one could cook up for a boy with a fascination for the ladies inside."

"It wasn't, as a matter of fact," Tommy agreed, and they all laughed, Imogen filled with a warm pleasure that she was here and she was welcome, and not simply by Rose and Esme, but now by Tommy, as well.

He didn't dislike her.

Indeed, as his blue eyes found hers, sheepish and sweet, it occurred to her that, perhaps, he *liked* her. Though surely that wasn't possible, was it?

Or maybe it wasn't possible that he like her as much as she liked *him*.

Their gazes locked for long enough that she had to tear hers away, clearing her throat and reminding herself of their positions. Of his role. "And after that? The straight and narrow?"

It was Rose's turn to speak with a little groan at the ceiling. "So straight! The most narrow!"

"What's that mean?" Tommy asked, affronted.

"Tommy." His sister leveled him with a firm look. "He was always on time, always immaculate, perfect manners, never snuck an apple from the fruit stand, never let us out of his sight, not even when we got older. Do you know how difficult it is to court with *that* following you everywhere you go?" She waved a hand in his direction.

"I wanted you to be safe!" He looked properly offended. "Truly, this is the only family that can make following the rules sound like a bad thing. It's a miracle Stanley is a vicar."

"A shock, to be sure, considering that he did not find the straight and narrow so easily," Esme agreed, looking back to Imogen. "I've another son, Stanley. He's a vicar in Croydon. He's often here for Sunday supper—Tommy will bring you back to meet him." She paused. "He is *also* unmarried."

Imogen laughed at the obvious suggestion, no small amount because of the laughable idea that she would be the appropriate match for a vicar. "I would enjoy meeting him very much."

"No, you wouldn't."

Everyone turned to look at Tommy when he spoke the words a bit too low and a bit too rough for the company. Imogen blinked. "I wouldn't?"

He took a visible breath. "It's just that . . . Sunday dinner is usually lamb."

"Oh?" she said, because it seemed she should say something, even though it was difficult to find anything at all to say in the wake of what felt like such a dismissal.

Tommy looked to his mother. "Miss Loveless does not care for lamb."

Rose's eyes were so wide, they threatened to come right out of their sockets, but Esme simply smiled a warm, welcoming smile. "Then we'll have something else."

A heavy knock sounded outside the door, and Rose went to the window to look down on the street below. "It's Wallace."

She was out the door as Tommy froze, casting a strange look at Imogen. She raised her brows in his direction. "Is there something wrong?"

"I don't think so."

She didn't believe him for a moment. "Is there something I should know?"

He could not answer, as the door swung open and his sister reentered, a look on her face that was equal parts anticipation and something Imogen could not name. Following behind her was a tall, older, portly man—one she immediately recognized. The superintendent of Whitehall, whom she'd met in the hallway outside the uniform closet.

He carried a small box in hand. Once inside, he removed his hat instantly and addressed the room with a boisterous "Aren't you all a refuge for a cold winter's night!"

"Come in, Wallace," Esme said, crossing the room to him, letting him claim her hand for an exaggerated kiss before taking his hat and the box he offered as he removed his coat, revealing a very simple navy blue wool suit with a flat gold medallion pinned to his lapel. Imogen's heart hammered with recognition in her chest. She'd seen the medallion before.

She had a matching one in the carpetbag she'd left by the door.

Her mind began to race as she started to connect the dots . . . dots she'd feared were connected for months.

Without thinking, she looked to Tommy, who immediately noticed the way she spun around. Concern in his gaze, he took a step closer to her. "Are you—"

His mother interrupted whatever he was going to ask with a too bright, "Look who is joining us for supper!"

"I say! It's been a tick since I've seen you at the Yard, Tommy." Wallace Adams made to step forward, but stopped midstride, the moment he saw Imogen. "Oh," he said, recognition flashing across his face. "Hello."

Imogen smiled.

"Introductions!" Rose insisted. "Miss Imogen Loveless, this is Wallace Adams. Wallace, Miss Loveless is Tommy's . . ." Rose paused. "Well, we're not sure. Something to do with work, apparently, so you likely know more than we do."

Mr. Adams's brows shot up at the words. "Work, is it?"

Tommy let out a sigh. "Adams is my superintendent."

The head of Whitehall. She pasted a smile on and dipped a little curtsy. "Mr. Adams."

Adams's attention flew to Tommy, then back to Imogen. Something flashed in the older man's eyes, so fast Imogen couldn't name it.

He knew who she was, of course. If he was Tommy's superior, he surely knew she was his assignment. Adams had likely been the person to assign Tommy the task of finding her that night in Covent Garden. And what's more, Adams knew she'd been with Tommy in Scotland Yard the morning of that assignment. When she was supposed to be missing.

It was a proper mess.

Imogen waited for him to reveal her identity and change the evening. Except he didn't. Instead, he smiled and said, "*Miss* Imogen Loveless. I'm very pleased to meet you."

Chapter Twenty

Within minutes, Tommy's mother had waved them all to dinner and they'd squeezed around the small, scarred table to one side of the main room of the flat.

Tommy couldn't keep his eyes off Imogen, seated across from him, eyes bright and curious as she fell into the evening as though she'd eaten a thousand meals in cramped flats in Shoreditch. As though she regularly scooped stew out of chipped earthenware bowls and tore hunks of freshly baked brown bread from a shared loaf passed round the table.

But she didn't do those things. They could lie to his mother all he liked—he could call her *miss* and she could hold back the truth of her birth—but Imogen Loveless was a titled lady, daughter to an earl. Sister to one. And every minute she sat in this house, at this table, their legs so close together beneath the table that he could feel her skirts against him, he had to remind himself that she didn't belong there.

Because every minute that passed made him imagine what it would be like if she *did* belong.

Which was impossible.

And even as he tried to keep that truth in his mind, he knew he was actively avoiding looking at Adams, who, despite calling Imogen *miss*, knew the truth, and would have more than a few somethings to say about her presence at dinner in Tommy's family home.

Tommy was certain that Adams would be the first to point out that traipsing all around London with an aristocratic lady was the fastest way to ensure that Tommy never got his promotion.

All that, and Imogen seemed to fit in perfectly, laughing at Annabelle's silly jests, making conversation with Rose, asking questions that revealed more about Tommy than he would ever share on his own.

Questions like, "How long have you lived here, Mrs. Peck?"

"David—that was Tommy's father—and I moved here the day we were married." She smiled at the door, far away for a moment before she laughed. "He nearly toppled me down the stairs when he carried me over the threshold."

Tommy's chest tightened at the words. At the way Imogen smiled, small and wistful, as though she understood how the memory of his father remained so large and present despite the distance of time.

She met Tommy's eyes. "How long ago did he—"

"Eleven years," he answered, even as he knew it would make everything more complicated. "Rose was fourteen, and Stanley was twelve."

Imogen nodded with a frank understanding that came with having lost someone of her own. "I'm sorry. My father has been gone for eight," she said. "It seems both an open wound and a long healed one."

"We were lucky to have Tommy," his mother said, reaching to squeeze his arm. "Stepped into his father's shoes instantly."

It wasn't true. David Peck's loss had been keen. "We were *lucky* to have Wallace," he said, turning to look at his mentor at the end of the table. "He pulled me off the streets and gave me honest work."

"Nah. I just did what David would've wanted." Wallace's eyes filled with something like pride as he looked to Imogen. "Tommy's father and I came up together. When we lost him, I did all I could to bring Tommy to the Yard. And we've never seen his equal." The superintendent turned back to Tommy. "And now look at you. Detective inspector and on your way to superintendent of the branch. Your da would've been bursting with it."

Around the table, everyone looked to Tommy, surprise and delight in their eyes. Everyone but Imogen, who had returned her attention to her bowl. Knowing how he was to get the promotion. Knowing that it would come on the back of doing her brother's bidding.

He couldn't look away from her as Esme said, "Head of the Detective Branch!"

"I expect so, if he's careful," Wallace replied, and Tommy's attention snapped to the other man, who was watching him with a gleam in his eye. A warning gleam as he slid his gaze to Imogen and back to Tommy. "But he's never been anything but careful."

Tommy didn't misunderstand. Imogen shouldn't be here. She was too close. And he liked it too much. And ruining the woman was not an option.

"So, soon, then?" Rose prodded, looking to Adams. "Come on, Wallace. You've got the ear of the commissioner."

"You've never met a question you wouldn't ask, have you?" Tommy said to his sister.

Rose grinned. "Not yet, but there's hope!"

"I expect Mr. Peck will receive his promotion just as soon as our work together is complete," Imogen said, drawing all attention. She smiled, and he was impressed with how real it appeared, considering it was forced.

"That's wonderful news!" Esme said.

"Even better if it means that the two of you will stop

talking as though work is all that brought you here to-night," his sister whispered in his ear as she got up to clear the table.

Imogen stood to help, and Rose waved her back, as though she could sense the truth—that Imogen Loveless had likely never cleared a table in her life. That she was simply visiting their world for a time.

"It was a lovely dinner, Mrs. Peck," she said to Esme. "Thank you very much for having me."

Tommy heard the unspoken preparation for goodbye in the words and he bit back a curse. The reminder of their arrangement—of his place in the world and at Scotland Yard—had returned her doubt. And now, he would have to take her home.

It was for the best, he knew. He knew it. *He knew it.*

"A bit rough and ready," his mother was replying with a laugh. "I imagine your meals are less chaotic than this group's."

"Not by choice," Imogen said. "I confess, when I am at home, I often eat alone."

Esme grew serious. That meals were to be shared was the most serious of her maternal commandments. "Your mother?"

"She passed when I was six."

Tommy wanted to reach for her. He knew what it was to lose one parent, but to lose both, and so early—no one deserved it. And he wanted to tell her so. Of course, he couldn't.

"So it is you and your brother, now?" Rose asked.

"In a sense." Imogen gave a little shrug. "He's ten years older. We haven't much in common . . ." Her eyes found Tommy's, and it was impossible to look away from her. He wanted to drink it all in, every bit of information she was willing to share. That, and he'd met her brother. They were nothing alike. She was legions brighter than him. Better than him.

"Suffice to say, our dinners are not as enjoyable as this one." She tossed a knowing smile at Tommy. "He adores lamb."

He laughed. "Well. I can't guarantee this dinner won't still go south," Tommy said, sliding a look to his sister. "Rose hasn't even begun her interrogations."

Imogen laughed. "I am more than happy to be interrogated."

Rose clapped her hands. "Oh, excellent! I've a list of questions!"

So did Tommy, if he was honest. There were a dozen of them he should be asking as he rifled through her carpetbag to find all the evidence she'd collected over the past few weeks.

But instead, the only questions that came to mind were dangerous ones.

Would you like to have dinner with me every night?

"It seems a fair payment for that delicious stew," Imogen offered.

May I kiss you senseless in the carriage on the way home?

"And there's cake, too!" Annabelle announced.

"I suppose I shall have to answer an extra one for that!"

Would you let me carry you to bed?

Imogen met his eyes, and must have seen something of his thoughts, as she flushed almost immediately and looked away before adding, "I have questions, as well!"

"Excellent! Let's go around then," Rose said, from where she was stacking the bowls on a table near a washbasin. "It shall be a game of sorts."

"I want to play a game!" Annabelle announced. "I have a question!"

Imogen included the little girl without hesitation. "And what is it?"

Annabelle hesitated for an endless amount of time. "I don't remember."

Where half the world, Tommy included, would have

laughed or grown frustrated with the reply, Imogen nodded seriously and said, "Would you like to see a trick instead?"

The table went quiet as Annabelle fairly shouted, "Yes!"

Imogen pointed in the direction of the door. "Do you see my bag over there? On the floor?"

Annabelle went up on her knees and craned to look. "It's very big."

Tommy gave a little laugh at that, and Imogen gave him a tiny smile before saying, simply, "Of course it is. Where else am I to keep my tricks? Would you be a dear and fetch it for me? Do you think you are strong enough?"

What? That bag was filled with God knew what—but Tommy would wager at least half a dozen things that would kill a grown man.

"Hang on," Tommy said, coming out of his chair as Annabelle leapt over the back of her own to do as she was bidden. "I shall get it for you."

"No!" Annabelle was moving with the inelegant speed that belonged to all children under ten. "She asked me!"

He squeezed behind Adams's chair, but his niece was already there. "Careful! Something inside may"—he couldn't say *explode*—"break."

Imogen laughed from her place, the tinkling sound drawing his attention like a siren's call. He was turning toward her before he could stop himself. Her big brown eyes glittered with amusement as she said, sounding like she'd sent his niece for an embroidery basket, "I think she will be fine, Mr. Peck."

He frowned, but Annabelle delivered the bag without event. Imogen set it on her lap and opened it, and Tommy lifted himself up in his seat to attempt to see its contents, an impossible task as the woman had her head practically inside the thing, extracting two pieces of paper, a small sharpened stick that looked like a leadless pencil, and a jar of white liquid that looked like milk but could easily have been poison.

This was Imogen Loveless, after all.

He returned to the table, watching, along with everyone else.

"I understand there is a cat in this house," Imogen said.

Annabelle nodded. "His name is Cat."

"An excellent name," Imogen said seriously.

"Uncle Tommy found him in the garbage and gave him to Grandma."

"With the name already attached, I imagine." Imogen slid an admiring look at Tommy, and he resisted the urge to preen. There wasn't anything heroic about finding the damn cat. Anyone would have saved him.

He leaned back in his chair and crossed his arms over his chest, and not because he wanted to reach across the table and push a curl from where it had fallen across Imogen's brow. "It was a perfectly serviceable name."

"I do not disagree," she said, and he heard the laugh in the words. Enjoyed it more than he should as she offered her hand to Annabelle, who immediately took it. Imogen turned it in her grasp and lifted the wooden tool from the table. With a quick look at Rose, she said, "It's goat's-lettuce juice. Perfectly safe."

Rose nodded her approval, and Imogen looked to Annabelle. "I understand Cat is too busy to visit with us this evening."

Annabelle nodded, but said nothing, too riveted to Imogen's actions as she dipped the pencil into the milky liquid and then began to draw on the back of the little girl's hand—the liquid clear as it hit skin.

The rest of the table watched Annabelle's hand, but Tommy knew better. He watched Imogen. Her pretty pink lips curved in a perfect smile, the hint of a dimple in the cheek facing him, the way her breasts rose and fell above the yellow wool of her dress.

The way her throat moved as she broke the watchful silence. "Mr. Adams, I could not help but notice the lovely pin you wear. It's very unique. Is it a saint?"

Tommy settled in, grateful for the turn to one of Wallace's favorite topics, giving him a chance to catalogue this woman who was more fascinating than any woman he'd ever met before. Whom he feared might be more fascinating than any woman he'd ever meet in the future.

Wallace leaned back in his chair and spread his hands wide over his torso. "It is, indeed. St. Michael."

"The archangel?" she asked, looking up at the older man's nod before dipping her pencil in the liquid again and returning to Annabelle's hand. "I confess, I don't know much more than that, as I am woefully unknowledgeable of Scripture." She paused and said to Annabelle, "Please don't tell your uncle Stanley."

Annabelle giggled, and Tommy's chest tightened with pleasure.

"Aye," Wallace said. "Michael, the archangel who sent Satan back to hell. Protector of warriors. Bringer of good luck. And so all the men at Scotland Yard get the medallion when they pass the five-year mark."

Imogen leaned forward. "And what does it say?"

"*Quis ut Deus.* Who is like God?" A gleam slid into the other man's eyes. "No one, of course. But St. Michael weighed souls for judgment, so he came the closest, I think."

Imogen's brows rose. "A heavy burden, weighing souls."

Wallace nodded with a grunt of agreement. "Luckily, he's the boys at Whitehall to help him."

"The long arm of justice," she said, her gaze flickering to Tommy, then back to Annabelle's hand, as though everything were perfectly ordinary.

"Exactly."

Tommy was watching Imogen carefully, thinking of the things she'd said in the hack about punishment and justice. About how it was meted out in the world. And suddenly, Wallace's tale of St. Michael rang differently than it had done all the times he'd told it before.

"Tell me, Superintendent Adams," Imogen said, and

Tommy knew what she was about to do. "When you weigh souls, do you find a difference between those in Shoreditch and those in Mayfair?"

The room went still, heavy with the question, everyone hearing the censure in the question. But Wallace did not blink. "No, Miss Loveless. A crime is a crime no matter the address."

She set the pencil down on the table with a little click. "Fascinating." She looked at Tommy, and their conversation from earlier rang in his ears. "You do not wear your medallion, Mr. Peck."

"Detectives do not wear any markings of the police," he said. "We're meant to blend in."

She lifted Annabelle's hand and blew a slow stream of air over the liquid, drying it before she said, "And how well it works," she quipped. "No one has ever recognized you."

"Certainly not the *News*," Rose added, picking up the jest. "That must be the reason for a Peek of Peck—you're practically invisible."

Tommy scowled as everyone around the table laughed.

"He's not invisible," Annabelle protested. "I see him quite well."

He looked to his niece. "Thank you, Annabelle."

"You're very big, Uncle Tommy," the little girl said, looking to comfort him.

"Well, either way, it's a lovely medallion," Imogen said, releasing Annabelle's hand. "And I'm happy to have learned of it tonight."

"Wallace is always happy to regale people with the legend of St. Michael," Esme said, and Tommy could hear something small and tight in his mother's voice, something that might have been akin to exasperation if she weren't so embracing.

"St. Michael brings me luck," Wallace said, leaning back in his chair and spreading his hands over his well-fed stomach. "I wear him every time I come to dinner—hoping that he'll help me convince Esme to marry me."

Though Imogen's jaw dropped at the words, they were not a shock to anyone else at the table. Rose waved away her surprise. "Don't fret, Wallace asks Mama to marry him at least once a visit."

"One day, she's going to say yes," he said, turning a desiring gaze on Esme. One Tommy had seen a thousand times before. One he feared would never be returned. "I've even bought her a house."

Esme reached out to pat Wallace's hand where it lay on the table. "It's too much."

"Nonsense," Wallace replied, and Tommy found he understood the words more than he had before. He looked to Imogen as Wallace repeated himself. "It's where you should be, Esme. A nice little house in Brixton, with a garden and kitchens and a fire ready to warm you whenever you like." He looked about the room, assessing. "Bigger than this place. Nicer, too."

Esme smiled, and for the first time, Tommy noticed the tightness in the expression as she stood from the table.

Wallace spread his hands wide and looked to the rest of the table. "She says she doesn't want me to feel like I have to take care of her."

"You *don't* have to take care of me," Esme said from where she pulled a cake down from a shelf and unwrapped it, and Tommy heard a thread of irritation in her voice. As though she were tired of this conversation.

Which of course she would be.

He looked to Imogen, taking it all in.

They stared at each other for a beat, and he marveled at her in stillness. Like a hummingbird alighted on a flower—paused for a heartbeat to be seen by only the luckiest of men. Stunning.

And then she returned to motion, changing the room

the way she changed the world, and turned to Annabelle. "Is your hand dry?"

Annabelle looked. "There's nothing there."

"Hmm." Imogen put a finger to her lips. "Are you quite sure?"

Annabelle lifted her hand to look more closely. "Yuh."

"Words, Annabelle," Rose said, coming to stand behind her daughter. "It's rude to grunt."

Annabelle gave a little irritated huff. "There's nothing."

Tommy leaned over the table, curious.

"That doesn't seem right," Imogen said, feigning confusion. "Thank goodness we have a detective inspector here." She turned to Tommy, a gleam in her eye that made him want to lift her up and thoroughly kiss her. "Uncle Tommy, would you mind very much . . . inspecting?"

Playing his part, Tommy very seriously looked over the little girl's hand before telling the truth. "There's nothing there, I'm afraid."

"That sneaky cat must have come and taken it," Imogen said to Annabelle. "Did you see him?"

"No! He didn't come!"

"Hmm. Well then. Let's see." She plucked a cake plate from the pile in Rose's hand and pointed to the candle at the center of the table. "Would you mind very much passing that candle over here, Detective Inspector?"

He did as he was told, and she set one of the pieces of paper she'd placed on the table aflame, setting it on the plate. As they all watched it burn, she said, "Did you know, Annabelle, that cats often leave their signature when they steal something? They can't help it. Some think they're not very clever, but I think it's something else entirely."

Annabelle was riveted.

So was Tommy.

This woman . . . she was perfect.

"What do you think?" Annabelle asked.

Imogen looked to Tommy. "I think they are extremely

proud of themselves." He thought of the women she worked with. Of the way they marched themselves into crime scenes and did as they pleased. Of the way they took justice into their own hands.

The embers had faded, leaving only the paper's ash, and Imogen put out her hand, palm up, and Annabelle immediately put her hand atop it. "Now, I don't know if the cat did steal my work, but if he did, he won't have been able to keep quiet about it . . ." She pinched up some ash and then rubbed it on the little girl's hand.

Everyone leaned forward, watching.

Rose gasped.

Wallace said, "I say!"

Esme chuckled.

And Annabelle announced, "A cat!"

There, on the girl's hand, in ash, was the face of a perfectly drawn cat. Ears and whiskers and all. Imogen sat back with a satisfied smile, and winked at Tommy before offering a teasing "And you call yourself a detective inspector."

She was magnificent.

"Mama! Do you see?" Annabelle brandished her hand.

"I do, love," Rose said, running a hand over her daughter's hair and looking directly at Tommy. "Miss Loveless is terribly clever, is she not?"

Captivatingly clever.

Imogen was blushing now, and he couldn't stop looking at her. Marveling at her. He wanted to take her somewhere and have her teach him every trick she knew. And teach *her* some of the tricks *he* knew.

"How did you do it?" Annabelle asked. "Was it there the whole time?"

At the question, Imogen tore her gaze from Tommy's and sat forward, lifting the other piece of paper and tearing it cleanly in two. She handed half to Annabelle. "Would you like to try?"

"Yes!"

If he wasn't careful, she'd captivate him for longer than a dinner.

And Imogen Loveless did not belong here, in Shoreditch. She belonged in Mayfair with her duchess friends and her earl brother and the rest of that world. It didn't matter that she fit perfectly at his mother's table, or that his sister looked as though she wanted to invite her to tea immediately. Or that his niece was now, officially, in love with her.

It didn't matter that he was coming to like this woman and her particular brand of delight a great deal.

It couldn't matter.

She was work. He had brought her here for a reason. To show her that he was worthy of her trust. To encourage her to share what she knew. To help him bring those terrorizing the East End to justice.

She wasn't for him.

"Excuse us, ladies," Wallace said, drawing Tommy's attention. "A moment, if you will, Tommy?"

And Wallace was about to remind him so, Tommy told himself as he pushed back from the table and followed his mentor out into the hallway, closing the door—and their chatter—behind him with a quiet *snick.*

The other man spun on Tommy as the door closed. "What in hell are you doing bringing that girl here?"

Tommy lifted his chin, not liking the sneer that came when Wallace said *that girl.* "It wasn't intentional."

"I hope not." Adams looked away for a moment, collecting his thoughts. "Goddammit, Tom. A *lady*? What happens if she tells her brother that you brought her to fuckin' Shoreditch in the dead of damn night?"

"First, it isn't the dead of night, Wallace. It's suppertime."

"Something could happen to her. Then what?"

"I'd never let anything happen to her," Tommy said instantly, the words like a whip, out faster than he could think them, and he knew instantly he'd said the wrong thing.

Adams froze, leveling him with a stern look. "Christ, Tom. You can't be thinkin' . . . Jaysus."

"I'm thinking of keeping her safe."

"Yeah, safe in your *bed*." The other man closed in on him, raising one long finger in Tommy's face. "Listen here, Tom. I can't protect you if you touch her."

"I don't need you to protect me anymore, Wallace," he said. "I'm perfectly capable of doing the job. On my own."

"Are you?" Wallace hissed. "Because this ain't how you please a toff."

Tommy hated the words. Not because he was keeping Imogen safe—God knew she required it. But because they made him feel dirty, as though he was only doing it because some rich member of Parliament needed a hound from Scotland Yard to do his bidding. "I shouldn't have to please a toff, Wallace. I should be good enough for the job, or not."

Wallace scoffed. "You're just like your father. He never took the easy way."

Tommy looked at the man who'd taken care of everything in the wake of his father's death—the man who'd been his mentor and trusted friend for years, and said, "I'd rather earn it. The lady knows things about a case that should earn it for me."

Adams's icy blue gaze narrowed on him. "What case?"

"The explosions in the East End."

A beat. "Och. Those damn explosions. I told you to wave off them. They ain't nothing. And now, what, you've got some lady detective filling your head with nonsense?"

"That's the thing," Tommy said, willing this man who'd taught him everything about investigations to hear him. "I don't think it *is* nonsense."

"It is," Adams said, unexpectedly firm enough to startle Tommy. "You're this close to being a superintendent, Tom. Stay out of the East End and close to Mayfair, where the titles can see you. Stay on this path. Get the girl home, and for God's sake—I don't care if the gel's writhing with it. Don't fuck her."

The way Wallace said the words, dripping with disdain and disrespect, made Tommy want to put a fist through something. Preferably his mentor's face. Every muscle in Tommy's body tightened as he took a step toward his superior, teeth clenched. "You don't talk about her that way."

Adams's brows shot up. "What are you going to do? Hit me?" He gave a little laugh. "In your mother's flat? Shit, Tom. You're in it, aren't you?" He shook his head. "That girl . . . she ain't just a *girl*, Tom. She's a *lady*. And you're a Peeler from Shoreditch. How do you think this ends? With her doin' the washing up in your mother's basin every Sunday night, wearin' a frock that costs more than the rent?"

Obviously not. Tommy knew the score.

Adams looked to the ceiling and cursed. "Do I need to take over watching the girl?"

No. She's mine.

No one was guarding her but Tommy. Not while he breathed air.

He stilled as the response coursed through him, barely keeping it in. Terrified of what it meant. He took a deep breath. Forced himself to relax. To loosen his fists. To rock back on his heels. "No."

Adams watched him carefully. "You're sure?"

"I'm sure," he said.

"Uncle Tommy!" Annabelle called from inside. "Come look!"

Tommy didn't move, letting a long moment pass until Adams exhaled harshly. "Alright. You take the girl home now. And you never bring her back. Jesus, Tom. Use your head."

The door burst open, Annabelle on the other side of it, waving a piece of paper in her hand. "Uncle Tommy! Come see! I wrote you a note!"

Tommy took it from her and forced a smile, stepping from the dark hallway into the warm golden light of the flat, his gaze immediately finding Imogen, who stood on the far side of the table, an expectant light in her eyes. As though she'd been waiting for him.

What would it be like to have this woman always waiting for him?

You're a Peeler from Shoreditch.

He swallowed and tore his gaze from her, looking down at the blank paper in his hands. "What's this? Did the cat steal my message?"

Annabelle shook her head, an enormous grin on her face. "I wrote you a letter in invisible ink!"

"Did you? I don't think so."

"Miss Loveless! Bring it here!"

"I'm coming." She laughed, lifting a candle from the table and crossing toward them, so plump and pretty in her yellow dress, looking like a lemon sweet. Something tightened in his chest.

No. Don't come here. Don't come closer.

But she did, closer and closer, until she was right in front of him, a carefree smile on her face. She extended the candle between them, low enough so Annabelle could watch. "Hold it over the candle."

He did, looking down. "Nothing."

"Patience, Detective," she teased, and it took all he had to watch the paper and not her. Not her silky curls, or her rosy cheeks, or her beautiful skin, or those breasts that would haunt him forever.

She's a lady.

You're a Peeler from Shoreditch.

And then he saw it. Words, appearing on the paper.

Annabelle clapped, delighted, and Imogen grinned up at him. "Do you see, Uncle?"

He did see. *I love you*. Written in the unmistakably messy, sloping scrawl of a seven-year-old.

"Isn't it wonderful?"

He sucked in a breath. "It is. It's wonderful." Ignoring the concern in Imogen's eyes, he turned to pull Annabelle close. "I love it. And I love you, too."

Annabelle beamed, and Tommy willed his heart to stop the pounding that had started the moment he'd seen the message and he'd imagined, unbidden, for a wild moment, how it might be to get that message from a different little girl . . . one with big brown eyes and a riot of beautiful black curls and a sweet round face.

Just like her mother.

Shit.

He had to get away from her.

Chapter Twenty-One

Outside, it had begun to snow, heavy, wet flakes that were already collecting on the cold cobblestones, and Imogen turned her face to the fast-darkening sky, breathing in the crisp January air, feeling oddly on the precipice of something as Tommy came to stand at her shoulder.

"That dinner . . . your family . . ." She shook her head and peered up at him, feeling breathless, something bursting in her chest. A *fizz-whee.* "How wonderful they are."

"Not the calmest of meals," he offered. "But I should have expected you to enjoy their particular brand of chaos."

"Oh, I did!" Imogen replied with instant breathlessness. "I did. So very much. It's just . . . things feel different now. Like there was a before tonight and an after. Does that make sense?"

Say something, she wanted to say to him. *Show that you noticed it, too. That you feel it, too.*

Silence stretched out between them, snow falling at a pace all around them as he guided her toward the hack he'd gone to fetch by himself and paid to wait—refusing her offer to join him with a stern insistence that he did not wish her to be too long in the streets.

A shout sounded in the distance, angry and deep, words impossible to make out, and she turned toward it as Tommy flinched next to her, quickly yanking the door to the hack open. "Let's get you home, my lady."

My lady.

No more Miss Loveless, the woman he'd introduced to his mother and sister. The woman who'd pulled on her coat and said her goodbyes upstairs, his mother and sister and Annabelle making her feel like a queen, thanking her for coming and urging her to return.

The woman who'd fallen into Esme Peck's embrace, lingering perhaps a touch longer than might be encouraged for a woman she'd only met. But it had been a lifetime since Imogen had received anything approximating maternal affection, and Mrs. Peck smelled of rosemary and thyme, and for a heartbeat, Imogen imagined that she would be back here, in this house, with these lovely people again. Soon.

That Tommy would invite her back.

She was Lady Imogen again. That strange, aristocratic oddity whose brother had begged Scotland Yard to keep out of trouble while he found her a suitable husband.

Still, she couldn't help the little thread of hope that she might be wrong. That he might have enjoyed himself there, too. That he might have enjoyed *her* there.

And that little thread of hope was why, when they were both settled in the carriage and it had begun its slow ride back to Mayfair, and Tommy was staring out the window as though there was something fascinating in the snowy night beyond, she couldn't keep herself from adding, "That was the loveliest dinner I've ever attended."

He did not look away from the street beyond the window when he replied, "It almost sounds like you mean it."

Imogen's brows snapped together. "I do mean it." When he did not reply, a whisper of irritation curled through her. "I do mean it, Tommy."

"Mr. Peck," he said. "Or Detective Inspector."

The correction was icy, and set her cheeks blazing with embarrassment. "What?"

"You shouldn't call me Tommy."

"I—" She shouldn't. She knew it. And still, the idea that he would choose now, as they rode in the dark away from that place where she'd seen so much of his world—the place he'd taken her so that she would think of him as more than a detective inspector—to correct her familiarity . . . The sting was undeniable. "I see," she said. "Of course."

Silence stretched between them, the only sound the carriage wheels on the cobblestones outside, muffled by the snow. She watched his profile in the darkness, marveling at the straightness of his spine, of the sharp edges of his beard, the hard angles of his face, the straight slash of his lips, pressed together, as though he had nothing more to say.

Was it possible that he had nothing more to say? When she had so very much she wished to say? And how could he be so still when she was so desperate to move? When she was resisting the urge to fidget with her skirts, or her gloves, or the sleeves of her coat. Or to lift her bag from where it sat at her feet and rummage through it— anything to distract from his resolute disinterest.

When she thought she might go mad, he said quietly, "We should not be so familiar."

The words were a blow. "What?"

He shook his head, just barely. "We would do well to remember our stations."

Their stations? Imogen's heart pounded in her chest. The reminder of their arrangement. The reminder that he was there only because of an arrangement with her brother. That he tolerated her only as a means to an end, in pursuit of the promotion he wanted so badly.

"It was a mistake to bring you there." How was it that she had just moments earlier wished he would speak? Now she wished he'd shut up.

He regretted introducing her to his mother. To his sister. To his niece.

Regretted giving her a look at his life—a look she had treasured. A look she feared she would keep locked away forever, bringing it out on high days and holidays when she wondered what her life could have been if only she'd been the kind of woman Tommy Peck might choose.

The kind of woman Tommy Peck might—

But she wasn't.

That was the problem with her, wasn't it? She wasn't the kind of woman any man would choose, which was how she'd landed in this place, with a brother who couldn't stomach her searching for a man who would suffer her, all while this man—this perfect, glorious man whom she couldn't stop looking at, or thinking of, or talking to—regretted her.

Regretted kissing her.

Regretted bringing her pleasure.

Embarrassment and frustration and shame and no small amount of anger coursed through her, and as she considered each of the emotions, she cast them aside, refusing to allow them purchase. Until the last.

"What right do you have to decide what is a mistake when it comes to me?" she asked, the question cutting through the dark carriage. She saw it hit him. Recognized the barely-there straightening of his spine. The hardening of his jaw. The tightening of his muscles beneath the sleeve of his coat.

Good. Perhaps he would be angry, too. In this, she would not be alone. "What right do you have to label what we have done a mistake? Was it a mistake to sit with me at the table in your mother's home? To introduce me to your niece? To save me from a carriage, from an explosion, from a collapsing building? Is it a mistake to take my help when I offer you a criminal, tied up and delivered along with all the evidence you need to send him to Newgate?"

He didn't look at her. Kept his gaze riveted to the city beyond.

Coward.

He wasn't going to give her the fight. And that made Imogen even more angry. "You needn't worry that you'll offend, *Mr.* Peck." She punched the title. If he wanted it so much, she'd give it to him. "I assure you, this is not the first time men have regretted me. I have spent most of my life being regretted by men. I've made something of a career of it."

His throat worked, but still, he did not speak. And he did not look.

"My brother regretted me when our father died and he was saddled with me. And so I steered clear of him. Plenty of men have regretted dancing with me, dining with me, being forced to partner with me in stupid games at country house parties. And so I have stopped dancing. Eating their dinner. Attending their parties. And that is before we discuss the men I have happily brought to justice. God knows they regret me more than all the others. And that, I assure you, has been a delight.

"And so. You play at being noble and decent and you tell me you regret me," she added. "Make no mistake, Detective Inspector, it does not make you special."

She was on course now, headed straight for danger, hot with indignation and refusing to let this man be yet another who would make her feel less simply because he could not bear being out of control. She looked out the window, searching for something familiar. They were in Holborn, a perfectly respectable neighborhood, where another hack would not be impossible to find.

And then she set her final bomb, one that would squeal and hiss and be impossible to ignore.

"You regret it? Kissing me in the carriage as we sailed across London earlier tonight? You regret putting your hands beneath my skirts the other night? Touching me where no one had ever touched me before?" She paused. "Terribly *familiar*, that."

A low growl rumbled from his chest as his fist clenched on his thigh, and a keen satisfaction rioted through Imogen. Good. He didn't like that she'd said that. Didn't like the memory she'd dredged up.

She wouldn't, either, after this, she supposed. And perhaps that would be for the best.

"No worries, Detective Inspector," she said to his profile. "You are not alone in your regrets. I find I have them, as well."

He snapped his attention to her then, his gaze suddenly riveted to her. *Too late.*

"So you are able to turn your head. I had wondered." Imogen lifted her hand and knocked twice on the roof of the carriage. The hack immediately slowed.

Tommy's brows shot together. "What are you about, Imogen?"

"That's *Lady* Imogen to you," she retorted, feeling petulant. Not particularly caring as she threw open the door, grabbed her bag, and leapt down into the snow, the carriage barely stopped behind her.

"Imogen!"

She closed the door on his bellow and hurried away from the vehicle, calling back to the driver, "Thank you! Carry on!"

Before the man, barely visible inside his hat and scarf and heavy coat, could reply, the door burst open once more, banging back against the carriage, Tommy landing almost instantly, his long legs already eating up the distance between them. "Imogen!"

He was bearing down on her, his words coming like rapid shot. "Do you know how dangerous that was? Leaping out of a carriage into a main road, without looking? In the dark? In the damn *snow*? What if there'd been another carriage going by? You could have been run down!"

"Ah, well, we couldn't have that," she said, lifting her chin defiantly. "How would you get the information

I have about your case? How would you win the day? How would you convince the home secretary that you have what it takes to do aristocratic bidding and become superintendent of the Detective Branch?" He froze, surprised by the words, no doubt surprised she'd found a spine, and she took the opportunity to shake him off. "What more must I say? *Go away.*"

"Where in hell do you think you're going?"

Oh, he was *furious.*

Likely angry that he wasn't getting his promotion after all.

Imogen did not look back. Instead, she increased her pace, her boots sliding in the snow. She would not be able to outrun him, but she could give him a merry chase in the meantime. There was a tavern across the street, a gleaming lantern indicating that it was open, despite the weather.

She headed for it, ignoring his shout. "Answer me!"

Imogen did not slow down as she looked over her shoulder and shot back, "Away from you. You'd best get back to your hack, *Detective.* As you know, I'm perfectly able to find my way."

He went still at the retort, and she couldn't help but turn a bit more to take him in, handsome and hulking in the middle of Theobalds Road, snow falling all around him, catching the brim of his hat and finding purchase in his beard. "I'm not going anywhere without you."

"Get stuffed."

She turned and made for the tavern, and for a moment, it seemed as if he would not follow her. There was no sound except the crunch of her own boots in the fast-accumulating snow.

Looking back, she saw that he hadn't moved.

Good.

"Good riddance," she said softly to the night. To herself. To convince herself that it *was* good that she was rid of him.

The door to the tavern burst open and a pair of men tumbled out, laughing and shouting their drunkenness to the night. Imogen pulled up short to avoid them, but her boots in the snow and the weight of her bag threw her off, and she slid, tipping into them.

One of them caught her, a tall, craggy-faced white man who did not hesitate to pull her close with a delighted "Look what I've found, boy-o!" He reached his hand around and clasped her bottom, firm enough for her to feel the pinch of his strong fingers through her coat and skirts and underthings. "I wasn't expecting such a warm surprise on such a cold night!"

His friend laughed, urging him on as Imogen squirmed in his grasp. "Release me!"

"Now is that any way to thank a man for keepin' you from falling in the snow?" He leaned in and pressed his mouth close to her ear. "I can think of a better way."

Disgusting.

She pulled her carpetbag back, gaining momentum, ready to whack him with it, and free herself to fight, but it was gone from her grasp before she could take the swing. Tossed aside as Tommy Peck took hold of the man's arm and pulled her out of his grasp. Before she knew what was happening, he'd set himself between her and her attacker.

"It was a mistake touching her, *boy-o*," he said. "And now, I'm going to have to break your arm for it."

The drunk reeled back with the shock of Tommy's arrival, immediately throwing his hands in the air as Tommy advanced. "That ain't it! She came for me! Rammed right into me! I just kept us both from going down . . . I wouldn't've grabbed her if I'd 'ad a look at her!"

Tommy didn't look. "Choose your next words wisely."

"I'm simply sayin' . . ." The drunk did not, in fact, choose his next words wisely. "Bit much, ain't she?"

Imogen barely had time to feel the sting of the words.

She was too busy being shocked by the wicked crunch of Tommy's fist landing directly in the center of the man's face, knocking him clear back into the snow.

She gasped.

The man's companion stared down at his friend, then back at Tommy, whose hand remained fisted at his thigh, ready to fly again. "Crikey!"

"Get gone. Both of you."

When he turned around, Imogen couldn't help stepping backward. He looked . . .

Enraged. Unhinged. Feral.

Glorious.

She swallowed as he stopped in front of her. "Thank you."

The sound he made should have been terrifying. He grabbed her hand and leaned over to fetch her bag from the ground before straightening and pulling her away from the tavern. Out of the lantern light, where he pushed her against the stone facade, blocking her from light and snow and anyone who might be looking, one hand coming to her face—*was he shaking?*

"You never run from me again." The words came ragged, as though they'd been ripped from him, and Imogen could not resist meeting his gaze, thankful for the way the snow lit up the dark night. "I can't protect you . . ."

It was hard to breathe in the wake of the words, the ache in them setting a similar one in her chest. "I'm sorry," she whispered. "I didn't mean—"

He shook his head, that hand threading into her curls as he stepped closer, pressing her back against the stone, tilting her face up to his. "I can't leave you. I can't . . . stop. When I said that—that we should not be so familiar—I meant *I* should not be so familiar," he said, the words low and hoarse, like it was difficult for him to speak them.

"I meant it would be safer if I kept my distance. Don't you see? You don't belong in Shoreditch. In the East End. You belong in a palace."

She shook her head and opened her mouth to correct him, but he was still talking, the ridiculous, wonderful man. "I meant it would be safer *for me*. If I kept my distance. To remind myself of all that so I don't—"

So he didn't what?

His thumb traced over her cheek, leaving fire in its wake. "And then he put his hands on you, and I wanted to . . ." His throat worked. His gaze raked over her face. "Did he hurt you?"

She swallowed. Shook her head. "No." Her hand came to his arm, where she'd stitched his wound. "Are *you* hurt?"

He ignored the question, instead watching her, as though she might disappear. And then, "I should not have touched you. I should not have kissed you."

Imogen opened her mouth to protest, and his gaze flickered down to the movement, to stare at her lips, and she forgot her words. He looked like he was starving. "I should not," he whispered. "But I will never, ever regret it."

He was so close. She could feel the words on her lips as he spoke them. "God forgive me, I won't ever regret any of it."

He closed the distance between them, his hand holding her still as he claimed her mouth, and her hands were on his shoulders, in his hair, toppling his hat to the ground, and they were kissing, hot and angry and frustrated and urgent, and Imogen wanted nothing more than to crawl into him and stay there.

She knew, as she sighed into his mouth, going soft against all his hard planes, that whatever they were doing was not forever. She knew that Tommy Peck would never be for her. That eventually, she would bring him trouble. But she would take what he offered now. Tonight. And she would savor it.

His hands were large and hot on her, singeing her through her coat and dress, pulling her tight to him, his tongue sliding over her bottom lip, willing her to open for him. When she did, they both groaned, and the kiss grew wilder, deeper, more frenzied.

Explosive.

And then he was pulling away from her. "We can't. Christ, Imogen. We're in the middle of the street."

"I don't care."

"We have to get you home. The snow—"

She shook her head. "I don't want to go home. I want to be with you."

He closed his eyes for a heartbeat, and she knew he was willing himself to be noble, the wretched man. He took a deep breath and then said, "We'll tell the driver to go . . ."

He trailed off, turning toward the hack. Which was gone, of course. Normally busy Theobalds Road was empty. The snow was coming faster and heavier. And it was immediately clear to both of them that there was no way Imogen was getting to Mayfair that night.

He cursed into the night.

"What will you do with me now?" she asked.

He looked down at her, closed his eyes once more, and whispered, "*Fuck.*"

She could not resist. "Really?"

He let out a bark of surprised laughter. "I didn't mean— Come to think of it, ladies are not supposed to know that word."

She grinned. "Does it help that I only know it in theory? Not in practice?"

"It doesn't. At all." He paused, looking up to the sky, snow falling into his beard as he thought, and she loved the play of emotion over his face. Determination, desperation, and desire. He wanted this almost as much as she did.

Please, she wanted to say. *Please, don't take me home. Please keep me with you.*

And then a final emotion appeared, as though he'd heard her. *Surrender.*

Taking her hand once again, he pulled her through the snow to the corner.

"Where are we going?" she asked, but her heart was already pounding. She knew what he was going to say. They were in Holborn, after all.

"To my rooms."

Chapter Twenty-Two

By some stroke of very good luck, they'd made it in the main door, up the stairs, and into Tommy's apartments at Mrs. Edwards's rooming house without incident. No one had seen them, and Imogen, for her part, had understood immediately that there was no time for chatter as they made their way through the dark, quiet house.

The last thing they'd needed was Tommy's landlady popping out from her own rooms in her stocking cap and tossing them both out into the storm beyond.

Closing and locking the door behind Imogen, he moved immediately to light a candle, and then the little stove in the corner, eager to get her warm.

She crossed the small room slowly, inspecting the space as she went, and Tommy tried to imagine it from her perspective. The frayed high-backed chair near the fire. The neat pile of books on the small table next to it. The larger table in the corner with a single, uncomfortable wooden chair, adorned with a coffeepot and a biscuit tin. A bookshelf with more books, ordered and even. A few frayed carpets on the floor, but not enough to muffle the sound of her exploration. A mahogany cupboard containing a neat row of ink, a pile of newspapers, a box of candles.

It was a far cry from her family's palace in Mayfair.

Fucking hell. He'd failed, completely, in his task today.

Instead of seeing the woman home safely, he'd taken her to supper in the East End and seen her stranded in a snow-storm. And attacked.

He was, quite possibly, the worst guard anyone had ever had. Including every royal who'd ever been assassinated.

Finished with his task, he stood, unable to bear the silence of his thoughts. "Are you—"

Imogen snapped to attention where she stood, her gloveless fingers trailing over a neat row of shelved books. "I'm sorry." She dropped her hand immediately. "It's very rude of me to—"

She was nervous.

Because of him.

"Would you—"

"Do you—"

They both stopped. She looked away. He wondered if he'd ever be able to look away from her again. He cleared his throat. "I would never hurt you."

Her eyes flew to his, beautiful and brown and wide with surprise. "I know that."

"I did not mean to frighten you. Outside." He flexed his hand, where his knuckles were already bruising. The movement caught her attention. "I wish you hadn't seen me . . . like that."

She looked up. "Do you wish you hadn't done it?"

"No." It made him a monster, he knew. Coarse and brutish.

Something lit in her eyes. "You would do it again?"

"A dozen times," he said. "A hundred."

A small smile. "I shouldn't like that."

She should, though. He wanted her to like it. He wanted her to like *him*.

"Is it because of your deal with my brother?" She was moving toward him. Slow and easy. As though this conversation were perfectly normal. As though it wasn't killing him.

"No." Her brother had nothing to do it. Not now. Not

ever, Tommy feared. "It is because no one hurts you. Ever again."

"My guard," she said softly, reaching for his hand. Taking it up in her own. Her touch impossibly soft as she circled his knuckles with her fingers. "My blade."

Mine.

It took all he had not to say it.

Mine.

He would have given anything for her to say it.

But she didn't. Instead, she lifted his hand and pressed a kiss to the back of it, above his knuckles, red and raw.

Fucking hell. She was going to destroy him. How was he to keep himself from taking her? From claiming her?

"You're shaking," she whispered to his skin, the words like fire. "Are you cold?" She pulled back and stroked over his wrist, and her touch did impossible things to him. Made him ache. Made him hard as steel.

"I am not cold," he said. "I am nothing near cold."

That whisper of a smile. Those lips that were so wide and pink and perfect. A mouth that made him want to do wicked, unspeakable things.

She released him, pushing past him, the impossible scent of fresh pears in her wake, and he followed her like a dog on a lead, unable to stop himself as she moved to the door between the front room and his bedchamber.

Dammit. He couldn't survive her in his bedchamber.

And still, he followed her.

She stilled inside the dark room, and Tommy moved to stoke another fire, even as he burned with the knowledge that she watched him. When the tinder caught and a flame was burning, he stood. "Let me light a candle."

"No." She held up a hand and crossed to the washbasin at the far side, near the window, barely discernible in the light from the fire. She fiddled at the basin before approaching with a length of cloth. "Sit," she insisted, and he did, on the small, uncomfortable chair that stood at the end of the bed, rarely used.

He placed his hand in hers once more, the slide of her touch setting his heart pounding as she turned it toward the light and stroked the cloth over his knuckles, the ice-cold soothing their sting. "You must take better care," she whispered as she came to her knees before him, to tend his wound.

He nearly came out of his skin.

He should tell her to stand. She was a lady, for Chrissakes. But he couldn't find the words. And he couldn't stop himself from looking at all the parts of her he shouldn't. Her dark lashes, shielding her eyes, her pink lips, full and tempting, her body, round and lush, and her breasts, shadowed and straining at the line of her dress inside that yellow coat.

She was perfect.

"I would have done much worse if you hadn't been there," he vowed.

She pressed carefully at the worst of the sting, and he sucked in a breath. Her gaze found his. "If I hadn't been there, you wouldn't have had to do anything at all."

He'd do it again. To anyone who touched her. Anyone who harmed her. Any time she required it, forever. All she would have to do was summon him. Her guard. Her blade.

"You did very well," she said softly, seeming to understand that he needed her praise.

He exhaled. "I didn't get you home."

But he was not sorry for it.

She stayed quiet, watching her work. And then, "Have you ever had a . . . woman? Here?"

Her head was bowed and he stared at her silken curls, gleaming in the firelight, knowing what he should say. He should tell her that he had women here regularly. Disabuse her of the notion that she was the only one. Confess to a long line of women frequenting the bed that was an arm's length away in that small, dark room made smaller by her presence.

But the lie would not come.

He told the truth. "No."

She took a deep breath, and he reveled in her relief.

He should tell her that it was because of his landlady. His neighbors. The way the floors creaked and the walls let every sound in. He should keep the rest a secret— that instead of bringing women here, he lay in that bed and took himself in hand and closed his eyes and imagined *Imogen*—her soft skin and silky curls and that smile that made him hard every time she gifted him with it.

That, at least, he could keep from her.

"I have imagined it, you know," she said.

What? Had he spoken aloud? What had she imagined?

"You, with another women," she went on. "I've imagined her. Beautiful and clever. Graceful and calm. Tall and lovely. She is magnificent."

You are magnificent.

"She is nothing like me."

"She does not exist," he insisted, louder than he planned, and he immediately stopped, lowering his voice. There were others in the house. They would have to be quiet.

Another reason that he should put her to bed.

"I know I should not be happy for it," she said to his knuckles. "But I am."

She finished her work and sat back on her heels, setting the cloth to the side before unbuttoning her coat and sliding out of it, letting it pool on the floor, giving him a full glorious view of the line of that dress the color of sunshine and lemons. A color that should not exist in the winter for the way it tempted a man.

Of course, she tempted him in every color, as though all else in the world was grey, and then Imogen came through and gifted it with her vibrancy. Like Persephone in hell.

"Imogen," he whispered again. "I cannot see you home tonight. The snow—"

She shook her head and removed the obsidian brooch that was always pinned at her neck, taking a moment to refasten it and set it on the low table by the fire. "I shall have to make do with this home for tonight."

Tommy groaned at the words—a delicious punishment for the way they made him imagine that this was her home. That *he* was her home. That he might give her all she needed. Food and shelter and pleasure.

The things he would do to please her.

She smiled up at him. "I like that sound you make. That rumble that sometimes makes me wonder if you cannot bear being with me and sometimes makes me wonder if you cannot bear being without me."

He fisted his hands on his thighs, resisting the urge to reach for her. "It is both." Something flashed across her face. Something like sadness, and he hated it. Hated that she might doubt her power here. Her worth. "I cannot bear being with you, because I am afraid of what I might do. How I might . . ." He trailed off with a deep breath. "Christ, Imogen. The things I wish to do to you."

Sadness became curiosity. "What kind of things?"

Every muscle was tight with his restraint as he refused her. "I cannot say. If I do, I might not be able to keep myself from doing them. And you would be . . ."

"Ruined?"

God, that word. The images it conjured. Imogen, naked and lush and his. In his bed. By his fire. Her hands fisted in his hair as he feasted between her thighs. Riding his cock.

He made a noise that was more animal than human.

She came up onto her knees once more, straightening her spine. "Oh," she said softly. "That's a different noise."

She was so close. The fabric of her dress brushed against his knee. "You should go to sleep," he said. "You may have the bed."

Her brow furrowed. "Where would you sleep?"

On the floor. Where he belonged, punished for all the things he wanted to do to her. With her. For her. For thinking even for a moment that he was worthy of her.

"In the other room."

"And if I asked you to sleep here?"

"We would not sleep," he said. "God forgive me, but I am not decent enough to resist the temptation."

Her eyes lit with pleasure and he bit back a curse. "Of me?"

He shouldn't have said it. "Of you." And he certainly should not have *confirmed* it.

"But what if—"

"No." His refusal was unequivocal. "If we— If I—" He leaned forward, coming closer to her. Urgent. "Imogen. Surely you see."

"It is strange how we call it ruination," she said softly, and his heart began to pound. "When it is so clearly the bit that is not ruined. It is the bit that is ripe and fresh and full of life." She paused. "How can the path of my own choosing, the one that makes everything seem brighter and fuller and more exciting . . . how can it be the bit we call ruin?"

He whispered her name, because there was nothing else to say in the face of such a tempting argument.

"Tommy," she went on in a soft whisper, her eyes the color of rich sable, pure temptation. "The way I feel . . . the things I feel . . ."

How was he to resist her? There wasn't a saint in Christendom who could resist her. She was temptation and sin and something far more dangerous. Something he dared not name.

"I find I am . . ."

He gritted his teeth. *Tell me. Say it.*

She did worse. She touched him, her fingers on his knee, and he jolted, nearly leaping from his skin.

She snatched her hand back, and that—*fuck*—that was worse. He reached for her, stopping her retreat, returning her touch. Placing his large hand over her smaller one, pressing her palm flat to him.

Her eyes flew to his.

"Finish it," he growled. Knowing he was too rough. Unable to find softness for the demand. "What do you feel?"

Her gaze lowered to her hand on his thigh, where his muscles flexed, eager for more of her touch. She squeezed and he went impossibly hard, aching, everything in him screaming to move her hand higher, to show her what he felt.

"I do not have the words," she said, shaking her head.

It was for the best. "Try."

Her fingers flexed on his leg and he sucked in a breath. Something flashed across her face. *Recognition.* "That," she whispered. "I feel that. As though I am nothing but the place where we touch. And at the same time, not nothing. I am something terrible in all the other places. Aching. Raw."

It was over. He knew it even as his fingers tangled in her curls, holding her still as he closed the distance between them. Whatever she asked for, he would give it to her.

He paused a hairsbreadth from her lips.

"I need you, Tommy."

He captured the words with his kiss, coming off the chair, dropping to his knees, his hands on her cheeks, hers clinging to him. Wild. Desperate. She met his kiss with her own, opening for him, meeting his tongue as he licked into her, as he stroked over her slow and sinful, and gave in to his own ache. His own raw need.

She cried out and he swallowed the sound before breaking the kiss, leaving them both gasping for breath. He ran his lips over her cheek to linger at her ear. "Be certain," he said. "I am not one of your pretty men who can play at this. I am coarse and rough. I lack the refinement required to deny you what you ask." He sucked at the skin there, below her ear, soft and perfect and sensitive. She made a little noise that threatened to take him out. "Be certain of what you need."

Her eyes opened, dark and sinful and so full of desire that he was grateful he was already on his knees, as she would have sent him to them. "I am certain," she said. "I have been certain for months."

Months.

"Fourteen months," she said, the words soft and shy. "Thomas Peck, I have been certain since the moment I laid eyes on you." A little smile. Like a fucking queen. *"I need you."*

There was no resisting her.

No desire to.

"Get in my bed."

Chapter Twenty-Three

Imogen trembled at the order, a fuse, bringing a heady rush of anticipation and sound. A frizzle that had her catching her breath.

He noticed, reaching for her like she was a gift he could no longer wait to open, helping her to her feet and then clear off them. He carried her to the bed that dwarfed the rest of the small room, large enough for a man his size. And for her, too, she thought as he set her to the edge and returned to his knees before her.

She leaned over and caught his face in her hands, kissing him deeply as her hands stroked over his shoulders and then inside, pushing the coat off him, being careful of his wounded arm even as she urgently wanted him free of fabric. So she could touch him. Claim him.

Tommy did not hesitate, kissing her deep and wild and lush even as he shucked the garment down his arms and tossed it away, across the room, unbidden. They worked together for the rest—waistcoat. Cravat. Shirt, up over his head and sailing the distance to meet its brethren in a wrinkled heap.

And then, Imogen set her hands to his skin, warm and smooth and broke the kiss, loving the way he chased her lips for another, and then another, before she put her palms to his shoulders and pushed him away. He went, putting space between them, breathing heavily and looking like he wanted to do crime. Like he would punish anyone who kept them apart, but since it was Imogen, he would allow it.

Because he would allow anything, as long as she asked.

Her heart pounded in her chest. He was stunning.

"I want to see," she said. "Let me look."

God help her, he did. He leaned back, just enough for the firelight to play over his wide chest and muscled arms. She'd known he was strong—the way he carried her like she weighed nothing—but seeing the proof of it . . . his thick arms, one sporting the bandage from the night on the docks, the dark hair over the planes of his chest and down his torso, where it narrowed between muscles cut in a deep V, disappearing into the band of his trousers . . .

She met his gaze. "You are so beautiful."

He looked away. It was not easy to tell, but she thought he might be blushing.

"Has no one ever told you that?" she asked. "You are. I—" She reached for him, her fingers trailing over his skin, through the coarse hair on his chest. "May I—"

"Anything you want," he said instantly. "Take it."

She was greedy for it, tracing the hard lines of his body, reveling in his fast, deep breath and the way his muscles tightened and he held himself back from her. "You are not interested in the details of my desires?"

"I am riveted to your desire," he replied, a dark laugh in the words. "But whatever it is . . . it is yours. I will not deny you."

She traced down his chest, stilling on a puckered circle on one side of his torso. Her gaze flew to his. "You were shot."

He grasped her hand and pressed a kiss to it. "Barely a scratch."

It was a lie, but she let him tell it. Loved that he did not want her to worry. She continued her exploration, lingering over a long line of raised skin. The result of a sharp blade. "And here? Another scratch?"

"Exactly," he panted. "Imogen, you're destroying me."

"I don't care for this," she said, letting her words go firm. "I don't like you hurt."

His stunning blue eyes found hers. "You sound like you're staking a claim, my lady."

Imagine if she could? Imagine if he were hers to claim? The idea sent a thrill through her. "And if I did? Would you take better care?"

He reached for her and kissed her deep and thorough, and once they were both breathing heavily, he pressed his forehead to hers. "I would have no choice, would I?"

"You wouldn't," she said, feeling playful and wild. "Because you would be mine."

Mine. The word was delicious, food after a long journey without it.

"I would be yours," he said at her ear. Agreeing. Strong and hot and perfect.

Her fingers stroked lower, dancing across the front of his trousers, making him pant with the way they avoided the hard, straining length of him. And then, a surprise. There, peeking out from one of his pockets, a piece of paper. One she recognized.

She picked his pocket, brandishing the white square between them. "You saved your note."

He claimed it in one fist, crumpling it with the force of his grasp, as though he did not have time for notes. But instead, he pulled her hand to the side with it and kissed her again. This time, like a reward. "You were brilliant tonight," he said softly.

He opened the paper and she watched as he ran his thumb over the words. *I love you.* He stared at the message for a long moment before turning an admiring gaze on her. "That was very clever. The invisible ink."

A thrum of pleasure came with the praise, and she

smiled, her hand sliding down his arm. "An ancient trick. Roman. Pliny the Elder."

His brows rose. "And here I thought your interests lay in ancient Greece."

"They lay anywhere I can learn about secrets," she replied. "And this one—it is not simply a party game for children." She stopped, her cheeks growing warm.

His gaze turned knowing. "Imogen, are you blushing?"

She pressed a hand to her cheek, willing the heat away. After all, she was on this man's bed and he was half naked before her. What room was there for embarrassment? "It is said that lovers used to paint messages on their bodies with it. A game for adults, as well."

"Hmm." Tommy's dark brows rose in curiosity. "And what were the rules?"

"I don't know—it wasn't in the book."

"Pliny the Elder, always leaving out the most important bits," he replied, leaning forward and pressing a kiss to the soft skin of her neck, sucking gently until she sighed. "You imagined it, though. How they made themselves a canvas. How you would make me your canvas."

I could make you my canvas. She'd said it to him the other night, on the docks, as she'd stitched him closed. Her fingers traced down his forearm, along the fast-healing wound there. "Yes."

"So tell me, my oracle," he asked, a low rumble. "What prophecy would you write on me?" He pressed a kiss to the skin above her dress, where her breasts strained for him. And another. And another. "What truth would you paint me with?"

"I would—" He was unraveling her. "I would—"

He gripped the fabric of her dress and pulled it down, revealing the straining tip of her breast. "Tell me," he whispered there. A command. A threat.

I would paint you with my love.

She bit back the words, desperate to say them and still knowing they would ruin everything. She looked down at him just as he turned his cheek and ran the thick pelt of his beard over her aching skin. She cried out.

He stole the cry with his kiss, swallowing it before he lifted his head and said softly, "Shh, love. We will be heard."

"I'm sorry," she replied. "I didn't mean . . ."

And then he was returned to her breast, running his beard over her skin like torture. "You misunderstand," he said, his hands at the hem of her skirts, sliding the fabric up her legs, his hands big and warm on her skin, leaving fire in their wake. "I would give everything I have to hear you scream, Imogen. But those sounds—they're all for me." He pressed her thighs apart and turned toward her breast, licking over the straining tip. She bit her lip and let out a tiny, soft sound. "They are my secret messages. How quiet do you think you can be?"

As quiet as she had to be for him to never stop.

And then he opened his mouth and sucked her nipple into his mouth and she nearly came out of her skin, immediately finding purchase in his hair. "Tommy," she whispered, his name strangled and aching.

He released her and licked over the tight bud. "I thought you were going to give me my prophecy?" His hands stroked higher, finding the edge of her stockings, making quick work of the ribbons at her thighs. "Tell me my future?"

It was all so much. "It is difficult to think of your future when I am so desperate for my own."

The scoundrel grinned, a flash of white teeth as he scraped them against her skin and she sucked in a breath. "Yes . . ."

"Tell me your future, then, Oracle." Another lick. Another suck. The slide of silk down her leg. "Let me make it come true."

He was giving her permission to ask for anything she wanted. Free rein.

Except . . . "I'm afraid you will be disappointed."

His hands stilled in their path up her other stocking. He lifted his head. "By what?"

"Not what. Whom." A pause. She closed her eyes, hating it, but having to say it. "By me."

"Imogen," Tommy whispered, releasing her legs, reaching for her face, his eyes searching hers. "There is nothing about you that could ever—" He let out a little huff of disbelief. "The way I want you . . . I could never . . . It's impossible."

"It's not, though. I have . . . never done this." She hated her lack of experience. "I've heard of things. Seen things, even. But I don't know . . ." She looked down at her lap, where her skirts were bunched and he was on his knees between her thighs. "I don't know how to please you."

He swore, soft and wicked, and the word alone sent pleasure pooling to her core. "You already know, love," he said. "You've pleased me before, coming apart in my arms in the library at the ball."

She shook her head. "But you didn't—"

He stole another kiss. "You, finding your pleasure, Imogen. You, letting me please you. That will please me."

"But what about *you*?"

He kissed her, long enough for her to forget herself. "Would you like to see how well your pleasure pleases me, my lady?"

She could lie. She probably should lie. But she didn't want to.

She told him the truth. Painted him with it, her fingers on his torso again, reveling in the way his muscles tensed and rippled at her touch. "Yes."

She gave herself up to him, and the way they crashed together was like an explosion, his hands on her knees, her thighs, removing another stocking, pulling her closer to the edge of the bed and standing her up, turning her back to him.

He stood, the heat of him so close as he leaned into her, pressing kisses along the back of her neck, her shoulders.

And then his hands were at the fastenings of her dress. "Would it please you if I undressed you, my lady?"

"It would," she whispered.

And he did, unbuttoning the gown, letting it pool at her feet. He paused, and she felt his tongue at the edge of her corset.

"Don't stop," she said, the words out before she could stop them.

"If it pleases you," he replied, humor in the words.

It was a game. Their game.

The corset was gone, followed by her chemise.

He slid a hand down her spine, and she sucked in a breath.

"Tell me," he whispered.

She knew her line. "It pleases me."

"And me." And then he was on his knees again, his large hands on her bottom, grasping her there, setting her aflame. She tried to turn, but he stopped her with his kiss, pressed to first one globe and then the other. He swore again, dark and wicked against her skin. "Do you know how many times I have had to stop myself from looking at you here? From watching this sway beneath your skirts? Hidden from me? Do you know how long I've wanted to . . ."

He pressed another kiss to her skin, his hands sliding around her hips, down her thighs, between them, cupping her tightly in his hand.

She gasped at the feel of him there. Everywhere. "Wanted to what?"

A pause, and she would have given anything to hear what he was thinking. She tried the game. "It would please me to know."

"Bend over." The command was soft and steel.

"I—"

"Let me please you," he whispered.

She did as he asked, folding over the bed, feeling the

rough fabric of the counterpane against her belly, her breasts, her cheek.

He let out a shaking breath. "You are . . . so beautiful."

She almost believed it. And then he was parting her thighs, and his fingers were there, at the place she ached for him, and she closed her eyes, wanting him there. "If I touch you here . . ." His fingers slid into her and she made a tiny noise. "Shh, love. Someone will hear. And then where will we be?"

How was it that the question made her ache more?

"Oh, you like that," he said, low and dark, like he'd discovered something wicked. And maybe he had. "What pleases you, Imogen? Having to be quiet?"

His tongue was stroking at the back of her thigh. "Yes."

"You don't wish to be heard?"

"No," she panted.

"But you like this . . . the threat of being found."

Yes. Yes. She liked it.

"You know I'd never let it happen, though, don't you?" His fingers stroked back and forth, maddening, circling the spot where she was desperate for him. "Because this is for me." A scrape of teeth. A little nip at her backside. And his fingers, stroking. Teasing. Perfect. Agonizing.

She turned her face into the bed and made a noise of frustration. "Please, Tommy."

And like that, the game was over. He flipped her to her back as though she weighed nothing at all, and spread her thighs wide, his gaze riveted to her core, to her hips, arching toward him. "Please," she whispered again, but she didn't have to.

Because he was already there, spreading her wide and setting his mouth to her hot, aching core, licking long and firm over her, setting her on fire. She thrust up to meet him as he made love to her, the sensation so wonderful that she threw an arm over her mouth to keep from screaming at the pleasure he gave her, sucking and stroking with tongue and fingers, grunting as she found his head with her free hand, clutching his hair and holding him close as he moved faster and faster.

His fingers worked inside her in a slow, sinful thrust as he found a breathtaking spot, and she gasped his name to the room, barely there and feeling loud as gunshot. With the knowledge of her pleasure, he pressed her thighs back with his broad shoulders, repeating his movements again and again, deep, rough licks, over and over, firm and strong, like the rest of him. Like his body. Like his mind. Hers for that moment, as she trembled with anticipation of what was to come.

An explosion.

Brighter, bolder, stronger than the ones that brought down buildings, and Imogen was bucking against him as he growled against her, the sound pure sin.

Pure pleasure.

"Tommy!" she whispered, and one of his hands came to hers at his head, threading his fingers through hers there as he rocked against her, bringing her back from the edge, steady and firm and present, until she was returned to the moment. To the room. To him.

It was like nothing she'd ever experienced.

And all she could think was . . . *more*.

Chapter Twenty-Four

She was the most beautiful woman he'd ever seen, coming apart in his hands, against his mouth, on his tongue, holding back screams until they escaped in little, perfect sighs, leaving him hard and aching for her.

He would spend the rest of his life holding this memory—this night—close. Because there would never be another one like it. And it would end here, with her a soft, lush promise in his bed, and him, using every bit of strength he had to resist claiming her, even as he intended to hold her through the night and thank God and the universe for sending snow to keep her in his arms.

Tommy eased back from her, his hands wide, gripping her thighs, reveling in the way they trembled. He couldn't deny the deep satisfaction that came with the knowledge that he'd made her weak with pleasure. He would do it again before the night was out, he vowed.

He would drink the sighs from her lips and memorize her taste.

And maybe she would memorize something of him, as well.

If that was all he won, it would be enough. It would have to be.

Leaning over, he pressed a kiss to the swell of her belly, reveling in her touch as her hands came to his head, fingers tangling in his hair once more, no longer gripping. No longer stinging. Now soft. Loving.

He, too, could be loving. He might not be able to speak the truth aloud, but he could show it to her. He could press another kiss, lower, letting his tongue linger until she sighed.

A third on the flesh of one soft thigh, loose and open to him.

A fourth on its match.

And then he let her go, sitting back on his knees, taking one last look, one last deep breath before he made to stand. To collect himself. To steady his thoughts. To prepare to give more and never take.

Lie. He would take. Every moment of this was for his taking.

"Wait." Before he could distance himself, however, Imogen set one small foot to his bare shoulder. "Don't leave me."

His hand rose to grip her ankle, holding it firmly, his thumb circling the inside of it in a slow, even slide. She was soft even there, dammit. Irresistible. "I am not leaving."

Her beautiful brown eyes searched his. "You are, though," she said. "Even if you stay—you are leaving. You are retreating."

He shook his head. Lied again, but this time it was worse because he lied to her. "I am not."

She sat up, slowly, reaching between them, her fingers curling into the band of his trousers and fisting the fabric there. "Prove it," she said. "Take these off."

"No." If he did that . . . if she touched him . . . There would be nothing noble in how this ended.

She read his thoughts. "Tommy?"

He reached for her, unable to stop himself from stroking his thumb over her cheek. "Imogen—"

"It would please me," she said, the words a wicked blow.

Not a blow. A stroke. A slide. A lick. *Perfection.*

He took a step forward, drunk on her desire. On his

own. "Then it would please me." And then did as he was asked, removing the rest of his clothes, tossing them away.

"Stop," she said as he stood straight once more, and he did, following the command without hesitation. She held up a hand, her only movement her hungry gaze, over his body. Tommy had never much cared for how his body looked. He knew people found him appealing. He rarely had trouble finding a lover, and he was not a fool—he understood all the double entendre in the papers.

But suddenly, he cared very much what Imogen thought. He stood under her inspection, imagining what she might be thinking as she took in his broad chest. His flat stomach. His muscled thighs, all dusted with coarse dark hair. What if she didn't like it?

"Let me—"

He rubbed a hand over his chest when she stopped, not knowing what to do. How to be.

Her gaze darkened, tracking the movement.

Another slide of his hand. Another hungry look as she followed it.

She liked it.

The knowledge crashed through him, and he remembered the rest of it. What else she could see. Without thinking, he stroked down over his torso, the light of curiosity and desire in her eyes making his own touch— usually perfunctory and utilitarian—powerful. Charged.

He stilled as he reached his stomach, not wanting to startle her.

"Don't stop," she whispered. "You're beautiful."

He wasn't. *She* was, bare and perfect on his bed. Not an oracle. A goddess.

He did as she asked. Lower. Lower still.

Imogen's eyes went wide. "It is . . ." She shook her head, her eyes on his cock, straight and thick and aching for her. ". . . nothing like I imagined."

He couldn't help the low rumble. "Have you done a great deal of imagining it?"

"A very great deal," she said softly, her jaw soft and slack, making him want things he had no right wanting. And then Imogen, his perfect girl, swallowed, as though she, too, wanted those things, and said, "That is . . . I've spent enough time with married women to know that this particular appendage cannot be predicted with a knowledge of classical art or a visit to the British Museum. But yours . . . It is . . ."

Tommy closed his eyes and took himself in hand, stroking himself in a long, slow slide, crown to base, unable to resist it as she finished her thought. ". . . *significant*."

His laugh came on an exhale of pleasure. It was not the first time he'd been assessed in such a way, but it was different now, with Imogen. Eager for her approval in a way he'd never been before.

He stroked himself again, loving the way she watched. Aching to give her everything she wanted.

Her eyes went even darker. "Do that again."

She was going to kill him, but he did as she asked, a drop of liquid revealing itself at the crown as he did. She leaned forward.

Oh, God.

"Does that feel—"

"Yes," he grunted with another stroke.

"May I . . ." She reached for him, and he exhaled harshly. She froze at the sound, her fingers mere inches from his.

She wanted to touch him.

Her gaze slid to his, and Tommy stared down at her, all soft skin and softer curves, her enormous eyes and her dark hair and those lips that made him want to do terrible, wonderful things. He reached for her, stroking a thumb over her full bottom lip, dipping just inside her mouth. "Would it please you?"

She turned and pressed a kiss to his palm, her little tongue sneaking out to lick at his skin and he cursed in the darkness. Something flashed in her eyes. Mischief. "Shh," she said. "You must be quiet, or someone will hear."

Not a goddess. A siren.

Singing him to his doom.

And he went with pleasure when she returned her attention to his hand, where he continued to stroke himself before she said, "Let me."

There wasn't a man alive who would deny her this. She took him in hand, working him, learning the feel of him. Another drop formed at the tip and she rubbed it into his skin. "Like that?" she asked, her eyes flickering to his, and he was laid low by the doubt in her gaze.

He leaned down and took her mouth in a searing kiss, delving deep with his tongue before he said, "Yes, love. Like that. It's perfect. You're perfect."

She blushed at the words, her grip tightening to perfection, and he wrapped her hand in his own, revealing all his secrets. Their breathing came harsh and ragged as she worked him, as he gave himself over to her, reveling in her touch, his free hand sliding over her soft skin, her shoulders, her arms, playing at the tips of her breasts, at the silken curves of her thighs.

Soon it was too much, and he stayed her movements. "Stop, love."

Her gaze flew to his. "But don't you—"

"Yes . . ." He leaned down and kissed her until the doubt was gone from her beautiful face. "Christ, I've never wanted anything like I want this. Like I want you. But I . . . can't. We can't."

Her brow furrowed. "Not *can't*. *Won't*."

"Shouldn't."

"What nonsense," she said, releasing him and coming to her knees on the bed, tempting him with her lush body even as he ached for her touch again. "Have I not made clear what little interest I have in should?"

"Imogen," he protested, drawing closer to her, cupping her face in his hands. Wanting to explain it. "You deserve so much more than this. Than me."

"I know quite well what I deserve."

Tommy raised a brow at the firm words, suddenly full of Mayfair after her day playing in the East End. Which was the point, was it not? "Dammit, Imogen, I ain't for you," he said, dropping his own mask. Letting Shoreditch into his voice. "I'm a boy from the East End who's only ever dreamed of touching a woman like you. This is more than I ever even let myself imagine. You, here, naked and sweet in my bed." He kissed her again, unable to stop himself, loving the way she pressed into him, stroking over her body, sneaking every bit of her he could. "You're so fucking perfect—too perfect for me."

It was her turn to kiss him, her turn to stroke over his body, singeing him with her touch. "You say you have not dreamed of me," she said when she broke the kiss and they were both gasping for breath. He closed his eyes and resisted the urge to deny it. To confess his lie and all the ways he'd imagined her since the moment he met her. "But I have dreamed of you, Tommy." Her fingers tripped over his skin. "I have dreamed of you in a thousand ways. Do I not deserve a taste of those dreams? While the world is at bay?"

She was back to goddess. Making him want to drop to his knees again. To worship her again.

"Do I not deserve to find pleasure?" she pressed on. "In this moment? With you?"

Yes. God, yes. She did.

"What if this is my only chance for it?" she asked, caressing his cheek with one beautiful hand. "Don't I deserve it? Don't you?"

How was he to deny her?

And then she whispered, "*Please*," and it was soft and sweet and full of an ache he recognized as the twin to his own.

He pulled her to him, lifting her up and over, following her down until they were beside each other on the bed, and a little triumphant noise sounded in her throat, and he matched it with a growl of pleasure before lifting his head and saying, "I will keep you safe."

Whatever it took.

She met his eyes, her gaze clear and beautiful. "I have never doubted it."

Kisses came long and slow and slick, and he took his time with her, grateful for the snow outside making the night endless, eliding time so he could worship her in every way possible, with his hands and lips and tongue, until she was writhing on his bed, her fingers fisted in his hair, forcing him to meet her gaze, unfocused and eager.

"Now, Tommy. Please."

She was ready for him. He was sure of it, but still, when he rose up over her, every muscle taut with restraint, he was consumed with fear. "I don't want to hurt you," he whispered as she parted her lush thighs, making room for him.

"You could never hurt me," she replied.

He leaned down and kissed her again, deep and slow, until she was arching up into him. "Talk to me," he commanded, soft and harsh at her ear. "Tell me everything you feel."

If it was only once, he wanted all of it. Everything she could give him.

"I feel full of you. Already," she whispered. "I feel you inside me everywhere. A part of me. How could that be?"

"I don't know, love." The closest he would ever get to the truth. "But I feel it, too." He closed his eyes and pressed his forehead to hers. "I never want to stop feeling it."

And then he was there, where she was sweet and soft and so wet, and he cursed as she whispered, "*Oh.*"

"Tell me," he commanded.

She writhed against him, and somehow, impossibly, he held himself from her. "Hot. And heavy. And . . ." A tilt of her hips, and they both groaned as the tip of him kissed her, finding purchase at her entrance.

Imogen's groan became a gasp as he eased into her, sweat breaking over his brow as he filled her with just the tip of him. "That feels *very good*."

He laughed at the analysis. He couldn't help it. "I could not have said it better myself."

"It feels good when you laugh, as well," she said. "As though you like me."

He stilled at the words. "Imogen . . . fuck . . ." She blushed and began to look away. He dipped his head to catch her gaze. "I do like you. I—" He bit back the words before he leaned down and kissed her, quick and sure. "I like you."

Her brows rose and she gave him a little smile. "You do?"

"Very much." *God, she felt good.* But he held himself still, knowing that what they discussed was more important than what they were doing. He repeated himself. "Very much. *Too* much."

"You aren't only exasperated by me?"

"I am *always* exasperated by you," he said. "Exasperated by how you run circles around me. How you keep secrets from me. How you tempt me."

A light in her beautiful eyes. "I tempt you?"

Because he was not a saint, he let himself go, sliding deeper—just a touch—not nearly enough— into her. She gasped and he groaned. "You are a vixen."

"Oh," she said, soft silk. "A vixen. I like that."

Another slide, and she stretched around him, warm and wet and fucking perfect. "I know you do," he said at her ear. "You like how you scramble my thoughts."

"I don't mean to," she said, one of her hands coming to his hip, her fingers curling into the flesh there, holding him tightly.

"But you like it—" A tiny thrust.

A little sigh. "I like the way you look at me," she confessed, her thighs tilting toward him. "Like you've never known anyone like me, but you want to understand me. Like you want me peculiar. And odd. Like I'm not too much."

"You can tell that, can you? What I'm thinking?" He thought he hid it better, how she moved him. How she perplexed him. How he sought out her challenge. "Not too much. *Not enough.* Never enough." He pressed deeper and she sucked in a breath. Concern chased away all his other thoughts. "Love—if it hurts—we can stop."

Her eyes flew to his. "Don't you *dare.*"

He gave a little huff of surprised laughter that turned into a deep grunt when she wiggled against him, adjusting to his size. She stilled, staring up at him, a dangerous discovery in her face. "You like that."

"I fucking love that," he said. "But if it hurts—I know I am—"

"It does not hurt," she said, quick. "It is full and—" Another move. "Tight."

Another groan. "God, yes it is."

"Do you feel that?"

"I've never felt anything so magnificent."

"Interesting." She shifted, as though she wanted to investigate.

Oh no. He did not think he could handle an experiment. "Imogen," he panted. "Be careful."

Curiosity. A cant of her hips. "Or what?"

"Or I won't be able to . . ." He trailed off, then growled, "*Yes.* Do that again."

Gorgeous girl, she did.

"You will, though," she whispered. "You promised you would keep me safe."

He had, and he would. And she knew it. And her knowing made him feel like a fucking king.

"Let me—"

"Anything." *Everything she wanted.*

Another lift. Another circle. He sank into her, deep and smooth, until he was seated to the hilt and consumed with pleasure at the feel of her beneath him. Around him.

"Tommy." She sighed. "That is . . . I never imagined . . ."

"I should be sainted for this." He panted, sounding like he'd run from one end of London to the other.

She tossed an amused look at him. "For what?"

Another laugh. Had he ever enjoyed himself like this? Doing this? "For my patience."

"I do not think they saint people for this particular act," she said.

He leaned down and sucked at the tip of one of her beautiful breasts. "But think of how many more people would pay attention in church if they did."

"Tommy?"

He switched to her other breast. "Mmm?"

"Do you think you might try . . . moving?"

He stole her lips again, and did as she asked, a small thrust, pressing deep into her. "Only if you promise to tell me everything you feel."

"I feel perfect."

"You *do* feel perfect."

She giggled, and he grew impossibly harder. "I meant—"

"So did I," he replied. "Let's see how much more perfect we can get, shall we?"

He pulled out, slow and punishing, making them both ache for the thrust he gave her, smooth and even, and she threw her head back, baring her throat to him. He leaned down and licked up the column of flesh as he thrust again. She sighed, and he gave her another and another, watching her throat, listening to her breath, loving the way she moved beneath him, soft and sweet and . . .

Perfect.

He would never survive this.

He would never survive her.

"More," she whispered, and he gave it to her, knowing

he would give her everything she asked, forever. Sure, deep strokes, over and over, until time slowed and she was clinging to him, a sheen of sweat on both their bodies as they rocked together.

Her pleasure became his only goal, and Tommy lifted himself over her, coming to his knees and pulling her up over his thighs, sliding into her again, watching the place where they were joined as he set his fingers to the straining bud at her core, rubbing tight circles there, timing them with the short thrusts he'd discovered she loved.

Imogen slid her hands over her body, toward the place where they were joined, and he thought he would spend then, in that moment, watching her shiver and writhe beneath their combined touch. Her eyes flew open, finding his gaze. "Look at me," he whispered down at her. "Let me watch you come apart."

He slowed his thrusts and he could see her losing herself. Turning herself over to pleasure. "Tell me, sweet. Tell me what you feel."

"So much," she panted. "So full."

One hand found purchase on his thigh, squeezing. "More."

"My greedy girl," he said. "Aching for me."

"I am greedy," she confessed. "I do ache. Don't stop. Don't ever stop."

"Never," he grunted, moving harder now, deeper, his fingers still working over her. It was the closest thing to heaven he'd ever felt. "You are so beautiful," he whispered. "So perfect. Do you feel it, love?"

She went tight, strung like a bow. "Tommy!"

Her back bowed to him, as he worked her, making good on his promise, giving her everything she wanted. She flew apart in his hands, around his cock, thrusting to meet him. "Please," she panted. "I want— I need—"

She didn't know, but he did.

He did, and he would always give it to her. Anything she asked. Everything she needed.

"Come for me, love," he growled, stroking over her once, twice, and then . . . "Now."

She did, shaking in his arms, whispering his name in the darkness as she came, hard and fast and stunning, clinging to him, one hand grabbing hold of his wrist holding him tight to her as she bore down on his cock, taking her pleasure, convulsing around him, milking the hard length of him over and over.

And in her pleasure, he found his own, pulling out to thrust once, twice against her beautiful, lush curves and come, her fingers in his hair, claiming his groans with her kiss, as though he were the virgin.

Fucking hell.

She made him feel like one.

And perhaps he was, in a sense. Because it had never been like this.

Clutching her to him, he rolled to his side, pulling her against him and kissing her, deep and sweet. When he released her, she said softly, "Thank you. For showing me. For giving it to me."

Tommy's breath caught in his chest at the idea that she might think he'd done her a service. "You are the most beautiful thing I've ever seen," he said softly, pressing another kiss to her cheek. Her temple. Tilting her chin up and running his tongue along the underside of her jaw. "My goddess. My siren. My oracle."

Her fingers ran through his beard, and she replied, "Yours."

A prophecy.

Mine.

He knew better than to say it aloud. Knew that if he did, he might never be willing to take it back. Instead, he kissed her once more, thoroughly, and left to add wood to the fire and fetch a length of cloth, rinsed in clean water.

When he returned to the bed, he washed her carefully, leaving a trail of kisses behind, kisses that led to him worshipping her again as she lay back and let him, whispering to him and to the dark room.

There.

Yes.

Again.

More.

Yours.

When she'd claimed her pleasure without shame or hesitation, she fell asleep, and he lay beside her, watching the firelight cast dancing shadows across her smooth, soft skin. He wasn't tired. He wouldn't allow himself to sleep. Not when he could stay up all night and watch her . . . too precious and fleeting a gift to waste.

And when she turned toward him in slumber, seeking his heat, fitting herself into his arms, as though they slept like that every night, he could not help the sigh that came, a bone-deep satisfaction that he knew he would not find again in his lifetime.

Knowing she was safe. Knowing she was loved. Knowing that, even in sleep, she understood those truths.

Imogen had been right. She was not ruined that night.

But Tommy was. For the rest of his life. For the rest of time.

Chapter Twenty-Five

When Imogen woke, the fire had died and the room was still, a barely-there light burning at the bedside. A candle that had not been lit when she'd fallen asleep. The first thing she noticed was how warm she was, as though she were in full sun.

Memory came fast and impossible and delicious and startling. She was in Tommy's bed. In Tommy's *arms*, wrapped in the heady scent of him, her face pressed to his warm, bare skin.

She stiffened with surprise, unaccustomed to this particular scenario, but before she could sit up, one of his enormous hands stroked over her shoulder—also bare!—and down her side, slow and sure.

"It's alright," he said, the words a low rumble at her ear. "I've got you."

For a moment, she believed him. She gave herself up to the words and to his touch and to the dim light and let herself imagine, just for a moment, just for this night, that he did have her, and that this was her life. That they lived in these rented rooms at the top of the stairs in Holborn, filled with perfectly ordered stacks of books and tables full of her work and a bed large enough for them to sleep tangled in each other.

She moved against him, stretching, reveling in the little changes in her body, the tension and twinges, the evidence that what had happened between them had actually happened. Like an explosion.

In this case, however, she had witnessed it. She'd heard the sounds—the sighs and groans and whispers, the gasps of pleasure and the slide of sheets and the press of his kiss against her temple.

She'd felt this explosion, too. Continued to.

Wanted to experience another.

But first, she wanted the aftermath.

"Did I wake you?" she asked, feeling like she should apologize if she had. Not that she was sorry. If they only ever had these hours, pulled from time by the storm that continued outside, if the wind against the window was any indication, she wanted him awake.

Tommy made a little noise of denial. "You were so still," he said, the words impossibly soft and perfectly clear in the darkness. "I couldn't stop watching you." She turned her face into his warm skin, embarrassed, and he caught her before she could protest. "It was magnificent—so different from how I have experienced you in the past."

She slid her gaze to him. "You don't care for my chaos?"

"On the contrary, I have spent fourteen months undeniably drawn to your chaos," he said, a low laugh in his quiet words. "Resisting your chaos because of what it might reveal. What you might see."

She lifted her head and looked at him. "And what is it that I might see?"

He looked to the ceiling above the bed, suddenly fascinated by the dark inlaid wood there. "The way I look at you."

Her heart threatened to beat from her chest. "And what way is that?"

He turned to her, then, meeting her eyes, fire in his own. "Like I've never seen anything like you. Nothing so bright. Nothing so blazing. Nothing so tempting, like I would follow you into hell if it meant being able to watch you. I am beginning to think it's not chaos, though," he added. "I'm beginning to think chaos is the way you hide in plain sight."

The words stuttered through her and she looked away from him. "I don't know what that means."

"I think you do, though," he said. "I think you play this role—the wild Lady Imogen, who might set off a bomb or put a knife into a villain to save the day—"

"I've never knifed a villain," she interjected. "It is not my preferred method of handling them."

"No. You prefer putting them to sleep with your latest concoction."

"In my experience they are more likely to stay out of my business if I do that."

"You see? That's not chaos," he said. "That's something else entirely. You hide your competence in chaos. You hide your keen sense of justice there. You hide the heroine you are there."

It was almost too much, the way the observation threatened to unravel her. The way it cut. "I am not a heroine. Heroines are bold and beautiful and brave. Captains of their own fate." She paused, and then, "You forget, I am surrounded by them."

"Tell me about your Belles."

She stilled against him.

"The Hell's Belles," she said softly. "When you gave us that name, you could not have imagined how we would delight in it."

"I'm happy to have been of some use," Tommy replied, hand stroking over her back. "Considering that night also provided me with less serious mentions in the *News*."

She giggled. "If only the ladies of London could have a Peek of Peck *now*."

He growled and rolled her to her back, leaning down and setting his teeth to her shoulder, nipping playfully at the skin there until she gave a little squeak and he lifted his head. "Tell me about them. I will keep your secrets, Imogen. I swear it."

She wanted to believe it. "Duchess would say you are the last man in Christendom I should trust."

"I'll worry about winning Duchess tomorrow."

Imogen smiled, ignoring the tiny explosion in her chest at the words. *Pow.* At the wild idea that he might one day stand by her side the way Caleb stood by Sesily. The way Clayborn did with Adelaide.

At the wild idea that he would, indeed, win Duchess.

As if it were possible.

Imogen answered more easily than she should have, but knowing, instinctively, that whatever happened beyond the walls of these quiet rooms in Holborn, what was said here was theirs alone. "They are the heroines."

"I am not so sure."

He was wrong, of course. "That night you named us . . . that was the night Sesily walked through fire to save Caleb."

"Blew up my jail, you mean," he said dryly, no doubt thinking back to the rubble Sesily and Imogen had left in the basement of Whitehall when they had broken Caleb Calhoun out of one of the cells there.

"As I recall," she said, "that particular explosion was simultaneous to the arrest of a viscount who'd murdered several former wives and committed any number of other crimes. A damaged cell door is a small price to pay if you think of it."

"Less damaged and more blown to bits, but I'll allow it." A pause. "But yes, it coincided with the delivery of a now familiar blue dossier, inked with an indigo bell, and containing an unimpeachable amount of evidence against the viscount."

She smiled and ran her fingers through the hair on his chest. "That's very lucky."

"Mmm," he said. "Well, considering your penchant for

explosions, I have a theory about that particular crime. Namely, it was not Mrs. Calhoun who committed it."

"I cannot say," she said breezily.

"You won't say, you mean," he said. "I'd appreciate you telling me how you did it someday."

The fact that she made her own gunpowder was for another time.

"You're wrong. It was *Sesily* who was the heroine that night. Coming in like an avenging queen, planning an absolute coup, and looking like she would burn London to the ground if that was what it took to save Caleb."

It had been a magnificent job they'd done. And Sesily wildly in love, the kind that came from a storybook. The kind that made Imogen wonder dangerous things in the dark of night, when she let her quietest thoughts run wild . . . things like whether she might have a similar love for herself someday.

"And then there is Adelaide, born a solitary princess to the king of the South Bank," she said. "Never hesitating to leap into the fray—to take down a villain. To stand for justice. And never once worrying that she might not have the strength for it."

"She went up against her father?" Everyone knew Adelaide's father. Alfie Trumbull, the head of The Bully Boys—the most dangerous gang in the South Bank.

"And it worked," Imogen said, matching his admiration. "He stopped offering muscle to the highest bidders north of the river." She did not add the rest—that when Alfie had stopped, others had stepped in. More powerful than before. Instead, she said, "And to think, I can't get out from under the yoke of my brother, who wouldn't know how to run a crime ring if he were offered all the money in Britain."

Tommy gave a little laugh at that. "Some of us don't find that to be a bad quality, you know."

"You miss the point," she said. "Adelaide's strength. It

is no wonder Clayborn tumbled into love and would not let her go."

She resisted the urge to meet Tommy's gaze. To beg him to do the same.

"I do not miss the point," he said. "In fact, I think you do."

She did lift her head then, feeling something close to affront. "I beg your pardon?"

Tommy caught her face in his big, warm hand, urging her to look at him. "What did you call them? Bold and beautiful and brave? Captains of their own fate? You forget I have watched you, Imogen Loveless. I have witnessed your boldness. I have been laid out by your beauty." They were pretty words, but they were not for her. She blushed and tried to look away. "Wait," he stopped her. "As for bravery . . . there are few who would run into burning buildings to save the day. Even fewer who would run into collapsing ones to save me."

"You cannot be trusted to save yourself, Thomas Peck. You are too noble."

"Only when it comes to saving you," he whispered.

She kissed him then, rewarding him for the words and the way they warmed her even as she knew it wasn't true. She knew that his nobility ran to his core. Had recognized it in him from the start—which was why he was the only man at Scotland Yard the Belles came close to trusting.

Well. Not Duchess. Duchess didn't trust anyone until they'd proved themselves.

"And so you are heroines together," he offered. "A team of women bent on serving justice in the dark corners where it is rarely found."

"Are they dark corners?" she replied. "They do not feel dark to those of us who frequent them. They feel like bright worlds, ignored by the rich and powerful."

"You mean Scotland Yard."

She hesitated. *Tell him.*

No. It was too much. If he did not believe her, it would put them all in danger. "I mean men with money and power and privilege."

"And so the four of you—all women with money and power and privilege—take up the fight."

"As much as we can," she said. "Alongside others, who often know the fight better. But money and power and privilege come with benefits—namely, resources for the battle."

"Tell me about the battle."

"There are too many to name. A tapestry of threads to be unraveled." She paused. "So we do what we can to pull as many as possible, and unravel the whole thing."

"How?"

"You know some of it," she said. "Safe places for wives escaping husbands, daughters escaping fathers. Fair work in bawdy houses, in workhouses. Better work for servants with vicious employers. A dozen other things."

"And now, O'Dwyer and Leafe, doctors in hiding."

She nodded. "A moving clinic for women in trouble. And for women who aren't in trouble, but have different plans."

His serious, knowing gaze did not waver. "They've enemies."

"More than they can count."

His eyes turned to flint. "Which means you have enemies."

She flashed him a smile. "Ah, but I also have a blade at my thigh and a keen understanding of explosives."

"And me," he said. "You have me."

Not forever.

She looked away. "Perhaps I do hide in my chaos. In my movement. But more and more, I find there is no time for stillness."

"Why not?"

"Because the fight is in the movement."

"For justice."

"It does not always feel like justice," Imogen said, thinking of the girls who had lost their doctors. Of Mithra, without her ale. Of Maggie, with her added security. Of women meeting villains tumbling out of taverns, without Tommy Peck at their backs. Of those gold medallions, and what they represented. She spoke to the darkness. "Sometimes it feels like vengeance."

Silence fell with the words, heavy and honest. And he took a deep breath, letting it out and leaving her wondering whether she had gone too far. Hoping she hadn't. Willing him to understand.

"Sometimes, it feels like vengeance is the best choice."

She lifted her head and met his gaze, the meaning of the words rioting through her. He understood. *He understood.* It wasn't possible, though. He still woke every morning and went to Whitehall, and banged the drum of right and wrong. Legal and illegal. Did he not?

And then he added, "I told you I would keep you safe, Imogen. I claimed the role of your guard. I pledged you my blade. If it gets to be too much, you can always summon me."

Even if it means fighting everything you are?

They lay in the silence, their thoughts like screams between them, until Imogen could no longer bear it. "When your father died," she began, not wanting to ask but knowing she must, "you said you were lucky to have Adams. That he pulled you off the streets."

"Mmm," he agreed, shifting beneath her, and sighing.

She placed her palm flat on his chest. "You don't have to tell me."

"I do, though," he said, and strangely, it seemed like he was talking to himself and not to her. "I have to tell you so you—"

She waited for him to go on. To finish the sentence.

He decided against it. Instead, he said, "My father was a street sweep."

Imogen had not lied to him when she'd told him the Belles had a file on him—a file that revealed dozens of things about his current life. The location of this flat, the story of his rise through the Metropolitan Police and his accomplishments there—his enemies and friends. And of course, the myriad events relating to Mayfair ladies' favorite pastime: a Peek of Peck (the last was entertainment more than anything else). But it did not include his childhood—a failure of the file Duchess had never hesitated to point out.

But Imogen had never been more grateful for a failing of the Belles in that moment, as she waited for him to tell her this story. To trust her with it.

"You've seen where we lived," he said. "When we were growing up, it was a palace. *Three rooms*, think of it. My mother and father in one; Rose, Stanley, and me in another. A window out the back."

"Not just any window," she teased him. "One that held treasures."

He chuckled and moved to put a hand beneath his head, making it impossible to ignore the thick biceps that appeared when he bent his arm. "You can't blame me for that crime. Those stockings were the prettiest I'd ever seen."

She placed her chin on her own hand, still on his chest, loving the warmth of him against her. Savoring it—this quiet, secret night, the two of them against the wide world. "Of that, I've no doubt."

"Until I saw yours the other night," he said, as his free hand stroked down her spine, lingering at the small of her back, tempting her with the possibility that he might stray lower. "Those ribbons the color of sunset will be the last memory I recall."

She smiled. "I am happy to be of service."

Another laugh died away, and he returned to his story. "My da hadn't known his family—he'd been born in the gutter and raised in an orphanage, until he was old enough to be tossed into one of the rookeries to fend for himself." He scoffed. "*Old enough.*"

Imogen understood. David Peck hadn't been old enough. No one was old enough for those rookeries. They were virtually inescapable. "He must have been a remarkable man."

"He met Adams in the rookery. They came up together, and Adams was caught picking the pocket of the right man—someone with connections to the Bow Street Runners." A pause as he looked to the ceiling, choosing his next words in the flickering candlelight above. "My father didn't have such good luck. He took work as a sweep.

"He met my mother in Covent Garden—he was sweeping outside a theater on the Strand and she'd been inside, watching the play. He used to say he knew the moment he saw her that there'd never be another woman." He paused for a moment, lost in a memory, and Imogen hung on the next words. "He followed her back to Marylebone, where she lived in a big house owned by her merchant father."

"Your grandfather," she said. All the talk about the East End and Shoreditch, and his grandfather was a wealthy merchant?

Tommy shook his head. "I never met him. He disowned my mother when she married my father . . ."

Her throat went tight with understanding, and anger, and resentment for an old man who could have had a bright, beautiful family with daughters and sons and grandchildren . . . and a *grandson* like this—strong and noble and good—but instead chose upward mobility. The kind that she imagined left him bitter and alone.

Tommy looked down at her and huffed a little laugh. "You look like you'd like to take up a blade."

"I'd like to give your grandfather a piece of my mind," she said.

"Thank you." He pressed a kiss to the top of her head. "But you can't. He's dead."

Good. That she didn't say it aloud was surely a sign of great character.

"My parents married," he said, returning to the story, sliding Imogen a look. "I was a five-month birth."

"If your father looked anything like you, I am not surprised," she said immediately.

He gave a little laugh. "That's why I—"

"I understand." And she did. She didn't wish for a child. Not then, at least. *Not yet.* She pushed the thought aside.

"But what I didn't know then, when I was stealing petticoats off the washing line, was that the flat was more than any street sweep could afford. I'm not sure my mother did, either. She took work as a laundress, but two jobs weren't enough to make ends meet. I'm sure my father didn't tell her that he was fighting in underground rings to make up the rent every week. Brutal work during the days, brutal bouts at night."

Imogen was instantly cold. "What happened?"

"Some said it was a bad punch. Others said he'd thrown the fight, and his opponent didn't let up. But it was a bad fight." He paused, his fingertips stroking over her skin, distracted. "Better than dying of something he caught in the gutter."

She didn't move. Didn't know what to do, except to whisper his name in the darkness. She knew the keen loss of a parent. Knew the ache that never seemed to leave, even years later. But this . . . no one deserved it. And the idea that this wonderful man had suffered it . . .

"I was nineteen," he said.

Nineteen, and suddenly the man of the house. She wanted to gather him up and hold him. But she knew he wouldn't have it. So she waited for him to finish.

"So that was to be my life. I would sweep streets and then fight in them. And care for my mother and Rose and

Stanley, and pay for that flat that suddenly didn't seem like a palace so much as a prison." He gave a little self-deprecating laugh. "Of course, now I live in two rooms myself."

"Don't you disparage this place," she said. "I'm very fond of it."

"I don't need more than it," he said. "But if I had a wife . . . a family . . . I could afford more. I'd buy a house somewhere. With a garden. Not like Mayfair, but enough to keep a few little girls happy."

The words, easy, like he'd thought of them before, made her chest tight. She imagined herself in that garden. Imagined those little girls with blue eyes like their father and black curls like . . . She swallowed around the knot in her throat and was grateful that they had to be quiet. "That sounds wonderful."

He looked at her for a long moment and she would have given the entire contents of her carpetbag to know what he was thinking. Instead, he looked to the ceiling and said, "I used to dream of it back then. I'd come home aching from the work and I'd fall into bed and I'd think . . ." He took a deep breath and kept going, the next bit coming quickly, like if he didn't let it out it might go wild within him. "Maybe, someday, I'd find a girl and she'd ignore my filthy boots and the calluses on my hands from the broom, and the raw knuckles from the fights, and she'd give me a child or two and we'd revisit the sins of my father."

She did reach for him, then. She couldn't stop herself, her fingers tracing the edge of his beard, the long line of his nose, the angle of his jaw. "But you didn't revisit them."

He shook his head. "My mother was terrified of the prospect. She summoned Adams, and he took me to Whitehall, where Peel was building the police. I resisted the job at first. I'd been roughed up on more than one occasion by Runners drunk on limitless power." He paused. "But after a few weeks, I could see a path that my father hadn't had. A way to change everything. A new destiny. Rewrite my future, and with it, have enough for my mother not to have to work any longer, for Rose to find a good man, for Stanley to have a different life. I thought I might be able to make a difference. I thought I might . . ."

He trailed off, and she recognized something in his expression. "You thought you might change the world."

He looked to her, amusement in his eyes. "Changing the world isn't a dream for a boy from Shoreditch. You start with changing yourself. Your path."

"We unravel the thread we can." She lifted her chin. "The world looks different for different people."

He was quiet for a moment. "I'm beginning to see yours is much bigger than mine. And still, you work to change it."

"It's a more tempting goal than any other I've imagined."

Tommy watched her for a long moment, his eyes searching hers before he said, soft and dark and wicked, "I've one closer to home."

Could he mean her?

She blushed, unable to believe it. Too afraid to face the words in her reply.

Too eager for them to be true.

So she settled for "You know, there's nothing wrong with filthy boots, Tommy."

He stared at the ceiling, the candlelight flickering above them, his hand rough over the impossibly silk skin of her shoulder. "When was the last time you cleaned a pair of boots, my lady?"

I would learn. For you.

She didn't say it. But he heard it anyway. "Imogen," he said softly, urgently. "I told you all this because tonight . . . what we did . . . what I did . . . *Christ.* I was supposed to . . ."

No. She could hear his guilt in the words, and she hated it. He was going to apologize to her. He was going to make it all seem like a mistake. "Don't," she said. "Please."

"Imogen—you are so far above me . . ."

"Stop," she whispered. "It is my turn to talk. My turn to tell you that I have dreamed of this. Of being here, in your arms."

He took a deep breath, his arm pulling her closer. "Imogen—"

"Don't," she repeated, knowing what was to come. Knowing he was going to dismiss her. Knowing that it was for the best. There were too many secrets between them. Secrets that, when brought to light, would change everything.

So she didn't confess her feelings. She didn't say what she wanted to say.

Didn't tell him she wanted to be that wife. Or give him those children. Or live in that house with the garden that he'd built in her mind, so real that it felt like a memory.

She didn't tell him she loved him.

Instead, she simply said, "Please, Tommy, let me hold tomorrow at bay. Just for a moment. Let me imagine, just for tonight, that this is real."

He was silent for an age—long enough that she wondered if he'd fallen asleep, even as she could feel the tension in his body, at all the places where they touched.

And then, finally, *finally*, he stroked his big, warm hand over her skin once more. A decision. An agreement. A vow.

"Tonight," he said. "I shall imagine it, too."

They did imagine it, falling asleep once more, wrapped in each other's arms, until dawn crept over the horizon, and Imogen slid from his bed before the rest of the house woke, slipping out into the snow, knowing everything had changed.

Loving him.

Seeing him clearly.

Believing him.

And hoping that he would believe her, too.

Chapter Twenty-Six

When the girl knocked at his office door, Tommy had never been more grateful for an interruption.

Imogen had left him that morning, somehow sneaking from his arms, leaving him in the deepest sleep he'd had in a long time, sated by her touch and satisfied with her nearness. He'd woken with the scent of her on his sheets and still hanging in the cool air of the room, the only sign that she'd been there at all.

The moment he opened his eyes, he'd sensed her absence, coming to his feet almost instantly, a desperate frustration flaring in his chest. Where had she gone?

I have dreamed of this. Of being here, in your arms.

Why hadn't she waited for him to take her home?

Let me imagine, just for tonight, that this is real.

Was she safe in the snow? On the streets? In the cold? Had she found her way home?

Of course she was. She was Imogen Loveless. But it didn't change the fact that he worried.

Tommy had washed and dressed in scant minutes, leaving his rooms and hurrying downstairs, eager to get to her. To be certain she was safe. To fetch her. To bring her back and tuck her into his bed and keep her there, where he could see her. Touch her. Kiss her.

Love her.

Of course, none of it was possible. The night was over and outside the streets had been swept of their snow,

and in the cacophony of morning carriages and hawk-
ers making their way through Holborn, Tommy was reminded that she wasn't for him to love. That she wasn't
for him to keep.

That she wasn't for Holborn, and five-month babes, and
coming down from her Mayfair palace to love him. Even
if she said she didn't want an aristocratic marriage, the
alternative—justice, vengeance, world saving—it was too
bright for him. Too bold. Too much—not because she
was too much, but because he was not enough. It was
best that she'd left, because the more time they spent together, the more difficult it would be for him to let her
go in the end.

So he'd gone to work, throwing himself into the files
he'd compiled on the explosions throughout the East End,
knowing that whatever Adams and the rest of the Yard
thought of his obsession with these particular crimes, he
would do anything he could to solve them.

To bring whoever was harming women in those bright
worlds, out of view, to justice.

For the East End, yes. But now for Imogen, as well.

To try, however impossibly, to be more for her. To be
enough.

She'd given him more to work with—now he knew
that O'Dwyer and Leafe operated a moving women's
clinic, providing illegal tinctures and tonics and proce-
dures to women who were in difficult situations. Who
needed care. Who wanted to change their futures, or
protect them.

That, combined with the knowledge that whoever was
wreaking havoc on the East End was well funded and
skilled, suggested that Tommy was looking for aristocrats. Men who were angry and vocal about women.
About suffrage. About freedom. About equality.

Men who could easily have used the law to punish,
but instead chose a simpler, less public way—a way that

would protect their reputations if they could keep their hands clean.

Which begged the question—*who was getting dirty?*

He'd made a list of a dozen lords, every one of them rich and furious, and with each name his breathing came faster, as he realized that whoever Imogen was up against, she was in more danger than he'd imagined.

And still, she faced that danger without hesitation. Heading toward it—and justice—every time. What had she said? *The fight is in the movement.*

She was magnificent. The way she'd stitched his arm on the docks after dismantling the explosives in Mithra Singh's warehouse as though she did it every day. How she'd come running to save him from the original O'Dwyer and Leafe's. The taste of her when she'd kissed him on the street last night.

The feel of her naked in his bed. Taking him. Meeting his movements—not a fight. A gift.

And still, she'd left him. And he had no reason to go to her until the following evening, when he would play guardian and suffer watching her attend a dinner filled with men who did not deserve her, each vying for her hand—a toff's version of a medieval tourney.

If only it was a medieval tourney.

He might not hold a candle to these men when it came to land stewardship or buying a damn horse or reciting fucking Shakespeare, but in combat? With a sword in hand? A lance?

He'd crush them.

And he'd go to her, covered in sweat and blood, and kneel before her for even a moment of her approval. Hell, if it were a medieval tourney, he'd toss her over his shoulder and steal her away, his strength all he needed to be worthy of her.

But it wasn't a medieval tourney. It was 1840, and sweat and blood were now money and power and privilege, and

Tommy Peck was not invited to vie for Lady Imogen's hand.

The night was over. And it was tomorrow.

And he would be smart to give her up.

But if he found something he could share with her about the crimes they were both so committed to solving . . . then he wouldn't have to wait to see her.

For business. Not pleasure.

He cursed in the empty room and returned to his files, searching for something new in the reports and scant eyewitness accounts. He grew more and more frustrated, and his mind turned again and again to Imogen, who still hadn't told him everything she knew. Who kept secrets from him.

Punishment cannot come from within.

What did it mean? Together, they'd brought down several of the most powerful men in Britain—she'd come to him with those files, blue, inked with an indigo bell. And each one had sent a man who deserved it to prison.

He did not imagine for one moment that the Belles had failed to compile similar files for those behind these crimes. She knew more than he did.

Of course she did. She'd tampered with his crime scenes, unraveling his control over them with her carpetbag full of vials and jars and whatever else she'd collected. And that lack of control should have infuriated him. But it didn't.

Now, he was infuriated that she'd brought chaos into his world and hadn't let him watch. That she didn't trust him to stand by her side as she meted out her justice.

That she didn't offer him a place in her chaos.

Tommy cursed harshly in the empty room, and a knock sounded on the door, equally harsh.

He shot to his feet, his heart pounding. *Imogen.* "Come."

The door opened, revealing a young girl, no more than

twelve or thirteen, with a round face and an expression in her bright brown eyes that he recognized immediately. She knew things he did not, and was enjoying it.

His pulse raced. He'd seen that particular expression in Imogen's eyes a dozen times. There was no question that she'd sent this girl, who crossed his office with efficient speed that reminded him of the lady herself, as though she had important business and he was a mere stop on the way to it.

She dropped a tiny curtsy as he stood to greet her. "Detective Inspector Peck?"

"You've the better of me."

A flash of a smile, so familiar. She wasn't going to tell him her name. The Hell's Belles trained their vast network of informants and spies and runners well. There was absolutely no need for this girl to be noticed by Scotland Yard, so names were irrelevant. Indeed, they were a liability inside this building. Instead, the girl dug into a pocket sewn deep into her skirts and extracted a small square of paper.

"For you."

He took it, his heart racing with anticipation. "Thank you."

The girl nodded once and, task complete, took off. Tommy followed her to the doorway, watching as she snaked through a group of constables who barely had time to notice her before she was off, down the hallway, headed for the exit onto Scotland Yard.

In and out in seconds, her work done, leaving barely a trace. In that, she was nothing like her employer, who had no hesitation being found in the uniform room, and preferred calling cards the size of holes in the side of jail cells.

Full of anticipation, Tommy looked down at the square of paper in his hands. He opened it, confusion flaring for a heartbeat as he turned it over, revealing that it was blank on both sides. He couldn't help the wide smile that came with the understanding of what she'd done. A thrill rioted through him, and he reached into his desk drawer, extracting a box of matches.

It was a secret message.

Maybe it would read the same as the last, but with a different author.

I love you.

He pushed the ridiculous thought away and struck a match, holding it beneath the paper as he held his breath.

Words appeared.

Not just words.

A bell, just like the ones that had been inked on the files she'd provided him in the past. But this one, not in indigo ink. This one, in goat's-lettuce juice. And beneath it:

Salisbury Steps
4 o'clock

She was going to tell him what they knew.

Dropping the paper to his desk, Tommy sucked in a breath and pulled out his pocket watch. Half-past three. If he hurried, he'd get there before her.

He snatched his coat and hat from the hook by the door and was down the hallway before he had them on, stopping only when someone shouted his name behind him. He turned to find Adams standing at a distance, a stack of papers in his hand, approaching at a clip.

Tommy shook his head. "No time, Wallace. I've somewhere to be."

"Somewhere to be? Or *someone* to be with?" Something must have flashed on Tommy's face, because Adams lifted his brows with a knowing look. "I know that look; don't get that girl in trouble, Tommy."

"On the contrary," Tommy replied to the older man, unable to keep the smile from his face, already turning away, eager to get to her. "She's finally going to let me keep her safe."

Twenty minutes later, Tommy pushed his way through The Brazen Beaver tavern, which stood at the top of the Salisbury Steps, a well-trafficked set of Waterman's Stairs that were the closest access point to Covent Garden from the Thames. The tavern's rear entrance—or front entrance, depending upon how one looked at it—opened onto a small courtyard into which anyone coming up from the river would be welcomed for food or ale.

Imogen wasn't inside the tavern, and she wasn't in the courtyard behind, so Tommy stepped to the edge of the embankment, leaning over the low stone wall to check the steps themselves. The top few were covered with a layer of well-trodden snow from the night before, and though the river was not yet low, it had receded enough to reveal another handful of steps that were usually under water, slick with the green muck that was sure to give anyone who wasn't careful an icy dip.

A bone-chilling wind whipped up the Thames, and Tommy pulled his coat tight around him.

"I did not expect it to be so cold." He startled at the words, so close, her shoulder barely an inch from his arm—so close that if he leaned in, they would touch.

He could keep her warm.

He cleared his throat and turned toward her, blocking as much of the wind as he could, and he took her in, her face turned to the sky, the sun setting in the west casting a golden glow over her dark curls. Her lips and cheeks were bright red as she flashed a smile up at him, and he distracted himself from the way he wanted to kiss her by cataloguing her clothes—a thick, fur-lined, grass green coat over a purple dress—the skirts bright and beautiful like the prettiest summer lilacs.

One did not have to be a dressmaker to know that the colors were not considered appropriate for winter, but they were appropriate for Imogen, and that was all that mattered. "You don't look cold. You look like a summer garden."

He immediately regretted the words, and then felt a different thing altogether when she grinned and ducked her face into the fur collar of her bright green coat. "Be careful, Mr. Peck, or I'll start thinking you like me."

"I am on the record for liking you, my lady," he said, keeping the words quiet, loving the way her cheeks pinkened in their wake.

"I like you, too," she said simply.

His chest tightened and he asked the question he should not. "Then why did you leave me last night?"

After a moment's pause, Imogen looked over her shoulder, indicating the path along the embankment. "It will be warmer if we walk."

"It will be warmer if we go inside," he said, even as he followed her as she started down the path. He didn't like her out here in the cold.

She shook her head. "Not inside."

"We could have met at my office."

She shook her head. "Definitely not your office."

"Are you afraid someone will remember the time you were there? Raiding the uniform closet? Or the time you blew up the jail?"

"You've no proof of the last one," she quipped, and he couldn't help his laugh, or the way he imagined putting his hand to the small of her back and guiding her around the piles of snow the wind had collected.

But she wasn't his to touch here, in public. Not even if last night, he'd touched her everywhere, and she'd come apart in his arms and then spent hours in his arms, confessing her secrets.

I am not a heroine, she'd said to him, and as he watched her make her way upriver, skirts swaying, the idea that this woman did not see how much of a heroine she was— that she might think herself too much or not enough—was madness.

She was bold and beautiful and brilliant. Captain of her own fate.

And, he feared, captain of his, as well.

"You never wear a uniform," she said, stepping around a pile of snow.

He held out his arm to keep her stable. "Detectives don't wear the uniform."

"Not wearing it doesn't seem to hinder you getting what you require."

"You're here, are you not?" he teased, drinking in her smile.

Once they were at a distance from the tavern, she turned, facing him, the wind whipping her curls into a frenzy, making his fingers itch to smooth them.

"I have things to tell you," she said, and he was shocked by the hesitation in the words—hesitation he'd never witnessed in her before.

Did she not understand that he would never betray her trust? He searched for the right way to settle her. "The message," he said, moving to block her from the wind. "It was business."

"Yes." She nodded once. Firm. "It was business."

"I confess," he said, trying for levity, disturbed by her seriousness. "I was disappointed."

A tiny smile flashed. "I fear you will be even more disappointed when you hear what I have to say."

He shook his head. "Imogen. Whatever it is. We are together in it."

She took a deep breath and nodded again, as if encouraging herself to go on. She reached into her skirt pocket and extracted a piece of paper. Handed it to him.

"Another secret message?"

"Secrets," she said, shaking her head. "But not a message."

He opened it to reveal three names, aristocratic and immensely powerful. Names he had known before he'd seen them that night at the Trevescan ball, in conversation with Commissioner Battersea.

Beneath each name, a location.

Bethnal Green. Whitechapel. Spitalfields.

He immediately recognized the sites of the explosions. "Are you sure?"

She nodded. "But we cannot prove it. There is a missing link."

He looked down at the list again. "Motive?"

Imogen looked to the river, pulling the fur over her face. "No. Motives are clear." She set a finger to the top name. "This one owned the factory where a dozen seamstresses died in a fire last year." She slid a finger to the next address. "Mayhew's print shop where the remaining workers met to plan their demands for better conditions.

"This earl—he is the money behind a bawdy house in Seven Dials. Didn't care what happened to the girls who worked there, as long as he got his money." The next address. "When they fought back, saving enough money to run, his muscle exploded the waypoint in Bethnal Green where they were waiting to be smuggled out of the city. And took eight girls with it."

Fucking hell. "Linden's bakery."

Another name. "This one is a monster, so untouchable thanks to title and fortune that his wife can't escape him. But she can keep him from tormenting a new generation." Two addresses beneath. "He discovered she'd been to O'Dwyer and Leafe's. Blew it up and went looking for proof so he could have her committed."

Tommy's teeth clenched at the words. "Did he succeed?"

She shook her head. "The records were hidden in an underground safe. We got to them before they could."

"The morning I found you," he said, remembering the Duchess of Clayborn climbing into a carriage with a stack of papers.

A little nod, a flash of surprise that he'd put it together. "Yes."

"Why explosives?" He looked to the paper. "He could have had her arrested. O'Dwyer and Leafe, as well."

"And risk the scandal?" she asked. "Even if he was willing to bear it . . . the violence is the point. These men . . . they don't want solutions. They want suffering."

He knew it was true even as he loathed it. There, on the paper, a second address. Mithra Singh's brewery on the Docklands. A flash of memory, O'Dwyer outside. "The clinic moved. You went up against him again."

She gave a little shrug. "What else could we do? They're the ones doing the work—all we can do is stand with them."

"You should have come to me," he said.

A small, sad smile. "We couldn't."

"The missing link." Something more. Something more *dangerous*.

Imogen nodded. "We didn't know how they did it. We didn't know who they were using. But now . . . we do."

He reached for her, remembering where they were just in time to keep from touching her. Wishing he hadn't remembered. Wishing they were inside, anywhere but in full view of the world.

She reached into her coat pocket. "You said we were together in it," she said softly, opening her hand to reveal a small gold disk, gleaming in the setting sun. "I fear you will feel differently now."

Tommy's stomach dropped.

He knew the St. Michael medallion instantly. From Wallace's lapel. From the drawer in Tommy's own rooms where he kept the one he did not wear. From countless other policemen.

He spoke to her hand. "Where did you find it?"

"Underneath the cistern in the brewery, where Mithra keeps the wheat."

"Where I found you," he said, his gaze rising to meet hers. "Where you were dismantling explosives."

Anger flared, hot and nearly unbearable. She could have been killed that night. And by— "Who?"

"Mithra surprised him, Tommy. He'd set the fire above and had placed the explosives on the lower floor— exactly what you would do if you were trying to blow the whole place to the ground, and anyone who was trying to save it along with it." A pause. "The fuse in the warehouse matched the fuse I found at the seamstress— fabric."

The words shattered through him as his mind raced. "From the uniforms. That's why you were in the closet."

She nodded. "We've confirmed the match of the weave. And the chemicals there—the explosive mix— they are the same from the bakery. And the print shop."

"Mercury fulminate," he said.

She nodded. "And the blasting oil—once I had it in hand, it was easy to match."

The weight of the proof was heavy and devastating. And still, he struggled with the shock of the truth. "The men I work with—the ones I've trained—" He trailed off, knowing as he spoke that he could not vouch for them all.

One did not climb the ranks of Whitehall without witnessing the way power consumed people. The way it made different shapes of monsters: Those born with privilege and power, unable to stop themselves from misusing it. And those who had come up on the opposite path—with nothing but strength and hunger—desperate to claim it.

"These men." She waved a hand over the files. "We cut off their line to muscle. When Adelaide married her duke, her father agreed to set The Bully Boys straight—"

"The Bully Boys aren't straight," Tommy said. They were the most notorious gang on the South Bank, run by Alfie Trumbull, a criminal with a code, but no discernible conscience. "They're claiming more turf every day, and giving Whitehall a run for it."

"You're right," she agreed immediately. "Alfie Trumbull will never cede power. But he's going to be grandfather to a duke someday, so playing muscle to the aristocracy doesn't work well for him any longer. That, and he knows that if he came for places the Belles protect, Adelaide and Clayborn will take him down without hesitation." A long pause. "So the terrible, powerful men who'd used The Bully Boys as hired guns for years . . ."

"They needed another gang," Tommy said. "One that would be tempted by proximity to power and unfathomable amounts of money."

"Yes. And we think they are paying handsomely for it."

He looked directly at her. "Who? How many?"

"We don't know. We're looking for the records."

"Where?"

"In their houses. While they are . . . otherwise occupied."

His mind was racing, following the plan. "Occupied with seeing you find a husband."

She lifted one shoulder in a little shrug. "I told you I had no intention of marrying."

"Imogen," he said, hot with anger and denial and a keen, furious faith that she was right. "What you're into—this isn't one toff and a handful of thugs."

She paused and looked out at the river. "We know very well what we're into, Tommy. Duchess isn't even sure we can trust you."

He met her eyes, his chest tight.

"I trust you, though," she said softly, staring up at him with her enormous brown eyes in her beautiful open face. "What they did to these places. To O'Dwyer and Leafe's. To Mithra's warehouse. They could just as easily do it to Maggie's tavern next. And a dozen others . . . if they knew what we kept at Duchess's . . ."

They would come for them. Without question.

Fear and frustration clouded her gaze. "Tommy—I have to trust you. We are running out of safe spaces. We are running out of people to stand with us."

He reached out to her, unable to resist touching her, stroking a finger down her arm, hating that he couldn't pull her close. "You have me."

"Do we?" she asked. "Are you with us?"

"Yes." The reply was instant. He knew what she asked. "*Yes.*"

Over the years, Tommy had made himself a name across London as a decent man and a good detective, and here was the test of it. He could turn his back on the evidence and swear by the good of the Yard. Or he could see the truth. Believe her. And turn his investigation toward what he knew was true. To unearth the corruption inside Scotland Yard.

And so, he faced the question: Was he a decent man? Or a decent detective?

Was he willing to turn his back on Scotland Yard—on his career, on the men who had pulled him from the streets? Was he willing to set a bomb himself? Punish those inside the Yard, standing with those who were outside of it?

Was he willing to stand with Imogen and choose justice? Vengeance?

He'd pledged her his blade, had he not?

The answer was unequivocal. He was with her. With these women who worked with honor and did more good in more places than Whitehall ever could.

Of course he was with them.

With her.

Before he could say it all, footsteps pounded toward them. He turned, sliding her list of names into his coat pocket, instinctively pushing Imogen behind him as he came to a crouch, fists up, ready for whatever was to come.

If they wanted her, they would have to come through him.

What came was the heavy blow of a truncheon, wicked and devastating at his side.

He sucked in a breath at the pain and threw a punch, knocking his foe back. *Foes.*

There were two of them, both wrapped in heavy coats and scarves, their faces difficult to see. Not so their clubs and fists, which came fast and vicious, quickly revealing to Tommy that this was no game. That they would put them down right there, in broad daylight, and not think twice.

He dodged another blow. Landed one of his own. And witnessed the truth he'd already known—that Imogen had already revealed. These weren't mere thugs. Not bullies from the South Bank. Not run-of-the-mill criminals from the East End, trading money for muscle.

These were policemen.

Tommy might not know their names, but he recognized the smoothness of the movements. The lack of fear. The certainty that even if they were caught, they would not face the same consequences as a common street fighter.

Even if Tommy hadn't recognized the club at the larger one's side—a Yard-issued truncheon—even if the brute didn't ring a bell with his broad, pale face and his nose, flattened by force sometime in the past, Tommy would have seen it.

It was confirmation; Scotland Yard was on the take. On the take, and willing to do anything to prevent being discovered.

And if there were two Peelers here, fighting in broad daylight, there could be any number more of them. At every level.

The realization crashed through Tommy along with

a horrifying thought—that they would keep coming as long as they were threatened with discovery. Which meant Tommy would have to do all he could to keep Imogen protected. If that meant blood on his hands, so be it.

Consumed with a feral fury, Tommy knocked the larger man into the dirt and made for the smaller of the two, memorizing his features—the dark hair on his pale, freckled face, his bulbous red nose, his small dark eyes.

They grappled with each other, Tommy calling out to Imogen, "Run!"

"I absolutely will not!" she said, too close for comfort.

He threw a punch, sending the man stumbling back, and turned to look over his shoulder. She was unbuttoning that coat—the one that looked like spring and summer all in one. The one that made him wish he could lay her down in a field and have his way with her.

"It wasn't a request, you madwoman!" he shouted, coming back around to block a heavy punch and land another of his own—one that rang with the crunch of a jaw going out of whack. "Get gone!"

The big one was up again, and this time heading for Imogen. A fucking mistake. If he laid one hand on her, Tommy would personally see it removed from the bruiser's body.

Imogen was backing away, toward the embankment. "Who do you work for?" she asked brightly, as though they were all at goddamn tea.

Tommy was going to lose his mind. "The police. He works for the fucking police. They both do."

His own foe didn't hesitate to reply, "Yeah, but you won't anymore, will you, Peck? You should've let us take you out with that carriage . . ." *The carriage outside The Place*. It hadn't been aiming for Imogen. The bruiser grinned, wicked and cruel. "Pride of Whitehall?

Not when we're done with you. Not when we're done with your girl."

The threat roared through Tommy, and he went for the man without holding back. All thoughts of justice gone as he fought with a single goal. To protect Imogen.

Her guard. Her warrior. Her vengeance.

Tommy made quick work of his opponent, putting him into the snow, already turning into a dead run, headed to help her. At a distance, she was nearly at the embankment wall, backing away as the other copper headed for her, arms outstretched, a wicked, playful grin on his face, as though they played a game. As though when he caught her, the cruelty would be the point.

She was too close to the low wall. If she wasn't careful, the bastard would push her into the river, and with her heavy skirts, she'd be dead before Tommy could save her.

Except, of course, Imogen had no intention of requiring saving. As Tommy watched, she reached up and yanked on the obsidian brooch she always wore at her neck—the one she always took care to keep out of reach.

It came off without any effort, and she opened it with a deft movement.

Not a brooch; a box.

Without hesitation, Imogen flung the contents of the box in the direction of the villain, who lifted his hands to his face just as . . .

Boom!

She'd blown the man off his feet. He now lay on his back at a distance, looking dazed and deeply worse for wear.

Tommy pulled up short, staring at the man for a long moment before turning to look at her. "Fucking hell."

"It won't kill him, but one must always be prepared." She waved away his shock and raised her voice in the direction of the prone policeman. "You really should make better choices, sirrah!" Turning a bright smile on Tommy, she said, "I suggest we tie them up and take them to Duchess's for questioning."

"I don't want to question them," he said. "I want to kill them both for thinking to threaten you."

Her gaze went soft on him. "That's very sweet, Tommy. But I think you'll find we need them alive if we've any hope of finishing our investigation."

She was right, of course. But Tommy struggled to care about the investigation in that exact moment. Instead, he was vibrating with anger and frustration and no small amount of admiration for this glorious woman. Instead, he cared about getting her to a private location and keeping her there for a long time. Possibly forever.

Nevertheless, if Imogen wanted to tie these men up, Tommy would do it. He'd do whatever she asked.

Christ. He was gone for her.

He made for her, eager to do as she suggested as quickly as possible so he could tell her just how gone he was. The words were right there, on his tongue.

I love you.

Except she wasn't looking at him anymore. She was looking over his shoulder, her soft gaze going hard, and then wide. He turned, knowing what he would find.

His opponent had found his feet again, along with his club. Tommy didn't have time to block the blow, nor the shove.

The last thing Tommy heard as he tumbled was Imogen's scream, and then he was in the river, the water like ice, stealing his breath and his strength, pulling him immediately down into the current.

He fought for a moment, with singular purpose.

Imogen.

He had to get back to her.

He kicked off from the riverbed, breaking the surface, forcing himself to take a deep breath. Shouting for her.

Except it was barely sound. The cold had taken his voice.

"Tommy!" She was there, running along the embankment, tracking him.

Being chased.

No. Not being chased. Chasing him.

He focused on her, in that dress—that color, bright purple. Not the aubergine or lavender that would be worn by a different woman.

By a woman in mourning.

Dammit, it was cold.

Would she mourn him?

He drank her in, his arms starting to go stiff. He wouldn't be able to keep himself afloat much longer. And still, he watched her.

If he was going to die, he wanted to die looking at her.

His boot hit the riverbed and he used the last of his strength to dig into the silt, to resist the current, thankful for low tide. But low tide or no, there was no one to help him. He closed his eyes.

"No! Tommy!"

The words were closer. She was closer. He opened her eyes and saw her, above him, on the Salisbury Steps, where she'd summoned him earlier.

No. If she waded into the river, she could easily be lost. If she was swept up, he wouldn't be able to save her. They'd die together of the damn cold. He tried to shout to her. "Don't—"

He struggled, but couldn't move. That had been quick. How long had he been in the water?

Wait. Now *Imogen* was in the water, a thick rope in hand—used to moor boats by the steps. She was wading toward him. "N-no . . ." He couldn't scream. Could barely make the word out for his teeth chattering. "Don't come further. The current . . ."

She ignored him, and then she was there, reaching for him. "Tommy," she said, her hand finding his. Gripping

him tightly. Feeling hot like the sun. "Please . . ." Her
voice was far away as she dragged him toward the bank.
"I can't do this by myself. Please . . . The tide is low
enough . . . Can you stand? Please, my love . . . Please
stand up."

My love.

For the rest of time, he would remember those words
on her lips.

And the way they brought him back to life.

Chapter Twenty-Seven

They did not have time.

By some miracle of location and tide, the current hadn't taken him far, allowing Imogen to wade into the river and save him. After helping him out of the water, she looked back toward the spot where she'd taken out the attackers. The first was still unconscious in the muck, but he would rouse soon enough, and the other was gone, the blade she sank into his thigh gone with him.

There was no time to care about it; Imogen wagered they had ten minutes before the whole of Scotland Yard was after them, and they had to find somewhere nearby to hide and get warm.

They were halfway up the steps before the cold wind claimed most of Tommy's mobility. He stilled as the wind whipped through him, swaying from the force of it, sucking in his breath.

"Tommy," she said urgently. "You have to move. Quickly. We'll be seen."

Somehow, the words propelled him forward. "Leave me. You have to g-get inside." His teeth were chattering so much it was difficult to understand him. "Out of s-sight. They're coming for you."

They were coming for both of them, she had realized on the embankment, which terrified her no small amount. The Belles had made a life of facing the wrath of powerful men over the years, but the idea that she'd brought Tommy into their fight—the fact that Scotland Yard had turned against him, as well . . .

"I'll be inside when you are," she said, setting herself beneath his arm, urging him to lean on her. "Christ, you're big," she said, looking down the embankment, assessing the threats that might present themselves at any time. And she didn't have a weapon. "It's not far, but we must move, love."

They had to get inside the maze of labyrinthine streets between the river and the Strand. Fast.

"We can't go to Whitehall," he said.

She gave a little laugh. "Tommy Peck, I have no intention of ever setting foot in Scotland Yard again."

"You were right," he said through the work of movement. "It was the p-police. They've been following me the whole t-time. You weren't in d-danger; I *put* you in danger."

"Some guard you are." Imogen was hurrying him forward, desperate to get him away from the curious attention of those who worked on the riverbank. She flashed a bright smile at an elderly woman standing in a nearby doorway before saying, under her breath, "Can you move more quickly?"

"C-cold."

"I know," she said. "It's worse in the wind. We have to get you inside and dry. And warm."

"C-can't move my arms," he chattered. "Can't keep you safe. Sh-shit, Imogen . . . We have to get you safe."

Wonderful man. Half dead from the cold, and still only thinking of her. "The faster you move, Tommy, the sooner I'm safe."

He moved.

They skirted around the pub at the top of the stairs, and headed north along Dirty Lane. When she recognized where they were, Imogen whispered, "Thank God."

"Where are we g-going?"

She raised a fist and pounded on the unassuming door

to an unassuming building, willing the door to open. Holding him as tightly as she could, she checked the street again. Empty in the twilight, but that didn't mean there weren't a dozen unseen witnesses.

The door opened. A keen set of eyes greener than any Imogen had ever seen tracked over them both, stopping on Imogen's face. "What kind of trouble are you bringin' to my place, Imogen Loveless?"

Imogen pleaded, "The kind the Belles will pay handsomely for."

The beautiful woman looked to Tommy. "Is that *Peck*? You brought a fucking *Peeler* here?" A pause. Then, "What happened to him?"

"He went for a swim," Imogen said, unable to keep the fear from her tone. "Please, Lorelei."

A sigh before Lorelei Wilde, tall, powdered, patched, and wearing a rose-colored dress that revealed a stunning bosom, opened the door wide. "Alright. But Duchess will owe me."

"*I'll* owe you," Imogen said. "Whatever you like."

"I want a batch of that stuff you use to send men to sleep," Covent Garden's most skilled madam negotiated.

"I would have given you that for free," Imogen replied. Whatever the girls at Wilde's needed to stay safe while working.

"Back to work, lovelies. For every man you distract this afternoon, the lady will pay handsomely." Lorelei waved several curious faces back into the main receiving room and indicated the center staircase. "Can he get up the stairs?"

"Of c-course I can," Tommy stuttered. "And I can hear."

The madam gave him a long look. "'S about all you can do right now, old man." She lifted his other arm and draped it over her shoulder, wrinkling her nose in disgust. "You're going to pay for this dress, too, Imogen, when your Peeler gets the stink of the river all over it."

"I'll p-pay for it," Tommy said.

Lorelei cut him an amused look. "Even if I were certain you would live, I wouldn't take that promise. This frock cost more than your yearly salary."

They made it up the stairs and down the hallway, to a dimly lit room with a large bed, a wardrobe, and little else within. "Who's coming after 'im?"

"With all due respect, Lorelei," Imogen said as she helped him to the bed, "it's best if you don't know this particular story. But it's quite warm in here."

"It's n-not warm," Tommy interjected.

She met his gaze. "It will be. Just as soon as we get you out of your clothes."

"Too warm?" The madam leveled Imogen with a look. "As warm as a Peeler in my place?"

Imogen turned away, already shoving his coat off his shoulders and letting it fall in a wet, sopping mess to the floor as she made for the buttons of his waistcoat. "As warm as a crew of them."

"Bloody hell, Imogen." Lorelei cursed, moving to the bed to pull back the counterpane and sheets.

"I know," Imogen said, frustration and anger flooding her. She knew she'd done the wrong thing bringing him here. Bringing the prying eyes of Scotland Yard here. "But he would have . . ."

She couldn't finish.

"Still might, God willing, then we can give him up." Lorelei sighed. "You're lucky I owe you four. Get him in that bed as soon as possible. I'll send up a brick or two to help get him warm. And you'll tell Duchess my debt is clear."

"It's better than that," Imogen said, throwing his waistcoat wide and pulling it down his arms. He was shaking enough to make the floors creak. "Now the Belles are in debt to you."

"If we survive this, I'll be sure to call it in." Lorelei gathered the coat and waistcoat in her arms and leveled

Imogen with a look. "He'll need a bath. If the cold don't do him in, the river will."

With that assessment, Lorelei left them alone. "They'll be looking for us." He shook beneath Imogen's touch. "They'll know we haven't gone far."

She nodded, but did not stop her work, unraveling the cravat from around his neck. "You must get dry. And warm."

"I can't lift my arms."

"In romantic novels," she said to him, grasping the open neck of his shirt, "the villains are always ripping bodices in two."

"You should go, Imogen. Get far from here. To your brother. Out of the city."

She ignored the stupid suggestion, chalking it up to his cold-addled brain. Instead, she said, "Layers of silk and linen and whalebone, just . . . pulled apart like a Chelsea bun. I've always wondered how that would feel."

"Imogen. The f-further you are from me, the less likely they are to hurt you."

She yanked at the collar of the shirt, rending it down the middle with a single, long *riiiiiiip*. "Oh," she said softly. "That is a delightful sound. I might like it better than an explosion." She tossed him her best flirt. "I certainly like the result better." Another pause as she tossed the shirt and ran her fingers to his bandage, which she immediately unraveled. "We need this off—you likely pulled a stitch."

"Imogen." No stutter there. Good. He was getting warmer. Or angrier.

She could find anger, too. "Tommy, you imbecile. I'm not leaving you. The further I am from you, the less likely I am to keep you alive, you lummox," she argued softly, finishing with the bandage and moving to work the buttons of his trousers.

She pushed the fabric down over his hips and shoved

him back to sit on the bed. He went, unable to stop her, his strength barely there. "Imogen," he repeated, his voice cracking with frustration. "Listen t-to me."

"No, you listen to me, Tommy Peck," she said urgently, pulling one boot off and then the other. "I am your guard now. I am your blade. Right now, *I* keep *you* safe." She looked up at him. "You call me Oracle? Here is my prophecy. You will get warm. And you will survive. And we will fight. And we will *thrive*. Together."

She had to believe it. There was no other choice.

A knock at the door prevented him from replying. She stood and flung his wet trousers away as it opened, looking for a weapon. *Dammit.* The one day she didn't bring her bag.

Thankfully, it was Lorelei, massive blond wig in hand, followed by two girls, one with firewood and the other with an iron basket of bricks.

The girls moved with immense speed as the madam handed Imogen the wig and waved her hand in the air. "Turn." Imogen did as she was told, "Best put that hair on and get yourself into bed as soon as you can. It's warm outside."

The police were looking for them.

"Dammit," Imogen replied, bending over and inspecting the wig, high and caged, as though it had been sent from a palace lady in waiting. "That was fast."

"Where are they?" Tommy asked from the bed.

"Why? Are you planning to do them in, Peeler?" Lorelei worked at the buttons of Imogen's gown as Imogen tucked dark curls up into the blond hairpiece. "I'll do what I can, Imogen, but you're going to have to give them something."

Imogen understood, stepping out of the bright purple dress—a color they would not miss. "They'll be looking for someone wet and cold."

"Take the clothes," Lorelei said to the girls who'd come with her as she crossed to the room's wardrobe, pulling a handful of menswear, a red silk dressing gown, and something else from within.

She tossed the clothes to the floor and the rest to the bed, returning to the hooks on Imogen's corset, adding it to the pile of clothes in one of the girl's arms. "He needs a mask. And you'd best put on a show. Chemise."

Imogen pulled it off without hesitation.

"Wait—" Lorelei reached up and adjusted the wig, tucking in the last few strands of black curls, stepping back and assessing Imogen's nude body. "Let's hope they don't go looking to see if it matches."

Imogen rolled her eyes and turned for the bed. There was no time to be embarrassed as she climbed in, reaching for the dark mask and leaning over to tie it over Tommy's eyes.

"Pity there's no time for a shave," Lorelei said. "Pull the curtains, make sure he stays in the dark, and hope the Yard sends idiots."

"Do they have anything else?" Imogen quipped.

"I can hear you," Tommy chattered.

She grinned. "You're not the Yard anymore, Mr. Peck."

"This isn't f-funny, dammit," he said, looking to Lorelei. "Get her out of here."

"So sorry, I don't take orders from men," Lorelei retorted, fiddling with the curtains around the bed, and stepped back to look at the tableau they made. "You make a good-looking pair. Try not to muss the wig."

As he could not move, Imogen highly doubted they'd be getting anywhere close to mussing the wig. He shivered beneath her as she straddled him, his eyes widening as he realized what was happening. She forced a smile. "You hear that, Tommy? You've been here for five minutes and you're already gaining admirers."

"I'd like to see what you deliver when you haven't been swimming in the ice," Lorelei said, her assessment a distracting gift to them both. "Maybe I'll come back and have another look when the lady has warmed you up."

"You absolutely will not," Imogen said.

"*Really.*" Lorelei leaned over Tommy's face. "Stay awake, man. She's making threats on your behalf."

He gave a little huff of laughter. "Sh-she's allowed to."

The madam's dark brows rose and she looked at Imogen. "Is she, now?"

"I am," Imogen said, unable to stop herself, nerves on end as Lorelei pulled a blanket over them both. Imogen pressed herself down to his body, cold and hard. Like marble. "He's mine."

Lorelei's eyes went even wider. "Isn't that a thing."

Imogen wrapped him in her arms, aiming to touch him in as many places as possible. To warm him however she could. He sighed, and she could not ignore the thrum of pleasure that coursed through her. "Send a message to Duchess. We need help."

"Already done," Lorelei said, and the door closed.

Silence fell inside the room, but outside, belowstairs, she could hear footsteps. The bang of a door. A few shouts of outrage, both deep and high-pitched.

"They're here," he said.

Searching the place. Imogen lifted her head. "Talk to me," she said. "You can't fall asleep."

"I c-can't get warm."

"You will," she said.

Another little huff of laughter that gave her hope. "Another prophecy."

"That's right. And they always come true."

"Not always in the way they are expected," he said. "For example, earlier t-today, I would have r-reveled in a prophecy that said that you and I would be naked in bed together this afternoon . . . but this was not quite how I would have imagined it . . ."

More footsteps. Closer. Another door banging open down the hall. Her mind raced. No weapons. No strength. No disguise.

"Tommy," she whispered, looking back over her

shoulder to the door—directly facing the end of the bed. She lifted up off him. "You said you were with me, at the river? Do you remember?"

His eyes found hers behind his mask, blue and beautiful. "Always."

"Right then," she said, sitting up as the boots came closer. "Stay with me."

She tossed the blankets back, revealing them both from the waist up, and went upright, straddling him. Leaning over the edge of the bed, she grabbed the red silk sash from the dressing gown Lorelei had pulled out of the wardrobe.

She positioned Tommy's arms above his head, taking heart when he sucked in a breath at the movement. "You can feel that, my hands on yours?"

"Yes," he said, the words rough as she wrapped his wrists quickly in the red ribbon, tossing the end over the edge of the bed. It wasn't perfect, but it would have to do. When she leaned back, he said, "I can see you, too."

She flashed a quick smile down at him. "Getting warmer, are you, Mr. Peck?"

"Mmm," he said, gasping when she pressed her hands flat against his chest and sat up straight, arching her back. "Fucking hell—that's—"

"Distracting?"

His muscles rippled beneath her hands, and she raised a brow in his direction. "Possibly lifesaving."

She couldn't laugh at his little joke. Couldn't do anything but hope that he was right. That it would be enough to save his life. And still, she forced a quip. "Let's hope they are not looking for a blonde."

Footsteps came closer, and Imogen began to move, gazing down at him, his gaze on her, drinking her in. "I don't want them to see you like this," he said. "I want this for myself."

She leaned over him. "It is for you," she whispered, and it was the truth. "I am for you."

The door blew open, and Tommy's gaze flew over her shoulder. The air shifted immediately, and he growled. "Get out!"

It didn't sound anything like a man who'd just been for a swim in the Thames. Nor did it sound anything like a man who was in hiding.

It sounded like a man who wanted to finish what he'd started.

It sounded *perfect*.

Imogen turned and looked over her shoulder, through the darkness of the canopied bed to the room beyond, where a few candles lit the faces of two young men, no more than twenty. No doubt young Yardsmen convinced early to take money for thuggery.

Two sets of eyes went wide as saucers. "Miss." One cleared his throat. "Beg pardon. We've been told to search the place."

"Be quick about it then," she said, holding her gaze as she rocked against Tommy and injected her very best South Bank accent into her words. "But no dallyin'. If you want to be watchin', luvs, you'd best 'ave coin."

"Fuck that," Tommy said like sin from beneath her. "They can't watch. This is mine."

He punched his hips beneath her and she bounced with the force of it. *His strength was coming back.*

She giggled. And somehow, impossibly, it wasn't forced. "You 'eard the man," she said, brazen as she could. "Get it done and gone, moppets."

She turned her back to them, staring down at Tommy as she kept her rhythm, rocking against him. "Alright then, love," she said, loud enough for them to hear. "I can keep you entertained through the distraction. You ready for a good fucking?"

Something flashed in his eyes at the words. A dark promise, like if they got out of there alive, he was going to take her up on the offer. "Untie me."

Warmth flooded through her at the demand and it was a heartbeat before she remembered that he wasn't tied. Whatever this was, it was for show. She reached over his head and pulled the red tie.

Was that—*Oh, it was*—his beard stroked over her nipple as it hung above his mouth. She gasped, pulling the ribbon from around his fists. Free, his arms moved, just enough to set his hands to her body. Barely there. He couldn't lift her, so she gave him what he seemed to want, leaning down over him. Turning her head to watch the police open the nearby wardrobe and close it, turning to watch.

"Go on, then," she said, the words low in the dim light. Urging Tommy on. It was for show, after all.

And then his mouth opened over her nipple and he licked at the straining tip, and she threw her head back. The Peelers weren't doing anything like searching anymore. Now they were watching.

Imogen made a show of holding Tommy's head to her breast, trying not to let herself get distracted by the icy cold of his hair. "Like I said, boys," she said, low and dark, "if you're goin' to stay, you're goin' to pay."

Tommy let go at that, and she couldn't help the way she squirmed for more. "Like *I* said," he replied in a low growl. "Get out. She ain't for you."

The words were dark and nearly feral, and the young Yardsmen did not linger as they followed the instructions, leaving the room and slamming the door behind them.

Imogen and Tommy froze, listening for their footsteps, not moving, not daring to speak, until they'd searched the next room, and the one after. And only then, when Tommy shivered beneath her, did Imogen pull the blanket over them both once more, pressing her body to his, willing him warm again.

She took comfort in the fact that he could move his arms again when he slid them across her back and held her tight to him. "That was incredible," he whispered at her ear. "And here I was, thinking you needed me to keep you safe."

"Don't fret," she whispered, unable to keep the relief from her voice even as she knew whatever was to come would be worse than what they'd faced. "I shall still write you a letter of reference."

Chapter Twenty-Eight

"They're gone."

He held her tight to him, his mouth at her ear. "Not yet." She lifted her head, and he feared she'd move entirely away, and whether it was cold or fear or some kind of unbearable combination of both, she said, "They may do another sweep. If they don't find us."

"Then we—"

He didn't have the strength to stand, let alone fight, and the knowledge that his body might betray him at a time when she was threatened was enough to make him wild. His hand moved of its own accord, and he reveled in the simple stroke of it over her back, in the feel of her against his fingers—fingers that had not been able to feel twenty minutes earlier. He pressed a kiss to her lips, desperate for the feel of her, trying to keep the animal inside him at bay.

"Talk to me," he said softly, when he released her.

She pressed her cheek to his chest, the powdered hair of her wig rough against his shoulder. Another sensation to enjoy, even as he counted the minutes until he could toss the thing across the room and revel in the softness of her sable curls.

"Are you . . ." She searched for the words. "Do you . . . believe me?" He took a deep breath, hating the sound of the question, small and urgent and full of worry. As though she still did not trust him.

He could not blame her for it, of course. But still, he ached for her faith.

Before he could speak, she was talking, the words coming at a clip, as though she was desperate to get them out. "I know you think I am mad. I know this . . . the names, the addresses, the uniforms, the medallion, the explosives. I know it seems like chaos. Like I'm bringing you a stack of files again, but this time, with very little proof. But Tommy—"

"Stop. I believe you. Of course I believe you." He pressed a kiss to her temple. "Imogen—I don't think you're mad."

She lifted her head. "You don't?"

"No." His hand found her cheek, his thumb stroking across the soft skin there. "I think the world is mad. But you . . . I think you are the best of it—you are hope, and passion, and purpose, and justice. And sometimes you are vengeance, too, and it makes me want to fight by your side. For as long as you need me." He shook his head. "For too long, I believed all of it was fleeting. Justice? Hope? Passion? It was all available in small doses only if I walked a narrow path. But now . . . I see there is another path. Another way. And it comes with all those things. And with joy, too."

And with love.

He couldn't say that bit. Even now, in this place, with her pressed against him, keeping him warm, hiding alongside him from what was in the world beyond. Especially now that he'd nearly gotten her killed and they had Scotland Yard searching for them. And so he would keep that . . . his final confession . . . his most important one . . . secret.

So he gave her a different one. "I believed you," he said into the darkness, "the moment you showed me the medallion. Before they came for me."

"You did?" She lifted her head and met his eyes, and he caught his breath at the hope he saw there.

"In my experience, the Hell's Belles rarely get things wrong." He pressed a kiss to her temple. "Thank you. For trusting me."

The moment was punctuated by the ringing of a bell in the hallway beyond. A familiar sound, made more familiar by the way Imogen inhaled sharply and released a long, relieved breath. "Finally."

"Bells," he said. "They follow you."

"They're going to follow you, too, if you play your cards right." He didn't understand, but he didn't have a chance to before she added, "She's here."

Whoever it was, Tommy knew they would end this quiet, perfect moment, Imogen naked in his arms. And he didn't want it to end. "Tell them to go away."

Imogen looked to him, a smile on her lips. "I'm afraid this particular visitor is not easily commanded."

A knock at the door, and it swung open.

Dammit, didn't bawdy houses have locks?

"Are you decent?" The Duchess of Trevescan entered, followed by two footmen carrying a bathtub and what seemed like a battalion of housemaids hauling buckets of water.

Tommy ripped off his mask. The woman, uncommonly tall and blond, was dressed head to toe in white—an ermine hat and a wool coat with fur trim over a white gown, finished with pristine white gloves and, he was certain, white boots. It was the kind of attire one did not see in London, because it was impossible to imagine it remaining white after thirty seconds in the city air.

Not so for the Duchess of Trevescan, who apparently terrified dirt.

Her gaze fell to the bed. "Ah. I see you are not decent." A pause. "That's a nice wig."

Imogen cut her friend a look and pulled off the wig in question, tossing it to the end of the bed as she moved off him, sitting up and holding the blankets to her chest. Tommy resisted the urge to pull her back to the spot where she'd been. "The river is like ice, Duchess," she said to her friend. "He would have died of the cold if we had not done something."

Duchess raised a cool blond brow. "Well, now that that's sorted, I fear he will die of the things in that river that are not cold if you do not get him into a bath. With soap."

"Are they gone?" Imogen asked.

"For now," Duchess said. "And truly stupid if that wig worked. Honestly, is it any wonder that Scotland Yard has taken up the yoke of The Bully Boys? Do they just have a team of imbeciles employed at Whitehall?" She paused. "Present company excepted, of course."

"I find I am quite happy being excepted from that particular group of villains, Your Grace." It seemed odd to use the honorific here, in a bordello, while he was naked, but he didn't imagine there was a place on earth where the Duchess of Trevescan did not look like a duchess.

"Mmm," Duchess said. "I understand you've had a run-in with your colleagues, Mr. Peck. And do you see now what we have known for a while? That whoever is part of this corruption, wherever the line begins, with boys just out of leading strings searching a brothel on the riverbank, it ends with someone much more dangerous?"

Tommy nodded. "I do."

"But you do not have that name."

He shook his head. "Whatever this is, I have been kept from it."

There was a long silence before Duchess nodded. "So it seems. Which begs the question: *Why?*" Before anyone could answer, she looked to Imogen. "For what it's worth, Imogen believed you were to be trusted from the start." The woman, tall, blond, and cool as ice, did not hesitate when she looked back at him. "Considering Scotland Yard sent a collection of thugs to kill you today . . . I'm leaning toward believing her."

"Thank you."

"Do not thank me," she said. "It gets more difficult now that you're out from under their cover."

He swallowed at the words, a thrum of understanding exploding through him. Scotland Yard was no longer his dominion. He no longer knew whom to trust.

The duchess seemed to understand the cacophony of thoughts that came with the realization, and her cool smile turned just a touch warmer. "I've guards on the roof and at both ends of the street, however, so they won't come back without being seen. At least, not tonight." She looked to Tommy. "I assume you don't know the names of the men who tried to kill you?"

Tommy shook his head. "No. They're constables outside of the Detective Branch. But I intend to find them."

Duchess's blond brows rose. "Planning to walk into Whitehall and ask the villains to step forward, are you?" A little smile played over her lips. "I don't presume to tell you how to mete out justice, Mr. Peck, but I would suggest you rethink returning to a place where your death would make things much easier. I suggest you have a look at the gift I've brought you before you do anything rash." Lifting Imogen's bag in her hand, she said, "In here. Oh, and all the rest of your tinctures and tonics as well, Im."

A long exhale signaled Imogen's gratitude, no doubt at having her arsenal returned.

Duchess was not done with Tommy. "Should you require assistance with anything, I suggest coming to see me. I've an excellent relationship with the *News*." Her gaze flickered to Imogen. "As you both have seen. Honest to God, it took the two of you long enough to . . ." She waved a hand toward the bed. "You may thank me when we are finished with this bit of work."

They looked at each other. Was the Duchess of Trevescan admitting to feeding the gossip columns and cartoonists? She brushed a speck of lint from the sleeve of her pristine white coat and stepped out of the way as the housemaids left, having filled the bathtub.

"Imogen, I've sent word to your brother that you are a guest at my home tonight." Her icy blue gaze flickered to Tommy in the bed behind them. "Though you do understand you are going to have to face that particular problem sooner rather than later. In the meantime, I'm sure Lorelei will find you a French letter should you require one."

"Duchess!" Imogen exclaimed.

The duchess spread her hands wide in a sign of utter innocence. "I'm merely attempting to be a good friend!"

"Start by leaving!"

The other woman turned for the door. "You will all miss me when I am gone, you know."

"You're not going anywhere," Imogen retorted.

"Not yet," Duchess said, pausing to look over her shoulder and giving Tommy a wink. "We've far too much work to do. Do try to make good choices!"

The door closed behind her, leaving Tommy feeling as though he'd just been through a hurricane. "Why do I feel like I've just been commandeered?"

"Because you have been," Imogen said, urging him out of bed, stopping only to pull on the red dressing gown Lorelei Wilde had left for her. "Be warned. Duchess does not care for taking no for an answer."

"Is that how she convinced you to join the Belles?" he said, following her lead, crossing the room and stepping into the bathtub, full of tepid water sure to finish the job of warming him.

She reached for a length of linen and some soap, and moved behind him to wash his back. As though everything that had happened that day was perfectly normal. Including this—the two of them alone, sharing secrets in a bawdy house.

Christ. He wanted it to be normal.

He wanted it to be daily.

Well, maybe not the bit where they were nearly killed . . . but everything else. And certainly the bit where she told him her stories.

"Duchess collects people," she said fondly. "She is the most loyal, honest, noble person I know, and when she decides she wishes someone in her orbit—and it does seem like orbit, like she is the sun and the rest of us simply gravitate toward her—she makes it impossible for you to say no."

"You, Sesily Calhoun, the Duchess of Clayborn . . ."

She washed his skin in long, lingering strokes before saying, "It's a far broader collection than that. Throughout London, across Britain." A pause, and then, "A collection of misfits who, together, make sense. Thanks to Duchess."

He didn't think Imogen was a misfit, but he held his tongue. "How did she find you?"

"My mother died when I was six—too young to remember her—and so I was raised . . . differently." He didn't like the assessment, but he did not correct her, not wanting her to stop. "It's possible I might have been raised differently anyway, but Charles turned out the way he turned out, so I doubt it."

Tommy thought her brother had turned out rather differently as well, but he held his tongue.

"Everyone says my father loved my mother beyond comprehension. That he would have done anything for her, and when she took ill with fever and died, a bit of him died with her. He had always been a scientist, but after that, he threw himself into his studies. Spent most of his time with other scientists—chemists and physicists and astronomers and doctors."

"I understand that," Tommy said. "Losing someone so important—all you can think to do is throw yourself into something that will distract from what you've lost." It was how he had climbed the ranks at Scotland Yard so quickly—anything to keep from thinking of the life his father might have had.

She nodded. "Charles was already away at school, and I think my father feared losing another, so he brought me with him wherever he went. And I adored it. I followed him about and learned what he would teach. I set off my first explosion at the age of eight." Her pride was palpable, and he couldn't help but feel it as well. "By the time I was ten, I was blowing things up in the cellars."

His brows shot up and he looked over his shoulder at her.

"Nothing living," she qualified.

"That's a relief." He sank beneath the water, coming up for air and raising his hands to lather his hair and wash the last bits of the river from it. Silence fell, and he raised his eyes to Imogen's where she stood now, at the end of the bathtub, staring.

"My lady?"

She swallowed. "It's just . . . you've a great number of muscles."

"No more than the usual amount." He'd never admit it, but he slowed his motions, flexing his biceps as he washed the rest of his body, enjoying her distraction. It served her right. He was in a constant state of distraction with her.

Her gaze tracked the movements as he dipped back into the water and rinsed his hair, ignoring all the parts of him that had been restored by the bath. And by Imogen. She was in the middle of a story, and he intended to hear the whole thing.

When he resurfaced, he came to his feet, stepping out of the bath and taking the towel she offered. "Go on."

"Hmm?"

Pleasure and pride hummed through him. He knew he wasn't a bad-looking man, but there was something remarkable in the idea that he could scramble her brilliant thoughts with a bath. "Explosions in the cellars."

"Oh!" she said, moving to her bag and rummaging inside before returning with a roll of bandage for his arm and making quick, efficient work of dressing his already healing wound—the stitches miraculously unbothered by his exertion that afternoon. "When we discussed experiments, it was the only time he paid attention to me."

His chest tightened at the words, and he reached for her, taking her hand and leading her back to the bed. She let him guide her beneath the sheets, turning toward him as he followed behind her. "Are you warm enough?"

"Yes."

"Are you sure? You were—"

"I'm sure."

"But the river—"

"Imogen," he said, stroking a hand over her cheek, setting one finger to the furrow in her brow. "I am well. No worse for wear."

Her gaze tracked over him. "You nearly died."

"You saved me." He leaned forward and kissed her, gently. "Tell me the rest."

She nodded. "You know much of it. I didn't care for dancing or pianoforte or needlepoint or learning to keep a house or any of the rest of the things young unmarried ladies were supposed to care for." She paused. "Truly, I don't think they do care for them. I think they go along with it because that's what they're supposed to do."

He nodded. "Men have a good lot."

She cut him a look. "Rich, moneyed, powerful men, especially." A pause as she returned to her story. "My father didn't mind my lack of interest. He was more than happy to hire me tutors for Norse myth and anatomy and fencing—did you know I could fence?"

"I did not, but I am unsurprised to learn it."

She smiled. "I'm not good at it like I am with pyro-technics."

A memory returned. "You exploded a man this after-noon!"

"I didn't *explode* him," she insisted. "I *stunned* him. His ears will ring for a bit, but I'd have needed something a bit stronger to actually harm him."

"And you without your carpetbag."

She laughed, tiny and sweet, and he couldn't stop himself from pressing another kiss to her forehead. "And so? What happened to turn you to a life of crime?"

"I beg your pardon, is it crime if you're meting out justice?"

"It absolutely is crime, but I'm warming to the idea."

Another smile, and then she said, "My father died." She took a deep breath, her eyes going distant. "In his sleep. They said it was peaceful. His heart just . . . stopped." Her fingers played absently at the collar of the silk dressing gown as she spoke. "And then I didn't have anyone. Charles returned from wherever men in their twenties go, but he didn't know what to do with me—a girl who made gunpowder in the cellar? I think he hoped that if he ignored me, one day I'd disappear, and he'd never have to worry about me having to step into a ballroom. Or a chapel.

"I did try, for what it's worth. To be the kind of sister he could love." A flash of humor in her dark brown eyes. "I would have liked for him to have been proud of me. To have thought highly of me. To *think* highly of me, instead of thinking of me only as a weight about his neck." She sighed. "I ate a great deal of lamb for the man."

He couldn't find a laugh. He was too busy imagining putting his fist into the Earl of Dorring's face. Because if there was one thing in the world that was easy, it was loving Imogen.

"Your brother is an imbecile."

Surprise lit her face. "Not a very kind thing to say about your employer."

It occurred to Tommy that the Earl of Dorring was no longer his employer. Even if he were staying at Scotland Yard, he couldn't imagine Imogen's brother would take kindly to the number of hours Tommy had spent naked in the company of his sister. And aside from all that, "I wouldn't take a penny from him. Not now."

Her fingers skated over his beard, tracing the line of his jaw. "Because we are even now that I've pulled you from the Thames?"

"Because you're perfect," Tommy said, knowing it was a mistake. Knowing he should dress and leave this place now, before he fell further under her spell. "Explosions and gunpowder and whatever you keep in that bottle that I hear knocks men out cold be damned."

A blush chased across her cheeks. "You always say such nice things."

"You deserve to hear nice things. Now finish your story."

"Duchess found me. Duchess is how the Belles find anyone. And, it seems, she is how the *News* finds you." She gave a little shrug. "I'm not sure I should tell you this part."

She absolutely should tell him this part. And everything else she had in her magnificent head. "Why not?"

"Well, it is not the *least* criminal of my activities."

He tugged her closer, full of her. "You forget, my lady. I, too, have a criminal past. I am a known thief of unmentionables."

Her laugh rang through the room. "That is true. Imagine what the world would say! Noble Tommy Peck, corset stealer. Alright," she said. "She stopped me from blowing up Charles's carriage."

His eyes went wide.

"It was an experiment!"

Tommy had been a detective long enough to know a lie when he heard one, so he stayed quiet.

"It wasn't an experiment," she confessed almost immediately. "I was young and angry and rebellious. And I wanted someone to pay attention to me. Thankfully, Duchess was doing just that, or we might have met at Whitehall long ago, under very different circumstances."

"For six years with you instead of fourteen months," he said quietly, "I would have taken my chances with young and angry and rebellious Lady Imogen."

She smiled, soft and tempting. "I would have liked that." And then he was consumed by all the other things about her that were soft and tempting. The taste of her. The feel of her. The way she wrapped herself around him and gave herself up to him.

The way she looked at him, like he was a god among men, not seeming to realize that it was he who was the mortal. That it was she who was divine.

"Tommy," she said softly. "I wonder if you would mind very much if . . ."

"Anything," he said. "All you wish."

She closed the distance between them, her kiss heady and sweet, her tongue stroking along his lower lip gently, carefully, as though he might break.

He growled and deepened it, pushing her back to the bed and coming over her, working at the tie of her dressing gown, parting the silk so he could slide one hand over her warm skin. God, the things he wanted to do with her.

Except . . .

He lifted his head, breaking the kiss. "Wait."

"No," she retorted, lifting into his embrace once more.

He resisted. "Imogen . . . sweetheart. Last night—are you . . . uncomfortable?"

Imogen blushed, and Tommy knew he shouldn't like it. He knew he should be concerned by her pink cheeks, an answer in themselves. He'd done his best to take care of her the night before. Made certain she'd come apart in his arms . . . more than once. But he knew his size, and no matter how careful he'd been—

She finally looked to him, her dark eyes, the color of rich sable, meeting his. "A . . . touch?"

He cursed in the quiet room, pulling her close, intending to whisper his apologies into her hair. He was too big for her. Too much a brute. Too coarse.

And he'd hurt her.

"Love," he whispered. "I am—"

"Don't you dare apologize," she said, the words sharp. "That's just the sort of thing you would do, Tommy."

Confusion flared. Wasn't that the gentlemanly thing to do?

If he were honest with himself, the gentlemanly thing was not to have fucked Imogen Loveless in the first place, but now that he had, he could certainly tell her—

"When I say I am uncomfortable it is not unpleasant. It is . . . I am . . ."

He thought he might die in the way her words trailed off.

". . . aware of . . . myself."

Aware. Christ . . . had that word ever been more devastating? Imogen, aware of herself. Aware of her heat. Her slick softness. Of that place that had tempted and tormented and ruined him.

"Aware of yourself," he whispered.

"Yes," she said, and it was the prettiest confession he'd ever heard. And then she closed her eyes tightly and asked, "I wonder if you might be interested in *also* being aware of me."

As though there was a possibility he might ever say no.

Chapter Twenty-Nine

She closed her eyes when she said it, because she couldn't bear looking at him. What kind of a person made such a brazen ask, and of someone who had just nearly died in a river . . . situation?

The words hung between them, bold and shameless, and her heart threatened to beat out of her chest in anticipation of . . .

Tommy was not moving. Nor was he speaking.

Oh, no. Embarrassment flared, hot and unyielding. She'd asked for too much.

"My lady?"

He used her title.

Awful.

"Yes?"

"Open your eyes, Imogen."

"I don't think I can."

"Hmm," he said, and the low rumble did something unreasonable to her insides, which should have learned a lesson of some kind by now, should they not?

He was moving, the whisper of his skin against the sheets like an explosion. And then he was there, touching her. A hand at her side. The sleekness of his beard at her shoulder. The warmth of his lips beneath her ear. "Alright. Don't open them, then. Don't watch."

He pressed little, wild kisses along her jaw before

taking her mouth again, slow and deep, until her arms were wrapping around him and she was sighing her pleasure.

When he broke the kiss, it was to say, "Don't watch me touch you here." His fingers stroked over her hip, along the swell of her backside. "Don't watch me kiss you here." He placed little, sucking kisses down her neck. "So soft," he said to the swell of her breast as he stroked his beard back and forth across it, setting her on fire.

"Don't watch me part you here." His fingers tracked down her thigh, and she opened to him, writhing against him as his fingers slid to her core, where she ached. "Or here," he said as he slipped a finger through her folds, drenched with her desire.

They both groaned then, and her hand moved to meet his to urge him on as he touched her. "I have to be gentle," he said, low and dark. "I have to take care while you are so . . . aware of yourself." One delicious finger slid inside her, and she gasped. "Are you aware of this, sweetheart? Of how wet you are? Of your impossible heat?"

She cried out and canted her hips up to him, her fingers on the back of his hand, as he petted and stroked her, making her beg, "More."

"Of course you can have more, love," he said. "But wouldn't you like to look?"

Yes. She did, opening her eyes just in time to meet his gaze as he licked over the straining tip of her breast, sending a sizzle of heat through her before he claimed it, sucking, soft and rhythmic, in time to the glorious circles his hand painted over her, making her wild.

"Tommy," she whispered.

He released her and stroked his beard to her other breast, his magnificent hand not stopping. "It's better when you watch, isn't it?"

When he claimed the other nipple, he changed his

strokes, and the wild pleasure had her arching up off the bed, her free hand threading into his hair, holding him tight to her as she rocked against him. "Tommy, I cannot . . . oh . . . please . . ."

He growled, and the sound, a dark promise, sent an explosion through her as she cried out his name again and again, and rode the climax to the end—to the moment when the pleasure became too much and he shifted against her, holding her tight to his palm and whispering his wicked praise at her ear. "That's it, love. You're greedy for it."

"I am," she confessed.

His hum of pleasure was enough to rekindle her aching desire. "You told Lorelei I was yours."

Heat spread across her cheeks. Not embarrassment this time. Indignation. "She was looking at you."

His blue eyes met hers, the pupils blown wide. "You didn't like that."

"I didn't." She'd hated it. "You *are* mine. I am greedy. For *you*." And she was. She wanted to drink him in, to keep him close. To spend every minute with him. She wanted him for herself, like the villain in a gothic novel. "It makes me feel a bit mad."

He shook his head. "And if I told you I am greedy, too?" He was over her now, sliding down her body, pressing kisses over the swell of her stomach, setting her on fire with his tongue and the glorious pelt of his beard. "Because I am, Imogen."

He spread her thighs apart with his shoulders, staring down at her like she was a feast.

"I am greedy for your brilliant mind and your beautiful smiles, and the taste of you. I am greedy for the way your sinful mouth feels against my skin, and the way your sinful body feels against my hands, and the taste of you." And then his hands were under her, and he was tilting her up to his gaze, and staring at her with a hunger she recognized, because it was akin to her own.

"I am yours," he said, hovering there, where she was desperate for him. Again. Already. "And fucking hell, I would do anything to make you mine."

"I *am* yours," she said, her eyes meeting his. "Whatever you wish. However you'll have me."

Something flared in his eyes, something bleak. Something she didn't like—there then gone—his hunger returned. "Like this," he said, and set his lips to the soft heat of her.

She did watch, then, the view of him, worshipping her, nearly sending her over the edge before he began. She reached down to put her hand to his hair, and he grabbed it with his own, lacing their fingers together as he worked her over with the flat of his tongue, strong and stunning until she was writhing against him, unable to stop herself from moving against him, over and over, again and again, faster and faster until she screamed his name in the darkness and collapsed into the sheets, liquid with pleasure.

He shifted, pressed a soft kiss to her stomach and whispered, "Mine."

Yes.

"Tommy," she sighed, his name the only word she could find when he rose over her and pulled her into his arms, wrapping her in his warmth.

She had been ruined after all, she thought as she closed her eyes and turned her face into his chest, reveling in him. Ruined for all others. Forever.

The realization made her want more. "What of you?" she said softly. "Are you . . . aware of yourself?"

His muscles tensed at the question. "I am fine."

"What you are is a terrible liar," she said, sliding her hand down the side of his body, delighting in the intake of his breath at the touch, and the low groan that rumbled at her ear when she found what she was looking for, the hot, heavy weight of him, so hard and impossibly soft at the same time.

"Imogen." He hissed her name, his hand coming to hers as she encircled his shaft, testing the size of it. "You don't have to . . ."

"And if I want to?" she asked. "If I want you to show me?"

His grip flexed on hers, tightening, and he groaned again, the sound simultaneously encouragement and protest. Her gaze flew to his. "Like this?"

A grunt of approval as he helped her find the pressure he desired.

"Like that," she said, the lesson feeling like a reward.

He cursed in the darkness. "Yes."

She shook her head. "It's not enough."

"It's more than I can—" He lost the words when she shifted, mimicking his movements from earlier, her lips tracing over his torso as they worked him together. "Imogen," he gasped when he realized what she was after. "No. Love—" But his free hand belied his words, coming to her hair as she moved lower, breathing him in, reveling in the tremors of his muscles as he held himself still.

And then she was there, kissing his hand over her own, urging him back so she could see—so she could marvel at the size and strength of him. She stroked her fingertips over the straining tip of him. "You are . . . beautiful."

Before he could reply, she licked up over him, salt and sweet, temptation made headier by the way he said her name like a prayer, like she was a goddess. His hands were in her hair as he cursed, filthy and delicious— tightening with unbearable gentleness as she took him deep, testing the taste and feel of him on her tongue.

He groaned. Blasphemy. Prayer.

And Imogen felt more powerful than she'd ever been, desire humming through her as she claimed Tommy's pleasure, following his lead, licking and sucking and drawing him deep, wanting to give him everything he had given her. Wanting to ruin him, as well. For all others. Forever.

Wanting to keep him with her. Forever.

When his hands tightened in her hair with a deep groan, she could not hold back her own, even when he said, dark and fierce, "That's enough, love . . . If you don't stop . . ."

"Don't stop me." She pressed a kiss to the tip of him, and he bit back another curse. "I want it. I am greedy for it. *Please*."

"Yes," he said, harsh and aching. "Take it, then. It's yours. It will only ever be yours."

The words sent them both to the edge as she found a rhythm that made them both wild, and he gave himself over to her and to his release.

When he'd returned from his pleasure, he reached down to lift her back into his arms, his hands stroking over her skin as he whispered her name and kissed her in long, lingering pulls until she was sighing in his arms.

They lay there for a long time, Imogen's thoughts untethered and quiet, her pleasure having stolen her wits for a bit.

And perhaps it had, because she did not expect it when Tommy swore in the darkness, not at all quiet, not at all untethered, and said, "This must be the end of it."

Shock had her immediately looking at him. "What?"

"I have put you in danger, keeping you here. This has to be the end of it. I mustn't take advantage of you again."

She sat up. "You believe you have taken advantage of me?"

"Imogen—what I have done to you . . ."

"What we have done *together*."

He closed his eyes. "Fine." Opened them. "What we have done together . . . None of it should have happened.

What you have given me . . . what I have taken . . . it is not for me."

Her eyes went wide. "Who is it for if not for the person I have given it to?"

Sitting up, he faced her. "You misunderstand. I am saying you deserve more."

"I understand you deserve to be hit in the head," she interrupted, climbing out of the bed and pulling the red silk dressing gown on once more.

He followed her, unbothered by his own nudity, reaching for her, pulling her to face him. "Imogen."

"No. Whatever this"—she waved a hand in the air between them—"misguided nobility is for, don't make the mistake in thinking it is for me. Not when I've been very clear about what I want. *Who* I want."

She paused, her throat tight, wishing it were not. Dammit. She would not cry. Why did women always *cry* when what they should do was *rage*?

"It is for you," Tommy was saying, and if she was less consumed with her own aching sadness, she might have heard his. "It is for you, because I am *not*."

Instead, she heard the words themselves, and felt their sting. "I see." She turned away, her chest tight, her throat tight, a hum in her ears. "I see."

"I don't think you do," he said. "For God's sake, Imogen. Think of it! I am the son of a street sweeper . . . was to be a sweeper myself until I was plucked from the gutter and sent to Scotland Yard, which has turned out to be dirtier than the cobblestones of Shoreditch. So now I'm a man with nothing. No title, no future. A rented flat in Holborn, and I nearly got you killed today!"

She blinked. "So?"

"So?! Are you mad?" He seemed headed there. "So, that's not how it should be for you. You shouldn't be running from men with clubs and knives! And now, beside me, you'll always be in danger. You think the Yard will stop coming for us? They won't."

"Let them come," she said, raising her chin. "We meet them together."

"No." His reply was full of frustration. "You should be somewhere far from me. Somewhere—"

"Dancing and doing needlepoint?" she asked. "How many times must I tell you—I don't want that. You think that if you are not with me, I will not face down men with clubs and knives?" She shook her head. "You say you want to keep me safe? Keep me safe, then. But you're right. Whatever you think marriage is, Tommy—it is not for me. I am not going to wait at home for you to fight your battles and then tell me about your day. I want my day. I want my battles. And I want us to come home *together.*

"You have severely misread my interest in men with name and fortune, Thomas Peck. So today, for one terrifying minute, when I thought I had lost you to the river before I'd even had a chance to have you, you weren't my guard. You weren't my blade. It didn't matter."

She was hot with anger, and she couldn't bear it. "It didn't matter because you were my—"

Don't say it.

She bit back the word. She didn't want it to be like this. In anger. In pain. In the waning minutes of whatever they might have been, before he ended it before it could begin.

But Tommy saw it, anyway. And when he asked for it, when he said, "Say it," she couldn't resist giving it to him.

". . . you were my love."

The words slammed through him. She saw them land, sending him back on his heels. He fisted one hand at his side and shoved the other through his hair.

"It's not enough, though, is it?" she asked. Knowing the answer even as he pulled her into his arms, curling his huge body around her.

"When I said I'd never take a penny from your

brother . . . it wasn't because we're even," he said reverently, into her hair. "Imogen . . . we'll never be even. I'll always owe you for deigning to look at me. But you . . ." His words came ragged, like they were torn from his chest. From hers.

"You will meet someone better than me. Someone worthy of you. Not because your brother decrees it, but because you choose it. You'll go to some dinner or some ball a month from now, and you'll wear a dress the color of sunset because you look beautiful in orange."

"I do?"

He ignored her. "Or purple or green or yellow or blue. Because you look beautiful in all of them, like a jewel in a crown."

She caught her breath at the words, more than she'd ever imagined anyone ever saying to her . . . let alone Thomas Peck. So why did they hurt so much?

"You're wrong. I will never marry, Tommy." Her eyes met his and she willed him to understand. "Not if I cannot marry you."

She wanted to fight. To scream and yell and do her best to convince him that he was wrong. She wanted to explode his nonsensical logic. She wanted chaos. Mayhem. All the things in which she so regularly found comfort.

But it would change nothing. And even if it could, even if she *could* convince him, it was not what she wanted. It was not, as he had said, what she deserved.

And so, Imogen nodded and chose stillness. "I once told you that heroines captain their own fate," she said softly, straightening her dressing gown and pulling the sash tight.

He nodded, seeming to sense the shift in the room. "Yes."

"Then I shall begin doing so here. Now. With you."

His beautiful blue gaze went wary.

"I am tired of asking for people to love me. Just once,

I'd like someone to love me freely, in all my truth, without my having to ask for it."

"Imogen—" Her name was broken on his lips, and she turned away from it, knowing that if he touched her again, she wouldn't be strong enough to leave.

"I'm going home. To my brother's."

A lie. She'd called that place in Mayfair home for her whole life, and it had never felt like his mother's flat in Shoreditch. Had never felt like Tommy's rooms in Holborn. Had never felt like this dockside bordello on Dirty Lane. It had never felt like Tommy's arms.

"I'll take you," Tommy said, already moving to follow her. "You're not safe."

She shook her head. "No. *You're* not safe." He was a danger to her heart.

He sucked in a breath, understanding what she meant. The words landing like a blow. Good. Later, she'd regret the wound. But right now, she wanted it. Wanted him to hurt like she did.

Imogen pulled the dressing gown around her and made for the door, knowing that when she opened the carpetbag that Duchess had delivered, she would find a fresh change of clothes—Duchess was always prepared. She would beg Lorelei for another room in which to change, but first . . .

She extracted a stack of blue files from within the bag. They were copies of the original files held at Trevescan House, each one about one of the names on the list Imogen had given Tommy on the riverbank earlier that day.

She lifted them out and set them on a nearby stool. "For you."

He stared at the files for a moment, knowing instantly what they were. "Imogen."

"They're not from me," she said, knowing she sounded petulant, and still wanting him to know that though she was the messenger of these files, she had not chosen to be as she had so many times before. That game was over.

He'd made sure of it.

She turned to the door. Spoke to it, and not him. "Goodbye, Tommy."

"Goodbye, Lady Imogen."

The reply might have broken her heart, if he hadn't already done that so well.

Chapter Thirty

Though Imogen could have headed to Trevescan House after leaving Lorelei's bordello, she saw no reason to put off the inevitable, so she returned home to Dorring House, hoping that she would find her brother in residence.

He was not, because of course he was not. But his valet insisted that he was expected back that evening, so Imogen washed and dressed and waited in the library by a fire that had been stoked to roaring, just off the main foyer of the house, doing her very best to forget that she had come embarrassingly, dangerously close to begging for Tommy Peck to love her, to choose her, to believe her when she said she chose him.

The old adage was right, it seemed. Beggars could not, in fact, be choosers.

She'd begged. She'd chosen.

And she'd been rejected.

So, in the wake of it, Imogen sat in her brother's library, recommitting to the life she'd already committed to—the one she'd been perfectly happy with before *he'd* come along and ruined everything. She would be a vigilante with a penchant for chemistry and explosives, and a lifelong spinster. Perhaps she'd get herself a dog to carry about in her carpetbag. She could call it something delightful. Like Pyroglycerine.

The main door to the house opened and closed, and

within seconds, Charles appeared in the doorway to the library. "What on earth are you doing in here at this hour?"

She looked up from the fire and decided not to reply, *Moping in the dark*, as Charles had never indicated even an ounce of empathy and she did not expect him to find any just then. Instead she said, "As it happens, I was thinking about the name for my dog."

He made a face. "You've a dog?"

"No, but I am thinking of getting one."

There was a beat of silence before he entered the room. "What's wrong with you?"

She'd had her heart broken.

Was it possible Charles was more interested in her than she thought? "Why would you ask such a thing?"

"Well, for one, you're wearing a normal color."

She looked down at the muted rose gown. She hadn't worn orange. Or purple or green or yellow or blue. She'd stood in front of her wardrobe, staring at a rainbow of colors, Tommy's words filling her thoughts like the buzzing of bees, and she'd chosen this in an act of rebellion. Though Tommy wouldn't see it.

But the fact that her brother had noticed it was a shock.

He was still talking. "Nor are you in the cellars with your laboratory—"

"You told me the cellars are off limits."

"Oh, and was I also to believe you would listen?" She didn't reply as he continued. "Nor are you with your friends in Covent Garden, or with your Peeler doing whatever it is you think I have not been told you are doing."

She opened her mouth to deny the truth and he raised his hand. "Whatever you are about to say, Imogen, I would remind you that you are not the only brilliant child in this family."

Her brows rose. "I thought you thought I was odd."

"I absolutely think you are odd. In part because you are so brilliant. Why do you think I want you married?"

She shook her head. "Charles, I—"

"I know," he said, crossing the room to pour a drink. "I assume you drink this?"

"I do," she said.

"Of course you do." He poured a second glass of whisky and crossed the room to deliver it before taking the chair opposite her in front of the fire. "Tell me. Do you expect me to let you ruin yourself for a Peeler from . . . God knows where?"

"Shoreditch."

"Where in hell is Shoreditch?" He waved the question away. "I don't care. If you think doing whatever you've done with him is enough to convince me to let you marry him, you might not be brilliant. You might just be madder than everyone thinks."

I don't think you're chaos. I don't think you're mad.

She sucked in a deep breath, resisting the sting that came instantly, shockingly, to the spot behind her nose at the words and the memory. Tears? Because of something *Charles* said? What an indignity. Absolutely not.

Her brother clearly felt similarly. "Dear God, Imogen," he said, horrified. "Surely that's not necessary?"

"Even if you could *let* me marry him," she argued, ignoring the question, "he won't marry me. He thinks I'm too good for him."

A beat. "Well. At least one of you has sense."

"He's wrong though. He's wonderful. I would be very lucky to call him my—"

Oh, no. She *was* going to cry.

"Oh, for God's—" Charles shifted uncomfortably in his chair. "Stop this right now. You cannot weep in the library."

"That's a strange rule. I have no intention of weeping. Here or anywhere else," she lied. She would very likely weep later. Alone. But she wasn't about to admit it.

"Good," he said, taking a drink.

She tilted a head in his direction. "May I ask something?"

He slid her a look. "Do I have a choice?"

"Do you really think me brilliant?"

"It's not a matter of opinion," he said, flatly. "You've always been so. Since you were a babe. A natural head for maths and science and languages and logic and about a dozen other things that the rest of the world must work for . . . and all of it coming so easily to you. You think I have not seen what you're up to in the cellars?"

She shook her head, unable to keep the surprise from her tone at her brother's kindness. "You never seemed to care . . ."

"Of course I cared." He sighed. "But I do not know how to be a father to you. Especially not like our father was."

"I had a father, Charles. I do not require another. But I would not have minded you deciding to be my brother."

He did not reply, which did not surprise her, considering Charles was not the kind of person who said things that would be considered in any way emotional. Instead, they sat in silence for a long moment before he said, "May I ask *you* something now?"

"Do *I* have a choice?"

He did not laugh at the jest. "How ruined are you?"

She didn't hesitate. "I hate that word."

"Yes, well, we can discuss issues with verbiage at a later time."

She met his gaze—bright blue and serious. "Some might say I am *thoroughly* ruined."

He sighed again.

"Don't sigh at me, Charles. You have an entire mistress. Probably more than one."

"That's different." A pause before he added, "And only one."

"It really isn't," she said. "At least, it shouldn't be. The only reason why you're not also *ruined* is because you are rich. And male."

"That kind of thinking is why you'll never find a husband."

"That kind of thinking is why I have no interest in a husband," she retorted. But the lie of the words crashed through her even as they still hung in the air. Because there was a man she would marry. There was a husband she would choose.

Except he had made it clear he was not for choosing.

"I could force him to the altar, you know," Charles said.

Imogen recoiled, instantly. "No."

"Why not? You wish him yours?"

Desperately so. She wished him her husband, her partner, the father of her children, her friend, her guard, the man who would stand by her side as they fought for justice. But more than all that, "Because he must wish me his, as well."

Something flashed on her brother's face, and for a moment, she wondered if he might have something to say that was not cool or unyielding. And for a moment, she wondered if she might like it.

But before he could, a shout sounded in the hallway.

Charles extracted his pocket watch. Imogen looked to the clock in the corner of the library. Half-past twelve. No one should be shouting in the hallway.

As one, they stood, perhaps the only time they'd done anything in step, ever.

The door to the library opened, and a footman rushed in. "My lord—"

But before he could finish, he was pushed out of the way by three men of varying heights and builds and ages, all in uniforms of navy wool—a fabric Imogen knew well.

The police had arrived.

Charles immediately stepped between Imogen and the men, in a movement that surprised her with its easy, instinctive protection. "Gentlemen," he said, Mayfair clear and smooth in his voice. "You seem to have lost your way."

One stepped forward, his gaze already settled on Imogen, angry and mercenary, and she instantly recognized him. Or, rather, she recognized the raspberry across his cheek—the result of the blast from her obsidian brooch that afternoon.

A brooch she was no longer wearing, unfortunately. She made a note to replace it with more than one the moment she was out of this particular situation.

Imogen's brows rose and she said, trying for her most charming, "Look at you! Barely a scratch. And with friends."

He scowled and returned his attention to Charles. "Lord Dorring. By order of the commissioner of police, we are here to arrest your sister, Lady Imogen Loveless."

Bless her brother for his unflappable poise. "I beg your pardon? Arrest my sister? A lady?"

"Yes, sir. We've instructions to search the premises for evidence relating to a series of explosions across the East End of London."

Charles's laugh was full of aristocratic superiority. "I assure you, that's *not* going to happen. Not ever, but certainly not in the dead of night."

So this was how it was to end, Imogen thought. *They were going to do it in front of all of London. Aboveboard.* They'd find her laboratory in the cellars. All her experiments with the explosive liquids from the blast sites. The strips of uniform from Scotland Yard—where she'd been inside the uniform closet.

And whatever they did not find, they would make sure was found anyway.

And they would be believed when they blamed Imogen for everything. Because of the uniforms. And the power. And the will of those who paid handsomely to keep them on the leash.

The proof was right there—three policemen, fanned out in the library belonging to one of the most powerful men in Britain, as though they had every right to be there.

"If there is reason for my sister to be taken in for questioning at Whitehall," Charles was saying, "I shall deliver her there, tomorrow. But you must be mad if you think I will turn her over to you lot in the dead of night. And even madder still if you think I'll entertain this intrusion in the dead of night."

"Commissioner Battersea believes the lady is at risk of fleeing the city," the man she should have exploded a bit more said. A pause. "She's gone missing before, by your own testament. And this afternoon, she assaulted two members of the Metropolitan Police."

"My sister, assaulting the police!" Charles laughed. "Really, gentlemen. Have you seen my sister? She's half your size. What kind of policemen are you keeping over there at Whitehall?" He turned to Imogen. "Sister, have you been assaulting policemen?"

"In my defense, only one of *these* policemen," she said happily, lifting her chin and staring down raspberry-cheek. "And I assure you, he deserved it."

Charles's brows rose as he followed her gaze to the man who had been speaking. "I have no trouble believing that."

The retort seemed to bring the Peeler to the end of his tether. "Grab him," he said, indicating the earl, even as he headed for Imogen. She eased sideways, toward the mantelpiece, where a ceramic vessel sat long forgotten.

Three men attempted to subdue a now struggling Charles as raspberry-cheek came for her.

She let him push her back, toward the fire. "You really didn't learn your lesson this afternoon, did you?"

Confusion flashed across his face. "And what lesson's that?"

"Never assume a lady is unarmed."

His gaze skated over her dress and still, he pressed toward her. "I'll take my chances."

"Alright, but I will warn you . . . taking your chances that I won't hurt you is about as good an idea as my taking the chances that you'll actually be delivering me to Scotland Yard if I go with you."

He was almost close enough to touch. She didn't have more time.

Imogen pivoted and grabbed the vase on the mantel, praying that the housemaids weren't thorough. Without hesitating, she shouted, "Eyes closed, Charles!" And tossed the vase into the fire.

Pow!

The noise that shook the house paled in comparison to the bright flash of light that crackled through the room, leaving the villains instinctively throwing their hands up.

"Shit!"

"Aargh!"

"What in—!" The last was from Charles.

Imogen didn't have time to savor the responses, or the beauty of that particular explosion. She was too busy grabbing her brother's hand and pulling him through the smoke and out into the hallway, slamming the door to the library behind them.

Charles proved immediately resourceful, sweeping one arm off the top of a heavy mahogany credenza in the hallway and pushing it in front of the door. "Tell me, sister," he said as Imogen leaned in to hold it firm—the men within were already attempting to escape. "Are there explosives all over the house? Or just in the rooms with the most flammable items?"

"Now why would I ruin that surprise?" she quipped, turning to find a group of sleepy-eyed servants converging on them. She looked to her brother. "Charles—I will explain everything. But right now . . . this is the Police. We need help."

The words were barely out when his valet, a man Imogen had never realized was as young and strong as he now seemed, shouldered her aside to hold the villains at bay. "How many within?"

"Three," Charles replied. "Easily taken, if you ask me." He looked to Imogen, who was shocked at the very idea of her brother taking down a trio of bruisers. "Where there are three, there are more, sister. It's time for you to return to hiding."

"No," she said. "No more hiding. It's time for us to end this."

"Then you'd best fetch that help you mentioned."

She needed her crew.

Holding tight to that thought she flew through the dark hallway and down the rear stairs to the quiet, uninhabited kitchens . . . out the back door into the mews behind Dorring House.

She was two steps into the alley, already headed to the street, when a hand grasped her arm, firm and painful, and she cried out, spinning back toward her captor.

Her eyes went instantly wide in recognition when the man spoke.

"It turns out they're right: If you want something done properly, you must do it yourself."

Three things occurred at once: First, Wallace Adams, Tommy's mentor, was running the corruption at Scotland Yard.

Second, Imogen was about to be kidnapped.

And third, she didn't have her bag.

Dammit.

Chapter Thirty-One

H e'd bollixed it up.

She'd left him earlier that night, when he'd pushed her away, and Tommy had told himself that she'd be better off without him, and safer, too, considering any number of Scotland Yardsmen were searching for him, intending to kill him.

He'd watched her depart Wilde's from the window of that room he'd never forget, every muscle in his body screaming to follow her. To take her somewhere far away and make a life with her and hang whatever mess they faced here in London.

But he held onto his thin thread of control—the last he could muster—and told himself it was for the best. Her friend the Duchess of Trevescan had guards everywhere to keep Imogen from danger, and she would be better off with them. With her friends. With her brother.

A villain could tip Tommy into the Thames and no one would think twice, but Imogen? An aristocratic lady? Sister to one of the home secretary's closest friends? They couldn't disappear her.

Unless the home secretary was in on it.

The home secretary, the commissioner of police.

If they thought Imogen had a line to their crimes, to the no doubt vast amounts of money they were making from aristocrats looking to use the police as hired guns to cover up scandal and keep truth from discovery, there was nothing that would stop them from coming for her. For her friends. For the extensive network of the Belles.

Not her brother, the earl. Not the Duke of Clayborn. Not Alfie Trumbull and his Bully Boys across the river. In this, the Hell's Belles did not have enough power to keep themselves safe.

They would need an army.

And he would be a part of it.

Tommy was out of bed, calling for a razor—the best tool for disguise for a man who'd had a beard since he could grow one. Once he'd shaved and dressed in a collection of gentleman's clothing found in the wardrobe at Wilde's, he disappeared into Covent Garden looking nothing like Detective Inspector Thomas Peck. Files in hand, he was grateful for the cover of night, unable to go back to his rooms in Holborn—no doubt tossed over or under watch—unable to return to Whitehall, even if he could stomach the thought of it. Unwilling to go anywhere the Belles might frequent, for fear of bringing a corrupt gang of policemen into their world.

As though he hadn't already done just that.

Instead, he disappeared into the winding streets of Covent Garden, then into a hack to find the only person he believed could answer his questions—Wallace Adams. Once they'd passed the dark windows of Adams's flat, he'd had the driver head east, to his mother's home in Shoreditch.

Adams had been a Bow Street Runner and survived the corruption that destroyed the group, and he'd been a senior member of the Metropolitan Police from the start. He believed in the police. In their work. And he would see in the proof what Tommy saw. A St. Michael's medallion. The fabric used as fuses. The similar blast sites.

What they needed was to follow the money, and that was where Adams excelled—he knew every powerful man in Whitehall and most of the powerful men in other police precincts across the city. Tommy needed him, and quickly. The faster they rooted out the corruption at the Yard, the sooner the East End was safe.

The sooner *Imogen* was safe.

Christ. He shouldn't have let her out of his sight.

After a moment of failing to recognize his clean-shaven face, Esme Peck had hurried her elder son inside, knowing instantly that something was wrong. Adams wasn't there, and Tommy lingered by the door, knowing he remained on borrowed time there—eager to leave before villains came looking for him in Shoreditch.

Worry etched in her pretty face, his mother asked, "Are you over your head, Tommy?"

He shook his head instinctively, and they both knew it was a lie. "I need Adams."

She knew from experience that he wouldn't tell her more. "Where's your lady?"

The question surprised him, making it impossible to feign ignorance. "How did you know?"

Esme tossed him a look that only mothers claim mastery over. "It hasn't been so long since I was shopping on Bond Street myself, Thomas. You think I can't tell a girl from Mayfair when she steps in my house?"

"I thought—" he started, but Esme waved the words back.

"You and Wallace in here thinking I didn't notice her shining boots, or her frock made from the softest of lamb's wool and dyed yellow as a daisy in the dead of winter?"

He shook his head. "But she didn't act like Mayfair."

"She didn't have to," his mother said. "She walked like Mayfair. Talked like it. And, she was pretty as a picture and pure money, though she ate stew out of my chipped bowls and played games with Annabelle and asked me about your da, and smiled at you as though you'd hung the damn moon." She paused. "Reminded me a bit of myself, if I'm telling the truth."

That had been his fear.

Imogen *had* smiled at him that way. He ran a hand back and forth over his chest to release the tightness that came with the memory.

"So what did you do wrong, Tommy?"

He shook his head. "There are a great deal of differences between us, Ma."

"She didn't seem to care much about them."

"She would," he said. "Eventually, she would come to care about them."

"Ah. An oracle, are you?" His gaze shot to his mother at the words. She couldn't have known what the word meant between him and Imogen, and still, the question shattered through him.

"I'm not," he said. "If I were, I would have stopped so much of what has happened."

"Oh, Tommy." A long silence stretched between them. "Loveless, you said her name was?"

"Sister to Earl Dorring," he said with a nod, a helpful reminder to speak that title here, in the three-room flat where he was born. "Lives in a palace in Mayfair. Two of her closest friends are duchesses."

"And what, we're to punish the girl for being born into a title?"

"She doesn't care about the title," he said.

"I noticed that when she walked in here and made sure everyone thought her a miss." Esme scoffed. "She didn't seem much interested in ceremony."

"She isn't," he said. Indeed, the only times he'd ever seen Imogen happy were in places where her title meant nothing. And still . . . "She deserves better than me. What do I have that she could possibly want?"

Esme sighed and set a warm hand on his shoulder. "Tommy Peck, sometimes you are so like your father, I could spit."

He turned surprised eyes on her. "What does that mean?"

She smiled. "Only that you're smart and strong and

noble and righteous . . . and you spend your days carrying the heavy weight of the world all by yourself, believing that there's no one out there who wishes to shoulder it with you . . . and you're dull as a spoon when it comes to knowing what women want."

I've been very clear about what I want. Who I want.

"I can't give her what she wants," he said. "Not without taking everything away from her."

"Is that what you think you're doing if you love her?" His mother's hand came to his cheek. "Is that what you learned from your father and me?"

Tommy put his hand to hers, closing his eyes. "He worked so hard, Ma. And you, too. A girl from money, in three rooms in Shoreditch."

"Don't you dare disparage this place," Esme said, and Tommy's eyes flew open at the words. Words Imogen had spoken herself in his own rooms in Holborn. "This place gave us a roof over our heads and space to love each other and make a beautiful family and three beautiful children. And the only regret I have, Tommy, is that your father didn't trust me with the weight of his worry. He didn't tell me enough so we could face what came together."

She dropped her hand and stepped back, tears in her eyes. "Think of what we could have been if we'd been side by side."

Tommy was silent, filled with an ache like none he'd ever experienced.

Finally, Esme sighed and moved to the washbasin. "I'll tell Wallace you're looking for him if he comes round."

He nodded and approached, pressing a kiss to his mother's warm, soft cheek. "I love you."

"I love you, too, my boy. Be careful." He'd made it all the way to the door when Esme called out to him. "Tommy—if you ask me, Loveless is a strange name for a girl who is so well-loved. She ought to change it."

I will never marry, Tommy. Not if I cannot marry you.

"It should be Peck," he said aloud. Surprising himself as much as his mother. "She ought to change it to mine."

His mother nodded. "She ought to at least have the choice."

He might not be worthy of her, but he was going to spend the rest of his life trying to be. And he was going to do it by her side.

If she forgave him.

He met his mother's warm blue gaze. "I bollixed it up."

She nodded. "It is not uncommon. You'll set it right."

He would. He'd do whatever he could to fix it.

And they'd face what was to come together. He hailed a hack and made for Mayfair, intending to find her and beg for forgiveness, and ask her to have him not as her guard, not as his assignment, but as her partner. As her husband. As father to her children—to the children they raised to believe in honor and fairness and justice and hope.

And though she was not there to hear it, Tommy vowed, in that moment, to stand by her side, whatever her fight. As long as she wanted him.

And if it was too late? If he couldn't win her back? The truth was that he would guard her forever. He would stand behind her forever. Even if she never knew he was there. Because he would never stop loving her, even if it meant having her in barely-there doses: glimpses of her going in and out of carriages, sips of her alongside her crew on the Docklands, breaths of her shopping on Bond Street. Whispers of her in Covent Garden.

He'd take crumbs of her while the rest of the world was able to feast.

And he'd keep her foes at bay.

Starting that night.

The carriage slowed unexpectedly, coming to a stop up the square, before they reached Dorring House. He threw open the door and jumped down, already looking up the street. "What's happened?"

The driver peered down the dark street.

"Peelers, sir. Police wagon blocking the road."

Cold dread landed in Tommy's chest. "Where?" But he already knew the answer.

"About where you're headed."

And everything became clear. They were going to arrest her for stabbing the policeman on the riverbank. Probably for exploding the other one. They'd take her to jail, then happily serve her up to the *News* as a dangerous woman. A lady with a penchant for violence.

They'd commandeer her carpetbag, filled with gunpowder, and call it treason. Imogen Loveless, a modern Guy Fawkes, a cautionary tale for what happens when you let women think.

He'd been around Whitehall long enough to predict the play.

To know, also, how well it would delight the audience.

"Fucking hell."

"My thoughts, exactly."

Tommy turned toward the words. At a distance, backlit by the lantern light of the row houses beyond, was Caleb Calhoun, easing his way toward Tommy, as though this were all perfectly normal.

Or, more likely, as though he were enjoying Tommy's discomfort immensely.

"I hardly recognized you. Bare face and all that." Caleb waved a hand in front of his own face while taking in Tommy's clean-shaven jaw and luxurious clothes. "You could pass for a toff if not for the fuckin' size of you."

"You're one to talk," Tommy said, tucking into the darkness to survey the scene. "Have you ever met a doorway you didn't have to duck through?"

"Can't help it. This is how they make those of us who don't come up with titles and money."

That much was true.

"I don't suppose you're still friendly with that crew?"

the American said, tipping his chin toward the police wagons and uniforms down the row. His jovial smile, as though Imogen weren't in danger, made Tommy want to throw a punch.

"No."

The American tipped his hat back. "Good. It was only a matter of time before you saw that the 'good men' aren't really the good men, eh?"

"I suppose so."

"The Belles will be glad to hear you've decided to stand for justice."

He had, of course. But it wasn't just that. "Decided to stand with Imogen."

Calhoun tilted his head in the direction of the wagon ahead, a handful of men standing guard outside of Dorring House—and God knew what going on within. "I'll tell you, Peck, your timing could've been better. This would be much easier if we had a senior member of Scotland Yard to stop whatever show they've got on."

Reminding himself that Caleb Calhoun was the closest thing he had to a friend in that moment, and it was best not to maim friends, Tommy said, "Why are you here?"

"To help you," Calhoun said.

Tommy's brows furrowed and he bit back his instinctive *I don't need your help.* Because he did. Obviously. "Thank you."

"What else is there to do? I've an outstanding debt, don't I?"

It was meant in jest, though Tommy couldn't find a response in kind. Fourteen months ago, he'd looked the other way when Caleb and Sesily Calhoun had broken out of the jail on the lower level of Scotland Yard.

"We didn't have a debt," he said. "Not even then. If not for that night, when you landed in my jail and tore the place apart, I wouldn't have seen all Imogen was. I wouldn't have become fascinated by her. I wouldn't have made sure that, anytime anything happened in London that might bring me in proximity to her and your wife and their crew, I was the lead investigator."

"You really are gone for her, aren't you," Caleb said, his tone full of understanding and no small amount of pity. "Take it from me, you should tell her so. As soon as possible."

"Get me inside that house and I'll do just that," Tommy replied. He'd tell her everything. As soon as he held her in his arms and apologized for all the mistakes he'd made. As soon as he told her how much he loved her.

"Well—you can't go through the front door. They've likely got a club or two with your name on them."

"Then we go through the back, and hope the kitchens aren't busy." Tommy was already headed for the shadows and the narrow alleyway that marked the mews behind Dorring House. As they crept through the shadows, he asked, "How did you know I would be here?"

"You'll learn soon enough that Duchess has eyes and ears everywhere—including on Scotland Yard—so the moment that wagon rolled out, messages were spreading through the network." Caleb paused, then added, sounding almost English, "But even if she didn't—of course you would be here, Peck. You'd be here, because Imogen would need you. And that's what we do, bruv. We go where they need us."

"You all say that," Tommy said softly. At the other man's questioning look, he clarified, "*We*. You bandy that *we* about as though you've never for a moment had to go it alone."

Calhoun's face split in a wide grin—wide enough that it made Tommy angry, because there should be no amusement as long as Imogen was in danger. "When we are out of these particular woods, you'll realize that it's *them* who are one crew, and we who are lucky enough to be along for the ride." He leaned in, like he was telling

Tommy a secret. "But here's the truth. Once they let you in, you'll do everything you can to make sure the Belles never let you out."

Imogen's ladies, in their bright silks and satins. What had she called them? Her Vigilante of Belles.

And her, a damn queen.

"She loves me."

"That's good, isn't it?" Calhoun asked.

"I told her it was a mistake," he said. "I let her go."

"You cocked that up."

"Yes."

"Too good for you, hmm?" Caleb understood. Likely because he, too, was married to a woman so far above him he shouldn't even attempt looking at her.

"Better than I'll ever deserve."

"God knows that's true," Caleb said. "But it's funny how those women are . . . They don't like it when you tell them that. In fact—they go out of their way to show you just how wrong you are."

"I'm not wrong," Tommy said, full of rage and desperation and a wild kind of love that he feared would burn him up. "But I'd rather spend the rest of my life trying to be worthy of looking at her."

"Like the damn sun, eh?"

It was nice to have someone who understood.

They turned up the street to access the mews, Tommy beginning to feel like he would lose his mind. "I have to get inside. To her. To fix it."

The words were barely out when a rumble sounded in the distance, from the direction of Dorring House. Both men stilled, immediately knowing what had happened. One didn't spend any amount of time with Imogen Loveless and not know that sound.

"Well. At least we know your girl is still in charge."

Tommy was already headed through the darkness at a clip, toward the sound, hiding in the shadows of the buildings even as anger and fear coiled tighter and tighter, until he feared he might rip the whole of Berkeley Square down if that's what it took to get to her.

There was a carriage sitting at the center of the lane, the horses unmoving despite the way the explosion had shaken the buildings around them. Horses trained by Scotland Yard to be unflappable.

And that's when he saw the man ahead, tucked into the shadows himself, so well that a less perceptive man would have missed him.

A less perceptive man wouldn't have recognized him, either.

And definitely wouldn't have taken such a blow with it.

Tommy crouched low instantly, telling himself it was strategy and not shock, pressing himself to the flat stones of the house and taking a deep breath, trying to calm his racing thoughts.

Calhoun followed suit, quiet concern in his words. "What is it?"

"It's Wallace Adams."

"Wallace Adams, the superintendent of Whitehall?" Caleb's brows rose in recognition. "You're sure? Isn't he . . ."

"My superior." Tommy trailed off, shock fading into disappointment. This was his mentor. His father's closest friend. One of the only men in the world Tommy trusted. A man who was supposed to be decent. Just. Disappointment became rage. "The bastard wants to marry my mother."

The American stayed still and said nothing, which was for the best, as there was nothing to say.

Tommy looked to him, jaw clenched. "If he touches her, I'll kill him."

Caleb nodded. "And you'll have a crew by your side."

Before they could move, the door to the Dorring House kitchens burst open and Imogen flew out, headed for the road. Tommy knew instantly that she was headed for help. But she was also headed straight for them. Straight for *him*.

Eleven years of training stopped Tommy from revealing himself, from stepping into the alleyway to meet her. To be whatever she needed.

"That's right," the American said softly. "Wait for—"

As they watched, Adams came out of the darkness and caught Imogen by the arm, pulling her up short, wrenching her back toward him. Tommy sucked in a breath as Imogen cried out, the sound rending the night, and he barely bit back a wild roar as he made for them, ready to unleash punishment on Adams for touching Imogen. For daring to threaten her.

Only Caleb's quick reflexes stopped him, pulling Tommy back, holding him tight. "I know you want him. I *know*," the American said with quiet force. "But they have the house, the girl, and the men. All we have is surprise."

Caleb was right, Tommy knew it. But he could not find control, his emotions raging as the woman he loved turned to her captor—a man he'd trusted for a decade. Her words rang in the night. "Tell me, Mr. Adams, how does this end?"

"However it must," he said. "And it will be your fault, as all you had to do was let Tommy play nursemaid for a few weeks, and instead, you got him tied up in a mess that wasn't his concern."

Wasn't his concern? It was corruption at all levels of Scotland Yard. Did Adams really think he'd never uncover it?

"Where is he?" she asked, and he clung to the tiny hint of concern in the words.

"We don't know," Adams said. "Another thing that's your fault. But he'll come running when he discovers we have his girl."

A low growl sounded at the threat in the words. They thought to use her as bait? They thought to threaten her? He would not rest until he'd ruined their lives.

She met his gaze. "I'm not his girl."

Adams scoffed. "I've seen the way the boy looks at you."

Like she is the fucking sun.

"As have I, Mr. Adams, and I assure you, Thomas Peck has made it quite clear he has no interest in my being anything close to his girl."

Tommy hadn't imagined he could feel hotter rage than in that moment, as he heard the resignation in her voice and realized she was not bluffing—that she meant what she said—that she thought there would ever be a time when he did not come for her. When he did not fight for her.

"Fucking hell," Caleb said as he pushed Tommy back against the wall, sensing his frustration. His desire to tear the whole place apart. "Easy, Peck. *Surprise.*"

In the distance, Adams had had enough. "That's *Superintendent* Adams to you," Adams sneered at Imogen.

"Not if I have anything to do with it," she said as he pulled her toward the carriage.

Adams stopped at the words, turning back to her, his face—now visible in the light from the carriage lantern—full of malice. "I'll teach you to disrespect me, gel," Adams said, his backhand coming fast and furious, surprising everyone, and knocking her back hard enough that she would have fallen if he hadn't been holding her upright.

That was it.

Tommy detonated.

Chapter Thirty-Two

Wallace Adams knew how to take a whack at someone.

Imogen shouldn't have been surprised, considering the fact that the man had been a Bow Street Runner and then a Peeler, and then the head of a whole lot of Peelers, but somehow, when the blow came, hard and fast—*smack!*—over her right cheek, she wasn't prepared for how much it would hurt.

Nor for how it sounded, a sharp *crack* followed by a shocking roar that echoed all around her, bouncing off the stones of the buildings above. She reeled back from the blow, but Adams still held her tight enough that she couldn't escape, and she came back around with her free hand at her face, protecting it.

He reached for the carriage door, jostling her into position so he could force her inside. "I hope he doesn't come quickly. It will give me time to teach you to respect authority."

What she would not give for her brooch. Something more dangerous.

Imogen forced a smile in his direction, refusing to show pain or fear, but knowing that if he got her into the carriage, she would lose all power. Her best bet was to keep this man talking. "I should tell you, far better men have tried it. And it has not turned out well for them."

He pushed her harshly toward the carriage, and she

stumbled, using the movement to resist, her mind racing as she looked for a way out. That was when she heard the roar again—punctuated by heavy footsteps coming toward them.

Tommy.

Instantly, Adams was jerking her away from the carriage, whipping her around to place her in front of him like a shield, one arm across her neck, tight.

"Get your fucking hands off her," Tommy shouted, the words dark and threatening as he advanced, looking feral and furious.

Like tinder about to blow.

"Tommy, no—" There were men inside and God knew how many more on their way, and Tommy couldn't be there. "You're who they want!"

He didn't look at her, still advancing. "Let her go, and I might not kill you for touching her."

"Don't come any closer, boy." Imogen felt the kiss of steel at her throat and lifted her chin. Adams had a knife there. "I don't want to hurt her."

It seemed like a lie if you asked her.

"You've already hurt her." Tommy kept coming. He kept his eyes on Adams and Imogen realized that he was not tinder about to blow. He was the explosion in progress. About to take down half of Mayfair.

Pure chaos.

Later, she would marvel at the beauty of it—Thomas Peck out of control.

But right now . . . if she didn't defuse the situation, she feared Tommy was going to throw himself bodily at an armed and desperate man. "I'm right as rain, Tommy— though I sense the same isn't the case for you. What have you done to your face?"

Behind him, Caleb Calhoun snorted a laugh.

"Hello, Caleb!"

"Alright, Imogen?"

"Perfectly! Though I do wonder if you might hurry

inside and check on my brother? I exploded a roomful of corrupt policemen . . . and left him to deal with it, I'm afraid." She paused, flinching as the tip of Adams's blade pressed to her neck. "Too bad this one wasn't with them, honestly!"

"Fucking hell—" Tommy took another step toward them.

"Uh-uh," Adams said. "Keep your distance, my boy."

"I'm not your boy. Let her go."

"No, I don't think I will. You see, this girl, she's done you dirty, Tom. She got you into this mess with her running around all over the East End. If not for her, you'd still be clear of all this, which is what I wanted from the start."

What nonsense. Tommy was a superior detective and possibly the only decent man at Scotland Yard. "If not for me, he'd have sorted it all out sooner, you cabbagehead."

"Imogen—" Tommy said, sounding like he was coming undone.

"You'd best keep your mouth shut, gel," Adams said, his knife tightening on her throat. "You ain't in a position for clever quips, and you're out of your fancy concoctions."

"*Stop*," Tommy barked.

The blade stopped, but its bite did not ease. "I tried to keep you out of it, Tommy. I wanted you to be far from it, so you could rise in the ranks. How did you think the *News* heard of you? The pride of Whitehall! You've me to thank for it . . . and now this little"—he shook Imogen harshly—"*bitch* has gone and ruined everything." He paused. "For what? To save a few unfortunates? Fucking women. This is what happens when you let them off the lead."

"Enough," Tommy said, furious. "She's not part of this."

"Of course she is!" He was growing more desperate. She could hear it in his voice. Feel it in his hold. In the way the blade shook at her throat.

"You can't kill me in a Mayfair alleyway, Adams," she said, sucking in a breath as he gripped her tighter. "Even the monsters you've got paying you from the House of Lords won't stand for that. Your work is in the East End, remember?"

She could feel the stiff surprise that came over Adams. "How did you know the money was coming from—"

"Parliament? There are only a few groups of people in London with the money and power to bring Scotland Yard to heel. Tell me," she said, aiming for enough distraction that he might make a mistake, trying very hard not to think of the blade he held at her throat. "What do you think those men will do when given the opportunity . . . to take the blame? Or toss you and your men to the wolves?"

He shifted behind her and Imogen was consumed with a tiny thread of triumph.

Adams was not stupid. He understood her point—rich, powerful, evil men would never relinquish power, and they would never take responsibility. Not when there were working class, less powerful, equally evil men to take it for them.

"Wallace," Tommy said, seeing it too. Moving closer, "if you needed money—I could have helped you. You didn't have to do this."

"I tried to keep you out of it. I had plans for you to run Whitehall. Out of the way. You'd take care of the Detective Branch and keep your hands clean. We'd see you commissioner of police, son."

Tommy's gaze narrowed. "Don't you ever call me that."

"Why not? I was your father."

"You were *never* my father. My father was a good man."

"Your father was an idiot!" Imogen flinched in Adams's grasp at the sound of his high-pitched screech, and he let her shift her weight, giving her more freedom of movement in his own distraction. "Got your mother into trouble and married her with *nothing*. Not a farthing to offer. A *street sweep*," he spat. "She could have married me!"

Imogen could barely breathe at the last. There was something strange in the words. A meaning she couldn't find.

Perhaps because high above them, on the roof, a bell rang.

There. On the other side of the carriage. Through the hazy window. There was someone there. Imogen's gaze flew to Tommy, but he still wasn't looking at her. Hadn't looked at her from the moment he'd arrived.

Adams was still talking. "I took you under my wing. I sent your brother to school, got your sister married. All I wanted was to have your family as my own. To grow old making your ma happy. That's what the money was for. Enough to build a house. Live there with the woman I've wanted forever. It was a good plan."

It was a terrible plan. And not only because Esme Peck hadn't agreed to it.

Something dangerous flashed in Tommy's gaze. "You'll never get near my mother again."

"Your mother deserved better," Adams said. "You think your da made your mother as happy as I would have?" There. Again. The comparison. "As I *have done*? A street sweep? Begging me to get him into underground fights so he could pay the rent in *Shoreditch*?"

Understanding dawned for Imogen just as it clearly hit Tommy. This *monster*. "My father." Tommy's voice was hoarse, disbelieving. "You arranged the fights."

Imogen would have given anything for a weapon at that moment. For the means to punish this man the way he had punished Tommy.

"Your father needed the money. I found a way to get it for him. He knew the risks."

"And you stood outside the ropes," Tommy said. "You stood outside the ropes and watched him die and thought you'd win my mother in the balance."

"I wanted your mother from the start," Adams said. "From the moment I set eyes on her. She made a bad choice. It should have been me."

Wanted. Like Esme was a prize, not a person. "Come now, Superintendent," Imogen said, breaking her silence. "She chose not to marry you, which seems a top-notch choice, if you ask me."

"And *you*," Adams scoffed, low and menacing in her ear. "He never put a foot wrong until you came along and ruined every plan I had for him." He looked to Tommy. "You could have found another skirt to lift. There are plenty of plump ones with dark hair and wide mouths to be found."

Tommy's gaze darkened. "When I take you down, Wallace, it will be for many reasons. But don't for one moment think it won't be because of the way you disrespected my lady."

Imogen's heart pounded at the words.

Adams backed toward the open door of the carriage. "Oho, disrespected your lady! The lady who wades about in the muck of the East End? I ain't worried about her."

"You should have worried, Wallace," Tommy said, the words thick with warning. With promise. "You should have worried when you put her in danger. When you threatened her life. When you touched her. That alone was enough for me to wreck you."

"Bold of you to be making threats, Tom," Adams said. "As I'm the one with a knife to the bitch's throat."

Though she ordinarily took great pleasure in the moments when stern, serious Thomas Peck went all dark and growly, it was difficult to do that just then . . . as she could suddenly smell what was coming.

Gunpowder.

And not the kind she kept in the library.

"Tommy," she said brightly, "I realize you're in the midst of a whole to-do here . . . and I really do appreciate it, but . . . it is very, *very* warm out here."

Bless that brilliant man; he understood. He lunged for her at the exact moment the rear end of the carriage exploded.

Imogen ducked out of Adams's hold as he was knocked back from the blast, instinct sending her turning away from the explosion as pieces of wood splintered through the alleyway and Tommy collected her in his arms before they were both blown off their feet.

The horses, it turned out, *were* able to be shocked by something, and they tore down the alleyway . . . without the carriage attached. Thanks surely to Caleb, as once a stable boy, always a stable boy.

Then Imogen wasn't paying attention, because Tommy was there, crouching over her, blue gaze flashing with worry and fury and frustration and something wild that she might have been afraid of if she didn't feel it, too. He reached for her, wrapping one strong hand around the back of her neck and pulling her to him, tilting her face up to his. "Are you hurt?"

Ears ringing, she shook her head. "You?"

He didn't answer. Instead, he was kissing her, deep and lush—a wicked, wonderful kiss that stole her thoughts, save one.

He was growling.

When he broke the kiss, he pulled back to look at her, fury in his eyes. "Hear me, Imogen Loveless. You are *mine*. And I will always, *always* come for you."

"You could have decided that a bit sooner, Tommy Peck."

One of his dark brows rose just slightly—just enough to promise that they'd be discussing this at length later. "Stay right here. I'm coming back to tell you how much I love you."

Her eyes went wide. *Yes, please.*

He turned to restrain Adams, who had pushed himself to his feet, knife gone from his grip, lost in the blast.

"That was *excellent*!" Sesily announced happily from

the other side of the wreckage, where Caleb had her pinned protectively against the stone wall. "No wonder Imogen is so mad for explosions!"

"Fucking hell, Sesily," Caleb grumbled from his position. "You nearly got everyone killed."

"But I *didn't*. Instead, I did the job!"

Just then, the Duke of Clayborn burst through the door, brow furrowed, stopping immediately, blocking Adelaide and Duchess from any danger that might still be afoot.

Her crew. Arrived like cavalry.

Duchess came up on her toes to look over his shoulder. "A pity. We've missed the fun."

"Sesily nearly blew us up," Imogen said. "I wouldn't call it *fun*."

"You've nearly blown us up dozens of times," Sesily said.

"Yes, well, I use a bit less gunpowder, generally. But well done, Ses. It certainly got the job done."

And then Tommy was back, pulling her to his side, away from the chattering crowd and into the darkness as they headed back into the house for whatever was to come next—who did one summon to handle a gang of corrupt policemen and the powerful men who paid them to commit crimes?

The *News*, it turned out.

Because the only thing more powerful than Parliament . . . was the public.

The Belles would sort it that night, because that was what they did. And Imogen wouldn't mind missing it, because she was with Tommy instead.

He pulled her into the darkness, holding her tight, staring down at her, his hands running over her body as if to ensure that she was safe.

Which she was. Because she was his.

"Are you hurt?" he asked again.

She shook her head. "No."

"Christ, Imogen. You almost died tonight. Multiple times."

She smiled. "Nonsense. I didn't even lose consciousness."

He gave a little laugh. "Love, if you had lost consciousness, I think I would have torn down Mayfair."

"I had no intention of dying until you told me all the reasons you came back for me." She shivered in his arms, and he immediately moved to shuck his coat, draping it over her shoulders.

"You're cold. We should go inside."

"No—" she protested. "The world is inside and we will have to face it soon enough. I want to stay here, with you. A little longer." She tipped her face up to his and he kissed her, lingering on her sweetness until they both sighed their pleasure. When the kiss broke she said, "You came back."

He nodded. "I couldn't stay away."

"Why not?"

"Only one reason," he said. "I love you."

"Did you not love me earlier when you let me go?"

His chest grew tight at the words. "I thought you would do better without me."

"And look what happened," she teased. "I was nearly kidnapped."

He pulled her tight to him, giving her a stern look, turning her face to the distant light and running a thumb over the bruise blooming across her face from where Adams had struck her. "I'm not ready to laugh about it. I still want to kill him."

She reached up to hold his hand to her cheek. "Instead of killing him, I'd rather you'd kiss me."

He did, slow and deep, turning her out of the wind, pressing her to the wall behind them and blocking her from everything but him—his warmth, his scent, the sound of his breath in her ear as he whispered his love.

"I love you." A stroke down her neck. "I love you." One warm hand sliding into his coat, wrapping around her waist. A dark curse, full of passion and promise. "I don't deserve you. I'll never understand why the universe delivered you to me. But I'll be damned if I let you go."

She turned to catch his lips, to drink in the sweet words. "I'll never leave you."

"Promise me," he said.

"Better than a promise," she replied, pressing herself tight to him. "A prophecy."

"My oracle," he whispered, pressing a kiss to her lips. "My heroine." To her jaw. "My love." To the soft skin at her neck.

Another shiver, full of desire. "Tommy . . ."

"Captain of your own fate," he whispered. "What course do you wish to set, my love?"

"One with you," she said. "Together."

And so it was decided.

Thomas Peck was having a very good day.

Epilogue

As it turned out, Imogen Loveless was wrong about her future. She did marry, and her brother found he had no choice but to approve of her husband. After all, on that night in January there was only one man in all of Britain—possibly in all the world—who could be trusted to keep Imogen safe from the chaos of the world.

And so it was that Charles, Earl Dorring, happily announced the marriage of his sister, Lady Imogen, to Mr. Thomas Peck, former pride of Whitehall, now thorn in the side of it. And on the first Saturday in April, the two were married at St. George's, Hanover Square.

The ceremony was performed by the groom's brother and followed with a lavish luncheon at Dorring House attended by a small group of the couple's closest friends and family, including the Belles, Maggie O'Tiernen, Mithra Singh, the proprietors of O'Dwyer and Leafe's Seamstress's, and John Phillips, the newly appointed superintendent of Whitehall.

A vast exposé, inspired by dozens of dossiers delivered by late night messenger from an anonymous informant to

Duncan West, owner and editor of the *News,* brought corruption at Scotland Yard to public light. The color of the files in which the evidence was delivered? Blue, of course.

Londoners of all ilk began questioning the aristocracy's inappropriate use of the police for personal criminal gain, and the home secretary, commissioner of police, and superintendent of Whitehall were relieved of their positions on the same day they were named subjects—along with a marquess, two earls, and dozens of others—of both a criminal investigation and a far-reaching parliamentary inquiry, helmed by the Duke of Clayborn and other reformers . . . and Earl Dorring, who was beginning to sound like a reformer himself now that he was spending more time with his sister . . . and warming to her marriage.

On the Tuesday following the serious aristocratic ceremony and reception, Tommy and Imogen's marriage was celebrated in a very different way, with a raucous, exclusive ball at Trevescan House, filled with wild laughter and loud conversation and dancing and rich wine and lush food and a bride and groom who, even then, months after they'd professed their love to each other in the dead of night in a Mayfair alleyway, only had eyes for each other.

They even danced together, much to the pride of his mother (who was happily toured around the room by half a dozen eligible young—and not so young—bachelors), and the satisfaction of her brother (who was happy to see that at least one of the myriad lessons for which he had paid had, in fact, stuck).

And when the happy couple paused at the refreshment table, Imogen feeding gougères and tartlets to Tommy, the Duchess of Trevescan appeared at their side. "I confess, I wasn't certain about you, Peck, but now that I've witnessed your devotion to our Imogen . . . I find myself warming to you. Are you certain you are not interested in running a security detail?"

Since leaving Whitehall, Tommy had hung out a shingle in Holborn, committed to continuing his work as a detective beyond the purview of Scotland Yard.

Imogen believed his private investigation firm should have been called Peck Peeks, and while Tommy was more than willing to give his wife whatever she wished in all things, he'd drawn the line at that particular suggestion. Peck Investigations was already doing a brisk business outside the purview of the police.

He lifted his brows in Duchess's direction. "What kind of security does a duchess need that requires an entire detail?"

"Come now, Tommy," she said with a wink. "You can't think the Hell's Belles are stopping now . . . we're just getting to the good bit."

With that, the Duchess turned away, dancing into the crowd of revelers, leaving the newlyweds to do the same, lost in each other and their friends and the music until Tommy finally danced his bride out the doors to the ballroom and onto the great stone balcony beyond, twirling her into his embrace to kiss her, deep and lingering, in the darkness.

"I love it when you carry me about," Imogen said, wrapping her arms around him as he lifted her to sit on the stone balustrade, bringing their faces nearly even. She ran her hands over his shoulders, down his arms. "It makes me feel like you've won me in a wager."

He laughed, the sound doing deep, sinful things to her insides. "Carried you out of a gaming hell to lay claim to you?"

"Mmm," she said. "Yes. That. Tell me more."

Tommy leaned in, kissing her again, then sliding his lips down the side of her neck, his beard—returned, thank *goodness*—making her sigh with pleasure. "I would like very much to show you how well I lay claim to you, wife."

"Wife," she whispered, shivering at the word. At his touch. "Say it again."

"My wife," he rumbled, pressing a kiss to her jaw. "My heart." Another kiss, at her breast.

"My love." He caught her ankle, sliding his fingers over the smooth skin there, beneath the hem of her dress, in the same peacock blue she'd been wearing that afternoon when he'd discovered her in the dressmaker shop on Bond Street.

"You love me," she said, breaking the kiss, her fingers trailing down his chest.

"More every day."

She warmed with the words, even as his touch slid higher beneath her skirts, up her calf, leaving flame in its wake. "I feel like it is I who won you, you know," she said. "I wanted you from the moment I saw you. In The Place." She set a finger to his brow, smoothing the furrow there. "Entirely made of muscle and control."

"No control at all." He snatched her hand and pressed a kiss to her palm. "Not from the moment I saw *you*, pure temptation, all fire and chaos." Lacing his fingers through hers, he said, "I still remember how wild I felt that night, like if I wasn't careful, I would lift you up, set you on the bar, and make love to you in front of the whole world."

Imogen gasped at the words even as he pressed her palm to his chest, where she could feel his heart thundering. "I still feel it. Every minute I'm with you, love. Out of control."

"I know." She reached for his hand, pressing it to her breast, where her heart thundered in the same, wild rhythm. "I feel it, too."

She leaned forward and met his kiss, a long, lush caress that consumed them both until the party and the gardens and the world fell away, and all they knew was the scent and taste and sound and the feel of each other.

Perfection.

He broke the kiss on a growl—a sound in which Imogen delighted, because it meant her steady, stern husband was coming undone. She smiled up at him and teased, "Why husband, you look like you're about to explode."

"Mmm," he said, reaching for her. "Good thing I have an expert in the field at hand."

She squealed as he pulled her from the balustrade and lifted her into his arms. "Tommy! We cannot! People will wonder what happened to us!"

"Nonsense," he said. "I'm certain they'll read all about how I ravished you in the Trevescan gardens at our wedding party in the next issue of the *News*."

She wrapped her arms about his neck and pressed a kiss to his cheek before whispering in his ear, "I hope they forgo the illustration this time."

He looked to her, and she caught her breath at the wicked intent in his eyes. "Then we'll have to make sure its unprintable."

And they did just that.

Hours after Tommy and Imogen disappeared into the gardens and then to their new home, Duchess stood at the edge of the ballroom, watching the remaining guests— none of whom showed any intention of leaving—and attempting to unravel her emotions. It should be said, this particular task was not something that Duchess generally enjoyed doing. Indeed, in the years since she'd become the Duchess of Trevescan, she'd attempted at all turns to *avoid* emotions. Especially the complicated ones.

That evening, however, the emotions were complicated.

Of course, there was happiness. She'd seen three of her closest friends married to men who loved them beyond reason.

But there was also concern. The more who joined their crew, the more likely they would be discovered. And she would do anything to keep her friends safe.

And then there was the other emotion. The one that never seemed to dissipate, even when she was in a ballroom full of triumphant delight.

Maggie O'Tiernen appeared at her shoulder, two glasses of champagne in hand. Accepting the drink, Duchess said, "I'm surprised to see you so far from Covent Garden, Maggie."

"I never miss a wedding," Maggie replied. "Especially when it's a love match. Those are the most entertaining."

The friends toasted and drank, looking out over the revelry for a long moment, Duchess considering what was to come. She took a deep breath. Exhaled.

"There's a man here," Maggie said.

Duchess turned. "There are many men here."

"Not like this one."

"Who is it?" Duchess's brow furrowed.

"No one knows. He says he'll only speak to you."

She sighed. They never seemed to know when they were not welcome. "Where?"

"There." Maggie tipped her chin toward the entry to the ballroom.

Duchess followed her friend's gaze and froze. To describe the figure crossing the ballroom as a *man* felt like a grave error. Like describing a lion as a cat, or a hurricane as a rain shower. This was not a man. He was a *force*—tall and strong, and pure, unadulterated power.

And he was coming straight for her.

"Shit," Duchess said softly.

"You know him?" Maggie asked.

Duchess shook her head. "No. But when a man looks like that, he cannot be good news."

Tearing her gaze away, she looked up to the second level of the Trevescan ballroom, where an observation hallway ran the entire length of the room. There Rahul Singh, her man of affairs, stood watch as he always did when the ballroom was in use.

He shook his head. He did not recognize the newcomer, either.

Duchess knocked back the last of her champagne and turned her brightest smile on Maggie. "Well. Whoever he is, it is time to show him that one does not simply *turn up* to see the Duchess of Trevescan."

Maggie laughed. "I'm looking forward to it."

The intruder was still looking at her, approaching not around the perimeter of the dancers, but straight through them. Who did he think he was? This was a wedding reception. Had the man been raised by wolves?

She stepped onto the dance floor and headed for him, refusing to show curiosity, or uncertainty, or the way her heart thundered in her chest as they came closer together.

They stopped inches from each other, orchestra swelling and dancers swirling around them, simultaneously attempting to look and not look.

"Sir?" she asked, lifting her chin and giving him nothing but cool disdain.

"I am told you are the Duchess of Trevescan," he said, the words low and smooth. Like the finest scotch whisky.

She raised a brow, ignoring the ice in his steely gaze. "I am."

"Fascinating," he replied. "As I am the Duke of Trevescan, one would think we would have met."

Author's Note

In all the years I've been writing historicals, I've never once had an idea that I could not find at least a glimmer of evidence for in history, and the Hell's Belles are no different.

They are based on the Forty Elephants, an all-women Victorian crime ring that operated for more than a century. Alice Diamond, the Forties' most famous queen, was an explosives expert herself—arrested for falsifying documents with the intention of stealing product from a London munitions factory. We don't know what she intended to explode, but I'm fairly certain Imogen would have some ideas. For more on the Forty Elephants, do not miss Brian McDonald's terrific resource, *Alice Diamond and the Forty Elephants*.

Regarding Imogen's literal bag of tricks: Readers of *Bombshell* will remember that she invented chloroform prior to that book—at the same time two other scientists were inventing it in Germany and the United States. Gunpowder, or black-powder, had been in use for centuries before Imogen started making it in her cellars, but in this book her use of mercury fulminate and other wildly explosive concoctions is simultaneous to the creation of blasting-oil (what we call nitroglycerin) now. I could not have filled her carpetbag without the help of Elena Armas, who is not only a superstar romance novelist, but also a brilliant chemical engineer who happily went down the research rabbit hole with me on nineteenth century explosives.

Imogen's invisible goat's-lettuce ink is real, and it really did come from ancient Rome. I found it in Amy Suo Wu's *A Cookbook of Invisible Writing*, an absolute delight of a resource that I snatched up a tiny Brooklyn bookstore years ago and have treasured since, knowing I'd eventually have a heroine with a carpetbag large enough to carry a jar of the stuff.

I am immensely grateful to Haia Shpayer-Makov for *The Ascent of the Detective*, which is an invaluable resource on the beginnings of the Metropolitan Police, founded in 1829 and nicknamed Scotland Yard for the location of its headquarters. The Detective Branch is real—formed in 1842 and staffed at first with eight men tasked with solving crimes, a new concept in policing which, until then, had worked to prevent crimes from occurring. Close readers will notice that I tweaked some of these dates to be able to fit this book into the larger, existing timeline of the Hell's Belles series—a choice I hope you'll forgive.

It will come as no surprise that corruption at the highest levels of the police began almost immediately after the founding of the force, disproportionately impacting communities in need. Police misconduct was as present in London in the nineteenth century as it is around the globe in the twenty-first, running counter to community empowerment, social justice, and public safety. Unchecked power corrupts and always has done, and we continue to see the scars of that truth in government and law enforcement today.

Historical romance gives us the gift of fantasy, however—of allowing us to show the past as we wish the future to be, and while Tommy would never return to the police, I leave the Scotland Yard of the MacLean-iverse to John Phillips, a decent man, committed to community empowerment rather than personal power.

A note on the Salisbury Steps and Waterman's Stairs, because I know many readers enjoy visiting the locations in my books. *Knockout* takes place before Victoria Embankment was designated for public use, when the space was full of bustling riverside businesses. Steps marked small docks where water taxis would drop passengers. All but twelve of the staircases were demolished, many of them bombed during the Blitz, including the Salisbury Steps. Even if they did still exist, however, they would no longer lead to Dirty Lane, but into the stunning gardens along the river.

As always, I owe a tremendous debt to the Museum of London, the British Library, and the New York Public Library for endless rabbit holes of research.

The Hell's Belles wouldn't exist without my incredible friends, for whom I would happily explode things. Louisa Edwards is the absolute best friend/reader/brainstormer a girl could ask for; she, Kate Clayborn, Sophie Jordan, Adriana Herrera, Meghan Tierney, and Erin Leafe have all had a hand in this book coming to life. I hope Imogen and I have done them proud. Special thanks to Kennedy Ryan, who dragged me over the finish line . . . *again*.

I am so lucky to have been with Avon Books since the start. Carrie Feron, Asanté Simons, Brittani DiMare, DJ DeSmyter, Eleanor Mikucki, Jes Lyons, Jeanne Reina, Liate Stehlik, Robert Alunni, Claudia Antunes, Gabe Barillas, Audrey Bresar, Sylvie Calder, Sandy Cooper, Anne DeCourcey, Ian Doherty, Kim Gombar, Leslie Greenfield, Sarah Gregory, Michael Guy-Haddock, Jim Hankey, Bethany Johnsrud, Onyew Kim, Dawn Littman, Katie McGarry, Barbara Meyers, Jessica Montany, Michael Morris, Deb Murphy, Carla Parker, Cathy Schornstein, Kaitlin Sim, Colleen Simpson, Andrea Smith, Robin Smith, Mathew Spadafora, Virginia Stanley, Rosalyn Steele, and Eric Svenson, who work tirelessly to bring them into the world. Rounding out this excellent gang are Holly Root, Kristin Dwyer,

Alice Lawson, and Linda Watson—I hope you know how grateful I am to each of you.

And finally, so much love to Chiara, Mark, and Mom for cheerleading; V for all the encouraging "you got this!" notes; Kahlo for all the supportive napping; and Eric, who, despite making fun of my explosion sounds, still makes my heart go *ratatat-whoosh*.

And finally, you! None of the books are real until you read them . . . thank you for bringing Tommy and Imogen to life, and for being so excited to see #TommyGoBoom. Duchess is next, and I really can't wait for you see what she's got cooking.

New York Times bestselling author

SARAH MacLEAN

THE HELL'S BELLES SERIES

BOMBSHELL, BOOK 1

Sarah MacLean returns with a blazingly sexy, unapologetically feminist new series, Hell's Belles, beginning with a bold, bombshell of a heroine, able to dispose of a scoundrel—or seduce one—in a single night.

HEARTBREAKER, BOOK 2

Sarah MacLean follows her highly acclaimed *Bombshell* with *Heartbreaker*, featuring a fierce, fearless heroine on a mission to steal a duke's secrets . . . and his heart.

KNOCKOUT, BOOK 3

Sarah MacLean returns with the next Hell's Belles novel about a chaotic bluestocking and the buttoned-up detective enlisted to keep her out of trouble (spoiler: She is the trouble).

New York Times Bestselling Author

SARAH MACLEAN

The BAREKNUCKLE BASTARDS Series

Wicked and the Wallflower
978-0-06-269206-1

When a mysterious stranger finds his way into
her bedchamber and offers his help for landing
a husband, Lady Felicity Faircloth agrees to his
suspicious terms on one condition: she believes in
passion, and she won't accept a marriage without it.

Brazen and the Beast
978-0-06-269207-8

Lady Henrietta Sedley has plans to make her own
fortune and to live her own life. But first, she
intends to experience a taste of the pleasure she'll
forgo as a confirmed spinster. Everything is going
perfectly . . . until she discovers the most beautiful
man she's ever seen tied up in her carriage.

Daring and the Duke
978-0-06-269208-5

Grace Condry has spent a lifetime running from her
past of being raised on the streets. Grace has a sharp
mind and a powerful right hook and has never met
an enemy she could not beat . . . until Ewan, Duke of
Marwick, the man she once loved, returns.